DEVOTIONS

Stories for the Amputee and Disability Admirer

By Hedera

Cover: Bruna Delvaux

ISBN: 978-1-257-98160-1

Illustrations: Facundo - Argentina

Copyright: Devotions by Hedera Books 2011

www.hederabooks.com

Let me introduce...

There are a lot of people who like the subjects amputation and disability very much. Those people are called admirers, devotees... officially Acrotomophiles.

Yes, indeed... people who are attracted in Amputees and find them even very attractive.

Probably you will find it strange if I tell you now that there are more then 1 on 500 people (sexual) attracted to Amputees and people with a disability. And yes, you find them back in both genders. Male & Female.

This book "Devotions", is the first book for them who are interested in those subjects, and like to read stories about the (fantasy) world of Amputee and Disability.

Many people like to write their fantasy stories down, but never got published. Devotions is a collection of 20 first and never before – in book published stories.

EDUARDO CRUCHOT

CONTENT:

A DREAM COME TRUE
by Vik

Harry awoke at sunrise. The weather had been mild and he had slept with the windows open. He heard the curtains rustling in the breeze and the swifts singing as they flew outside. There was the sound of a chick and the flapping of many wings. He smiled. he knew it was no chick but a hawk and the wings flapping were those of the pigeons that roosted on the roof of the building. That hawk sure scared the dickens out of those pigeons every time it came around.

He had been away for nearly a month and it was good to be back in his apartment, in familiar surroundings - his books, his computer, his sound equipment, his dark-room and his pictures hanging on the wall. Even though he was single he had a large flat with a queen-size bed in the bedroom and a hide-a-bed couch in the guest room.

He yawned, stretched and got up. Putting on his house robe he went to the kitchen. He got out a pitcher, filled it with milk and put it in the microwave. Setting it for 3 minutes at full power he turned it on. Then he put coffee and water in the percolator and turned it on too. While the coffee percolated he pulled a large breakfast cup and saucer, a bowl and two spoons from a cupboard and set them on the counter. He picked up the bowl and placed it on top of the saucer, then he placed the spoons inside the bowl and took the whole lot to the dining room table. From the sideboard he removed a box of cereal and placed it beside the bowl. Then he returned to the kitchen. The microwave had stopped. He opened the door, picked up the jar and without shutting the door took it to the dining room table.

The coffee took a little longer to percolate so he went to the table between the two recliners in the living room, picked up the remote and turned the TV on. He switched to the news channel, placed the remote beside the bowl and went to the kitchen. Noticing that he had left the microwave's door open he pushed it shut. The coffee was ready. First he pulled out the basket halfway so that the grounds would cool before they went into the waste bin and then he poured the coffee into the cup. He picked it up, went to the dining room table and sat down to have breakfast.

"Things take a little longer now," he thought. "'Normally I would have waited for the milk and the coffee to be ready, poured the coffee and put all the dishes, cutlery, milk jar and cup full of coffee on a tray and brought the whole shebang to the table in one trip. I would have also poured me a glass of orange juice but today it was too much trouble.

"Well, I've begun a new life. I wanted a change and I've got it. Everything else is going to be different too."

Placing some cereal on the bowl he poured milk over it and into the coffee cup. Opening the sugar bowl he spooned out some sugar, poured it into his café au lait and stirred it. Then, feeling quite happy with himself, he had breakfast while he watched the news. Afterward he smoked a cigarette enjoying the privilege he had been denied for two weeks.

He knew that the daily would come in at eight o'clock; he decided that she could do the dishes so he left them on the table, just putting away the cereal. He stubbed out the cigarette on the ashtray and very carefully stood up. He had left his crutch in the corner between the toaster and the wall. He picked it up and tucked the stump of his left leg between the staves, resting it on the hand grip. Lovingly snuggling the crutch under his armpit he held it by the front stave and swung slowly and easily to the bathroom. Previous to the operation he had discussed with the surgeon how long the stump was to be. He wanted a short stump and when he gave his reasons the surgeon agreed. The way he was walking now was the way he wanted to walk as a one-legged person, partly controlling the movement of the crutch with the stump of his leg. He had absolutely refused when the surgeon suggested the use of a prosthesis.

"That would negate the whole purpose of the exercise. Don't you understand? I want to be an amputee. I've practiced doing many things in my 'crippled' condition and I could get along very well pretending that I wasn't complete but now I want to be really crippled. Pretending is not enough. I'm twenty-two now and I don't want to wait any longer. I want to get along with what's left of my body and the most I'll do is use a crutch. It's not a question of saving money - I'm independently wealthy - it's simply a question that I want to be a cripple and live as a cripple."

He undid the robe's belt and pulled his right arm from the sleeve. Holding the crutch with it he pulled out his left hand and hanged the robe from the hook on the wall. Placing the crutch under his left arm he stood in front of the wash basin and looked at himself in the mirror. The image of the crutch confirmed that it was not a dream, that he was indeed one-legged, Yes, his body had been altered and he looked with satisfaction at the reflection of his new shape.

He looked at the shelf under the mirror. There were the deodorant, the shaving cream, the razor and the after shave lotion that he hadn't seen or used for a month. The tooth brush and glass were in their hanger on the wall, The nail brush and bar of soap rested on the washbasin's concavities.

He leaned the crutch against the wall to the left of the washbasin and placing his stump on the top edge for balance he opened both faucets so that the water would come out warm and wet his face. He then removed the top from the can of shaving cream and shook it. Bending his right elbow he looked at the stump of his forearm. It was four inches long. He smiled remembering how many times he had mentally practiced shaving and brushing his teeth before he entered the clinic. For two weeks previous to the amputation he had bent his fingers against the palm of his hand and bound his fist and wrist so that they couldn't move. It wasn't quite like having four-fifths of your forearm missing but it gave him a good idea of what it was going to be like to have a hand gone.

Pressing the button on the can he let the shaving cream fall on the stump of his arm. Holding it up he picked up some of the cream with his left hand and applied it to his face. He repeat-ed the operation until his face was covered with lather then he rinsed his hand under the water. He had a bit of trouble when he tried to rinse the stump of his arm. He had to bend very far to put it under the faucet. He leaned over supporting himself on the washbasin with his left hand and let the water fall over the remains of his arm. He straightened up feeling an enormous satisfaction as he ran his single hand over the stumps of his arm and leg, enjoying the absence of the limbs.

"I'm so glad I'm no longer a pretender," he thought. "Now I'm the real thing."

He took the razor with his left hand and started shaving. As he shaved he reminisced over the events that had brought him to this very much desired condition.

Ever since he could remember he had been all three: a devotee, a wannabe and a pretender. As a child he had lived in South America for many years. There he saw many beggars, Most of them were amputees.

Since he was ten he had pretended to be either one-legged or legless, mostly the latter. When his parents were away visiting friends in the evening he would bend either one or both legs and tuck them into his pajama legs knee-first. Then he would pull up the waist band and tie the cord, Finally he would roll up the pajama legs around his thighs and shins so that the knees stuck out, looking like he had stumps instead of legs. Sitting on his bed he would hold up his hand and say, "Alms for this poor legless beggar, please. Alms for this poor legless cripple."

Not content with this he would slide down the side of the bed and crawl on all fours around the floor of his bedroom. He thrilled at the feeling of not having any legs and crawling on his hands and "stumps". Sometimes he would swing his body between his arms, humping along and landing on his butt at every "step". The best part came when he wanted to climb back on the bed. He became very adept at hoisting himself with his hands on the edge of the bed and then swinging first one "stump" and then the other over the edge. One evening when he was about eleven he had been feeling poorly. His parents had an engagement so they asked the maid to look in on him occasionally. He was already in bed when they left and as soon as they did he performed his "legless" act. Half an hour later the maid entered the room to see how he felt. He was sitting on the bed and when the maid looked in he showed her his "stumps".

"Look, María," he said. "My legs have been cut off!"

"God protect you, child!" the maid said, bringing her hands to her face. She left his room and didn't look in on him again.

He devised another way of pretending he was crippled. His parents were used to the very long baths that he liked to take so he knew he would be left in peace while he was in the bathroom. He had the idea one day to sit on the floor and cross his left leg over the right one. He half bent his right knee, crossed the left leg over the right and tucked his left foot so that it rested against the left side of his right leg, just above the ankle. Then he twisted his waist to the left and leaned with both hands on the floor. Unable to walk with his legs twisted one about the other he dragged himself all over the tile floor resting on his hands, his left hip and thigh, and the inside of his right foot.

Another trick he pulled in the bathroom when his parents were away was to bend his right arm and put it through the sleeve of a short-sleeved shirt. He would then put his left arm through the other sleeve and button up the shirt. To diminish the bulge at the right shoulder he would cup his hand around it. Looking in the mirror and using a little imagination it looked as if his arm had been amputated at the elbow. He would raise it and lower it and jiggle it slightly as he had seen the stumps of real amputees do.

Whether he was pretending to be legless or one-armed there was always a time when he cupped the "stump" of his arm with his hand or the "stumps" of his legs with both hands, delighting in the feeling that his arm or legs were incomplete and that the hand or hands by rights had no business being where they were. He started another pretense. He would tuck his legs inside his pajama trousers and then put the jacket on so that it covered his right arm. He would put his hand behind him so that it was held in place by the trousers' cord. Now he was not only legless but strictly one-armed with not the ghost of a stump hanging from his right shoulder and the sleeve hanging empty as he crawled on the floor. Crawling on his two "stumps" and his left hand he would watch that empty sleeve flapping about and have an orgasm.

There were two girls who begged on the street where he lived. One was missing her left leg below the knee and her stump showed as she crutched alongside people asking for alms. She would bend and straighten the knee of the amputated leg at each step as if she were really walking on it The other girl was the one he really liked. She was a pretty thing who was also missing her left leg. She wore a wide-skirted dress and her stump didn't show so he couldn't tell how long it was or whether she had a stump at all. Then one day he saw her leaning with her back against the wall of a church. She was holding her crutch in front of her and the stump bulged through her skirt because she was resting it between the staves. It reached almost to her knee. One day she approached him to ask for money as was her wont. For some reason he noticed something odd in the girl. He was flustered and refused although he had given her alms before. The girl kept on crutching beside him, insisting. At times she would be practically walking backwards in front of him and slowing down, trying to stop him. He had the idea that the girl wanted more than a few cents. He was fifteen and she must have been about his age. The image in his mind of the stump drove him crazy. He wanted desperately to talk with her, to make love to her but he had always been bashful with girls and didn't know how to approach her. Besides his training had been that one didn't mix with the lower classes and he would have had a hard time explaining a prolonged absence from home.

He kept on giving alms to the girls but the one with the leg missing above the knee never insisted again.

There was another girl, not a beggar but a woman of about twenty-five, who also walked with a crutch. He deduced she lived close to his home because he ran into her every so often on the street. She must have had polio as a child or been born with a defect because her left leg was pencil-thin and about two feet shorter than her right leg. It hung limply from her hip ("Like wet spaghetti," he thought.) and even though the foot hung pointing down from the ankle there

13

were still about 18 inches of empty space between the toes and the side-walk. She wore high-heeled shoes and stockings on both legs and he thought that she would have to buy pairs of stockings and shoes of different sizes. The sole of the shoe on the crippled foot was always immaculately clean since she never set that foot on the ground. She wore a coat over her shoulders that reached down to her good knee and he suspected that she did so in order to hide the crutch.

She had a most elegant way of walking evidently acquired from many years of practice. Her right leg was very well muscled and she walked with a slow, sensuous sway that charmed him. Her left leg swung aimlessly about because she had no control over it. It was almost as if she had been born with a crutch in her hand. Very probably she had never been able to walk normally on two legs. He would follow her for a block or two when he was on his way home from school admiring how naturally she used her crutch or slow down his walk when he saw her coming head on but at twenty-five or so the age difference was too great and he never approached her.

When he was sixteen his parents left once more for the evening. They had a different maid now and she was very sexy. He walked into her room and started chatting her up. They sat on the edge of her bed. She tucked one leg under her, hitched up her skirt and started to unroll the stocking very slowly. He looked down at her leg and it looked like it had been cut off at the knee, just as he pretended his legs were cut off. She was raising and lowering her other leg enhancing the illusion that she was one-legged. He had a tremendous erection and put his hand on the girl's knee pretending it was her stump. Just then his parents walked in, having returned from visiting their friends, and caught them in the act. He got a good chewing out and the maid was fired.

When he had just turned seventeen he graduated from high school and his father sent him to college in the States. His father insisted that he live in a dorm so the times of pretending were over. However he still day-dreamed of being an amputee. He imagined all sorts of combinations. One leg off below or above the knee, both legs off with one below and one above the knee or both legs off above the knee. He wanted stumps so he did not day-dream about one or both legs disarticulated at the hip. In his day-dreams there were also images of beautiful girls similarly crippled and they would make love in the most outlandish positions because of their missing limbs.

The first week he saw a coed with her left arm amputated at the elbow. He was disappoint-ed because she wore a white stump sock but loved to watch her walk with her stump jiggling at each step.

During his four years at college he met and dated several girls and had his normal share of sex but amputee girls were very hard to find although he kept looking for them. In that sense he missed his years in South America. He wanted to go back, look for the one-legged beggar girl and make love to her. However his parents had moved to a different country and he couldn't find a good excuse to go back where the girl was.

He was a sophomore when one day he found himself drinking beer with some friends at a night club. A bunch of girls was sitting at the next table. One of them was sitting with her back to them but she turned her head sideways and he saw in spite of the dim light that she was beautiful. He got up and asked her to dance but the girl refused. He behaved like a gentleman and didn't insist. He returned to his table and resumed the chat with his friends. Somebody at the girls' table spilled a drink and the lovely girl stood up to avoid having the liquid fall on her lap. It was then he saw that the girl's right arm had been amputated halfway between the shoulder and the elbow. She was wearing short sleeves and the stump was beautiful - rounded where the arm ended and with a flat tip about half the diameter of the arm. He thought that maybe the girl had refused to dance with him because she didn't want to give anybody any unpleasant surprises. In the low light of the room he had not noticed her missing arm when he asked her to dance. Then he thought that maybe the girl didn't really want to dance. He was afraid of being rejected again so he kept his seat.

He was twenty-one in his senior year. His grandfather had set up a trust fund in his name when he was born and now he was given control of the money. To celebrate he was having tea with a girl when across the room he noticed a rather fat girl sitting at another table. She had a very pretty face but the rolls of fat disgusted him. She was holding her tea cup with her right hand and her left hand rested on her lap. Then she lifted her left arm to reach for her purse and he noticed that the forearm ended a few inches below the elbow. She pushed her purse towards her with the stump until she could reach it with her right hand. She reached into the purse while holding it open with the stump and pulled out a wallet. She opened it and pulled out some bills. The performance had made him forget that she was fat and to his dismay he realized that she was about to pay her bill and leave.

She did pay her bill. It was late autumn and the weather was getting rather chilly. She pulled out a single glove from her purse and using her stump with great dexterity she put it on her right hand.

He decided he had to meet her. He talked to Val whom he knew could get the information he wanted for him, and she wrangled an introduction. The one-armed girl's name was Dot.

They had several dates. As Dot realized that they liked each other she started losing weight and soon became quite presentable. Eventually she turned out to have a lovely body. Her face which had been pretty turned beautiful as soon as she lost her double chin and her cheeks hollowed out a little. She had a car and she showed him her driver's license with "Restricted to driving cars with automatic drive only" stamped on it.

One day they were having drinks at a bar and he felt confident enough to hold her hand. He held it for so long that at last she said, "May I have my hand back, please?" She wanted to have another drink from her glass.

He learned that she worked for the department store that ran the tea room where he had first seen her. She was of an artistic bent and designed the windows and the special exhibitions. Her hobby was making jewelry and she showed him some pieces of her own making. He was astonished at the fine work that it entailed and asked how she could do it with only one hand.

"I was born like this," she said simply, holding up her stump.

Just before Graduation Day they went to a rodeo. While they were roping and tying the calves he asked her whether she would rather go to dinner at one restaurant or another.

"I don't care," she answered. "You choose."

"Let's leave it to luck," he said, pulling out a coin from his pocket. "Heads the first one, tails the other."

He flipped the coin in the air but it arced towards her. She was seated to his right. He reached over with his left hand but missed catching the coin. Instead his hand fell on her stump. He left it there for a moment. She looked at him and giggled. Then she picked up the coin and said, "Here it is. Heads!"

He took the coin and put it in his pocket. Without really thinking what he was doing he raised his right forearm from the armrest between them and patted it with his left hand.

He said, "Come here, lass."

She looked at him and smiling shyly she rested her stump on the armrest. He lowered his arm so that the elbow was in the air next to her and his hand was resting on the front part of the armrest. He cupped her stump and gently caressed it. She looked at him tenderly and rested her head on his shoulder.

* * *

Graduation Day arrived and she was there to see him proudly flick the tassel on his cap from right to left.

That night they went out to celebrate and he asked her to marry him.

She was doubtful.

"I don't know, darling. All my life I've thought that I wanted to marry a one-armed man, one who would understand exactly how I feel about my condition. You're the perfect lover but you have too perfect a body to be my perfect husband."

His desire to be an amputee which had lain dormant most of the time during his last college years was exacerbated. So was his devotee aspect. To be no longer a wannabe or a pretender! He, an amputee, marrying a lovely amputee! The mind boggled.

He answered, "I'm perfectly willing to lose a hand for you but I'll ask for something in return. You don't know what it's like to lose a limb because you never had that hand. You grew up one-handed. I'll be losing a hand after having had two all my life. You want me to understand you but I also want you to understand me. So I must ask you to lose a limb as well. That way each one of us will know exactly how the other one feels. I don't think you want to lose your only hand so that leaves one of your legs. Since at least part of the time you'll be needing to use a crutch I suggest that you have your right leg amputated. That way you'll be able to handle the crutch on the side that your leg is missing. Losing both an arm and a leg on the same side can be very inconvenient."

She smiled, "Losing a limb is always inconvenient but I agree with you that losing a leg on the same side as my missing hand would be very inconvenient.

"However if I agreed to have my right leg amputated that would leave me with two missing limbs while you would be missing only one. Our problems would once again be different. To make sure we understand each other, would you agree to have a leg amputated as well?"

He felt more aroused than ever. The idea of making love to a one-armed, one-legged girl while he himself was similarly crippled was immensely seductive. More important, he was comfortable with the girl. She had a good sense of humor and was fun to be with. Their tastes and scales of values had very much in common. They were good friends. He had fallen in love with her. It wouldn't be such a tremendous sacrifice to give up a leg as well as an arm for her sake.

"Agreed. Tell you what. Since you'll be missing your left arm and right leg I'll have my right arm amputated just like yours and my left leg severed. How's that?"

"Suits me fine," she said as she caressed the back of his neck with the stump of her arm.

She ran her hand through his hair and said, "There are just two details that remain to be fixed."

"Which are?"

"We already know where you're going to lose your right arm and that we are going to lose a leg each. Question: at which level are you going to have your leg amputated and at which level am I going to have my leg amputated?"

"During the last summer vacation I saw a tall, slim one-legged blonde. She was dressed in a very tight fitting dress. Her right leg was almost totally missing. The stump was very short and as she crutched along the stump was resting on the hand rest. She held the crutch by the front stave. Since the dress was so tight it tented and I could see how her stump moved back and forth as she moved the crutch. I thought it was tremendously sexy."

'Fine. Now we know how you want to lose your leg. What about mine? I'm not sure whether I want a long or a short stump. I don't even know whether I want my leg amputated above or below the knee. What do you think?"

"Since the stump of my arm is going to be like yours perhaps the stump of your leg ought to be like mine. Then we would each be the mirror image of the other - as far as amputations go, that is."

She said with a serious mien, "One last thing. I have never used a prosthesis. I've always managed with my single hand and my stump. It's not possible to walk or stand up any length of time without some sort of aid. We'll limit it to a crutch - one crutch only. Not two crutches. We could handle them with our stumps below the elbow but no; just one crutch. No artificial legs, not even peg legs. Agreed?"

He was getting to love the girl more and more.

"You're a woman after my own heart. And no hooks or artificial arms. Just one leg, one arm and one crutch each plus whatever use we can make of our stumps."

She smiled wickedly.

"We'll make a splendid couple. You like amputee girls and you want to be an amputee too, don't you?"

"Is it that very obvious?"

"To me it has been ever since we met. When Val introduced us you couldn't keep your eyes away from my stump. I used it and waved it about just a bit more than necessary and you nearly had an orgasm. I was fat then so it couldn't have been my good looks.

"We're very much alike, you know. I was born without my hand and I've always wanted to be one-legged as well. When I was a young girl I would bend my right leg and bind it in place. I would hop about or crawl on my hand, the real stump of my arm, one knee and the 'stump' of my leg.

"I fell down from a fence and broke my right leg deliberately so that I could have a crutch to walk with while it healed. Of course I kept it afterward. From then on every time I was alone I would pretend that my right leg ended at the knee and I would walk about using the crutch. I wanted so badly to be dependent on that crutch. I wanted it to be my life-long companion. I would look at myself in the mirror and think 'You're not only one-armed, you're also one-legged.' Of course the stump of my arm was real but I loved to caress the 'stump' of my leg with my real stump. I learned to bend over far enough so that I could rub the tip of my stump against the knee which to my mind was the tip of the 'leg stump'. I'm getting all wet just thinking that someday I'll be able to do it for real. I never showed it to you but I have another crutch at home. The old one became too short when I grew up. When I'm alone at home I spend a lot of time with my leg bound up. I bought a pair of baggy blue denims and cut off the right leg above the knee. When I tie up my leg and wear them I look for all the world like a one-armed (which I am) and one-legged (which I'm not) woman.

"Did you ever play games like that when you were a child?"

"Very often. Sometimes I pretended to be one-legged or one-armed but most of the time I pretended to be legless. A few times I even pretended I was legless and one-armed.

But most of the time I sat admiring my knees or crawling on them. They looked like real stumps.

"I'm afraid I'm not very good at using a crutch. Could you give me some pointers before I lose my leg?"

She answered, "I'd be delighted to. Tell you what. To-morrow you and I will go to the drugstore and buy a crutch for you. We'll also have to get some baggy blue denims and a very wide leather belt. I have to go because I have to advise you on the right size for the crutch. Then you can move in with me. I have to go to work but we'll spend every spare moment of my time practicing walking with our crutches."

"Look, I have more money than I know what to do with. You could quit your job and we could spend all our time practicing. We would be ready sooner that way. I could also get some elastic bandages, a wrist splint and adhesive tape at the drugstore. I could fold the fingers of my right hand flat against the palm with the thumb in front of the first knuckle of the index finger. Between you and me we could bandage the hand and the splint up to about halfway up my forearm. Then we could tape over the whole shebang. It won't be exactly like having my arm amputated a few inches below the elbow but it'll give me a fair idea of how to handle myself with only one hand.

"That way we'll both learn how to be one-legged and one-armed before we have our limbs amputated."

"Smart boy," she said and kissed him passionately.

The following day he packed his clothes and drove to her house. He picked her up and drove her to the store where she resigned her job. He waited for her outside and when she came out they went to the drugstore. Then they went to the supermarket and stocked up on food, drinks, soap and all sorts of household articles. Last they bought his baggy blue denims and a very wide, flat belt. They went to her home and she locked the door.

"All right, it's time to practice," she said. "You have twice as much to learn as I do. I have to learn only how to be one-legged and I've practiced it quite a lot. So we'll begin with you. Go into the bathroom, take a good shower and come out in your shorts. Then we'll fix you up."

He did as he was told and when he entered the bedroom she had everything laid out on the bed plus a tape measure and a pair of scissors.

"Well start with the easy part first," she told him.

She measured the length of his thigh and cut off the left leg of the blue denims four inches above the knee.

"You're going to have to do and undo the strap around your leg with one hand only so we might as well put your hand out of commission from the beginning."

She took the splint and taped one end to his hand. She taped the other end to his forearm. Then she placed a third strip of tape just above his wrist.

"Try to bend your wrist," she ordered.

He tried. "I can't," he answered.

"Good. Now bend your fingers and your thumb the way you said."

He did so. She took the elastic bandage and with her hand and the stump of her arm she bound first the fingers, then the hand and finally the wrist and forearm to where the splint ended, about seven inches from the elbow. He was amazed at how tightly she had wound the bandage with only one hand.

"Try to move your fingers."

Again, he couldn't.

"Fine. Elastic bandages tend to loosen up and if they do they slip. We'll hold the bandage in place with the tape."

She taped the bandage, again very tightly.

He asked, "Are you sure you're not going to cut the circulation to the arm?"

She looked deep into his eyes.

"Does it really matter?"

He bent his elbow and looked at his bandaged arm. The hand was indistinguishable from the forearm. It just looked like he had a very long stump. He realized that putting on his shorts after the shower had been the last thing he would ever do with both hands.

He shrugged. "No, I suppose not," he said.

"O.K. Let's start on the leg. This will only take a few minutes. Let's adjust the crutch to your height. Put your socks and shoes on and stand up."

He put on his socks using just his left hand. His shoes were the moccasin type so he had no trouble with shoe laces. He stood up.

She picked up the crutch and held it vertically under his left armpit.

"Too short," she said.

He said sarcastically, "I thought you were going to advise me on how to buy a crutch of the proper length. What do we do now, go and change it?"

She laughed.

"No, silly. Crutches are adjustable in height within certain limits. You're six feet tall. I bought a crutch that could be adjusted for people who measure from five feet nine to six feet three inches. See where the staves join the center post? The three parts are joined by two screws that go from the front to the back of the crutch. The screws are held in place by butterfly nuts and pressure washers. The center post is perforated along a great part of its length. All I have to do is remove the screws, slide the center post up or down and replace the screws, washers and nuts."

She laid the crutch on her lap and very dexterously adjusted it to his height. It only took a minute, He couldn't get over his amazement at how well she managed with her single hand.

"One more adjustment," she said.

She again placed the crutch vertically under his arm pit.

"Let your arm drop naturally," she commanded.

She took a look at his wrist and the hand grip. They were at the same level.

"No adjustment necessary. Time to 'chop off' your leg"

She ordered him to take off his shoes and socks and sit on the edge of the bed.

"Now bend your leg under you and place the belt under your ankle with the buckle end to your left and close to the ankle."

"Aren't you going to help me do this? I'm one-handed now, you know."

"Only when it's absolutely necessary. You have to learn how to be both one-legged and one-handed. So get going!"

"You're a hard-driving teacher."

"Only because I love you, darling. Amputations are definitive. There's no turning back after-wards. Not many people are as lucky as we to practice being limbless before they really are."

He was mollified.

He placed the belt as she had told him to and brought the free end around and over his thigh. He inserted the end through the buckle and pulled tight. The buckle's pin was way beyond where the perforations ended.

"You'll have to start again. Wind the belt around your ankle first and then around your thigh."

The pin was close to the perforations but if he fastened the belt it would be too lose.

"Hang on a minute, my love."

She picked up the scissors she had used to cut off the leg of his blue denims. He pulled on the belt as tight as he could and with the point of one of the blades she punched a hole through it at the proper point.

He pushed the pin through the hole wishing he had his right hand to help. It finally went in. He raised his thigh and felt his foot moving under him but his knee did not move. He remembered his days as a child when he tucked his bent legs into his pajama trousers. Only this time he was not play-acting. He was getting ready to have his leg removed.

"'Amputation' and 'stump' are such sexy words," he thought.

He put on the blue denims. At least he could lean on the "stump" of his right hand while he did it. He understood then why they had to be baggy. His foot made a lump behind him and it would have been difficult to move the 'stump' of his leg if the seat had been tight. He drew up the zipper and put on his right shoe and sock. His left knee stuck out of the cut-off leg of the pants just like it had out of his rolled-up pajama leg many years ago, looking like a stump. She handed him his crutch.

"All right. Now stand up and start walking."

"That's all there is too it, huh? Just stand up and start walking!"

"No, my love, that's where you begin. There's much more to it. You'll have to learn how to go up and down steps, to pull out your wallet and pay the butcher, the baker and the candle-stick maker and then you'll have to learn how to carry home everything they sold you. You'll have to learn how to shower and go to the head with only one arm and one leg. You'll have trouble knotting your tie, pouring yourself a glass of water and a zillion other things. So that's not all there is to it. Now get up and walk."

He tried to stand up but lost his balance and fell back on the bed. He tried again, leaning on the "stump" of his arm and managed to stand up. He couldn't feel the floor with his left foot. He looked down and saw his leg ending at the knee. He raised the thigh but no more leg could be seen. Only the knee showed below the cut-off leg of the denims, looking for all the world like a stump. She was the perfect pretender and with her skill she had made him feel like his leg had really been cut off.

As he did when he was a child he raised his hand to beg for alms. He had always done it with his right hand and he did it again, raising his bandaged "stump". He also raised his bent leg so that the knee showed very clearly. He swung the 'stump' of his leg in an up and down arc from the horizontal to where he couldn't lift it any longer.

"Alms for this poor beggar boy, kind madam. Alms for this one-legged, one-handed boy. Look at me, madam. I have only one arm. I have only one leg. Look at my stumps. I can't work. Alms please!"

She laughed so hard she had to sit on the bed with tears in her eyes. She wiped them away with the stump of her arm.

He waved about both "stumps" enjoying the delightful feeling of crippledness. The crutch, replacing his shortened leg, felt wonderful under his arm. The sense that his foot could not touch the floor - that there was this huge empty space where his leg should have been - excited him no end. He wanted the feeling to be real, permanent.

"You'll make a wonderful cripple! The arm does look a little made up but your leg looks like it was really cut off at the knee. Are you sure you want your leg amputated so high?"

"Yes my love. With a long stump I wouldn't be able to place it on the hand grip and move the crutch with it. You have no idea what a sexy feeling it is. Besides we'll wear very short shorts when the weather is warm enough so that our stumps will remain in sight. After all showing off your stumps is one of the charms of being an amputee."

She too was excited by the idea of becoming one-legged.

"All right, time to start practicing. You're leaning to your left on your crutch. It's not vertical. Remember that the crutch replaces your leg. You wouldn't walk with your leg sticking out at the side. Straighten up and place the tip of the crutch where the heel of your foot should be. From now on it is going to be the heel of your foot."

He had a sense that it wasn't only putting on his shorts that would be the last thing he had done with two hands. He now understood that he would never again walk on two legs.

"I am not going to release my leg until its cut off. Is that it?"

"Yes. And when I tie up my leg it too will stay that way. From now on you and I are one-legged and one-armed. There will be a transition from the pretend to the real situation and then you, I and our stumps will live happily ever after."

"And how will that transition come about? We have to make arrangements for the operations. Are we going to go out in the street looking like this?"

"The arrangements have already been made, my love. After you went home last night I called a friend of mine at the clinic. All we have to do is make a phone call when we're ready and they'll send an ambulance to pick us up. Your surgeon will be a gorgeous one-armed blonde and mine will be an extremely handsome one-legged guy."

The idea of being maimed by a beautiful amputee struck him as delightful. Then he thought twice about it. He frowned, "Are you sure it's O.K. to have a surgical operation done by an amputee?"

"Don't worry. These people are good. They've been practicing for years."

"You do think of everything, don't you?"

'When I have the chance to make my dream of being one-legged come true and to boot I can catch a dreamboat like you who is going to lose an arm and a leg for both our sakes I try to be as thorough as possible.

"Now start walking. You'll have to practice and practice and I'm eager to get on with our plan. At first you'll take short steps, remembering to keep your crutch always vertical within a plane parallel to your direction of movement. In other words, move it backwards and forwards but try not to move it sideways unless you're about to lose your balance. Now move the tip of the crutch forward about twelve inches, lean on it with both your armpit and your hand and bring your foot to a few inches in front of the tip. Try to bear as much of your weight as you can on the hand and leave the rest to the arm pit."

Her instructions had been very precise. He did as he was told and to his surprise he moved very supply to a position a short distance in front of where he had been standing. The "stump" of his leg swung forward as he moved the crutch and backward as he moved his leg.

"That's the idea. The crutch replaces the leg so it and the stump must move together in the same direction. It's a bit awkward at first because with those unfortunate two-legged people the arm on the same side moves backward as the leg moves forward and viceversa. You now have to move your arm, the crutch and the stump in the same direction all the time. You'll get used to it shortly."

He started crutching, hesitantly at first, around the room. Soon he was taking longer steps. He delighted in walking with one leg and a crutch.

"You're doing great," she said. "Now go out to the living room. There's more space there for you to practice. I'll join you shortly."

He crutched all around the living room. He went around the sofa. He leaned over and tried to turn a table lamp on and off with his right hand. The bandaged "stump" prevented him from using it, reminding him he was not supposed to have a right hand. He went to the window, shut it and lifted it open again.

As he finished raising the window he heard a thumping sound behind him. He turned around and there she was, crutching toward him. The illusion of one-leggedness was perfect. The "stump" of her leg peeped enticingly from the bottom of the right leg of the blue denims and swayed in perfect unison with the crutch. She was wearing an espadrille on her left foot with the ribbons tied up around her slim ankle. A very tight white blouse with short sleeves and an astonishing décolletage completed the ensemble. The stump of her arm which was normally very quiescent waved about a little every time she brought her leg forward. She crutched slowly, swaying her body in a sensual manner at each step just like he remembered that girl with the crippled leg.

And the crutch! What a crutch! It was not an ordinary aluminum affair like they have in the hospitals. This one was made of red oak with very thin staves. The hand grip and the saddle were covered with the finest Cordovan leather. The wood had been varnished and it gleamed in the light. There was no adjustable center post, no nuts and bolts. The two staves melded gently into a thicker one twelve inches before they reached the floor. The crutch had been made to order.

He was dazzled. If this was what she looked liked pretending he couldn't imagine what she would look like after she had her leg amputated.

"You like?" she asked with a brilliant smile.

"I... I don't know what to say. Seeing you has left me speechless."

"I'm glad you approve."

She pointed at the crutch with the stump of her arm and said, "I have a collection of these; eight in all. There's another model. It's finished in shiny black enamel. I have four of each: for flat soles, one, two and three inch heels. I thought of having two more made to be used with four inch heels but I decided it would be too dangerous since I can use only one crutch to walk with.

"As you can see, I've been pretending for a long time."

He thanked his gods that he had met such a charming, delightful woman.

They spent the rest of the day crutching about her house. At one point she teasingly dared him to catch her. He tried to but she was much better than he at using a crutch and ran circles around him.

"Not fair!" he said. "You've had years of practice!"

She crutched up to him, put the stump of her arm around his neck and kissed him. The combination of a sexy crippled girl kissing him while he himself was on a crutch with a useless right hand was too much. He tried to pick her up to take her to the bedroom. His crutch was in the way and he tossed it off to one side.

He was strong enough to pick her up while she screamed, "Please don't, sweetheart, well fall!"

Fall they did. He had forgotten about his "missing" leg and when he tried to take a step with it they both came tumbling down. He managed to fall so that she came down on top of him.

"Are you all right?" she asked.

"Yes, I'm fine. A bit embarrassed but fine," he answered. "Are you O.K.?"

"I had a comfy cushion to fall on," she said with a smile.

He put his hand on her breast and gently squeezed the nipple. She was not wearing a bra under the blouse.

"As long as we're down here why don't we take advantage of the situation?"

"Suits me fine," she answered and started unbuttoning her blouse.

They made love for an hour, at the end of which both were exhausted. Making love when both partners have a leg tied behind them does not make it easy to find a comfortable position.

With the ease of long practice she picked up her crutch and stood up. He was still on the floor and she stretched out the stump of her arm.

"Place your crutch upright against the wall."

He did so.

"Now hold on to my stump so that you can get up."

While he was still teetering on one leg she pulled her stump away from his hand. He hopped to the wall and gratefully snuggled his crutch under his arm.

"I told you it was always inconvenient to lose a limb. We have, for all practical purposes, lost two."

"I don't care how inconvenient it gets. I really want to lose them!"

"Well, the sooner you learn how to get along with one leg and one hand the sooner we'll make our dream come true. Come on, let's practice some more."

By supper time he was getting to be quite good with his crutch. They were both quite hungry from the exercise.

"Time to cook dinner," she said.

"Cook? How?"

"We'll make it easy to-night. We'll heat some TV dinners and eat at the counter. There's apple pie for desert. There are plates and cutlery in that cupboard," she said pointing with her stump. "You get them and place them on the counter. In the meantime I'll put the dinners in the microwave and slice the pie."

The cupboard was over the counter. He managed to open the door without dropping his crutch. There was a stack of plates in the middle, a cutlery tray to the left and several glasses to the right. He tried to pick up a couple of plates but his crutch started to fall over. He thought that if he were already missing his leg he would be able to control the crutch with the stump. He tried the next best thing. He pulled the crutch away from him and opening up his bent leg he tried to thrust the knee between the staves. He was able to introduce about three inches of his "stump". It was enough. The crutch was away from his body and he was supporting it instead of the other way around but by now he felt stable enough standing on one leg.

He picked up two dinner plates at a time and set them on the counter. There followed two dessert plates. He placed one to the left of each dinner plate. Then he brought down two glasses. He lowered the cutlery tray and placed a knife, fork and spoon beside each dinner plate. He ended by placing the tray back on the shelf and shutting the cupboard door.

Retrieving his crutch he called out, "Ready!"

There was the sound of muffled applause behind him. She was clapping by beating her hand against the stump of her arm.

Eating with one hand was not hard for him. She, of course, had been doing it all her life.

Picking up the dishes and taking them to the dishwasher was another matter. He had to carry the plates, cutlery and glasses across the kitchen. First he went to the dishwasher and opened the door. Then he returned, picked up the knives with his left hand and holding them and the hand bar simultaneously took them to the dishwasher and placed them in the cutlery basket. He picked up the forks and spoons and did the same thing. He went back to the counter and contemplated the plates and glasses. Finally he took one of the plates and tucked it between the "stump" of his right arm and his body. There were remains of food on the plate and he dirtied his shirt. He shrugged in resignation.

"It's always inconvenient," he thought. "But what a small price to pay for achieving a life-long ambition."

He finished carrying the other plate and the glasses to the dishwasher, poured some dishwasher liquid into the bin, shut the door and turned the machine on.

She was in the living room, watching the TV, absent-mindedly running her right hand over the "stump" of her right leg. She too was wishing that the training period would be over soon so that they could both be double amputees and enjoy their lives as they wanted to.

He crutched in saying, "It's been a long day. I'm going to hit the hay so hard it's going to hit me back!"

"I'm right with you," she answered.

She turned off the TV and stood up. They crutched to the bedroom side by side.

Undressing was a bit difficult for him but not for her. When he finally lay on the bed he tried to do so on his back. His left foot got in the way and he turned to sleep on his right side. She was facing him and having had previous experience of sleeping with her leg tied up she lay on her left side. She touched his leg "stump" with hers.

"My stump loves your stump," she said in a low voice.

He answered, "All my stumps love all your stumps."

They went to sleep in each other's arms, whether complete, incomplete, bound or free.

They slept late the following morning. When he opened his eyes she was already awake, looking at him tenderly.

Suddenly he sat up with a start.

"What is it? What's the matter", she asked.

"My leg. I can feel it to the knee but I can't feel anything below."

"It's perfectly normal," she said. "The position in which you have kept your knee for the past twenty-four hours makes it difficult for the blood to circulate. Also your sciatic nerve is under pressure. The combination makes your leg numb. Actually this is very good because it enhances the realism of your 'one-leggedness.' From now on you'll feel as if the leg had been really cut off at the knee. My leg is numb too. I walked by resting my 'stump' on the edge of the bed and it felt like I had a real stump."

"But doesn't it damage the leg?"

She gave him the same answer she had given him on the previous day when she had bandaged his arm very tightly to make it look handless.

"Does it matter?'

"No, of course not. How silly of me to worry."

They had breakfast. He was getting good at setting the table and taking the dishes to the dishwater.

"Time to shower and dress," she said.

He showed his "handless" arm saying, "But it will get all wet."

She replied, "Not to speak of the leather belts strapped around our legs. When leather gets wet and dries it shrinks. Come to think of it, we could save some money on the amputations. Wet and dry the belts until they shrink so much they cut our legs off."

32

"Sadist!" he said.

"Not any more than you, my lord. It was you who suggested that we both have our legs amputated."

"Yes, but only after you suggested that I lose my arm in order to marry you."

"I didn't suggest it. I only said I had hoped to marry a one-armed man. It was you who offered to have your arm amputated. Anyway, let's not quibble over trifles. We've agreed on many things already. Let's just agree we're both sadomasochists, O.K.? Now let's get back to the showering business."

She crutched to the kitchen and returned with three draw-string garbage bags held in the crook of her left elbow. They were of two different sizes.

"This long narrow one is for your arm. the other two are for our 'amputated' legs. You put your stump in and pull the draw-string. That way neither the bandages nor the belts will get wet."

"You are a clever girl, aren't you?"

"I told you, I have been practicing this for lo these many years."

They breakfasted, showered and dressed.

She told him, "You've gotten very good at walking on a flat surface. Now I want you to learn how to go up and down stairs. Come with me to the garage."

A door from the kitchen led to the garage. He was glad because he would have felt self-conscious crutching out of doors. It wasn't the leg that bothered him so much as the arm. The tape that covered it was white and stuck out like a flag.

The garage was large and her sapphire blue car left plenty of space available between the grill and the back wall. She went to a corner and pulled out a set of wooden steps. There were five steps at each end with a fairly large platform in between. She pushed the contraption with the stump of her arm to the center of the available space.

"You don't know how to do this and I'm out of practice. I've been too lazy to come here as often as I should to keep in practice. I'll do it first and show you how. You stand nearby, ready to catch me if I fall."

She crutched up to the steps at one end while he crutched over to the side of the stairway.

"The fundamental principle is that while you're going up the leg goes first and then you bring your crutch up to the same level as your foot. It's quite the opposite when you go down. The crutch goes first and then you bring your foot down to the crutch's level. Don't do anything silly like trying to take two steps at a time, especially when you're going down. You risk breaking your neck. Understood?"

"Yes, ma'am. Leg first when going up, crutch first when going down. One step at a time."

It made sense. The crutch was rigid while the leg could bend at the thigh, knee and ankle. If you raised the crutch first while going up the saddle would be higher than your armpit. If you lowered your foot first while going down the crutch couldn't bend. It would swing like a vaulting pole and send you tumbling down the stairs.

She demonstrated. Her lack of practice didn't show. He admired the elegant way in which she handled her crutch.

He thought, "She'll make a splendid one-legged woman and with that hand she's already missing I couldn't ask for anybody better."

"Your turn," she said.

The first time he went up and down the "stump" of his arm waved all over the place. By the fifth he had brought it down to a gentle jiggle which he thought quite appealing. He hoped when had his arm amputated the stump would jiggle in the same way.

They practiced and practiced. They kept thinking of new and more difficult things to do and they found ways to do them. Not very orthodox ways at times but they worked. They found they could do things with their "stumps" that they had thought impossible. The bond between them grew stronger and stronger every day.

Two weeks to the day after he moved in with her they decided they were ready.

They removed the belts and unwound the tape and elastic bandage around his arm. Their unbound legs were thin and useless below the knee from lack of exercise. He could move his elbow but his wrist and fingers were locked in the position in which he had placed them.

She said, "We'll have to use our crutches to go to the clinic," and reached for the phone.

* * *

The doctor was a smashing redhead. The right sleeve of her white coat was empty. Her stump reached about six inches below the shoulder. It moved now and then and when it did the sleeve would rise and fall. He wondered if his stump would do that as well as jiggle.

She smiled when she saw the state of his arm and leg and said, "Welcome to the Dream Club."

He understood that she, too, was a voluntary amputee.

"I see from your registration form that you are in for the voluntary amputations of an arm and a leg. Also that you have pretended to be an amputee for a long time."

She pointed the stump of her right arm at him. The empty sleeve hung limply where her arm ended and she waved the stump about a little so that it swung from side to side

She said, "You understand, of course, that amputations are definitive. It's not like when you pretend, where you can always unbind your limbs and be back to 'normal.' Once you've had a limb removed there's no turning back. That limb is gone forever."

Harry understood that she was doing her duty in trying to dissuade him but the look in her emerald green eyes told him that she was itching to amputate his arm and leg.

"I understand, doctor, but I'm in love with a one-armed girl," he answered. "She's going to have her leg amputated so that we'll both be crippled in the same way. It's so that we can each understand the other one's problems perfectly. I've wanted to be crippled since I was very young and now I have the chance not only to be an amputee but to be with the girl of my dreams. I realize that pretending is not the same as being an actual amputee but this is a chance I simply can't miss."

The doctor lowered the stump of her arm and tucked the empty sleeve into the right hand pocket of her hospital jacket.

"Very well, then," she said and signed the form authorizing Harry's amputations.

She looked at the fundus, examined his reflexes, took his blood pressure and pulse, measured his breathing rhythm and ordered a clotting time analysis and an electrocardiogram.

"I'll start operating on you in a couple of hours if all the analyses come out well. Two hours after that you'll be as you've wanted to be for so long."

She rubbed the stump of her arm with her hand. There was a happy look on her face,

They took a blood sample, carried him to cardiology in a wheel chair and then took him to his room in the same wheel chair.

Two hours after he had left the doctor's office a nurse gave him a shot and wheeled him on a stretcher to the operating room. At the same time another nurse was wheeling Dot, who had been assigned the room next to his, to another operating room.

He woke up feeling a dull pain. He couldn't quite place the origin at first. Then he realized he was hurting in two places. He smiled with satisfaction. Just to make sure he lifted the sheet over his right arm. Yes, there was his arm or rather what was left of it. The stump was so short that they had to bandage it to above the elbow. He pushed the sheet away from him and looked at the stump of his left leg. It was precisely the length he wanted, allowing for the thickness of the dressings. He let go a whoop of exultation.

A nurse heard him and rushed in thinking something was wrong.

He apologized, "I'm sorry, ma'am. It's just that I've wanted to be one-armed and one-legged for so long and now at last I've got my wish!"

'Oh, you're one of those, are you?"

"One of those? Oh, yes. There aren't many of us around, are there?"

"Quite a few. They perform at least a dozen voluntary amputations every week in this hospital alone. Personally I can't see what you find in it."

"Look, ma'am, some people aren't happy because they're fat, others think they're too thin. So they go on a diet to change their weight. Some persons are black-haired and they dye their hair red. Others have brown eyes and they wish they were blue so they buy colored contact lenses. I wished to have only one arm and one leg so I had the extra limbs amputated. It's that simple.

"Could you tell me how the girl next door is doing? The one who had her right leg amputated?"

"Oh, she's doing fine. She woke up fifteen minutes ago and asked for her crutch. I never saw anybody who had just lost a leg handle a crutch with such finesse, much less so soon after her amputation."

"Well, yes, she was an expert before she lost her leg. She taught me how to use my crutch. Would you hand it to me, please?"

She walked to the corner, picked up the crutch and gave it to him. He got out of bed and crutched to the bathroom. He regretted that the bandaged stump of the leg would not fit through the staves. He moved it in unison with the crutch as Dot had taught him. He was still a bit woozy from the operation but he kept his balance. The stump of his arm jiggled a little as he walked. It was his first experience as a real double amputee and he was enjoying it to the hilt.

Three days later the nurse who had heard him whoop came into the room with a wheel chair.

She handed him what looked like an oversized diaper. It was actually something similar to a man's jockey shorts without a slit in the front.

"What's that?"

"'Jungle pants.' You're supposed to wear them at PT so you don't give an indecent show if your gown goes up above your hips."

He put on the garment remarking how easy it was to put the stump of his leg through the hole in the left side. Once he had it on he moved from his bed to the wheel chair.

"The doctor says it's time to start your PT."

"You keep talking about PT. What is PT?"

"Physical therapy. You have to learn how to walk with a crutch, do things with your remaining hand and eventually be fitted out with prostheses."

"But I don't need PT. I've been rehearsing being one-legged and one-armed for two weeks. I can use a crutch quite well, thank you very much - you saw that the day after my limbs were amputated - and I can get along very well with my single hand and the stump of my arm. And I don't want artificial limbs. My girlfriend and I decided we would get along with just one crutch each and our stumps."

"Look, I don't know what you and your girl decided. All I know is that I've been ordered to take you down to PT. You can discuss the matter with your physiotherapist and your doctor when you get there. Now sit straight on the chair and I'll wheel you down."

"May I take my crutch with me?"

"They have plenty of crutches down there. Now let's go."

He looked up over his shoulder at her, "You know, you're a gorgeous woman. You'd look lovely if you smiled instead of frowning so much."

The nurse arranged her lovely blond hair and smiled. She looked at his stumps with a touch of envy.

She pushed his chair into the hall. Dot was being wheeled out at the same time. She didn't have her crutch either.

The two nurses walked side by side, each wheeling her patient to PT.

Dot looked at him with a loving smile and said, "Hi, you handsome cripple! Long time no see!"

He waved the bandaged stump of his arm and answered, "Hi, you gorgeous amputee! Good to see you again."

The drop in their hospital gowns below her right hip and his left hip betrayed their almost absolute lack of a leg.

They both raised their short stumps so their gowns tented. She held the stump of her arm with her hand while he did

38

the same with the bandaged stump of his arm and they raised them above their heads in a sign of victory.

The nurses left them at the PT room. A stunning blonde approached them walking on a crutch. The stump of her left leg reached to mid-thigh and her right hand was off an inch above the wrist. She had the same slow, sensual, swaying way of walking that he had already seen three times before in his life: the "polio girl" as he thought of her, the one-legged girl with the tight dress and Dot when they pretended to be one-legged.

She said, "Good morning. My name is Arlene and I'm your physiotherapist. I know that finding oneself minus one or more limbs can be a great shock and there's a tremendous feeling of helplessness. I'm here to teach you how to adapt to your limitations and learn to live as normal a life as possible."

Dot looked about her. Everywhere there were groups of recent amputees doing various exercises. Each group was being led by a physiotherapist. It struck her that the amputees had been grouped according to the types of amputations. Three people with one leg amputated below the knee and another above the knee were doing their exercises together. Five people with both legs amputated above the knee were doing the same. Everywhere she looked the members of each group had similar stumps. In a corner a tall, slim brunette sat on a stool practicing writing with one of her feet on a sheet of paper that lay on the floor. She was wearing a bikini. Both arms were off at the shoulder. She had a physiotherapist for herself.

What struck Dot was that all the physiotherapists were stunningly beautiful girls who had suffered the same amputations as the members of the groups they were leading.

She said to Arlene, "How does the clinic find so many lovely girls who are both physiotherapists and amputees?"

Arlene smiled, "It's not hard. There are plenty of recent graduates and the hospitals are glutted. It's not easy to find a job in PT. The clinic looks for specific amputee physiotherapists and hires them. The idea is that a person with a disability can best be trained by someone with the same disability. "

"And suppose a specific amputee is not available?"

"Then the clinic places an ad on TV asking for able-bodied girls who are physiotherapists and are willing to have the necessary limb or limbs amputated. If they answer the ad and agree then the clinic pays for the operation, all their medical expenses and their rehabilitation. See that armless girl in the corner teaching the other girl how to write? She had her arms amputated a year ago. She says she's never been so happy in her life."

"And the girl she's helping?"

"That's a sad case. She was an amateur pilot and her light plane crashed. She's adjusting fabulously however."

"Are you a voluntary amputee too?"

"Yes. It's a well-kept secret but there are many more of us around, both men and women, than people think who have had one or more limbs amputated voluntarily. A year and a half ago I jumped at the chance to lose my hand and my leg."

"Are you going to take care of Harry while someone else takes care of me? After all he's missing his right hand and left leg like you but I'm missing my left hand and right leg."

"Normally there'd be two of us but my opposite number resigned yesterday to get married. So I'm going to take care of both of you."

He said, "Look, I don't think we need very much physiotherapy. Dot was born without her hand so she's used to being one-armed. We both practiced being one-legged before coming here and we only requested admission when were quite proficient with our crutches. I taped up my hand to get used to doing things with only one arm."

"Let me see," said Arlene. She called for two aides who wheeled Dot and Harry beside a walking bar and fetched two crutches.

"Please hold on to the bar and stand up."

They did so and Arlene adjusted the crutches properly. She handed them over and said, "All right, let's see you walk."

They raced each other around the room veering when they got to each group of amputees. They slowed down for the last twenty yards and aped Arlene's sexy walk.

There was a round of thundering applause from everybody. The handless people beat their stumps together and the two armless girls clapped with their feet.

"Great show!" Arlene said. "Now let's see you going up and down some steps."

They practically ran up and down the steps.

"One more test," said Arlene. "Do you see those two burned-out light bulbs in the ceiling? There are stepladders and bulbs in that closet. I want each one of you to replace one of the burned-out bulbs."

Dot smiled as she looked at Harry who had a dismayed look on his face.

"Just do what I do," she said.

Dot crutched over to the closet and opened the door. She placed the stump of her arm under the rung of one stepladder and lifting it off its hook she supported it with her stump and her left shoulder. Slowly she backed out of the closet, turned around and crutched to a place on the floor under one of the bulbs. She set down the ladder, opened it wide and pullled the tool shelf into a horizontal position.

Going back to the closet she picked up a new bulb, crutched to the ladder and placed the bulb on the shelf.

All the time Harry was watching her and repeating her movements.

"How do we go up the steps?" he asked.

"Easy. Just look for a rung that's at or just below the level of the stump of your leg, lean on it and bring your good leg up."

They raced up the ladders. Leaning on the top rung with the stumps of their arms the unscrewed the old bulbs, placed them on the shelves, screwed in the new ones and came down with triumphant grins on their faces.

'I'm convinced," said Arlene. "It's lunch-time. We'll go to the coffee shop and have lunch together. The treat is on the house."

They served themselves cafeteria-style, pushing their trays along the chromed railing with the stumps of their arms and holding up their plates so the personnel could serve them. They settled on veal cutlets with peas and mashed potatoes. They also picked up some buns and butter. For dessert they chose apple pie a la mode.

When they reached the cash register Arlene told the cashier to charge the meals to the clinic. The girl pushed some keys on the cash register with her wrists and let them through.

Harry asked, "Are all the personnel amputees?"

"Yes, except for some of the nurses. Sometimes we need able-bodied people to turn the patients in bed. The clinic is dedicated to amputations and with very few exceptions every-body who works here has to be missing at least one hand above the wrist or one foot above the elbow. The policy of covering all medical expenses for amputations and rehabilitation extends to anybody who is able-bodied but wants to work here."

Dot and Harry carried their trays to a table. Arlene had let them go first so they wouldn't see how she did it,

They both placed their single hand at one end of the tray and the stump of their arm under the other. Holding their crutches tightly under their arms they moved them with their elbows and their hips. They couldn't use the stumps of their legs to control the movement of their crutches because the thickness of the bandages prevented them from thrusting the stumps between the staves.

Arlene came up behind them doing the same thing. The stump of her leg was too long to place on the hand grip. When all three were at the table she pushed back her hair with her hand and the stump of her arm.

"Good show!" she said. "You two must have practiced for ages before becoming amputees."

Dot said, "Harry practiced being one-armed and one-legged for two weeks. I was born with a stunted left arm and for a long time I pretended that I was one-legged as well.

"You see, Harry asked me to marry him and I told him I wanted a one-armed husband. He said he was willing to lose an arm if I lost a leg. I told him that I would be left with two stumps to his one so he agreed to lose a leg as well. And here we are."

"You kids don't need very much PT. They'll remove the stitches and the bandages in a few days but your stumps will still be swollen. I'll show you how to wrap an elastic bandage to bring the swelling down. I'll also teach you some exercises to keep your stumps strong,

By three in the afternoon they were back in their rooms.

Four days later the doctors removed the dressings for the last time. The stitches were also removed. Their stumps were still slightly swollen but they were thin enough now so that they could rest them on the hand bars, between the staves. They bandaged their stumps as Arlene had taught them so the residual swelling would go down quickly.

To their disappointment the doctors insisted that they stay for another week.

"Just to make sure there's no sign of infection," the curvaceous redhead said. She was in her office, wearing a short-sleeved blouse. The stump of her arm wiggled when she moved in her chair and he found it enormously exciting.

They were checking out when Dot's doctor approached them on his crutch. His left leg had been amputated a few inches below the knee.

"Congratulations." he said. 'In another two weeks your stumps will be absolutely beautiful."

He unpinned his trouser leg, rolled it up and showed them his stump. There was not the slightest sign of a scar upon it.

"I had my leg amputated three years ago. You can expect similar results six months from now."

They paid their bills, called a taxi and went to her place. Each one had taken only a small valise with a change of clothes and a toilet kit. They carried the valises in the crook of the elbow of their missing arms.

When the taxi driver offered to carry the valises to the door of the house they refused his help.

"Thank you," she said. "We may have lost our limbs only two weeks ago but we're already expert amputees."

"It shows. You both have a lovely way of walking," the taxi driver said. "Between the two of you you'd make a great whole person."

"But we're not whole and we don't want to be. As a matter of fact that's why we each had a leg and an arm amputated."

She didn't trouble to explain that she had only had her leg amputated and that she had been born minus an arm.

The cabby replied, "The more power to you. Have a good day."

They went into her house eager to examine their stumps in private. They had taken looks at them in the clinic but the place was full of doctors and nurses who kept barging into their rooms at the most ungodly hours either prescribing or administering medicines or changing their bandages and examining the stitches for any sign of infection.

They both spoke simultaneously.

"Show me the stump of your arm."

"Show me the stump of your leg."

They laughed.

"Ladies first," he said and extended the stump of his arm.

She gasped, "It's beautiful! That surgeon did a splendid job even if she had only one arm to work with. Do you know that she was right-handed and that's precisely why she had her right arm amputated? She said it would be too easy to lose her left arm and she wanted things to be difficult for her after her amputation. She's considering having her left leg amputated below the knee, not because it's easier to use an artificial leg but because she wants the stump to show all year round. She has to use a crutch in order to do that and she's practicing beforehand like you and I did."

He bent his elbow and looked at the stump. It was a lovely stump, a most satisfying stump. He tried to close and open his fist and he could see the muscles at the tip contracting and relaxing. He remembered when he had put on his shorts the day he moved into her house. That was the last thing he had done with both hands. Going to the bed to have his leg bound with the belt was the last time he had walked on both legs. It had been only four weeks ago but somehow it seemed so far back in time.

She cupped her hand around his stump and caressed the part below the elbow with her stump. What they had done had joined them as partners for life with ties more binding than those of any marriage vows. She felt full of love for this man who had given an arm and a leg for her, and for whom she had lost a leg.

"I love you," she said, looking at him with glistening eyes.

"I love you too. I love you so much that I feel I could burst."

She tossed her head gaily. With a bright smile she said, "Your turn now. Let's go sit on the couch and you can look at the stump of my leg."

They sat side by side with her on the left and him on the right. Their two leg stumps were touching. She raised her stump for him to see. He placed his good arm around her shoulders and caressed her stump with the stump of his right arm. She shivered at the touch of the two stumps.

He said, "It's gorgeous! Look at how beautifully rounded it is. And the muscles still feel very strong."

"We'll have to be careful about that," she answered. "If we don't exercise them continuously they will become shriveled and pointy and ugly. I noticed that you tried to clench and open your fist when I was looking at the stump of your arm. I saw your muscles move."

"Yes, but I wasn't trying to exercise my stump. I just wanted to know exactly how it feels when you want to move a limb that you no longer have."

"And how did it feel?"

"Delicious. It filled me with joy. It's a sensation that those poor folks with whole bodies will never delight in."

He raised his stump and wiggled the muscles, again trying to close and open his fist.

"See? There's no hand to move. It's lovely!"

"Let me look at the stump of your leg," she said. "You have two new stumps to my one."

He raised the stump of his leg and it was she who put her arm around his shoulders. She caressed his stump with the stump of her arm and it was he who shivered with delight.

They looked at each other with desire in their eyes.

"Bed!" they both said as one.

This time there were no troublesome feet or bent legs to get in the way.

Harry rinsed the razor under the running water. He wiped it dry and closed the faucets. With a face cloth he wiped the remaining lather from his face. Then he unscrewed the top of the toothpaste tube. He placed the tube on the washbasin and holding the toothbrush with his hand squeezed out some toothpaste with the stump and ran the bristles over it. He brushed his teeth.

He got under the shower and reaching out placed his crutch nearby. The stall had been fitted with small stainless steel shelves at sundry points on the walls so that he could lean on them with the stumps of his arm or leg. They were there to help him keep his balance because he couldn't take his crutch with him under the water. He turned on the faucets and leaned the stump of his leg on one of the lower shelves. He reached for the soap and placed it in the crook of his elbow. Picking up the brush he ran it over the soap vigorously and scrubbed himself.

"It's a good thing Dot was born without a hand. Things would have been much different if she had been born with her arm missing from the shoulder," he thought.

He wondered if he would have been willing to match Dot's missing arm if that had been the case. He had always wanted to be an amputee but except for the few times that he kept his arm under his pajama jacket he had always pretended he had stumps.

After rinsing himself he reached for a towel. He had always dried his back by holding the towel behind him and rubbing it back and forth from side to side. They had warned him that amputees often try to use their missing limbs and that he could fall if he tried to walk on his missing leg but automatically he reached for the ends with his hands.

"What a lovely feeling," he thought as he looked at the stump of the arm. He straightened and bent the elbow enjoying the sight of the truncated limb moving. He closed his right fist and the muscles in the stump contracted.

Holding the towel between the stump of his arm and his body he picked up the crutch and left the shower stall. He dried himself bit by bit. To dry his back he bent his elbow double to hold one end. The strokes from side to side were much shorter but that was part of the inconvenience he had expected.

Being a self-sufficient double amputee was quite an art and he felt proud of himself.

He went to the bedroom and dressed himself while humming a tune. He was going to see his maimed girlfriend and he was happy.

It was late spring so he selected a pair of khaki Swiss army shorts and a beige short-sleeved shirt. The shorts were indeed very short and they would show practically all of the stump of his leg. He put the stump of his arm through the left sleeve of the shirt and rolled it up with his left hand. Then he put on the shirt, buttoned it up and with his left hand rolled up the right sleeve. He didn't like floppy sleeves so he had always rolled them up so they would only reach a short way below his shoulders. Now, more than ever, he wanted his arms to show - especially his incomplete right arm.

Before he left the apartment he took out his brand new driver's license and looked at it with pride. Stamped on it was the phrase, "Restricted to driving cars with automatic drive only."

He took the elevator down to the garage and crutched slowly to his car, enjoying the dull thud of the crutch every time he moved it forward and it landed on the concrete floor.

He got in, leaned forward and to the right to insert the key and started the car. He fastened his safety belt by reaching over his lap with his left hand. With the stump of his arm he shifted the gear lever. He reveled in the unusual way in which he had to perform ordinary, everyday actions.

They had an appointment in the park. He parked his car and crutched over to the pond self-consciously ignoring every envious stare from the men and every admiring gaze from the women.

He saw her from a distance. She was wearing hot pants that showed part of her buttocks. The stump of her leg, like his, was resting on the hand bar and jutted out just a bit beyond the staves. From her sleeveless blouse the stump of her arm was gently swaying at every step.

His right elbow was slightly bent and the stump jiggled gently just as he had wanted it to. He stopped to watch her admirable walk. Crutch - leg , crutch - leg. Step - sway, step - sway. The stump of her arm enhanced her crippled beauty. He was filled with desire and tender-ness for the beautiful, maimed creature that was approaching him.

He started crutching again and they met.

"Excuse me, ma'am, haven't we met before?"

"I don't think so, sir, but I think it's time we did."

"Would you like to take a walk?"

With a coquettish smile she answered, "I'd love to."

He offered her the stump of his arm. She tucked her stump under it and together, they crutched away down the lane under the spring light filtering through the trees.

A beautiful redhead waddling on knee-pads arranged her hair with her left hand while the stump of her right arm tried uselessly to help. She looked at them with her emerald green eyes and smiled.

THE SEX SURROGATE

By Jeff Keane

Forced by his wife to seek treatment after failing to perform sexually for three long months, a humiliated impotent guy rediscovers the joys of a hard-on with the help of a kinky, big-titted amputee sex therapist.

At 10 o'clock on a Saturday morning, Tony Decker more or less slunk into Dr. Janet Clarke's waiting room.

After checking in with the pretty reception☐ist, he sat down and nervously paged through a magazine. He felt like a whipped dog, and the reason was simple: Tony hadn't been able to get it up for the past three months.

He'd been to shrinks and medical doctors, and none of them had helped him worth a damn. And his wife, Sally, was more than fed up. Just this past week, she'd threatened to leave him if he didn't get his "pathetic weenie fixed," as she put it.

"Either your dick starts working," Sally had said, "or I start walking. I mean it, Tony. I'm not gonna spend the rest of my life fucking myself with dildos!"

Dr. Clarke was Tony's last hope. She was a sex surrogate whose advertisement he'd seen in the newspaper the day before. And

right now, just the thought of having to face her-him and his limp-noodle dick!-made Tony break out in a cold sweat.

"The doctor will see you now," the receptionist said.

"Right," Tony mumbled, and walked glumly toward the inner office.

Dr. Clarke was sitting behind an impos☐ing mahogany desk, backlit by sunlight slanting in through a window. For a moment, Tony just stood there and stared at her in open-mouthed astonishment.

The doctor wasn't simply good-look☐ing-she was flat-out gorgeous, with masses of shoulder-length auburn hair and huge brown eyes. Perfectly made-up, her lips and nails were painted cher☐ry red. She was wearing a diaphanous white blouse that didn't disguise the heaviness of her breasts.

Even from across the room, Tony could see her lacy brassiere through the sheer material of her blouse. "Man, what a fuckin' rack!" he thought to himself.

Smiling warmly, Dr. Clarke indicated a chair by the desk and asked him to sit down.

When he'd done so, she asked matter-of-factly, "You're currently impotent, is that correct?"

Flushed with embarrassment, Tony nodded miserably.

"That's right, ma'am. It's been about three months now, and my wife, Sally...well...she's getting a little impa☐tient."

"I'm sure she is," the doctor smiled. "Tell me, Mr Decker. When you were potent, how big was your erection?"

"Well, maybe about eight inches," Tony replied.

"Was it thick or slender?" the doctor asked.

Flushing again, Tony mumbled, "Pretty thick, I guess."

"Good," she said soothingly. "So in other words, as recently as three months ago, you were having substantial eight-inch erections. And you've been tested by medical doctors, and apparently there's nothing physically wrong. Correct?"

Unable to meet her eyes, Tony nodded and stared down at the floor. He was in an agony of embarrassment. Talking about his non-existent hard-on with a woman he'd just met- and a stunning piece of ass at that-made him feel like a wimped-out faggot asshole. Hell, even that cute little receptionist probably knew he couldn't get it up!

"Sometimes the problem is very sim☐ple," Dr. Clarke was saying. "I'm sure you love your wife, but there are times when a man needs a different type of erotic stimulation..."

While he spoke, the doctor casually unbuttoned her blouse to the waist, then reached into her frilly white brassiere and pulled out both of her breasts. As her flesh puppies popped loose, Tony blinked his eyes hard.

"Shit almighty, what a pair of knock☐ers!" he thought. She was carrying a pair of DD-cups at least, Tony guessed-big, pointy beauties capped off with dark brown pancakes.

Once she had her breasts freed, Dr. Clarke leaned forward so that her rub☐bery nipples were pressed against the papers on her desk.

Giving him a slow smile, she asked, "You're not by any chance getting an erection, are you?"

"No such luck," Tony said weakly. Despite the doctor's gorgeous titties flopped there on the desk, his cock was as soft as custard. The bitch of it was, he was unbelievably horny. He would have given a year of his life for just one killer hard-on-just one rock-hard boner that he could use to wipe that smug smile off her face.

"Would you mind disrobing, please?"

Dr. Clarke asked. "I'd like to inspect your genitals."

Rising slowly to his feet, Tony meek☐ly unbuckled his pants and dropped them to the floor, and then took off his underwear and stood there staring at his worthless pecker. A few months ago, the sight of a bare-titted woman like this would have had him as stiff as a frozen carp. And now shit, he now might as well have been a dickless eunuch!

"Step over to the side of the desk, please," the doctor murmured.

As he moved closer, Dr. Clarke put on a pair of glasses and then took his limp prick in her red-nailed hand. Leaning over to inspect his cock, she rolled back his foreskin and squinted at the glans, then lifted his dick and tightly gripped his balls in her free hand.

"Nice, heavy testicles," she said. "Have you had any wet dreams lately?"

"No, ma' am," he replied.

"Well, you undoubtedly have a lot of sperm stored up. Your next orgasm will certainly be a big one. Just stand still for a moment now..."

Reaching beneath his dangling balls, she began massaging his prostate gland with her fingertips. At the same time, she took his cock in her fist and vigor☐ously pumped the shaft. As she picked up speed, the movement of her flurrying hand made her big titties jiggle like two mounds of Jell-O. After hand-jobbing him for a good minute or so, she released his soft prick and then once again inspected his wrinkled penis.

"Turn around and bend over, Mr. Decker," the doctor said briskly.

"Ah, what's that, ma'am?" Tony asked.

With a sharp edge in her voice, she repeated, "Bend over. ..and spread your buttocks."

Totally humiliated, Tony turned away and leaned forward, and then reached back and spread the cheeks of his ass. He heard a snapping sound as the doctor pulled on a rubber surgical glove, and then suddenly ran a finger deep into his asshole.

When he instinctively tightened up, the doctor said, "Relax, Mr. Decker. I'll be just a moment...

"Yes, ma'am," he muttered.

For the next few minutes, red-faced with embarrassment, Tony crouched by the desk while the doctor probed his rectum. Now and then she reached between his legs and took hold of his cock, checking for any sign of an erec□tion. Finally she pulled her finger out of his ass and took off her rubber glove, casually tossing it into a waste basket.

"Alright, Mr. Decker," she said. "Step into the treatment room, and I'll be with you shortly."

Indicating an open doorway with a nod of her head, Dr. Clarke turned back to her desk and scribbled something in Tony's file. Feeling like a kid who'd just been dismissed from the principal's office, Tony walked into the adjoining room. Aside from a long leather couch against one wall, the room was com□pletely devoid of furniture. As he closed the door, soft elevator music drifted out of an unseen speaker.

When he sat down on the couch, Tony's bare ass squeaked on the leather cushion. He looked down at his limp dick and shook his head in dismay. The thought of what he'd just been through-bending over like a dip□shit geek while a gorgeous bitch fingered his brownie-was enough to make him blush all over again. By this point, she probably thought he was some kind of cock-eating homo. Fuckin' son of a bitch...

A few minutes later, the door swung open, and Tony got the shock of his life. The doctor was completely nude, bal□anced on two crutches! Her left leg was long, elegant and beautifully muscled, but her right leg ended in a blunt stump about six inches above the knee! Between her legs, she was hairless as a cue ball, with huge, puffy cuntlips that glistened with honey.

"As you can see, Mr. Decker," the doc☐tor said, "we all have our little problems we have to overcome. Don't you agree?"

"I...I guess so, ma'am," Tony stam☐mered.

Gimping into the room on her crutches, the doctor hopped a few steps closer, with her stump wagging as she bounced for☐ward on her left foot. With each hippity-hop step, her big, conical titties wobbled up and down. Tony didn't know where to look his eyes darted nervously from her jugs to her snatch and down to her one foot. For some reason, the fact that her toenails were painted made the lack of a second foot even more startling.

"I was in a car accident seven years ago," she explained. "At that time, I was planning to be a model. Imagine! But when that became impossible, I went back to school and got my degree in sexology. As I said, we all have prob☐lems we need to deal with."

"Yes, ma'am," Tony nodded.

When she finished speaking, Dr. Clarke hopped another step closer, bringing her hairless snatch within inch☐es of his face. Droplets of cunt-butter were drooling out of her slit, and her oversized clitty was already poking out of its fleshy hood. Face to face with her sex, Tony took a deep breath and inhaled the steamy odor of her tuna, thinking, "Man, the bitch is ripe!"

In a breathy voice, the doctor said, "Massage it for me, will you?"

"Ma' am?" Tony asked, stunned.

She arched an eyebrow in amusement.

"My leg," she said, pointing at her stump. "Massage it for me, Mr. Decker."

Tony blinked a few times and then reached up and gingerly took her amputat☐ed leg between his hands. He was startled to feel the hard bone beneath the tucked-in skin at the end of her stump.. and even more startled when he ran his hands upwards and felt the powerful muscles of her truncated thigh. Her stump was about the size and weight of a prize country ham, and as he began kneading the amp-flesh, the doctor swayed on her crutches and sighed happily. "That feels wonderful," she murmured. "You know, it's the strangest thing, but when you've had a limb amputated, you can still feel it sometimes, even though it's no longer there. It can drive you crazy because it gets so itchy and all."

While she talked, the doctor inched another half-step closer, until finally she had her hairless hairpie pressed up against Tony's mouth.

"Eat it up, Mr. Decker," she hissed.

Dr. Clarke didn't have to tell him twice: releasing her stump, Tony wiggled his tongue between her greasy labials. The interior of her fuckhole was hot as a fur□nace, and she immediately started pouring out honey faster than he could lap it up.

Gulping down her pussy-crude, Tony put his hands on the doctor's big female ass and mouth-fucked her all he was worth. Before long, his face was smeared with her slime, and between the rich aroma of her twat, and the tangy taste of her snatch-butter, he felt dizzy and high as a kite.

"Good boy!" she panted.

"Ooo...yes...YES!"

Dr. Clarke was fully in heat now, flex□ing her powerful cunt muscles and nip□ping at Tony's tongue with the walls of her pussy. Growing more and more excited, she finally tossed aside her crutches and stood there on one leg, holding onto his head to keep her bal□ance. Suddenly her pussy spasmed vio□lently, clamping down onto Tony's tongue and holding him in place while she convulsed into climax.

"Yee...eee!" she squealed.

"Yee...yee...yeeek!'

The force of her orgasm just about knocked her over. As her one knee buck□led, Tony quickly grabbed her by the waist. Standing up, he gathered her in his arms and helped her to the couch. When he had her settled into a reclining position, she laid there panting for a moment, titties heaving. Then she fluttered open her eyelids and broke into a wide grin.

"Why, Mr. Decker," she said coyly. "Look!"

Dr. Clarke was pointing at his crotch, and when he glanced down, he was stunned to see that his dead cock had begun to stir into life. For the first time in months, he could feel his pecker begin ning to swell with blood, at first gradually, and then more and more forcefully, until finally his meat was frozen upright. He had a hard-on, alright the first one in months, and it was a boner so stiff he could have pounded nails with it.

"My heavens!" the doctor laughed. "It looks like you're back in business!"

In business, and on her like white on rice: climbing into the saddle, Tony rammed his club into her hairless slit. She was buttery smooth and softer than rose petals, and as he tunneled into her fuck chute, she yelped with pleasure and gripped him between her stump and leg. He started plunging his bone in and out, humping away like a rabid hound. Within moments, he had her jugs jittering so wildly it looked like her big nipples might fly right off her chest!

"Harder!" she shrieked. "Fuck ine harder!"

Gritting his teeth, Tony went into overdrive, delivering his meat with such efficiency that his moving cock was nothing but a blur. Writhing beneath him, the doctor matched him stroke for stroke, humping her pelvis furiously and rubbing his flank with her bulky stump. Then her boobies and face flushed bright pink, and she threw back her head and howled with delight.

"Yeeek! Yeeek!" she shrieked.

Hearing her go off, Tony gave her three or four quick thrusts, then buried himself to the gonads and hung on tight. Three months of pent-up jizz boiled in his balls, and then his spunk came siz zling up his shaft and splattered deep in her cunt. Grunting like a rooting hog, he fired load after load, flinging gobs of white lava into the doctor's womb.

"Yeeek!" she screamed again. "Ow! Oo! *Yee-eeek!*"

Minutes later, still dazed from coming, Tony heard the doctor say, "I think you'd better return next week, Mr. Decker. Just to make sure your problem has been solved."

"Yes, ma'am," he said eagerly.

56

"In the meantime," she purred, "let's see if we can raise another erection, shall we?"

As he pulled his dick out of her sop☐ping snatch and rolled off of her, Dr. Clarke sat up and then bent over and sucked his spunk-covered pecker

between her lips...

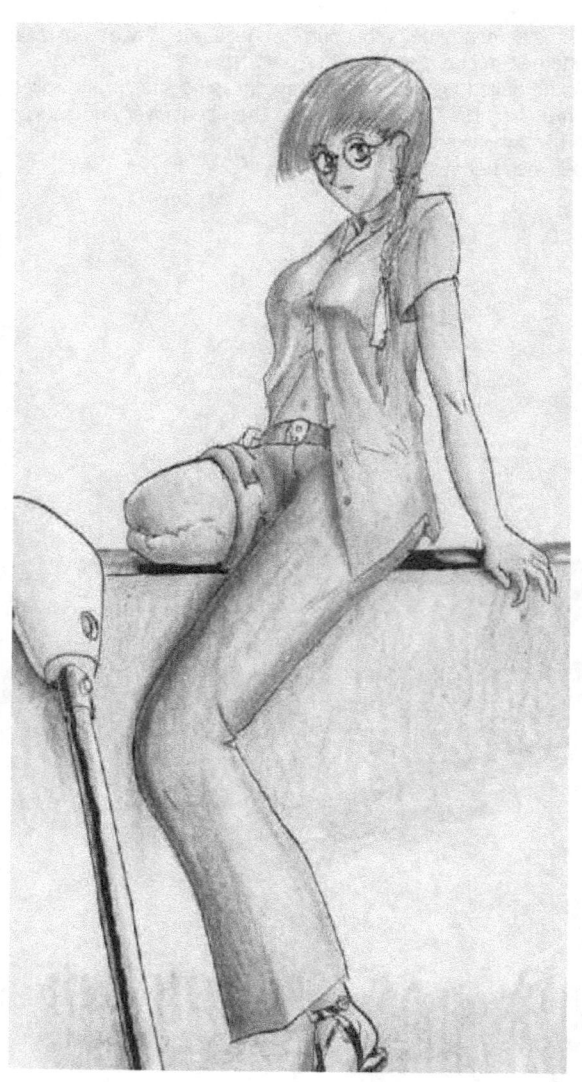

A FOOTHOLD ON LIFE
By Anon

We were so busy talking, stretched out on the grass there on the hill, that neither Sally nor I noticed the sky darken. We were reminiscing about the school year just past and the senior year ahead as 17 year old girls will, most of our conversation centering about the boys at school rather than the curriculum.

Then we felt the chill of the breeze and looked up to see that we were in for a storm. We jumped up, grabbed the blankets and the remnants of our picnic lunch and ran down the hill as fast as we could.

"Let's cut across the Martin place, Melissa," Sally said, "We'll get home a lot quicker." The Martin estate was ringed by a low iron fence. Sally climbed over and I handed her the things I was carrying. I had just put my hands on the top bar to swing myself over when the lightening bolt hit. I remember a brilliant flash and then nothing.

When I came to I was completely disoriented. For several moments I was aware only of... well... awareness. There were no thoughts, no consciousness of my body, just a vague notion of being alive. My mind was suspended above reality. Then my eyes opened and I saw that I was in a room, obviously a hospital room, but I had no knowledge of why I was there. For a long minute I was puzzled and then slowly my whole body seemed to come awake and my mind began to function. I remembered being at the fence and the flash, and strangely, I think I knew I had been electrocuted. I moved my head a little and saw the nurse by my bed who smiled at me but said nothing. Suddenly alarm went through me. Was I all right? I wondered.

I was far too weak to move but I began focusing my attention on different parts of my body. I could feel the sheets pressing down on my toes and feel my legs against the bed. I didn't have the strength to move them but they didn't hurt. My body felt all right and I didn't seem sick. I wanted to raise my head to see myself but all my muscles seemed limp and exhausted. I guess maybe I tried to move my arms because then I realized something was strange... I had no awareness of my arms or hands at all. I couldn't feel them against my body or against the bed. They must be asleep, I thought, and I tried to remember how to move them. With a feeling of dread I turned my head and looked sideways at my right shoulder. Horrified at what I saw I jerked my head over and looked at the left shoulder.

The nurse had seen my head move and she stood up and leaned over and stroked my hair. I looked at her unable to speak. I wanted to say it but the words wouldn't come out. I realized I felt ashamed. To speak of how I was now would be like finding myself naked in the street and then shouting to everyone to look. But the nurse said it for me. "Yes, Melissa, I'm sorry but... your arms are gone."

A wave of numbness went through me and everything swam in front of my eyes. I felt a sting in my leg and I guess the nurse must have given me a shot because everything faded away.

When I came to the second time consciousness rushed back. My parents were by the bed, their eyes sad, but a look of "we must be brave" around their mouths. I whispered, "Mama." Then my mother fell across me sobbing. It was then I felt that indescribable sensation of wanting and trying to use the arms I no longer had. The impulse to throw my arms around my mother was there but nothing happened. Even with my mother's face against mine I felt cut off from her. I wanted to hold her to me but I could only lie there helpless. When my father lifted her to her feet I wanted to reach out a hand to her and I guess I involuntarily tried because I felt a dart of pain in my right shoulder. I must have moved it under the bandages.

Dad said, "Now don't you worry, honey, everything will... work out. We'll get you some... arms, the best there are." He turned to the doctor who I noticed now for the first time. "They do wonderful things with... arti... artificial arms now, don't they, doctor?" The word "artificial" was as painful for Dad to say as it was for me to hear. The doctor nodded.

I whispered hoarsely, "I'll be all right, Dad... Mom. Don't worry about me." I couldn't have sounded very confident because I didn't feel confident, but I had to say something and there was nothing else to say. I still couldn't speak of my missing arms. I couldn't think about the future or artificial arms or anything except the shame, the embarrassment and the helplessness I felt. I wished I could pull the covers higher over my empty shoulders so no one could see them.

The doctor took my parents out then, my mother still crying. Then for the first time, I cried. The tears poured down my cheeks and my body shook with sobs. My shoulders began to ache and the shudders made them hurt worse. I cried until there were no more tears and then the nurse wiped my face with a damp cloth. I hated to have her do it. That was something I should do for myself but I couldn't.

The doctor came back into the room and sat on the edge of my bed. "Melissa, I think we should have a little talk... feel up to it?" I tried to nod and he went on. "I'm going to tell you just where we stand now, and where we go from here. I think you are a brave girl and want to know the truth and I know you will help us to help you. The lightning bolt striking the fence burned your arms, Melissa, so badly that we had to amputate them. We had no choice. We had to take them off at the shoulders. We... well, we couldn't leave any stumps at all. That will mean that it will be pretty tough to learn to use artificial arms and, frankly, there will be lots of things you won't be able to do with them. But we'll all work hard, and if you do, too, I think we can promise you'll be able to do lots of things that now probably seem impossible. Are there any questions you would like to ask?"

There were millions of them but none seemed like the right one to ask then. They were going through my mind so fast they didn't even get fully formed. Finally I asked, "When will I get... them?"

"Well, not for awhile. First we have to get you strong again and especially strengthen the muscles of your shoulders and back. You'll use them to operate the arms." I didn't understand just what he meant but I said nothing, just nodded. He brushed my hair back tenderly and left.

From that point on hardly an hour passed when my helplessness wasn't impressed on me more and more. The nurse fed me, wiped my chin, brushed the hair from my eyes and tended to my toilet needs. Even shifting my position in the bed was difficult not having arms with which to lift myself. When it hurt most was when I had to ask to have some personal chore done for me like holding a glass of water to my lips.

When they changed the bandages on my shoulders they carefully screened the operation so I never got a good look at them. But on the second day after the amputations the nurse said I was to sit up. She slipped a hand behind my neck and lifted me to a sitting position and helped me swing my legs over the side of the bed. For a minute I felt precariously poised as though I might fall over. I had never realized how important arms are to balance. I had been naked before under the covers so they could have easy access to my shoulders but now she put a hospital gown on me. Before she pulled it over my head, though, I looked down at myself and shuddered at the sight. I had always been proud of my body. My figure was slender but well-developed. My breasts were full and firm and I had a deep suntan. But now I looked... how to describe it. Now my breasts looked larger than ever before. Without my arms my body looked impossibly narrow. The white bandages at my shoulders contrasted with the tanned skin seemed to accentuate the slimness of my torso and call attention to the absence of my arms. When the gown was in place the sleeves hung flatter at my sides and I hated the sight of their emptiness. I was glad when I got back under the covers.

The same afternoon the nurse said I should get out of bed and walk a little. Again she sat me up, put scuffs on my bare feet and I stood up for the first time without my arms. I really felt armless now. I was unsure of my balance and my upper body felt ridiculously light.

Walking without any arms swinging at my sides was a strange and terrible sensation. I felt like a prisoner in my own body. The nurse opened the door and said, "Let's walk down the hall a ways." I didn't want to leave the room but she insisted and propelled me out the door. In the hall I faced the stares of patients and visitors and the more discreet glances of staff members who passed us. The shame and embarrassment of being armless, of having people see my mutilated body with the empty sleeves dangling from my armless shoulders swept over me now worse than ever.

From then on I was up more than in bed. I was so incredibly helpless, though. I could move about freely, but I could touch nothing and do absolutely nothing for myself. I couldn't even read until the nurse brought a stick with a rubber tip and put it in my mouth for me to turn the pages of a magazine she propped up in front of me. The word "freak" came to me. Here I was doing a simple thing like reading and I had to do it with a stick in my mouth. I thought wryly that I'd be a sensation in a sideshow.

After a few days the bandages came off and I got my first look at my empty shoulders. I didn't want to believe they be-longed to me... that these were the shoulders boys had circled with an arm or rested their head on. They came to a soft of blunt point. Below the tips thin pads of soft flesh covered the empty sockets, and thin horizontal scars where the amputations had been closed. My sides were virtually straight from the ends of my shoulders to below my ribs where my waist narrowed. My "hour-glass" figure was destroyed and I looked impossibly straight and slender.

They started me on an exercise program which from my point of view only exaggerated my feeling of armlessness. I did sit-ups using only my abdominal muscles. They had me twist my armless torso from side to side and had me shrug these ridiculous shoulders up and down and had back and forth countless times. The prosthetist came and felt my shoulders, measured me in a variety of ways and added to my embarrassment. I felt like a plucked chicken being examined.

Schoolmates and family friends came to visit but they never stayed long and were obviously as nervous in my presence as I was in theirs. Mom and Dad had gotten over the first shock of having an armless daughter and tried hard to encourage and cheer me. I went through it all in sort of a trance because I felt that any kind of useful or happy life was out of the question now. I didn't know what to expect of the artificial arms but I couldn't imagine ever feeling like I had arms again. My self-awareness stopped at the shoulders and I didn't see how it could be extended to inanimate metal and plastic arms.

This feeling was confirmed when they finally brought them and put them on me. They looked horrible and like anything but arms. There were large plastic caps which fitted over my shoulders and an array of straps which went across my chest and back and down to a wide belt they buckled around my waist. I looked like a Martian in all that apparatus and I hated it from the first day. By shrugging my shoulders in certain ways I could release springs causing the elbows to flex and the hooks to open and close. It certainly didn't feel like using arms though it was sort of interesting like a new game. I could clumsily catch small objects with the hooks and move them around but I had to twist my whole body to move the hooks to a new location. If a hook was on the wrong angle for a certain job I had to push it against a chair or something to swivel it on the "wrist."

On the day I was to "perform" for my folks the nurse strapped the hooks on me and then dressed me in a skirt and blouse and shoes. Now my shoulders looked as wide as a football player's and the material of the blouse stretched over them tightly. The blouse had long sleeves and the glittering steel hooks projecting from them made me look grotesque, I thought. My folks exclaimed over me and I picked up pencils and match sticks for them, dutifully, and tried hard to remember which shoulder to shrug which way to open which hook. I felt like I was controlling the action from a great distance. That is what I was doing, of course, because the only body sensations were in my torso and shoulders. There was no touch sensation in the arms or hooks, of course, and I watched them move as you would a machine.

My mother almost immediately asked the prosthetist if I wasn't to get "hands" that looked like hands. She was repelled by those steel hooks sticking out of my sleeves, I could tell. He told her they would make a pair that would look very natural, but they wouldn't function as the hooks did, they were strictly for looks.

After more days of training they discharged me from the hospital. The nurse dressed me and when my mother came she insisted that the hands with the plastic gloves that looked like skin and nails be screwed onto the ends of the arms in place of the hooks. Then she stood me in front of a mirror and said no one "would ever know..." I did look quite normal except for the extra-wide shoulders, but when I walked the arms and hands hung stiffly at my sides.

The rest of the summer was a nightmare. A nightmare of learning to live as an armless girl. I thought of myself as armless even with the artificial arms because they never felt like part of me and I could do very little with them. I was embarrassed to have people around to see my helplessness and I soon discovered my mother was, too. With the hooks I could clumsily feed myself except for cutting things and handling glasses and cups. I learned to write legibly though slowly and could shove and lift some things around. But I was still very helpless and if alone could accomplish very little. I read a lot and watched television though the channel selector was too slippery for me to turn and I needed help even with that. The arms were hot and heavy and the straps chafed me so that I welcomed bedtime to get out of them.

Mother would undress me, help me with the toilet, and then tuck me in bed since I couldn't even manage the covers. If I turned over and got the covers tangled I could sometimes wiggle out but usually ended up either with the covers all twisted or partly off me. I finally persuaded mother to cut the sleeves off my pajamas and close the armholes, She didn't want to very much, though I couldn't figure out why, but I insisted because the empty sleeves got so twisted around me in the night.

In the mornings I waited helplessly until mother came to bathe me, brush my teeth, fix my hair, put on my lipstick and then strap on the arms and dress me. I hated being handled like a baby, unable to do the simplest personal chore, and having no privacy of person at all.

66

I preferred to wear the hooks because they permitted me to do a few things, gave me some contact with the world around me, but my mother didn't like them. They were ugly and unnatural looking to her and most days she would put the dead looking, useless hands on the arms. I was helpless to do anything about it so she had her way most of the time. Especially if anyone was coming she would insist that I wear the hands. Some days I asked to go without arms entirely because they were so uncomfortable and of such little use. Rarely would mother agree. She didn't like the looks of my armless figure, I knew, and that pained me worse than the helplessness.

My social life had come practically to a halt. Occasionally we went to a movie and most people failed to notice my arms weren't real. One night, though, my mother left me in the lobby while she went to the restroom. A man was passing out free boxes of popcorn and he came up to me and said, "Here—on the house," with a smile. I said, "No, thanks."

"But you like popcorn, don't you? especially if it's free?"

"Yes, but..."

"Then here, take it." He grabbed my arm to press the box into my hand and when he touched the hard plastic and the arm didn't bend the strangest look of shock came over him. He looked at the other hand then and then saw the truth. He muttered, "Gee, I'm sorry," and hurried off. I nearly cried.

Sometimes Sally invited me to her place and she did everything for me and somehow it was easier to accept help from her than from my mother. Once I went to a party at Sally's but it was horrible for me and I think for everyone. Mother always made me wear the hands when I went out so I was completely helpless and had to be fed and everything.

More and more I hated being armless. Instead of getting used to it every new day seemed to bring new frustrations and embarrassment. Going back to school in the fall was the worst. Mother conceded that I would have to wear the hooks to school and then I began to feel about them almost as she did. Kids and teachers alike didn't seem to be able to avoid staring at them when they thought I wouldn't notice.

The other kids were very helpful, carrying my books, helping me eat and go to the restroom.

The big change in my life as an armless girl came one Saturday afternoon. Our back yard sloped down to a little ravine through which a small stream ran. There were bushes and trees along the stream bank and I liked to go there and sit by myself on nice days. That day I was sitting on the grass wishing I could throw twigs into the water when suddenly a boy stepped out of the bushes on the other side. A young man, I should say, and a very good-looking one. He saw me and smiled.

"Hi," he called, and the leaped across the stream and walked up to me. I knew he hadn't noticed my arms. I was wearing the hands because mother was expecting a friend for lunch and I had on a long sleeved blouse with capri pants.

"I'm Steve Carter. I just moved in that little place over there."

"I'm Melissa Logan," I said, nervously. Steve dropped down on the grass next to me in a very casual manner and began telling me about how he was fixing up his place and other chitchat and I tried to respond to his friendliness. It was almost impossible not to, he was so warm and pleasant. I knew he would discover my arms and I dreaded the moment of "exposure" as I thought of it. It came in an unexpected way. Steve reached into the pocket of his jacket and took out a candy bar. He peeled the wrapper back and then held it out to me.

"Here, I'll split it with you. Break off half."

"No, thanks," I said, almost hysterically.

"Come on," he urged, "It's a long time till lunch."

"No, really... I... ." And then I saw him looking at the stiff, motionless "hands" in my lap. He looked up at me, the smile gone, and said softly, "Artificial, huh?"

"Yes," I whispered. I wanted to run then, knowing that those pleasant minutes when I had been accepted as a normal pretty girl, were gone. But Steve surprised me.

"Well, we can get around that difficulty." The smile was back and he broke off a piece of candy and held it out saying, "Open up."

I wanted to laugh and cry at the same time and I think tears did come to my eyes but I opened my mouth and bit off a bite of the candy. No one had ever treated me like that. He acted as though my armlessness was just a nuisance to be circumvented. As he fed me the candy he asked, "Can you use those things at all, Melissa?" His manner was so casual I didn't mind talking to him about my arms—or lack of arms.

"I have some hooks I wear sometimes that I can use some, but these "hands" don't work at all. I... I can't do much even with the hooks. I guess they do for some people but you see... both my arms were amputated at the shoulders so I don't even have stumps and that makes a big difference."

"Yeah, it would... I can see that. Say, did you ever try using your feet?"

"Using my feet?" I was incredulous. "Don't be silly. What could I do with my feet. I push doors shut with them but that's about all they're good for."

"No, seriously. I've read about armless people who are real clever with them."

I winced at the word "armless", I guess simply because no one had ever said it in my presence. Steve was chattering on.

"They feed and dress themselves, do housework, write... nearly everything, and very efficiently, too."

"I don't believe it," I scoffed, "and even if it were true I wouldn't try it. I am enough of a freak as it is without doing things with my feet!"

"You are not a freak!" Steve said angrily, "and what's freakish about doing things differently so long as you get them done? And believe me, Melissa, you could do a lot more than you can with these artificial arms."

The idea appalled me but strangely I didn't resent Steve for suggesting it. I guess it was a relief to talk to someone about my condition even if nothing came of it. "I'd die of embarrassment. Just imagine sitting at a table and feeding myself with a bare foot!"

"Would it be any worse than being fed... or feeding your-self with a steel hook?" Steve's bluntness was a shock but his words made sense in a way. "Besides," he went on, "I'll bet you have very pretty feet. Let's see." He reached for my left foot and I quickly pulled it back under me almost upsetting myself.

"No, I shouted. I have to... to go in now." I started to get up but Steve calmly put his hands on my shoulders, against the stiff plastic shoulder cap, and held me down. His voice was gentle.

"Melissa, I wouldn't embarrass you for the world, but I honestly think you're passing up a chance to... well, achieve real independence for yourself."

He sounded so kind, I relaxed. "But Steve," I protested, "I can't make my toes work like fingers, and besides, I'd feel terrible going around barefoot and having people see me doing things with my feet, even if I could."

"At first, perhaps, but I think it would be easier to get used to than being helpless. And once you got good at using your toes I think people would accept it as natural, for you... and not feel as sorry for you as I'm sure they do now. Won't you just try? Let me take off your shoes. After all, you go barefoot when you go swimming, don't you?"

"I used to swim. I don't now, of course."

"Then you weren't born without arms?"

"No, I lost them about four months ago." I tried to smile. "I'm still quite a novice at being armless." There... I had used the word out loud myself. I extended my legs in front of me and Steve pulled the slippers from my feet.

"They are pretty feet," he said softly.

I have quite small, slender feet, smooth and soft with straight, regular toes. I wiggled my toes in embarrassment and said, "Well, don't just stare at them!"

Steve laughed and looked up at me. "Now, it won't be easy to learn to use them, Melissa. The people I've read about were all born armless and used their feet right from the start, but I'm positive you can learn to do many things with them if you stick to it and practice hard."

70

"I think it's pointless... even if I tried my mother would never stand for it. She is ashamed of me now for being armless and would never tolerate my using my feet."

"Well, you'll just have to stand up to your mother. Good grief, does she want to keep you helpless? Maybe you can practice on the Q.T. until you learn a little and then when she sees what you can do she might change her mind. Now here, let's try it."

Steve broke a long twig in half and tossed it on the grass by my bare feet. "Pick that up with your toes."

I must have been red with embarrassment but I pawed at the twig with the toes of my right foot and succeeded only in pushing it around. I could spread my first and second toes, but when I tried to bring them together around the stick they would cross over each other. A couple of times I did get the stick between them but when I tried to squeeze it enough to pick it up my toes wouldn't behave right and it would flip out. I was about to give up when suddenly my toes seemed to coordinate and I got a good grip on the twig.

"Swell!" Steve shouted, his eyes glued on my bare foot. "Now position it as though it were a fork and bring it up to your mouth."

I was engrossed in the challenge now and by pushing the twig with my other foot I maneuvered it so that it was positioned properly. But in trying to raise it up I couldn't get my foot very high off the ground.

"Cross your ankle over your other knee and then lean down to your foot." I did as he suggested, twisting my foot and ankle so the sole was turned toward my face. By leaning way forward I still could not touch my lips to the twig.

"These darned arms get in the way," I complained. Steve bent each arm at the shoulder back enough to get the forearms out of my lap. I had no control over the shoulder joints myself. They swiveled on friction plates and whenever I wanted to reposition them I had to push the arms against something. I tried again and this time could touch my nose with my toes. Suddenly I felt very silly, sitting there with my bare foot up by my face, a twig held between my toes.

"Steve, if I did learn to use my feet I would always feel ridiculous."

"No, you won't. I'm sure you won't once you get accustomed to it. It'll seem like a perfectly natural way of doing things." I had to admit it was a triumph to pick up something and be able to feel it. That was a sensation I hadn't felt in the four months my arms had been gone. When I did things with the hooks I didn't feel so much like I was doing it as like the hooks were doing it by themselves. The absence of feeling and the shrugging and twisting motions of my body which I used to control the hooks made every action seem remote and disconnected from me. Steve seemed to be reading my mind.

"Melissa, rub your feet against the grass." I did, looking at him in puzzlement. "Now reach out and touch my hand." I surprised myself then. I looked at his upturned palm resting on the grass and wanted very much to touch him. Almost without realizing what I was doing I dropped the twig from my toes and put my foot in his hand. As his hand closed around it I curled my toes in an effort to return his grasp... and for the first time the sensation of being cut off from human contact, of being a spectator instead of a participant, was gone. Again I was feeling the warm, wonderful contact of another person. Not the contact of being handled, as when my mother bathed and dressed me, but a contact that was mutual in which I was returning the touch.

But the touch of Steve's hand on my bare foot was even more than I realized. It was an intimacy between a boy and a girl. Steve looked into my eyes and smiled that gentle smile and his hand tightened its grip on my foot. I was drawn to him as I had never been to anyone else. I loved the warmth of his touch. I think that at that moment I fell in love.

But then sanity returned and the moment was gone, and it seemed like a ludicrous mockery of romance to sit there with a boy I hardly knew with my bare foot in his hand and pretending that this was normal, that I was normal or could ever expect anything like a normal romance with a boy. A fine picture, I thought, if you can't hold hands because your arms have been cut off, why just hold foot and hand. Everyone will smile and say 'aren't they a sweet couple' and the boy will accept it as perfectly natural to sit in a movie and hold his girl's foot, and... I shuddered to think how my armlessness had warped my emotions to the point where I was desperate enough to see normalcy even for a second in such a preposterous situation.

Again Steve seemed to divine my thoughts. He spoke softly, "Melissa, don't distrust your feelings. Don't think there can be only one way... that there is only one standard. You are different from other girls only in that you don't have arms. Your needs and feelings are the same. But because you are as you are, you must fulfill your needs in somewhat different ways. Try to accept your difference and not go on cutting yourself off or suppressing your feelings because you refuse to behave differently. Naturally, doing things with your feet seems strange to you but you can't alter the fact of your lack of arms, so you have to adjust your thinking and your actions accordingly. Otherwise, you'll cripple your personality and kill your chances for a normal life."

"Is it normal to pick up things with your toes or feed yourself with your feet?" I asked pointedly.

"Is it normal to pick up things with hooks, or worse, to have things done for you by someone else? I think it's far more normal to do things with your toes than to make a bunch of complex motions of shoulders and body in order to set some mechanism in motion to do things." His voice grew more gentle. "Melissa, I know a woman who is so short she stands on a stool to reach the sink. That isn't 'normal' either, in the sense that not everyone does it. But for her it is quite normal. She gets the dishes done. Would you have her stand around in frustration until someone takes pity on her and does them for her? Using your feet may not look as 'natural' to other people but to you it will soon seem a lot more natural than using the hooks ever would. And in time the people around you will accept it as normal for you, too."

"Using your feet will come to look and feel so easy and casual and ordinary that others will not only get accustomed to seeing you do things that way but they will forget about pitying you, which won't happen so long as you are struggling awkwardly to do things with the hooks."

Steve fell silent then, and smiled sheepishly as though he realized he had been lecturing. Much of what he said, though, expressed my own feelings more clearly than I had ever formed them in my own mind. Everyone had talked of how "natural" I looked in the arms but I always felt as though the real me stopped at the shoulders.

Maybe I could learn to accept my armless body as complete in itself, just different from others. My feet, if I could learn to use them, certainly put me in more direct contact with things. They had nerves and muscles and the sensation of touch just as hands did and if they could do many of the things that hands did it probably would seem natural.

I realized then that I had been staring at my bare feet and wiggling the toes in the grass, enjoying the sensual pleasure of the touch. Steve was watching me, an amused smile on his face. "Any of that make sense?"

"Yes, a great deal of sense. I have a lot to learn though, and I'll probably get awfully frustrated in the process."

"I'd like to help, if I can. Maybe we can sort of work on your lessons together."

I thrilled at his words. My embarrassment had gone and I was excited at the prospect of perhaps becoming more self-sufficient and less helpless. I was equally thrilled to know I would see more of Steve. His wisdom and gentleness were unlike anything in my experience. His desire to help without giving any impression of pity was wonderful. He seemed to accept me as a person... a person with a problem, but at least one with a right to self-respect. I guess that what it was more than anything... I felt more whole with Steve. Besides, he was a very attractive fellow and I wanted to believe that maybe he found me attractive... even though I was armless.

We agreed to meet the next afternoon at the same place. When I got there Steve was waiting and he had brought a number of things with him. He had a fork, some small empty bottles, a pencil and a pad of paper, and even a large safety pin. I lowered myself to the grass and extended my feet for

74

him to remove the saddle shoes and bobby socks my mother had put on me that morning.

"Oh, lesson number one is to take off your own shoes."

"But they have laces and besides, I have socks on," I protested.

"Well, use your ingenuity."

I propped my right foot on my left knee and started to maneuver a hook into position to grip the lace. My mother had put the hooks on my arms that morning for school and because no one was expected that day, hadn't thought to change them. She still didn't like me to wear them, but she was getting more weary of tending to me and my equipment.

"No, no. No using the arms, remember?" said Steve. I sat back, frustrated. Then an inspiration hit me. I shifted the arms out of the way, shoving them with my knees, and leaned down and caught the end of a single lace in my teeth. I gave a pull and it came undone. Smiling triumphantly, I repeated the operation on the other shoe and then by pushing at a heel with the opposite toe I managed to force the shoes from my feet. With the socks on it was hard to get my big toe in the elastic top, but after several attempts I succeeded and tossed the sock off my foot. With one bare foot it was easy to take off the other sock. When my feet were bare I laughed happily and said, "Gee, that's one job I could have taken off Mom's hands and I didn't even realize it."

"You'll be taking lots of jobs off her hands before long," Steve answered confidently.

"Take them off her hands with my feet, huh?" I felt good at being able to make even bad jokes about the situation.

We set right to work. First Steve had me pick up twigs with one foot and snap pieces off with the other. Then I picked up the pencil with my toes and laid it down again endless times. I was so clumsy and slow I think I would have given up if Steve hadn't been so patient and encouraging. He kept me at it for a couple of hours and my ties did begin to cooperate a little better. I got so I could pick up the pencil and maneuver it into writing position with only one try. I failed completely, though, when it came to unscrewing the bottle caps, even the smallest one. From forcing them into such unnatural positions and actions the muscles of my feet cramped several times and finally Steve agreed to call a halt. Then he took my feet in his hands and massaged them. Somehow it now seemed quite normal to have him holding my feet and the touch of his hands sent an electric tingle through me.

When dinner time came Steve pulled my shoes and socks on for me and I went into the house with a ravenous appetite. So ravenous my clumsy fumbling with my hooks to feed myself made me even more exasperated than usual. At bedtime I asked my mother to get me a glass of milk and while she was out of the room I succeeded in taking off my shoes and socks.

"Melissa" she exclaimed, when she came back, "You're bare-footed. How did you manage that?"

"Oh, with my feet," I said casually.

"With your feet? You didn't use your hooks?" Mom was incredulous.

The next day was Monday and a school day, but as soon as I got home I hurried out to the stream bank and Steve was waiting. This time he had brought a kitchen chair, explaining that it would be easier to work sitting on it than on the ground. This time my feet and toes seemed to cramp even sooner but Steve assured me that was to be expected until my muscles got adjusted. When we finished the "lesson" he began massaging my feet again. As he did he looked up at me and very casually asked, "How about going to a show with me tonight, Melissa?"

I was so surprised and excited I stammered for a few seconds before I was finally able to say, "I'd like that very much." I think Mom and Dad were even more surprised than I was. They had so avoided the subject of boys since I lost my arms that I knew they felt no boy would ever show an interest in me. When I told them he was a neighbor and 23 years old they were a little shocked, I think. I explained how I met him but said nothing of our "foot training lessons," as we now called them.

In his gruff way Dad said, "Well, we'll look this young man over when he calls. I was nervously hoping Steve would win their approval and could hardly stand still as Mom bathed me and dressed me in an organdy party dress with long sleeves. She had taken off my hooks and as I stood before the mirror while she fixed my hair I had a sinking feeling when I looked at the sleeves with nothing projecting from them. The rigid, unmoving hooks filled them but the appearance of handlessness made me look disgusting to myself.

I stepped into high heels and Mom said, "You look lovely, honey... Oh, I forgot your hands." She got them and I thought again how corpselike they seemed, severed and lifeless. When she had screwed them in place and the sleeves covered the ends of the gloves that looked like skin I looked very much like any other girl... if you didn't look too closely.

My fears about Steve's acceptance by the family proved groundless because he turned out to be the cashier at the bank where Dad did business and they knew each other casually. I tried to look poised and graceful as we walked out to the car but I was very conscious of the rigid motionlessness of my useless plastic arms.

With the proper shrugs I flexed the elbows, cringing at the mechanical sound of them clicking into place, and slid into the seat, my skirt twisting under me as it always did, but Steve, so full of surprises, casually slid in opposite me and asked me to raise up so he could straighten my skirt as though he had done it a thousand times. At the movie he fed me popcorn and whispered comments about the picture and made me feel that there was nothing strange about being out on a date with an armless girl.

On the way home he stopped at a drive-in over my weak protests, and fed me a hamburger and a malt. Somehow with him I quickly got over my self-consciousness in each new situation because he seemed to accept my being armless so easily and casually.

The thrilling moment came when we stood at the door and tilted my chin up to him and kissed me. I leaned into him his arms went around me in an embrace I wanted so badly to return. The stiff, unyielding arms kept me from closer contact with him and his hands must have felt the straps of the harness through my dress. I wished I could make the arms vanish and press my armless body against his and be held close, so close that I wouldn't mind not having arms to throw around him. But his lips were soft and warm against mine and that was enough. I knew then that I was desirable to Steve, even as an armless girl. His kiss assured me of that.

There were many kisses and many dates after that and I savored every minute with Steve, not permitting myself to think beyond, to what it might lead to or how it might end. I never questioned the genuineness of Steve's affection but I didn't dare imagine that even he would some day ask an armless girl like me to marry him.

We continued educating my feet and toes to do the work my amputated hands had once done and though it was slow and difficult I did make progress. Once my feet seemed to learn what was expected of them my skill increased at an accelerated rate. After about three weeks I was able to write with a pencil between my toes at least as well as I could with the hooks. It was then that I told my folks that Steve was helping me train my feet.

"Your feet?" Mother was aghast. "Why what can you do with your feet?" I told her it was beginning to look like I could do a lot with them and it was much better than using the hooks. Both Mom and Dad seemed to think it was nothing more than a game but if it kept me amused I might as well go on with it. I think I realized I was happier than I had ever been since my arms were amputated. They liked Steve and respected him and I suppose thought he was just keeping me entertained by helping me develop skill with my toes. I began kicking off my shoes and practicing writing and opening bottles, etc., in the evening, as I sat barefoot trying to manipulate a pair of scissors with my toes Mom came into the room and sat down with a serious look on her face.

"Melissa, honey, you are taking all this business of using your feet too seriously. Oh, I admit you are getting quite clever with them... your writing is almost perfect, but darling, frankly I think it's a little... disgusting. Feet weren't intended to be used as hands."

Tears came into my eyes and I wanted to hide my bare feet which so disgusted her. I screamed, "Neither were steel hooks! I don't want to be helpless all my life and if I can learn to use my feet then I'm going to... unless you can tell me how to grow new arms and hands out of these shoulders." My violent gesture released the elbow lock on one of the arms and it flew up almost to my face, the bright steel hook poking out in an eloquent, if somewhat macabre, testimonial to my words. Mom came over and patted my shoulder, but as her fingers thumped loudly against the plastic she raised her hand and rested it on my head.

"Honey, baby, I didn't mean to hurt you. I know how terrible it must be for you but daddy and I look after you, don't we? And you must admit you couldn't very well go around barefoot in public, doing things with your toes."

I sobbed, "Sure you take care of me... but don't you think I'd like to be able to take care of myself? Right now I'd die if I had to use my feet in public, but I think I can get used to it. I hate using these hooks in public too, and worse yet they can't do much and I'm awkward. With my feet I'm getting so I can do some things much easier... and it's more natural, to me, at least. "

I'm sure Mom didn't understand but she felt so bad about my armlessness she hated to see me more upset so she adopted a "let's let nature take its course" attitude. Part of her feeling was genuine sympathy for me but much of it was sympathy for herself, I knew, for having an armless daughter... a freak. I confided my feelings to Steve and he was as always, wonderfully understanding. He hoped my folks would come around but encouraged me to insist on my right to do as I felt right in this matter. We started having lessons in his little bungalow. My folks knew I went there but so long as the neighbors couldn't see me go the back way they didn't mind.

I got more and more capable in the passing weeks. At Steve's I practiced feeding myself, putting on makeup, washing my face and even combing my hair, though we both laughed at the contortions I went through to get my foot that high. I dusted furniture, ran the vacuum, holding the handle between my chin and shoulder, and by sitting on the drainboard with my feet in the sink, even washed the dishes, practicing first with plastic ones.

As I got more and more skilled and tried more and more things the artificial arms became more and more of a nuisance. I complained about then several times and finally Steve said, "Why don't we take them off, Melissa?"

"Oh, no," I gasped. I wasn't embarrassed about having him see me in just a bra, but I didn't want him to see my armless shoulders. "I... I don't want you to see... my shoulders are... ugly." I stammered.

"Honey, they couldn't be ugly to me. Haven't I told you that you are a very lovely girl? And I know what they must look like. Believe me, I won't be shocked or think you any less beautiful... in fact, I think you would be more beautiful just as you are and without all that apparatus." His voice was so gentle and sincere that I wanted to believe him. After a long moment I whispered, "all right."

He stood in front of me and unbuttoned my blouse and drew it down over the arms and tossed it to a chair. Now all the straps and steel and pink plastic of those horrible looking arms was exposed to him for the first time. He gave no reaction but started to unbuckle the waist belt and the other straps. He grasped each arm above the elbow and lifted them away, putting them down on a chair where they looked grotesque to me. He turned back to me and I shrank as his gaze took in my nearly nude torso. My breasts swelled up out of the bra cups and again I thought how heavy they looked for my unnaturally slim body.

There was nothing I could do to hide my naked, armless shoulders or to stop Steve as he put a hand on each of them. His hands covered the amputation scars and pressed gently in on the empty sockets which had once held my arms. For some strange reason it occurred to me that no other girl could be held in just that way—those places on her body could not be touched. Steve bent and kissed the point of each bare shoulder and as he did I pressed my armless body against him and tears came to my eyes. Steve embraced me and then turned my face up and kissed my eyes and my lips.

Then he stepped away and picked up my blouse. Smiling, he turned the sleeves inside out, saying, "We won't need those dangling," and draped the blouse around me and buttoned it. I had never seen myself like that except in pajamas and I turned to a mirror and stared at myself. Steve stepped up behind me.

"Don't I look terrible?" I asked.

"Of course you don't."

"But I'm so narrow. And besides, I look so different than anyone else. When you look at a person you expect to see arms and hands at their sides, but me... I just end at the shoulders."

"Well, honey, you don't have what everyone else has but what you do have is perfect and lovely. It can be appreciated, you know, without arms added to the picture."

"Not everything that I have is perfect. My shoulders are scarred and bony-looking."

"Now stop that," Steve said impatiently. "Those scars are hardly noticeable and will get fainter all the time. If you had them anywhere else on your body you wouldn't think them so disfiguring. It's just because they are associated with the absence of your arms that they seem larger and more vivid than they really are." He smiled and again put his hands on the ends of my shoulders and shook me gently. "I like your little shoulders."

Without the artificial arms I felt so much lighter and freer. I hated having Steve put them back on me when I left. I could do so much more without them being in the way. I told Steve, laughingly, that having them off was like having a great weight lifted from my shoulders. From then on whenever I went to Steve's the first order of business was taking off my arms and, of course, my shoes and socks. Sometimes we just let the sleeves dangle but most of the time Steve would tuck them inside or pin them to the back of my blouse. We both agreed it looked neater not to have empty sleeves flopping loosely around. Their flat emptiness was more startling looking, I thought, than not having any sleeves visible.

Around home I always wore the arms but I began to use my feet more and more. My mother stopped making a fuss about it unless someone was coming to visit. Finally one morning I told Mom not to bother putting shoes and socks on me. "I'll just be taking them off right away," I explained. She looked at me with a mixture of dismay and disgust but said nothing so I started the day barefoot and I ended it barefoot. I even walked over to Steve's in my bare feet and he was pleased. He said being barefoot was a much more natural state for me. From that time on the only time I wore shoes was to go to school or elsewhere out in public. My feet became less sensitive to cold and less sensitive to walking outside. Going barefoot became so customary I no longer felt partly undressed when my feet were bare. Using my toes as fingers had now become completely natural to me and I constantly amazed myself at how much I could do and how easily. When I had shoes on I felt like a person with arms would feel if someone tied them behind his back. I carried things from place to place by holding them between my chin and shoulders when I was at Steve's and not wearing my hooks. It was difficult with the hooks on.

The principal thing I had not learned was how to dress myself. When I mentioned it to Steve one Saturday afternoon he said very casually, "well, I guess we'd better do something about that."

I looked at him for a long minute and then finally said simply, "Okay." Steve had seen me naked to the waist except for my bra so I felt no embarrassment at the idea of him seeing me in just bra and panties. He took off my blouse as I stood helplessly in front of him, then he unfastened my skirt and let it drop from my hips. I stepped out of it and with my now agile toes picked it up and extended my leg to lay it on a chair. I knew Steve was trying to make this seem like just another of our "foot training" lessons but his eyes drifted up and down my nearly nude body and he said in almost a whisper, "You are fantastically lovely." While his words thrilled me, I no longer was so shy with him about my mutilated figure and I was able to reply with a gay, "Thank you, sir!" and a mock curtsy.

We started in on the task at hand, or at foot, and it proved to be tougher than I had ever imagined. We experimented with a number of different ways of arranging the clothes and several approaches to putting them on but each ended in failure. After nearly an hour of struggling into my skirt I fell back on the divan and with a wave of my leg sent the recalcitrant garment flying across the room Steve was weary too and he dropped to the floor beside me and put one arm around me. He looked at me for several seconds and then pulled me into a kiss that set me shivering with excitement. I still felt my armlessness more strongly at such moments because I wanted to throw arms around him and hold him close. Steve began caressing my waist and hips and his hands quivered warmly against my flesh. He leaned close to my face and said softly, "Perhaps we should start with the basics, honey. Maybe you should learn to put on your bra and panties first."

"Perhaps I should," I answered.

Steve lifted me up and unhooked my bra at the back. I lay back down and he slowly and sensuously drew it off me, freeing my breasts so that they pointed brazenly naked up at him, the pink nipples crowning them. I had no arms to disentangle from the bra straps but as he slipped them off my shoulders his hands caressed those places that were unique to me... those indented, soft surfaces from which arms should have projected but didn't.

Gently he kissed the nipple of each breast as his hands sought the waistband of my panties. He hooked his fingers in it at each side and drew them down over my hips, his hands caressing me all the way to the tips of my toes. I was completely naked now, more naked than any other girl could be for I was naked of clothes and naked of arms and hands. I lay there, a nude head, torso and long legs with carefully trained feet.

As I lay nude in armless helplessness, Steve's hands and lips caressed and explored every inch of my body. When both of us were quivering with passion he slipped quickly out of his clothes and stretched out on the divan beside me. I writhed sensuously against him as he held me. It was the only way I had of returning his caresses.

When our passion exploded with a delirious sensation such as I had never known before and again we lay beside each other, exhausted but content, Steve tenderly kissed my eyes and cheeks and lips and we whispered almost simultaneously, "I love you." At that moment nothing mattered, not even my lack of arms, for nothing existed but my love for Steve.

I spent many hours naked with Steve from then on. Some of them were spent in lovemaking, some in the effort to learn to dress my armless body and many for no reason other than the erotic pleasure of being nude in the presence of my lover.

I learned to manage my clothes finally—that is, many of them, but because of the design, or the position of buttons or zippers on some of my things, I would have been forever unable to put them on or take them off by myself.

Secure in Steve's love and confident of my skill with my feet and toes, I began next the campaign of abandoning the artificial arms completely. When Steve and I went out on dates we would go first to his place where he would take off my hooks and tuck my empty sleeves smoothly inside my dress or blouse. The first time I ventured forth in my "armless loveliness," as Steve called it, I wasn't sure I could stand the embarrassment of the stares at my unnaturally slim and armless shoulders. But I gritted my teeth and, relying on Steve's calm and casual manner and trying to emulate it, I survived and gradually became accustomed to it.

I did not, as yet, use my feet in public, but I did go out to dinner, where Steve fed me amongst the open-mouthed astonishment of waiters and other diners.

We even went dancing. Steve would put his right hand on my waist and his left on my armless shoulder. I had difficulty at first moving gracefully to the rhythm of the music because with-out my hooks I felt stiff and uncertain of my balance, but gradually this, too, disappeared and I danced as well as I had before my amputations.

Once I had conquered some of my self-consciousness I began to almost enjoy studying the reactions of people who noticed my lack of arms. Children, in their blunt frankness, would often ask their parents within my hearing, "What happened to that girl's arms?" Or they would come up to me and look carefully at one armless shoulder and then the other and with puzzlement written all over their faces ask, "Why ain't you got no arms?" Unless someone snatched them away quickly they would pursue the subject further as various limitations of being without arms occurred to them. "How do you eat?" "You can't open doors, can you?" and the best one, "How can you scratch when you have an itch?"

I laughed when a little girl asked me that, but actually it was a good question because until I began using my toes for such purposes I had often suffered tortures at having an itch I was helpless to scratch. At home I always ran to a doorway or something and rubbed against it, but at school or in public I still had the problem and such a little thing as that could make me feel very helpless and very armless.

One afternoon during the vacation between semesters my mother had some friends of hers to tea. She dressed me in a party dress and high heels and of course I wore my "hands." She fussed over me and fed me cookies and held my cup to my lips. She preferred that, to having people see me using my hooks. The minute the people left I kicked off my shoes. I knew my bare feet looked incongruous with the frilly party dress but I had to accustom myself to being barefoot on any occasion or with any outfit. Mother didn't change my clothes because she had to hurry to fix dinner. When I went to the table she noticed I was still wearing the useless hands.

"Oh, my," she exclaimed, "I forgot all about them. I'll have to get your hooks and put them on you, Melissa."

But I had an idea of my own. "Don't bother, Mom," I said, and promptly raised one bare foot up to the table, resting my ankle on the edge, and arching my instep sharply to pick up a fork with my toes.

"Melissa," mother cried, "You can't eat with your feet. I've let you run around her barefoot and watched you use your toes for lots of things but, after all, feeding yourself with your feet... it just... isn't done!"

"Isn't done!" I flared, "Because other people have arms and hands to feet themselves? I haven't got any, or haven't you noticed?" I was embarrassed enough, knowing what a strange picture I made, sitting there with my bare foot propped on the table, my toes holding a fork poised over my plate, and my mother's attitude made me feel worse... like a freak.

My dad came to my rescue. "Now, Martha, I think we should let Melissa do things in whatever way she can. Let's see how she does... that looks like quite a trick, handling a fork with those little toes." He reached over and tweaked my toes and patted my naked instep. I could have kissed him. Mom succumbed in silence and nothing more was said but I must have blushed red through the whole meal because they both continually watched my foot as I maneuvered the fork to pick up a bite and then twisted and flexed my foot to turn the sole toward my face while I bent low to the table to take the fork in my mouth.

The rigid, useless mechanical arms, hanging from my shoulders, made using my feet difficult so after my folks had accepted the fact that my feet were going to serve me as hands my Mom offered little protest when I asked her to leave the arms off. I wore them to school but the minute I got home Mom would take them off and I spent every evening and all weekend in what I now regarded as armless and barefoot comfort.

I took the final step a month later. I told my principal that I wasn't going to wear my hooks any more and asked him for permission to wear barefoot thong sandals to school. Normally they were forbidden as not being "proper" for school wear. He couldn't believe that I could write and do other things with my feet and asked me to demonstrate. It was the first time anyone had seen me use my toes except for the family and Steve. I slipped off my shoes and tugged off my socks with my toes as he watched with fascination, his eyes riveted to my feet. When I was barefoot I asked him to hand me some paper and a pencil. He tore a sheet from the pad on his desk and picked up a pencil but then looked flustered, not knowing how to hand them to me. I leaned back in my chair and extended both legs, my insteps sharply arched. He held the paper and pencil carefully, extending toward my waiting toes. I took them and laid them on the floor and then realized the carpet would not provide a solid background for writing so I looked around quickly and saw several books on a small stand beside me. By twisting around in my chair I was able to raise my feet and pull one of the books free of the stack. I had to position so I could grip it tightly between the soles of my feet in order to lift it down to the floor. I laid the paper on the book and then picked up the pencil with my toes and quickly wrote the first lines of the Gettysburg Address. Then as a final flourish I picked up the paper and held it out to Mr. Cooper who took it from my toes gingerly and studied it.

He was so pleased at my foot-writing and so flabbergasted at the same time he didn't know what to say. He complimented me finally on my skill and 'courage' and then asked how I would manage other things around the school. I convinced him I could dial the combination lock on my hall locker and feed myself in the cafeteria as easily, or more so, with my toes as I could with the hooks. Certain things I would need help with, but I needed the same help when using the hooks.

Mr. Cooper gave his approval and said he would notify all the teachers involved. I left his office feeling proud and happy but as I walked down the hall and passed other students I began to think about the days ahead when I would face them with for the first time as an armless girl, and when they would see me using my feet and toes as hands for the first time. Then my mood was not so gay but I was determined that that day should be the last I would ever wear those hated hooks.

When Mom took them off me that night I felt both apprehension and relief in the realization that they were never going back on. From here on for the rest of my life I would be completely, permanently, absolutely armless.

Mom had abandoned the hope of dissuading me so the next morning she silently turned the sleeves of my blouse inside out and then draped it over my shoulders and buttoned it up, the empty sleeves on the inside against my sides. I slipped my bare feet into the thong sandals and the die was cast.

I got through the day much better than I had expected. Kids and teachers alike stared with fascination as I pushed the books around on my desk with my chin and then raised a bare foot to the desk top to turn pages and hold my place. They were even more enthralled when I laid a sheet of paper on the floor and wrote with a pencil between my toes. The more fearless ones commented with praise and astonishment at how well I could use my feet. I was nervous but my feet, thanks to all the careful training and practice, never failed me and by the time the day was over I knew I would have no regrets about my decision.

After school I ran over to Steve's and for the first time he didn't have to take off my hooks because I had none. I told him excitedly about the day and he crushed my armless body against him and kissed me soundly in congratulation. To make the break with the past even more complete and to launch myself completely on my new way of life, that night I ceremoniously gathered up all my socks and shoes that had laces or straps and made up a bundle for the Salvation Army. From that point on my feet would serve as hands and my toes as fingers and, just like people with hands and arms, they must always be free. I still felt somewhat self-conscious about the idea of going through life practically always barefoot, but I was getting more and more used to it and there was some comfort in the knowledge that my feet were small, perfectly formed and quite pretty.

I went completely barefoot all the time at home or at Steve's place and wore only thong sandals to school and most other places. The only times my feet were ever covered at all was on the more formal occasions when I wore slip-on pumps with high heels.

Mom and I spent many hours altering my wardrobe, removing the sleeves from all my blouses, sweaters, dresses and coats. We closed the useless armholes with the material of the sleeves and they looked quite neat. All new clothes were bought with my armlessness in mind. Everything was made without sleeves and with zippers and buttons arranged so that I could reach them with my toes and my trusty long button hook. I preferred the new things which had obviously been designed just for me and had never had sleeves. But there was a rather odd feeling at first connected with wearing things which were so unique. It made me feel even more conscious of my anatomical strangeness to be wearing something that fit me perfectly and snugly but which no one else could possibly wear. In spite of my awareness of my preternaturally slim torso and narrow shoulders, I had everything made to fit smoothly and form-fitting because I realized it looked neater than having a lot of loose material around my shoulders.

Sometimes when putting on my makeup I would stop and stare at myself in the mirror and think what a strange sight I was sitting there with a bare foot propped up in front of my face, the small toes gripping a lipstick and my armless shoulders hunched forward so their odd, sharp outlines were clearly visible under the material of a sleeveless blouse stretched tautly across their contours.

My feet and toes seemed to learn new things every day. I became so adept at using them that it suddenly dawned on me one day as I was dusting furniture, the dustcloth held by my toes, that I no longer felt like a girl who had lost her arms but like… an armless girl. I no longer felt the urge to reach out with a hand but reached automatically with a bare foot.

I could do homework, wash dishes, and even cook if things were properly arranged. Mother never let me, at home, but at Steve's I had tried my 'foot' at it many times and managed quite well.

I had become so self-confident, in fact, that I raised little protest when Steve asked me to marry him. I was thrilled, of course, but I still had difficulty believing that a man could want an armless girl for a wife. I knew, though, that I could keep a nice home for him and there was no doubt of the love between us. My folks were pleased too, especially when we assured them we were going to wait until I graduated.

I spent nearly every evening and the whole of weekends with Steve, sometimes out on dates, but often just at his place. We played records, danced, ate, and made lots of love. One of my favorite outfits, because it was picked out by Steve, was a pair of snug fitting, high-waisted Toreadors. They clung to my hips and legs and came almost up to my breasts. I wore bright sashes around the waist to set off the black pants and blouses of almost any color. In this outfit and with my feet perpetually bare I looked quite exotic, we both thought. It gave me great freedom to use my feet and toes and as I moved about the house and yard, constantly using my feet for every act and with my armless shoulders outlined under a smooth fitting sleeveless blouse Steve thought me quite exciting.

One Saturday as we sat on the floor playing chess, me with one leg curled under while I moved pieces with the toes of the other, I looked up to see Steve studying me with an odd look on his face.

"Melissa, I was just thinking how delightful you would look in those slinky black Toreadors with the red sash of you were nude to the waist."

"Well," I smiled, looking down at my armless shoulders, "I'm helpless to stop you if you want to take off my blouse."

"No, you do it and I'll watch." Steve enjoyed watching me use my feet, especially when I was using them to undress myself.

I gave him a coy glance and crossed my right ankle over my left knee. Slowly I unbuttoned my blouse with my toes. I wore no bra. Steve enjoyed the movements of my full breasts as I went through the contortions of my armless activities. When I had the blouse open I took one side of the material between my toes and drew it slowly back, revealing one naked breast for an instant, then repeated the action on the other side, though that required using my other foot. It was a macabre strip tease but I could tell Steve was enjoying it.

Next, I hunched one shoulder and with my chin pushed the blouse off so it fell, disclosing my "bare spot," as we called those surfaces above my rib cage and below the points of my shoulders where my arms had once been attached. One breast was now completely exposed, too. I smiled seductively at Steve as I sat there, my blouse half off and my torso half naked. I shrugged my nude, armless shoulders toward him in a gesture of invitation and he kissed the scar of the amputation which was now quite faint. It always gave me a strange thrill, a mixture of embarrassment and excitement, when he did that, but it reassured me that my armlessness was not repugnant to him. We repeated the ritual on the other side, then I tugged the blouse free of the waist band with my toes and tossed it aside.

If I had had arms I would have leaned back on them and struck a pose, but I had to settle for throwing my helpless shoulders back and thrusting my bare breasts forward proudly.

"You do the most thrilling strip tease I've ever seen, darling... one other thing... do you know how the girls in the burlesques caress their breasts, lift them and wiggle them in such a sexy way? Do that for me, please... ."

"Steve!" I said with exasperation and a little dismay.

"Honey, don't tell me you're bashful."

"Well, don't tell me you've forgotten, as I sit here naked to the waist, that I haven't any hands to do what you ask."

"But you do have feet and you can be more sensuous with those cute little things than other girls can with their hands."

What he suggested was a novel idea but an interesting one. I had always secretly enjoyed admiring my breasts. I was quite proud of them. But that was when I had my hands. Since my arms had been amputated I had never touched them. Now, though, I propped a bare foot on my knee and ran the sensitive sole over the soft fullness of my breast. It was a strange and wonderful sensation and also gave Steve quite a show.

The rest of the day and all that evening I remained naked while my armless shoulders, breasts, and feet remained completely bare for Steve to gaze on and caress. That night I sat on the divan with Steve on the floor in front of me and we watched a movie on TV. Occasionally he reached up to caress my nude torso.

I tended to all his needs as was our custom. When he wanted to smoke I would extract a cigarette from the pack on the coffee table with my toes and put it in his mouth, then with both feet strike the lighter and hold it for him. I also held out pieces of candy to him which he would take from my toes with his lips. When they weren't busy doing something for him Steve held my feet and caressed them, now and then lifting them to his lips and kissing the curve of the instep, each toe individually, or turning the foot up and pressing the sole against his lips. He held and fondled my feet as most boys handle their girls' hands. But when I had got accustomed to it I wouldn't have traded my feet for hands for anything in that respect, because I think we both got more pleasure from his attentions to my feet.

Every action of Steve's indicated that he never once minded that I was so different from other girls... that I wore blouses without sleeves because I had no arms to fill sleeves, that I constantly went around in bare feet instead of properly shod because I had to use my toes as fingers.

The hardest thing for me to start doing with my feet instead of my missing hands was to undress Steve. Of course I knew it was normal for a girl to undress her lover—to open the zipper of his trousers and caress and manipulate his penis, But I was no normal girl, and the only way I could do it was the way I did everything else, with my toes. But Steve loved it, and in this he encouraged me too and I came to love fondling and caressing him in my unique way.

One day after school when I arrived at Steve's for our dinner date he was quite excited about something, I saw instantly.

92

"Melissa, we have a date after dinner. I learned today about a girl on the other side of town who has no legs. I spoke to her on the phone and told her about you, and she is just about your age, and she invited us over tonight. She is quite anxious to meet you."

I was anxious to meet her, too. I had never given much thought to other handicaps than my own, but now I wondered what it would be like to be legless instead of armless. I was inclined to think it would be less limiting but now that I was accustomed to my armlessness the idea of being legless constituted the frightening and the unknown.

It was a small, pleasant cottage on the outskirts of town, and as we approached the door I heard a TV set going. When I had slipped my foot from its sandal and raised it to press the bell with a toe (by agreement Steve did almost none of such little chores), we heard a small and very young voice call out, "Come In!"

We looked at each other and shrugged, but I curled my toes over the knob and swung the door open. We stepped into a charming living room to see a sight that caused us both to gasp audibly. An incredibly pretty little girl of about twelve sat on the floor in front of the television. Her light blonde hair was drawn back in a pert pony tail, away from a face of the most perfect and delicate features I had ever seen. She looked like a child from another world, she was so dainty and lovely. But we shuddered when we saw what had happened to her body. She wore a cute little quilted housecoat of pink silk, demurely tied at the neck with a blue ribbon. The way it draped flatly against the floor around her it was obvious that this beautiful little child had no legs.

She smiled radiantly at us and in a voice that was as pretty as she was said, "Oh, you're the armless girl... I've been so wanting to meet you. I'm sorry I didn't come to the door, but you see, my legs are cut off and I can't walk." She flipped the flatly betraying bottom of the housecoat with her hands. "Of course I scoot around... real fast, too, but with this long housecoat on it tangles me up sometimes and I didn't want you to have to wait."

The startling words, spoken with such casualness and frankness, caused my mouth to gape, but there was a trace of wistful-ness around the small, smiling lips. In a very ladylike manner she gestured from where she sat in her legless helplessness toward a couch and said, "Sit down, please."

Speechless, Steve and I sat and I unconsciously slipped my bare feet out of the sandals I wore just as I would at home.

Steve recovered his voice first. "But we thought you were somewhat older, Jill."

"Oh, I'm not Jill," the young girl laughed, "that's my sister. I'm Jackie."

"Well, Jackie," I put in, " we're delighted to meet you... but you see, we thought it was Jill who had... lost her legs."

"Oh, she did. You see we both had our legs cut off. . I mean, amputated." The word was obviously a new one for her and sounded strange coming from such a small and pretty girl.

She went on, "We were on the roller coaster together when the car went off the track and fell. You know that bar you hold? Well it hit something and came down across our legs and crushed them and they all four had to be... amputated."

The abrupt and blunt way she discussed all this was a little startling, even for me and all I could say was, "I see."

"I'll go get Jill. She's in her room and can't hear the doorbell from there. I'll have to take this housecoat off."

Her small hands pulled on the ribbons and unhooked the front of her housecoat and took it off. We got our first direct look at her slender young body, so badly mutilated. She wore flowered, flannel pajamas, the legs of which should have had small pink feet projecting from them. Instead their lengths lay flatly, crumpled and empty before her. The way the soft material outlined her stumps we could see they were very tiny—no more than a few inches of each thigh remained, at most.

Jackie raised her legless torso on her hands and swung herself forward. Her small buttocks plumped softly against the floor with each swing and the empty pajama legs trailed behind her, drawing tightly across the rounded ends of the short, thick stumps of her amputated legs and flopped limply

94

as she swung quickly along on her hands. While the girl moved with an odd grace and quite rapidly across the floor I couldn't help thinking how tragic it was that she should have to get about in such a fashion instead of flitting about on slim, capable legs and feet.

In a moment she came swinging back, the empty pajama legs now folded up in front and tucked into the waistband. Behind her rolled a bright, obviously new, chrome wheelchair. In it sat an older replica of the smaller girl. Every bit as lovely and delicate appearing, Jill had a fullness of figure and maturity of face that made her a beautiful girl with everything needed to make men pant—except legs. She was 18, we later learned, just a few months younger than I.

She wore a soft, full sleeved blouse of white rayon and a brown linen skirt. The skirt was as flatly empty, draped smoothly over the largely unused seat of the wheelchair, as her sister's pajama legs. Her stumps were equally short, we could see.

She wheeled over close to us and stopped her chair next to a coffee table, several small maneuvers being necessary to position it facing us. She handled it quite adeptly but still was obviously learning. The younger girl thumped across the room on her little bottom and propped her elbows on the coffee table. When the introductions were over Jill looked down at her sister and said in the manner of a reproving elder, "Jackie, will you please go get in your wheelchair? You'll catch cold on the floor." I knew it embarrassed her to have her legless sister swinging about on her hands. She went on to us, "I can't keep her in her chair. She just goes bouncing all over the house like that and the other day she even went into the back yard without her chair."

"Well, it's big and clumsy," Jackie protested, "I can get around better on my hands. Besides, with two wheelchairs in the house we always have traffic jams." But she dutifully went swinging out of the room, her soft little stumps thrusting forward and jiggling with each swing of her slim body.

"It is a problem, Jill said. "We have to share a room and we are always getting our wheels hooked or wanting to get at

95

the dressing table at the same time. And if we meet in the hall one of us has to back up to let the other by."

Jill went on, "Well, it's certainly nice to meet you, Melissa. Though you don't have the same problems we do it is nice to talk with another... amputee. Of course, Jackie and I are in the same boat but it's not the same as knowing someone new and someone my own age. I don't really know whether it is easier or harder to accept having no legs because Jackie is that way, too. At the hospital I found out later they debated whether to put us in the same room. On the one hand they thought realizing the same thing had happened to both of us might increase the shock, and on the other hand they thought maybe... well, "misery loves company," you know. Finally they decided to put us in the same room. I guess they figured we would wonder about each other anyway and they couldn't keep it a secret for long. We were both unconscious from the time of the accident until all the amputations were over with, so... ."

At that point Jackie came wheeling into the room in a wheelchair the mate of her sister's, though it looked larger holding her small and much abbreviated figure. She picked up the story.

"I came to first and my face was turned toward Jill's bed. I saw by the way the covers were so flat that her legs were gone. At first it sort of puzzled me but I could tell there couldn't be any legs there so I knew they must have been cut off." Jill visibly winced at Jackie's childish bluntness but the younger girl continued. "I felt awful seeing what happened to Jill and then suddenly I wondered about myself. I looked down and... sure enough, no legs on me either. I still couldn't really believe it and I tried to move my feet and wiggle my toes... but I couldn't feel anything happen and the covers still lay just as flat. Later my stumps started hurting and I could tell where they ended."

Jill then took up the story again. "When I came to and saw what had happened to both of us I started crying and so did Jackie and I guess we wanted to hold each other but of course with no legs we couldn't get to one another. Our folks tried to comfort us but they were as shocked and

96

unhappy as we were. When we left the hospital and people saw us as we were... are... I think we both felt better about not being alone in ... such a condition. Dad was even uncertain about how to lift us. He couldn't put an arm under legs we didn't have and besides he was afraid of hurting our... stumps. Finally he just lifted us like babies, holding us under the arms, you know, and sat us in the car. At home we were introduced to our wheelchairs and since then we have been learning how to get around and do things without ever standing up or walking."

They were certainly a strange sight, the two pretty, legless young girls, each in her own wheelchair, Jill's stumps moving nervously under her skirt now and then while Jackie was twisting and folding and tying knots in the long, empty legs of her PJs.

The smaller girl suddenly asked, "Were you born like that... without any arms, I mean, or were they cut off like our legs, Melissa?"

"They were cut off, just a few months ago. So I'm still a newcomer to the "club" myself. But I've trained my feet and toes, with Steve's help, to serve me instead of fingers and hands, and I get along pretty well."

"Gee." Jackie was wide-eyed. "Do something with your toes."

"Jackie!" Jill exclaimed.

"That's all right," I said quickly. "I do everything that way so I'm not sensitive about it." I looked around for something to pick up when Steve tossed his cigarettes and lighter onto the coffee table. For the first time I realized I had been sitting there with my feet bare. It seemed so natural to me now and somehow even more so in the presence of these crippled girls.

I raised my feet to the coffee table and quickly took a cigarette from the pack, rested my foot on my knee to take it from my toes with my lips and then with both feet struck the lighter and raised it to the cigarette.

Both the girls watched awestruck and made flattering comments. Little Jackie added, "You have very pretty feet, Melissa."

Steve giggled and winked. "I've been telling her that all along."

"We used to be quite proud of our feet," Jill put in wistfully. "A photographer saw me at the pool one day and said he had been looking for someone with pretty feet for an ad about Bermuda. He persuaded me to pose for him and he took a picture of just my lower legs and bare feet on some sand in which the words, "Come to Bermuda" were drawn, as though I had just done it with my toe. After that I got quite a few jobs where just bare feet were to be photographed... ads for thong sandals, etc., even grass seed. Then Jackie thought there ought to be some jobs for her so she went to the studio with me one day and took off her shoes and socks when I did, and sure enough, the photographer noticed how nice her little feet looked and she got several jobs after that, too."

"It's a good thing we did," Jackie said, "because now we have to look in magazines to see our feet." This bizarre thought made both girls chuckle.

"By the way, Melissa," Jill said, "I think my shoes would fit you. We were going to send all our shoes to the Salvation Army now that we can't wear them, but you are welcome to any you like. Most of them are like new. You see, after we started posing we seldom wore shoes. The photographers said shoes might rub red spots or blisters and so he practically forbade us to wear shoes except when absolutely necessary. So we almost always went bare-foot. All the time at home and on picnics and things. Mom enforced the rule. Jackie didn't mind much but I felt kind of silly at first, especially when guests came and I had to be barefoot all the time they were here. And of course the subject always came up for discussion, which added to my embarrassment."

"I know just how you feel," I said. "Because in addition to being barefooted nearly all the time, I have to use my feet as hands in front of people and in public... but I'm getting used to it now."

After that first visit I saw a lot of my legless friends. The very next Friday they invited me to come and spend the night. They usually slept in twin beds but that night, since

98

they were both now so short, having no legs, they slept in one bed, one of them at each end, their stumps pointing toward each other, and I took the other bed. I don't know who was the most fascinated, they watching me undress myself with my toes and putting on my sleeveless pajamas, or me watching them undress, exposing their stumps to me for the first time. All four were very short, blunt and rounded. They made a startling picture, side by side, the emptily hanging pajama legs dangling flatly over the side of the bed.

At breakfast the next morning the whole family hardly ate, they were so fascinated watching me feed myself with my feet. I was proud and a little embarrassed because I had never fed myself in front of strangers before. The girls' parents left after breakfast and said they would be gone for the weekend so the girls persuaded me to stay. We all dressed in shorts and I stayed barefooted as I would at home. Both girls looked very cute but rather pathetic, I thought, sitting in their wheelchairs with their stumps just barely peeking out of the brief legs of their shorts. I persuaded Jill to abandon her wheelchair so both of them spent the day scooting around on the floor swinging between their hands.

In the afternoon Jill proposed a sunbath. I quickly agreed and then got a shock. "We always sunbathe in the nude, Melissa. Our back yard has a high fence and is completely private." I was somewhat startled and yet the idea appealed to me so we all stripped completely. It was quite a sight to watch the two leg-less girls swing along in absolute nudity through the house, down the steps and across the grass, the sun glinting on their smooth, tanned skin. Jill's full breasts bounded and joggled as she hitched her legless torso along. Jackie hadn't quite developed her fullness yet, but I was amused to notice that her pert little nipples were distended and erect as her hormones began to kick in. I knew she would find a boyfriend to help them along. I felt my own bare breasts bobbing sensually as I walked behind them, and I was secretly glad I had someone to appreciate them.

When we stretched out on the grass I noticed both girls were covertly looking at my bare shoulders, my lack of arms being as novel a sight to them as their lack of legs was to me. Reading their thoughts, I said, "Armless shoulders make me look awfully narrow, don't they?" The subject out in the open, they asked if they could feel my shoulders. Intrigued, I guess, to see what a shoulder felt like with the socket empty and covered with flesh and skin. They alternately touched my shoulders, feeling all the contours and pressing the flesh into the empty sockets. When they were satisfied, Jackie asked, "Would you like to feel our stumps with your toes?"

I said I would and they both obligingly hitched closer so I could explore their stumps of thighs by rubbing the soles of my feet over them. Through the soft flesh I could feel the cut-off ends of bone. It was a strange and novel touch sensation for my feet. I had touched my own shoulders but they were not like stumps. Jackie giggled and said, "Ohh, your toes tickle!" She scratched the blunt end of her stump with her hand.

Just then the phone rang in the house, and shouting, "I'll get it," the smaller girl went flipping across the lawn as fast as her hands would carry her. Her slim little figure swung in a strangely graceful motion as she propelled herself along on her bare bottom, with pony tail flying.

With her sister gone, Jill got serious. "Melissa, you're very lucky to have Steve, but I think he is one in a million. One of the hardest things to accept about spending the rest of my life without legs is the certainty that I will spend it alone."

My eyes swept along the reclining figure from the perfectly modeled face, down the slender throat and over the full, up-thrusting breasts with their proud, rose-colored nipples. The flat belly and tiny waist which swelled out to full hips and... and then there was nothing. There the naked figure ended. Just below the hips there was nothing except two abruptly ending stumps. She should have had long, smoothly-curving legs and shapely small feet to complete the perfect picture. But what there was, was lovely. But it ended so shockingly, and the sight of her stumps made its beauty macabre and its

100

helplessness obvious and tragic. Nevertheless I tried to reassure Jill and did have the example of Steve to lend strength to my words.

"I know I'm pretty enough but who will find these pretty," she said, hiking both stumps up in the air in a grotesque gesture. Without thinking I stuck out a foot and pushed the nearest stump down. "Actually, you know, it isn't impossible that a boy might... find your stumps and your leglessness provocative. Steve and I, well, sort of play love games built around my armlessness. He kisses my shoulders and... well, the right boy will caress your stumps and tease you about the way you do things and you will find yourself loving it." Jill fell into a contemplative mood and in a minute Jackie came out of the house, still completely naked, bringing a tray of lemonade to us. She traveled by setting the tray in front of her as far as she could reach and then swung her legless little body up to it. In this slow and difficult way she came across the lawn, calling, "I thought a cold drink would be nice about now."

In the weeks that followed I saw a lot of my legless friends. Through the influence of Steve and I they adopted new wardrobes tailored to their new, foreshortened figures. Capris and slacks were cut off and the ends closed so the remainder of the legs formed "pockets" to accommodate their stumps. Skirts, too, they shortened so the long lengths of empty material was not in the way. Now they covered their stumps but that was all. They both looked darling in their special outfits, and less like they were wearing someone else's clothes.

Life for me became full and rich, secure in Steve's love. I now used my feet for anything, anywhere. In the nicest restaurants I could prop a bare foot on the table and with a fork between my toes feed myself without self-consciousness, in spite of the startled waiters and staring diners.

When I graduated, the best present was an engagement ring from Steve—sized, of course, for the third toe of my left foot.

When my wedding day came I was dressed in a gorgeous white bridal gown, unique only in that it was without sleeves or arm-holes and the smooth satin fitted snugly over my armless shoulders. Jackie and Jill were there, seated in their respective wheelchairs, in front of the first row of seats. At the appropriate point in the ceremony Steve took a tiny ring from his pocket and dropped to one knee in front of me. I raised my bare foot and he slipped the wedding band on my "ring toe." Thereafter, I would have both rings on always.

I had intended at first to wear slip-on pumps but then Steve and I both thought it would be an exotic touch and also symbolic of my new freedom to be married in my bare feet.

Since then we have known all the thrills and happiness of any young couple very much in love. And my armless shoulders and my skilled bare feet and toes have, if anything, only made our life uniquely fascinating and delightful.

BALI THIGH

by James Dawson

I almost drowned the first time I got a glimpse of Tamika 's perfect ass. I was snorkeling off the coast of Tahiti Nui in the clear, shallow waters guarded by the island's coral reef. One minute I was watching a school of bright orange clown fish darting way from my hand. What I saw when I turned my head, though, was even more exotic. At the time, I had no idea who this bronze-skinned Polynesian beauty was. She stood chest-deep in the still water and obviously thought she was alone. She wore a skimpy white bikini. An elaborate tattoo resembling a red lace garter encircled the upper thigh of her right leg. I assumed -it was some

sort of tribal marking.

From my underwater vantage point, I silently watched this nubile native push her bikini bottom down around her hips. She crouched slightly, using her hands to hold the firrn cheeks of her ass apart. In the diamond-shaped space between her thighs, I could see the thick lips of her pussy, which appeared to be shaved.

What excited me more, though, was the sight of her other opening. For most guys, a slippery cunt might be the main attraction a girl's body has to offer. Personally, though, I've always preferred the smaller, tighter pleasures of a well-greased asshole.

This pretty stranger's anus was dilated to the size of a quarter and bulging outward. It was delicious ly obvious why she had assumed her squatting position. I wished that I had brought along my under water camera. Then again, I had a feeling I'd never forget this sight.

Sure enough, the rounded tip of a thick brown turd soon emerged from the girl's puckered shithole. It stretched her anus open wider. At one point, the crap cigar stood straight out from her bare back side, swaying slightly in the crys tal clear water. Then her turd-cut ter clenched off that mud-colored tail. It floated gently to the fine white sand.

I reached to free my stiffening cock from the tight spandex of my Speedo. I hooked a thumb in the waistband of the stretchy material and tugged it down under my balls, situating it so the bulge of my scro☐tum would hold it in place. The upward pressure the suit put on the underside of my nuts felt good.

Keeping my eyes trained on the squatting girl's crack, I grabbed my cock and pumped it with my fist.

I was far enough away-about 30 feet that I saw what hap☐pened next before I heard it. Her asshole seemed to blow a huge air bubble that rose to the water's surface, followed by several smaller ones. Then the sound of those sputtering farts reached me. Since my head was below the water's surface, I obviously had to control my automatic urge to sniff them. I could only imagine how deliciously sharp and pun☐gent they must have been.

A bright yellow cloud began spreading around the tops of the girl's submerged thighs. Looking closely, I could see the transparent yellow jet of her piss stream shooting from between her cuntlips, disturbing the calm of the surrounding water. Her sweet urine surrounded her lower body like a dissipating golden fog.

At the same time, she pooped out a couple of pebble-sized turds that wafted downward to the sand, join☐ing the slick loaf she had passed earlier. The sight of her dainty, pink asshole spitting out those turds was enough to put me over the edge. As her anus flexed shut between the smooth globes of her asscheeks, my cock spewed a half-dozen ropes of cum into the water. I was breathing so hard through the snorkel's mouthpiece that I was surprised she didn't hear me.

Her urge apparently satisfied, the girl reached behind herself and gave her crack a vigorous rubbing with the edge of her hand. Perhaps to make sure she was completely clean back there, she burrowed her middle finger up inside the rim of her asshole and wormed it around a little. Then she rubbed both hands together underwater, tugged up her bikini bottom and waded to shore.

Staying under the surface and kicking my flippers, I quickly swam down-shore from where she was heading. She wasn't looking in my direction when I emerged from the water. Nobody else was anywhere in sight which was probably why she thought she could get away with taking an unobserved off-shore dump in the first place.

I found my duffel bag, toweled off, pulled on a polo shirt and ran a comb through my hair. The girl had her back to me and was gathering things into a straw beach bag when I attempted to casually stroll toward her.

"Hi," I called out. "I thought I was the only one who knew about this spot."

She looked startled. She was probably thinking about how thoroughly humiliated she would have been if anyone had caught her taking a shit in the surf.

"I...uh.. .I was just leaving," she stammered. She had a lilting but unplaceable accent. Her face was as beautiful as every other part of her tanned body. Her eyes were as dark as her shining black hair. She had a small, upturned nose and lusciously thick lips. She was the perfect image of a Girl Friday fantasy: bronze skin. big boobs, hard ass, long legs. Plus a few other attractions that she didn't know I had seen.

"By the way, I'm James." I said. "What's your name'?"

"Tamika," she said shyly, pushing a stray lock of hair behind one ear.

"Say, Tamika, would you like to have a drink with me?" I asked. "We could go..."

"No, I really have to be leaving." she said, hurrying away. She looked like something was on her mind. Maybe it was something she had come to the beach to try to forget.

I expected her to head for a car on the nearby road. Instead, she surprised me by winding through the brush and heading up the side of Orohena, the volcano at this end of the hourglass-shaped island.

I decided to follow her from a distance. What the hell: maybe I'd get the chance to see her do something else that would stiffen my prick. She might have to take another crap or feel a sudden need to piss on a bush. Hell, maybe she'd get horny and start humping the base of a palm tree with her bare crotch. There was always hope.

After an hour of climbing, I was drenched in sweat and ready to turn back. Then I heard the drumbeats.

106

Up ahead, hidden by a stand of trees, a t1at shelf was cut into the side of the mountain. A half-dozen men in feathered headdresses and loin clothes stood around a stone altar topped by a flat slab. One of the men held an ax with a foot-wide blade.

Standing silently behind the men were an equal number of women. They were naked, except for bead necklaces and string belts decorat□ed with seashells. Each of them was as young and beautiful as Tamika. Their tits were plump and firm, with big nipples that pointed upward. Their pussies were uni-formly clean-shaven.

There was one maior difference between Tamika and these girls, though: Tamika still had her right leg.

I stared in fascination as these six alluring amputees, who were leaning fetchingly on ornately carved wooden crutches. The smoothly rounded stumps of their right legs all ended above the knee. Those stubby thighs gave them a charmingly feminine look of utter helplessness.

In my life. I've only had the pleasure of fucking two amp girls. Both of them treated me like I was a pervert, just because I wanted to adore their stumps. Neither of them liked it when I tried rubbing my stiff prick over their smooth leg-ends. They could barely toler□ate it when I licked the bases of their stumps while I fucked them.

These native girls, however, seemed proud of their asymmetri□cal condition. They stood with their chins up and their chests out. Whatever strange tribe they belonged to, it was apparently one that cut off women's right legs as some odd rite of passage.

Tamika emerged from the brush and walked solemnly toward the altar. She had removed her white bikini. Now she was dressed the same way as the other women   or undressed the same way. Like them. she was naked except for a necklace and a belt of shells she apparently had gotten from her beach bag.

She bowed her head respectful□ly, then climbed onto the slab and lay tiat on her back. Her legs were spread. The leg with the thigh tat-too that looked like a red garter was closest to the man with the ax. After a few words of ceremony. the man raised the ax above his head. Then he let it fall, using the tattoo as his marker.

Tamika didn't even cry out as she was separated from most of her right leg with a sickening "thunk." The amputee women quickly gathered around her to tend to Tamika's new stump. The applied ointments to it and bound it up with a hooked needle and what must have been surgical thread. Then they dressed it with a flesh-colored cloth bandage.

Tamika grimaced during the pro□cedure. but managed to smile with pride as she looked down at her now-abbreviated limb. She cau□tiously raised and lowered it from the s l a b. The me n and w o me n around her smiled warmly and stroked her hair and shoulders.

I had my cock in my hand and was furiously jerking myself off. The sight of all those naked amp women hobbling about on their crutches with their stumps swing□ing free had made me hard as a rock. My balls were drawn up tight against my body and I was just about to shoot when I felt the tip of a spear in my back.

It was no use struggling. I had□n't even noticed that the three native men who found me had sneaked away from the others at the altar. I'd been too busy look□ing at the women.

One of my captors cupped a meaty hand over my mouth when I tried to shout. Before I knew what was happening, I had taken Tamika's place on the altar. Strong hands ripped my shirt from me and bound my wrists. The largest of the men yanked off my swim trunks, leaving me naked.

Ropes around each of my ankles were secured to the bottom cor□ners of the altar. My arms were pulled above my head so that the rope around my wrists could be tied to the other end of the altar. I was spread-eagled and naked on the warm stone slab.

The men backed away. To my shock and delight, the amputee women gathered around my nude body. One of them bent over my crotch and began sucking my cock. Another hopped awkwardly up onto the slap with me and sat on my face. As she rubbed her smooth cunt against my open mouth, I felt other hands and mouths on my balls, my feet, my nipples and my armpits. No one said a word.

Tamika was sitting nearby in a can□vas sling chair favoring her stump.

When a different native girl took the place of the one who had been squatting on my face, I called out, "Tamika, what's going on? Who are you people?"

"Don't you like our customs?" she replied.
"Well, I guess, but..." The new girl sat down hard on my mouth, obviously wanting attention. From the way she had situated herself, with her backside closer to my mouth than her pussy, it was no mystery what she wanted. I rammed my tongue up into her asshole and wiggled it from side to side. She liked that. She gyrated her hips, moving her ass in small circles. I kept licking and sucking her sour little shithole. She let out stifled moans of pleasure.

Two of the girls were licking my hard cock by now. Another two sucked my balls. One of the cock-suckers had shoved a finger up my ass. The last of the six girls was biting my nipples. I was in heav□en.

The girl who was nibbling my chest climbed onto the slab. On one knee, with the stump of her other leg hovering free, she hov□ered over my cock. The girls who had been sucking it held it upright, aimed at her crotch.

"She wants to know which hole you prefer," Tamika said.

She seemed to be enjoying the spectacle that was being made of me. I had the feeling that she was sorry she couldn't join in because of her delicate, just-amputated condition.

"I want her asshole," I said. "And I want to lick her stump while I'm fucking her."

The six girls gasped and looked at each other, their eyes lively with interest and approval. Apparently all of them knew English. They exchanged smiles. Two of them actually blushed. I had the feeling I was going to fit in just fine with this tribe.

"You have made the correct choice," Tamika said, somewhat enigmatically.

Before I could question her, my little nipple-biter started lowering her backside onto my cock. Two of the other girls held her ass-cheeks wide apart. My dick was sopping with saliva from the mouths of the girls who had blown me. I was well lubricated for this fanny fuck.

The muscular ring of her asshole dilated open around the tip of my erection. She paused, letting her self get used to my dick, and then lowered herself a little more. Her breath came in little pants as her anus stretched wide around my throbbing tool. Finally, she had taken my entire rod up her hot, tight rectum.

She tentatively extended the smooth, rounded stump of her right thigh toward my face. By bending my neck, I could lick and kiss and suck it. She reached between her legs to masturbate her clitty while I pumped her ass and tongued her lovely stump.

Another girl was squeezing my balls hard and pumping two fin gers in and out of my ass. It should have been painful, but in my present circumstances it only increased my excitement. The others were savagely biting my nipples. The other two still held my fuckmate's cheeks open, and helped raise and lower her on my thick cock.

The girl I was buttfucking cried out with an anal orgasm The girl who was squeezing my balls grabbed them even harder and twisted. I lost control and shot what felt like a quart of semen up into the clutching, slick asshole surrounding my dick.

The girl I had ass-fucked was raised off of my meat. She and others backed away from the altar. The native men stepped toward me again. The one with the biggest headdress gestured toward my still-hard dick.

'Now he has the ceremonial markings," the tribe leader said.

The other men nodded approv ingly. By craning my neck, I could see that my dick was ringed with brown and black shit stains from the native girl's asshole.

The man who had wielded the ax produced a small, jeweled knife. He grabbed the head of my dick, pulled my cock taut to its maximum length and raised his knife above his head. The blood drained from my face. I was too shocked even to scream.

Fortunately, Tamika did it for me.

"Wait!" she cried. 'We do not know if he has fulfilled the other part of the ritual!"

The men looked very annoyed. The chief narrowed his eyes and looked at Tamika. He grunted. It sounded like a question. Then he jerked his head toward me.

I looked pleadingly at Tamika.

"The chief wants to know if you took a shit in the ocean today. If you didn't, he can't complete the ceremony.

The funny thing is, I actually had taken an underwater dump out near the coral reef before 1 spotted Tamika dropping her own load.

As I prepared to give the chief my answer, I hoped like hell that none of the tribe members had been out snorkeling that morning and seen me!

HOT SPELL
By Bob Houghton

It was the hottest summer for a decade, the year I sat my finals. There was a hospice ban by the end of May and, in the evenings, there was a European feel to the city of Oxford - people sauntering about, licking ice creams, pausing to listen to busters rather than rushing past. Cafe owners moved tables and chairs outside, where there was room on the pavements. There was a real holiday feel to the place which was infuriating for those of us who had to revise.

Sod's law also dictated that, hot as it was, it was also the first summer that I had one leg. Twelve months previously I had a left leg, now I didn't. A car crash at the end of an all night student's bash had seen to that. Just what you want at twenty -- your finals coming up, temperatures to fry eggs on the pavement and having to get everywhere, do everything, on crutches.

I was studying English Literature at University and needed to work. Having lost three months swatting time in hospital and recuperating, by God I needed to work! I was not one of your brilliant students, but I was capable and diligent - and meant to get a 2:1 if it killed me. I would have given my right arm to get it. I'd already given my left leg, so what the hell.

"You'll never be able to concentrate", my friend Liz said as I left the hall of residence wearing a dress that just about covered my bum, carrying a string bag of books and tan lotion, a blanket thrown over my left shoulder. I always used to carry loads and loads of things, but crutch users just have to learn to travel light.

"I can revise and get a tan!" I laughed, crutching myself carefully out into the sunlight, concentrating on carrying the string bag and making sure the blanket didn't slip off, while maneuvering my crutches and trying not to fall over. "Anyway, this might be it, the only decent spell in an English summer!"

Liz nodded and grimaced and made her sensible way back to the library where the windows were closed and hot students lolled and drowsed over their books.

I unwound the string bag from my wrist and put it, and my crutches on the grass. I lowered myself down and, from a sitting position, did my best to spread the blanket over the prickly grass. Bumping myself into as comfortable position as I could find, I started to spread the sun tan lotion over my shoulders and along my leg. since they had let me out of hospital in all my new streamlined state, minus all excess lower limbs, the one thing I had still not got used to was how bizarre my solitary leg looked without its partner. As it stretched out in front of me with a huge, still unfamiliar gap where my other leg used to be, I thought for the millionth time how weird it looked!

I wasn't bitter about it. I don't know why, but I wasn't. Obviously the tears had flowed in the early days, but I had got used to feeling stupid, looking stupid -- when you live in a city of two hundred thousand people and you are the only one without a full complement of the old walking equipment, both are inevitable. But no doubt having one leg would have its good points. It's just that on a boiling hot day like today it was tricky to bring them to mind.

I lay on my stomach looking at the dazzlingly interesting pages of T S Eliot and William Shakespeare. It was very peaceful. There was the small of sun oil, the murmur of bees, a lawn mower in the far distance. I squinted at my notes, reams of them that I had written and forgotten. I closed my eyes for a moment, overwhelmed by how much I did not know. And I must have fallen asleep because I awoke with a start, feeling that I was being watched.

I lay still for a moment, trying to dispel the impression that someone's eyes were sliding over me. Despite the heat of the sun, I goose pimpled I sat up and crossed my arms in case my breasts were exposed. Suddenly I remembered the hem of my skirt which had ridden up and revealed the stump of what remained of my left leg. Flustered, I pulled down on the material of my ridiculously short dress, angry to have worn such an absurdly inappropriate article of clothing for an amputee! Then I saw him.

He was well built and blonde, good looking really. That's all I noticed before he turned and went. The way he loped away reminded me of a wolf, but perhaps that was because he made me feel very vulnerable, like someone's prey.
I felt disturbed, and felt like going inside. This was one of the main symptoms of losing a limb, I found. In any situation in which someone made me feel vulnerable, the feeling of helplessness, anger, humiliation, intimidation - all those things - ware hugely magnified. I could no longer leap up, impose myself, take the high ground. Getting up had to he done slowly and carefully, balance had to be ensured, crutches had to be reached for. Trying to gain control of any such situation propped up on those damn crutches was just so, so difficult.

Later, I saw him again. Liz and I and a few more friends went out for a drink just before closing time. It was nearly dark, but still hot. All the chairs outside the pub were full and I had to haul myself up onto nearby wall, leaning my crutches against it somewhat precariously. The roughness of the wall played havoc with the flimsy fabric of my cotton dress, and I had to carefully rearrange the material over the stump of my left thigh.

Stump. Now there's a word specifically designed to make a girl feel good! You have a car crash, which is bad enough. They take one of your legs off, which is now seriously bad. And they make you feel a whole lot better by leaving you with what they call a stump. Ugly word, or what! You would have thought that, by now, they would have come up with something else to call it, you know? Ok, call it that for soldiers who lose their leg in the war or something but could there not be a name just a teeny weenie bit more glamorous for a pretty girl of twenty with a great figure, nice personality and a life to lead?

116

I wouldn't mind, but my stump is actually very sweet. Don't laugh, it is! No bigger than a Playmate of the Year's tit and kind of pretty with a single fading scar like a nice smile and two dimples. And it wobbles like a firm pink jelly. I like that. Whether a firm pink jelly is an adequate substitute for a strong thirty inch leg with a foot that reaches the ground is open to discussion, of course. But the way I look at it is this -- this is me. My family knows it, my friends know it, and - most important, and hardest of all -- I know it. I can wish I had my leg back all I want, but it ain't gonna happen.

Half empty skirts, pinned up trouser legs, full length crutches, elbow crutches - all these things are now part of my life. Forever and ever, amen. And firm pink jelly is a lot better than a hideous grot bag of a stump covered in scars. But I digress.

We were all complaining about how much work we had to do, wondering which sadist designed the academic year so that the exams came at the hottest time!

"You wait," Liz said. "We'll put our pens down after the final exam and whoosh! the skies will open. Just you wait!" We all nodded gloomily.

I looked around at the people outside the pub. They were almost all couples. God, I so wanted to be half a couple. I had not had a relationship since I became one-legged. Correction. To be strictly accurate, I had not held a boy in my arms, kissed anyone, let alone made love. As I glanced about me, the guys were cuddling their girls, irresistible in their shorts and skimpy dresses, flaunting their long long tanned legs. How I missed that. My friends had been great and my social life had never been better. Invited everywhere, taken along, never excluded from anything. But hopping along on crutches excluded you psychologically however hard people tried. I was still the only girl at any party, at the pub, in the debating society, at the cinema, who had to pick up her crutches, get her balance and hop about to get anywhere. The guys seemed to really like me but none of them ever wanted to kiss me, put their hands round my breasts and squeeze, take down my pants and satisfy my sexual desires.

Then I saw him again. A lone figure, looking, staring at me. I don't know how long he had been there but it was long enough to have bought a pint and drunk half of it. My face grew hot. I jumped down off the wall and slipped onto my crutches. At least I was as in control as I could be, but I didn't know where to look how to be. I felt so stupid and self conscious like some circus freak.

The landlord called last orders. Liz went to buy another round. Someone went home, someone went to the toilet. I was left alone. I looked across at him and he should have looked away, but he smiled and nodded towards me. I felt his eyes on me, as firm and definite as a tongue sliding up the inside of my thigh. He kept looking down at the point where my left leg ended. A breeze kept playing with the thin cotton of my dress and several times the outline of my stump was emphasized. I was getting angry and confused. My face was getting redder, but he only looked at my body. Suddenly he just turned and walked away leaving me propped up on my crutches feeling stupid, angry, alone.

Liz came back and I smiled at her to convince her - and myself that everything was fine. I wanted to tell her about it, but she would probably say I was being over sensitive. When you lose a leg, it's very easy to think that everyone is staring at you, even when they were not.

I had wanted to be the center of attention for a guy for a long time now, but there was something creepy about this one. He did not look at my face. He didn't even stare at my boobs and, believe me, he wouldn't be the first. No. All he seemed interested in was the one bit that made me feel self conscious and uncertain about myself. The bit that gave him the upper hand, the high ground, the advantage over me. Blast him!

The following day, I got up and showered and washed my hair. I felt good! Looking through my wardrobe I chose a hugely, totally inappropriate dress to wear. Not that it was desperately short but it was one I used to wear a lot when I could count up to ten on my toes. It had a long split up the front and was just perfect for a girl with two great legs to flash. Well, I was only just short of the required number, so what the hell! I tied a scarf around my head, pulled a small leather purse over my head - see what I mean about travelling light? - and slipped onto my crutches.

I was still stirred up by the creepy guy, but today I was ready for him. I could not help thinking of the way his eyes seemed to lick my thigh - how dare he! But today, I felt great. I would go into town and buy myself something, and, if I saw him I'd stick a crutch up his ass and see if he could still stare with his eyes watering.

I was the best looking one-legged girl on crutches in Oxford! I knew that for certain. And I knew that I looked good as I crutched myself along, the split in my skirt showing my long, tanned right leg to it's maximum advantage.

I went into a big, cool store and sniffed perfume. I tried some eyeshadows on the back of my hand and chose one to complement my tan. I sat outside a cafe, under a striped sunshade, leant my crutches against the spare chair beside me, and ordered iced coffee. When it came it was cold and frothy, so thick with ice cream that it clogged the straw. I leant back in my chair and relaxed.

When I got back, I decided, and I would definitely go the library and do some work. Definitely. Well, probably. I closed my eyes and enjoyed the moment.

As I sat there, I could not shake the creepy guy out of my thoughts. sod him! Why was he getting to me in this way! I decided then and there what I had to do - I had to speak to T.H.

T.H. turned and smiled a greeting as the combination of my crutches and single shoe resounded across the ceramic tiled floor of the University Conservatory.

"Hi, Dumps!" she called out cheerily. "I thought that was you coming. Clunk click every trip and all that!" In the cathedral hush of the conservatory, which I knew that T.H. really appreciated, the noise I made as I crossed the floor was a bit of a giveaway.

If you're wondering why T.H. called me Dumps - well, it is a rather disrespectful abbreviation of my rather disrespectful University nickname of Dumplings. Most people in the college have disrespectful nicknames and I got mine within a week of arriving in Oxford. I was invited to a summer dance by the Captain of Cricket - an extremely eligible and dishy catch - who, in a state of slight inebriation, rechristened me Dumplings, a coarse but very thrilling reference to my rather prodigious boobs. His actual revelation was that I was the kind of girl to get in a stew over and my breasts were "good enough to eat!" Very cheeky for a first date, but I loved it! Most nicknames had an element of irreverence, even cruelty, to them - I have no doubt that if I had been minus a leg when I started at Oxford, my new label would have made some reference to my being a bit short in the lower extremity department!

I made my way across the conservatory and, slipping off my crutches, sat down next to T.H. who, after Liz, was my closest friend in college. I liked talking with her, and respected her views on life. Without doubt, she was the most breathtakingly beautiful and sophisticated girl in the whole University. Of South African parents, she came over to England at the age of sixteen to go to a very up market private school in Hempstead. Unfortunately, within two weeks of arriving in England, she had an appalling riding accident in which she and the horse she was sitting on changed places, leaving her paralyzed from the waist down, and sentenced to spending the whole of the rest of her life wheelchair bound. Consequently, she spent the first twelve months of her life in England in Stoke Manderville Hospital, where they retrained her for her new, and very different life.

Her actual name was a glorious Lydia Constance de Villiers, known to acquaintances as Connie, but to her closest friends as T.H., a nickname she had actually given to herself. It stood for Top Half, which she joked was basically all she was. She would say her legs may be useless, but what she could do to guys with her Top Half was something else! It was obviously true because she was without doubt the most sought after girl in Oxford. She had been out with every eligible bachelor in the City and was now engaged to the astonishingly handsome Simon Matthewson, captain of Boats and Rugby, and the single biggest catch at Oxford University. He really could choose any girl he liked - including me!   But he had chosen T.H., and loved her dearly.

It was really not difficult to see why. Apart from being amazingly beautiful, with long black, shoulder length hair and huge green eyes, T.H. was just so incredibly nice. She was charming company, laughed a lot and, if you wanted her opinion, she would give it willingly and without any messing about. She handled her wheelchair without fuss and, to my knowledge, no one had ever heard her even tut - - let alone complain -- about the terrible frustrations of not being able to walk.

The wheels of her chair squeaked an the tiled floor as she spun round to face me.

"We'd make a couple of good burglars, wouldn't we, Dumps!" she laughed. "People would hear us coming a mile off. Me squeaking and you clunking and clicking!" She put her hand on my arm. "Still using the crutches then? No sign of a false leg?"

"Nah" I answered dismissively. "I've frigged about down at the limb fitting centre but, with my third dumpling, I've got nothing decent to attach it to, really. To get a comfortable, decent looking leg you can actually walk on properly, you have to have more stump than I've got, you know?"

"Can't get comfy?" she enquired sympathetically.

"Hopeless, to be honest. Looks like I'm stuck with these!" I said brightly, patting the crutches I was holding. "Still, It's not too bad. Things could be worse." I thought of T.H. stuck in that bloody wheelchair. That must be worse, for God's sake.

"Oh, yes. There's always someone a lot worse off!" she said breezily.

"Anyway, look - I need your help." I thought I would get to the point of my visit.

"Oh, Good! I love giving people advice." she chuckled.

"I've got this creepy guy who's following me about." I really did respect her opinion on what I should do about it. "Several times I've seen him around, and he just stares at me."

"You're not just being paranoid?"

"No, I'm not!" I snorted indignantly.

"What I mean, is this," she went on. "You are twenty years old, absolutely gorgeous, nearly six foot tall, with the best damn tits in Oxford - for which I hate you, incidentally! - one magnificent leg that goes right up to your bum and you get around on crutches. Of course guys are going to look at you, you silly cow!"

"Yeah, I know." I replied. She was right, of course. "But, I don't know, this guy just seems creepy. I mean, he hasn't come up and tried to speak to me, strike up a conversation you know? He just stares and then goes off."

"Look, Dumps, I'm no Claire Raynor, right? But to me it's obvious. He would dearly love to speak to you, but he's just shy. I mean, it's got to be more difficult to talk to a girl with one leg, surely? What does he say? Anyway, he might think you'll dismiss him as some Devotee."

"Devotee? what's that?" I asked, puzzled.

"Come on. Dumps! Get real!" She threw her head back and roared with laughter. "Are you serious?"

"Yes, I'm serious." I said, baffled by what she was saying. "What's a devotee?"

"A devotee, my dear naive child, is a guy who fancies the pants off a girl who has got a leg or an arm off." she explained. "Have you honestly never heard of that?"

"You're kidding!" I was incredulous.

"Uh huh! I'm telling you that there are guys out there who think that to see you clunk clicking along on your crutches is

122

the sexiest, most provocative, sensual and inviting sight in the whole wide world." T.H. laughed to see the look of total disbelief on my face. "I'll tell you, Dumps, there are at least two guys at the Uni who would give anything to take you out. They've asked me for an intro, but I told them to deal with you direct."

"I just can't believe this!" I shook my head in amazement. "Do you know, not one guy has even asked me out since I lost my leg. Not one! I just put it down to the fact that, with all the gorgeous girls in Oxford, why would anyone want a girlfriend hopping around on crutches?"

"Therein lies your problem, Dumps," said T.H. "You give out vibes that you think no one wants you, or you think that, because you've got one leg, everyone is staring or creepy or a mad axeman!"

"Do you know, I think you're right." The more I thought about, the more I knew it was true. Sure, I had got over the physical problems of getting about without my leg but, psychologically, I guess my self esteem was much lower than it was before my accident. I felt inferior, substandard, second rate.

"Look at me." T.H. went on. "It never occurs to me that I'm not attractive to men and I can't even stand up! I have to go everywhere in this chair, squeaking about, sitting at the top of a huge flight of two steps waiting for someone to help me. But I soon found out that the guys were queuing up to help! They just love to be in control, have a girl they can protect, look after." She leant forward and put her hand on my arm again. 'But I tell you one thing, Dumps. I would dearly love to be able to get up out of this damn chair and get around on one leg and crutches like you. Perhaps, just perhaps, you don't know how well off you are."

"Of course you're right, dear T.H." I put my hand on hers, and gave it a squeeze. "I'm sorry for coming to you with my troubles."

"Not at all, sweetheart," she smiled. "My advice to you is go out and find this guy. If he's nice, then fill your boots - or boot, in your case! If he's not, then forget him. You'll be surprised what's round the corner."

I pushed myself upright and slipped my crutches under my arms.

"Thanks T.H. You're a real star." I leant down and kissed her on the cheek. Turning, I starting across the conservatory, once more the sound of my shoe and crutches ringing out on the tiled floor. T.H. called and I stopped, propped myself up safely and turned my head.

"Forget the burglary business, Dumps. You'd be the worst!"

"Good morning. I think you wanted to speak to me."

He spun round at the sound of my voice. His face went red and his mouth opened in amazement to see me standing at his side.

"Oh .... er, yes. Thank you," he replied, tongue tied, unable to say anything sensible. "I'd, I'd love to, yes. Yes, I would."

Standing next to him for the first time, I saw that he was about six foot or a fraction more. I'm about five ten on my high heel and always have my crutches set so that I stand full height when I'm on them. Some crutch users set them a little lower so they are a little hunched on their crutches, but I've always been proud of being tall, and was damned if I was going to start being ashamed of it because I had one leg. He was a good couple of inches taller than me, blonde, very good looking with light blue Steve McQueen eyes.

"Louise." I released my right hand and held it out towards him.

"I know." He smiled, and shook my hand strongly.

"Really?" I raised one eyebrow, determined to maintain the high ground. For the first time I felt that I had the upper hand with him, and didn't want to let it go.

"Yes. I know quite a lot about you," he said, rather sheepishly. He had regained his composure quickly, and seemed a little shy -- good old T.H., right again! -- and I found myself warming towards him. Already, he didn't seem at all creepy.

124

"Why don't you buy me a coffee," I suggested. "Then perhaps you can tell me exactly what you do know about me!"

We walked across the Square side by side, and stopped at the Blue Cafe, a little place tucked in the far shady corner, a regular haunt for students. Today, at this time, we had the place to ourselves.

I slipped out of my crutches, and he leant forwards and took them from me, holding my hand as I lowered myself onto a chair. I had successfully managed this basic manouvre a million times alone, but suddenly it felt nice to have someone to just give me a hand. He leant the crutches against the wall beside him.

"Are they all right there?" he asked, concernedly.

"As long as you promise to let me have them back when we go," I smiled.

"Sure." He smiled back. A nice smile. "I'll just pop inside and get a couple of coffees. Do you want a cake?"

"No, thanks." I patted my tummy. "I have to watch this you know." I had about the flattest tummy in Oxford. I had always been fit and I think that, since I had been getting about on crutches, I was probably in better shape than I had ever been in my life. It was hard work, like permanently working out! I looked down at myself to make sure everything was in good shape. I didn't have to worry about my boobs, they had been just fantastic since I was about fifteen! I rearranged the material of my dress, which was about calf length, to show the glimpse of my single leg to maximum effect and smoothed the bit that fell over the stump of my left thigh, emphasising the plump roundness of it. If this guy liked one-legged girls -- devotee, was that the word? -- then let's find out, huh?

"OK here you go." He leant forward and put the coffees carefully on the table. "By the way, I'm Adam."

"OK, Adam," I replied. "So - tell me what you know about me."

"Well, I know you're name's Louise. I've known that for about two years. I know you're taking your finals at the moment. I know you come from up north, because I heard you talking to some friends the very first time I ever saw you and recognised the Yorkshire accent. And I know that, when you first came to Oxford, you used to have a bike because, the second time I saw you, you were riding it and you had on a pair of the shortest shorts I had ever seen. I thought from that moment that you were the most beautiful girl I had ever seen. Then, about eighteen months ago you disappeared for ages and the next time I saw you, you were like you are now and I still thought you were the most beautiful girl I had ever seen!"

"That's very flattering!" I exclaimed. Fancy him knowing all that and thinking I was still beautiful. "The bike had to go I'm afraid, unless I wanted to keep riding round in circles! And the shorts. "There was something else I wanted to know. When you first saw me like this," I looked down at the material covering my stump. "Did you think I was more beautiful than before, or less?"
"Definitely more," he replied, without hesitation.

T.H. was right, I thought to myself -- he's one of these devotee sorts. I didn't like the idea. I could not get used to the idea of guys liking girls just because they had lost a limb. It didn't seem right. All that pain, humiliation, embarrassment - and it ends up with someone getting enjoyment from it.
"Why, for goodness sake?" I asked, a little irritably.
"Please don't get me wrong," he said, clearly worried about me getting the wrong impression. "When I saw you in your shorts, riding the bike, I really did think you were just perfect. Many others times I saw you with a group of friends, laughing and talking, and I just could not imagine ever getting the chance to speak to you. you were just so together, so sublime, so flawless that I knew you would never talk to the likes of me.'
"Gracious!" It was all I could say. "Do go on."

"Well, when I saw you for the first time on your crutches, I suddenly saw a glimmer of hope. I was heartbroken to see you like that. I know I didn't even know you, but you were already a part of my life, and to think of you suffering made me feel sick inside. But you were no longer perfect! There was a chance for me. That made you more lovely than ever. I wanted to hold you, protect you." Suddenly he stopped. "I ... I'm sorry, Louise. It's just that I've wanted to meet you, talk to you for so long..."

"It's all right, really." I reassured him. He was being so honest, and I had been very short of such attention and flattery for a year that I didn't want him to stop. "So, here was this poor crippled girl, with only one leg, having to struggle about on crutches," I pouted, mischievously. "And you felt sorry for her, right?"
"No!" he exclaimed. "I never felt pity. The way you moved on your crutches never suggested you wanted pity. I just wanted you more than ever. It's very difficult for me, with girls. I've always been looking for a girl I can look after. When I first saw you, there was no way that you were that kind of girl, but now I think perhaps you need someone to care after you. That sounds awfully patronising, doesn't it?"
"No, it doesn't," I replied. "Do you know, Adam, I'm really glad I've met you at last. If I'm honest, it sounds like what you need and what I need could fit in beautifully together. If you knew the number of times in the last twelve months that I've passed shop windows and seen my reflection, on crutches and with one stupid leg poking out of my skirt ... or the number of times I've absent mindedly tried to get up from where I was sitting and just walk to where I was going next, forgetting I've got only one leg. You have no idea of the despair I have felt, hopping to the loo at night, or getting onto my crutches for the hundredth time in the day. And it honestly never occurred to me that anyone would ever think I was beautiful or desirable again."

It all poured out. Adam had been so honest with me, It just felt right to tell him how I had been feeling since I lost my leg - I mean really feeling, behind the facade of normality I had erected around myself.

"I can't believe this is happening!" The relief in his voice spoke volumes. "If you just knew how often I had wanted to be with you like this. And now, here we are. You're more lovely than I thought you were, you're friendly and you're not telling me to get lost!"

"No, Adam," I said quietly. "I'm not telling you to get lost. I'm wondering where we go from here."

"At the risk of sounding corny," he smiled. "Louise, would you be my girlfriend? Please?"

"Please hand me my crutches." I pushed myself upright and balanced myself with a hand on the table.

"Sure," he said, looking a bit puzzled.

He gave me the crutches, and I slipped my forearms into them. I moved round a little just to be straight in front of him, covering the short distance with no more than a couple of small hops. I stood there, braced on my crutches.

"This is the reality, Adam. This is me. My leg's not going to grow back and I can't use an artificial limb. I've tried, but I can't. What I'm saying is that, if we go out together, I am always going to be on these crutches wherever we go, whatever we do. If it gets serious between us, you may be living with a one-legged girl, sleeping with a one-legged girl. If we get married I will be going up the aisle on crutches. If we have children, I will be trying to push the pram and using crutches at the same time. If we were together until the day I die, I will be one-legged every minute of every day of every year until then."

He got up and closed the distance between us. He leant forward and kissed me softly on the lips.

"Yes, please." he whispered.

LEGLESS IN LOGVILLE

by Pete Romastia

For the last three Saturday nights there had been a virtual war taking place out on the dance floor of Garveyls Saloon in Logville California. It was all because of the latest craze sweeping the nation-country and western line dancing. The rouble stemmed from the fact that local dancers were literally being booted off the floor by an obnoxious crowd of drunken revelers who swept into Logville from neighboring

Sacramento for the night. These rowdy visitors could not be both☐ered with dance floor etiquette. Their only concern was participat☐ing in the latest country and west☐ern fad.

As a result, scuffles were erupt☐ing all the time on Garvey's dance floor and a few fist fights had even broken out in the parking lot.

As owner of Garvey's just a very small country and western club in a very small California town, Jack Ross knew he had to stop the dance floor battles or say goodbye to the diehard local two-steppers who'd been patronizing his joint for years.

Tonight, the worst out-of-town troublemaker out on the dance floor seemed to be an attractive blonde in jeans and cowboy boots who was lurching about like a drunk. Jack knew he should proba☐bly just kick her out, but she was so good-looking with those huge tits bulging out of her low-cut top that he'd much rather ask her to two-step with him than leave the premises.

There was also something else about the girl that attracted Jack to her, although he couldn't quite put his finger on what it was. Still determined to read her the riot act, however, regardless of the fact that he found her extremely alluring, the club owner marched onto the dance floor and pushed his way through the crowd toward the unruly blonde.

"Hey, you're really pissing off a lot of people and I'm gonna have to ask you to leave if you can't be a little more considerate!" Jack screamed at the buxom blonde over the Merle Haggard song blar□ing over the sound system.

No doubt to disarm him, the girl immediately grabbed the club owner and began dancing with him. Jack went along with her ruse just long enough for her to fall flat on her pretty ass right in the mid□dle of the dance floor. Assuming she was bombed out of her skull, he helped her to her feet and escorted her to the door.

"I think you'd better leave, Miss. You've obviously had too much to drink," Jack said to the stumbling big-titted blonde.

"No, you don't understand. It's just that I think I broke my leg out there!" the crazy babe exclaimed, apparently sober and with a straight face. It was then that Jack noticed that her left leg was grotesquely twisted from the knee down.

"Jeez, we'd better get you to a hospital. How the hell did you manage to do that just scooting the boots?" he asked, shocked at the condition of her mangled leg.

"No, you don't understand," she replied. "Come out to the parking lot and I'll show you."

Annoyed by what had happened and perturbed at the thought of a possible lawsuit, the club owner followed the girl outside where she leaned against the wall of the club and rolled up a leg of her jeans to reveal the tell-tale metal of a lower-limb prosthesis.

Jack's heart immediately skipped a beat as his mind went back to his old girlfriend, Laura, who had also been a highly fuck☐able amputee. Despite the fact that she had left him for another man, Jack still found a female stump, together with a big pair of tits, highly arousing.

"Shit! It looks as though the foot-ankle assembly and the sus☐pension device both have prob☐lems. Wouldn't you know it!" the blonde said dejectedly.

"If it's an articulated single-axis unit, I should be able to repair it for you," Jack remarked without missing a beat.

The girl appeared stunned by his knowledge of artificial limbs.

"Yes, it is, but how the hell did a fine-looking hunk of man like you from a sleepy town like this come to be an expert on prosthet☐ics?" the blonde asked.

"Well, my ex-girlfriend had an amputation similar to yours and I was always having to fix her rick☐ety tin leg because she refused to get a new one, the bar owner explained. "By the way, my name's Jack Ross."

"Sally Jones. Pleased to meet you," the blonde purred, extend☐ing her hand. "This prosthesis is only two days old, so it shouldn't be giving me any problems at all. In fact, I came out here dancing tonight to break it in...not to break it off!"

"I tell you what," Jack said. "Let me tell my bartender and the doorman that I'm leaving for a while. Then we can go to my workshop over at my place and take a closer look at it, if that's okay with you."

"Sure," she smiled. "So you're both the manager of this joint and an orthotic technician'?"

"Actually, I'm the *owner* of this joint and I just tinker with artificial limbs as a hobby," Jack laughed.

Five minutes later, Jack was unlocking the door to the work shed in back of his house.

"I hope you don't mind, but I'm going to have to remove my pants to get the leg off," the blonde said as soon as they entered the clut□tered workshop. Sally immediately began to wriggle out of her tight-fitting jeans without even asking the club owner to look away.

Jack's jaw quickly fell to the floor at what he saw next. Sally didn't just have one artificial limb. She had two! Both were identical and attached to her truncated extremities by functional but cock-raising corsets.

"My other prosthesis is also a bit of a nuisance, so I'm going to slip if off too while you're working on it's twin," the blonde cooed.

Having stripped down to her panties and seating herself in a chair, Sally began to undo the laces of her left thigh corset. Attached to the socket and shank by a side bar and knee joint assem□bly, Jack noticed that the blonde also had a flexible waist belt and fork straps to aid in suspension of both prostheses, inadvertently making the entire ensemble look like some bizarre form of bondage gear.

The club owner was suitably impressed as Sally slipped off the broken limb and handed it to him. Then she began to seductively remove her other mechanical leg

Jack was having a difficult time keeping his eyes on the job in hand, especially when Sally finally slid out of her other prothesis and revealed two of the sexiest stumps he'd ever seen. The delineation of her thigh muscles was excellent and the club owner was amazed at how well-developed her rectus femoris and vastus lateral is were on each extremity.

"I bet your old girlfriend didn't have a matching pair like these," the blonde teased, noticing Jack's fixation with her legless condition and sensually running her hands around her silky ends.

"No...no, she didn't," Jack admitted.

Seeing the huge bulge in the club owner's pants as he leaned nervously against his workbench, Sally spread what remained of her lower limbs and began to rub her crotch in a highly masturbatory manner.

"Why don't you come over here and take a closer look at my thighs?" Sally suggested, seduc☐tively licking her lips.

It was all that Jack could bear and he immediately went over to the blonde and fell submissively to his knees. Without any further prompting from the gorgeous amputee, he began to kiss the tem☐porary welts that her thigh corsets had left on her stumps, at the same time catching a delectable whiff of pussy from her panty-covered crotch.

Then without hesitating, Sally pulled her low-cut top over her head and began to unfasten her black lace demi-bra. Before he had realized what was happening, two colossal udders flopped around Jack's head and nearly suffocated him with their meaty massiveness. For a moment, he simply wal☐lowed between the amputee's big☐nippled droopers, sniffing her per☐fumed skin.

Then, trembling a little, Jack began to touch the edges of her tits, probing their yielding heft with his fingers so as to fully appreciate their true size and weight. Jack slowly pulled back so he could view the blonde's monu☐mental bust, made to look even larger by her wasp waist.

The slim but stacked blonde's thumb-like teats were fully erect and pointed sexily at Jack. Her wide, puffy areolae were covered with nubs and because it was cold inside the work shed, Sally's fat nipples and bumpy dug-halos were extra hard and inviting.

Sally then gently pushed Jack away from her chest and picked up her discarded bra, placing its empty cups over the ends of her perfectly round stumps. The effect was incredible as her thighs were instantly transformed into what resembled two very pendulous breasts, apparently exploding out of a flimsy tit sling. Having a breast fetish as well as an amputee fetish, Jack was in seventh heaven upon seeing this sexy illusion.

Jack immediately plunged his face between Sally's brassiered stumps, nuzzling the blonde fox's tightly clamped thighs and grind☐ing his snout into her deep cleav☐age. Then Jack stood up and raised Sally's stumps, separating them ever so slightly. He next jammed his throbbing cock between them and squeezed them together for additional friction. He began to push his hips against her svelte frame, sinking his manhood into her accommodating thigh cleav☐age. Then the bra fell off to reveal her nippleless, substitute jugs. The illusion being shattered, perhaps it was time to hump the real thing, Jack mused.

Exchanging Sally's firm stumps for her far more malleable udders, Jack started to lustfully tit fuck the buxom amputee as she sat in his workshop chair. At the end of each thrust, when his cock peeked out of her frontal chasm, the blonde would lick its purple tip, probing his cock's weeping piss eye with the tip of her talented tongue.

Having acquired a taste for Jack's flavorful dick, Sally slith☐ered off the chair onto the floor so she could give the man a full-fledged blow-job while he stood. Perched precariously on her knees the end of her stumps-the busty blonde slurped and slob☐bered on Jack's veined member until it tingled and glistened with her viscous saliva.

Then just as she appeared to get a decent rhythm going with her bobbing head, Sally let go of him and hauled herself up onto a near□by workbench, knocking tools to the floor, and stretched out on the hard wooden surface. Removing her sopping wet panties, she allowed her splayed stumps to hang over the edge of the bench.

Jack could now see the amputee's wide-open snatch in glorious gynecological detail. Already glistening with cunt juice, her rose-colored pussyl ips peeked alluringly through the dense trian□gle of hair between her truncated limbs. Now Sally used her middle finger to roll her distended clit and probe the slick hole below.

Once more, it was all too much for the club owner and he immedi□ately buried his veined schlong up to the hilt inside Sally's flooded snatch. Humping her while stand-ing as she lay on the workbench enabled Jack to massage her big soft boobs, now delectably flat□tened due to her supine position. Jack grabbed handfuls of bosom, manipulating it in every direction as Sally's impaled hips bucked violently against him.

Without much warning, Jack felt himself starting to ejaculate. Before he could even attempt to hold back, his cock exploded and he emptied the entire contents of his bloated balls into the blonde's sopping twat.

When Jack realized that the amputee hadn't climaxed yet, he knelt down again and buried his face in her hirsute crotch. Sally's labia still gaped open from the extended reaming they had just received, and he easily penetrated her pouty folds with his agile tongue.

Licking the blonde's slug-like clit drove her wild, and she clamped her strong stumps even tighter around Jack's skull, mash□ing his nose to her musky mound. When Jack looked

136

up over her matted bush, he could see Sally's collapsed bust jiggling around like two giant blanemanges capped by cherries as she contentedly rocked herself back and forth on his sticky face.

Inevitably, an extended climax swept through Sally's body and her skin flushed bright pink in an orgasmic glow. Thrusting her gap☐ing pussy against her partner's mouth, she came again and again, groaning noisily and slamming her fists on the dirty workbench.

Now bone-hard again, Jack changed positions with Sally so she could fellate him again. This time, however, she placed her full lips around the tip of the club owner s swollen tubesteak and proceeded to swallow all of his impressive manhood.

Gradually the amputee took his entire shaft down her esophagus and used her throat muscles to skillfully suck him off while she playfully pinched his ball sac. This blow-job was a lot better than her previous one, Jack mused, when she'd no doubt been overtly impatient to get her rocks off herself. In fact, he rather felt as if he was attached to an out-of-control milking machine as Sally relentlessly suctioned his dick.

Then, sensing he was about to come, she disengaged orally from him and began to manipulate his obscenely large dick again with her inner stumps. Jack's heavily flowing jism spilled from his cockhead, lubricating her muscle-bound thighs and only then allow☐ing him to slip out of their vise☐like grip.

"So, are you going to be able to fix my prothesis, Jack?" Sally asked after they'd recovered from their torrid tryst.

"Sure," he smiled. "I just have to weld the broken foot bolt and reattach the patellar-bearing sock☐et to the torn thigh-corset. It shouldn't take more than a half an hour. However, I do want some□thing from you in return."

"Haven't you had that already?" Sally smiled mischievously.

"No, seriously, I want you and your friends to behave in my club when you come down from the city," Jack said. "You're driving away all my regulars."

"Sorry about that," Sally responded. "Those other bozos are my co-workers. I guess we have been getting a bit out of hand lately. I'll tell my friends to shape up, though I don't know if they'll be back again after this weekend."

"Why's that?" Jack asked.

"Well, I think I'm going to tell them they're all been banned from Garvey's. That way I can come back to Logville alone and teach you how to line dance with□out having them gossip about me back at the office. What do you think of that?"

"I think it's a great idea," Jack laughed. Perhaps you could teach me some more *horizontal* dancing as well. I promise you that my house is a lot more conducive to great sex than this grungy old workshop.

"In that case, why don't you show it to me anyhow," Sally said. "If you don't mind carrying me to your bed, I'll let you repair my artificial leg in the morning."
"Okay, that's a deal," Jack smiled. "Just as long as I don't have to repair my bed in the morning, too."

ISOLATED
By Ed Carlson

I had spent the better part of month hiking to get to the cabin. This place was so isolated that the wolves didn't know it was there. The hike had been up the frozen river. A river of ice. The supplies I had, I had pulled on the sled, every day for almost a month. A supply plane will parachute me in more in about two months.

The cabin was a cozy place made of logs. A couple of small windows let in the bright sunlight of the very short winter day. A fireplace on one wall did a good job of keeping the log cabin toasty warm when it dropped to forty below. The large bunk in the corner was comfortable enough. The cook stove provided ample heat to fix my meals. The hand pump at the kitchen sink provided water without having to leave the cabin. It pumped water out of a well directly under the sink and the foot valve had a slow leak so there was never a problem with freezing. The chair would be comfortable enough to pull up to the fire. The kitchen table and two chairs would be just right for my meals.

I was facing the isolation with mixed emotions. I enjoyed the solitude. I suppose that's the reason that I would spend the winter, until breakup and spring floods are over, in this very isolated spot. In the late spring or early summer, I would build a raft and float back down the river to what they call civilization. The way I had done it in previous years. My other emotion is that I longed for someone to talk to. A gorgeous female would be nice. I can dream can't I? But what kind of a gorgeous female would subject herself to the rigors of the isolation and loneliness. She would have to be out of her mind.

I spent my first day settling in. I put my supplies away. The frozen meat that I brought was stored out in the cash. The canned goods were put neatly on the shelves in the cabin. The dishes had been put away in the cupbord and were just the way I had left them. I checked out the mine. At least when you got underground a ways it was above freezing, even though it was pitch black when you turned off the light. A blackness you could almost cut with a knife.

The fire felt good and I started on one of the paperbacks that I had lugged with me. I fixed my dinner and read for a while longer. I gave thanks to the Lord for the safe jorurney. It was cozy and warm and I stoked up the fire before I turned in for the night.

The next morning was beautiful. The mountains shown in all their glory as the morning sun made the snow pink. I was one of those sights that you need to etch thoroughly in your mind so that you may visit it when you are far away and the pressure of society are weighing you down. I stood on the cabin porch taking it all in. I noticed clouds building on the backside of the mountains. Soon the mountains will be enveloped and the magnificent view reduced to a fog bank that hangs just at the tree tops. I enjoyed the splendor while I could. At least when the ceiling drops I'll be in the mine and it won't mater anyway.

I went in and fixed breakfast. The bacon and eggs tasted good. Eggs are something I won't have much longer. I don't have refrigeration as such. Only frozen, out up in the cash, or room temperature, in the cabin with no in-between. I finished up my breakfast and washed up the dishes. I had stalled long enough and it was time to get to work in the mine.

When I went out on the cabin porch I noticed how quickly the storm had blown in. The ceiling was about two hundred feet above the trees. A good day to be underground. I picked up my pick and shovel, and had just started for the mine entrance when the silence was shattered by the sound of an airplane engine. My first thought was, is that fool high enough to make it over the mountains. The more that I listened to the plane the more I knew he was too low, way too low. I decided not to go into the mine quite yet.

As I stood there I heard the plane's engine start to sputter. It would catch for a moment but would soon be sputtering again. I walked back to the cabin porch in hopes of getting a glimpse of the plane. I had just set my pick and shovel down when I saw the plane break out of the low clouds. It was a narrow two place plane. The kind that has the pilot in the front and passenger behind. I could see two people in the plane. He was trying for the frozen river but clipped the top of a tree instead. There was a loud tearing noise and then a deafening crash as the plane went down. The plane crashed within a hundred yards from where I was standing.

I picked up an ax and started running toward the plane wreckage. It was a horrifying site. It seemed like there were twisted pieces of broken airplane everywhere. I had a quick flashback of my days as a volunteer fireman and some of the car wreaks we were called to. There was a strong smell of gasoline. I determined that it was coming from the detached wings that were now laying in two different places about fifty feet away from what had been the plane's fuselage.

I found the pilot and quickly determined that there was nothing that a mortal such as me could do for him. He was with his maker.
His passenger was unconscious but breathing and was slumped over toward the dead pilot's seat. I straightened the passenger up to try and maintain a good airway. The passenger was a woman. She had facial lacerations and had suffered deep and sever cuts on both arms above and below the elbows and had been caused by the glass from the broken side windows. The wounds on both of the her arms were bleeding profusely right through her nice down coat. I knew that I had to act quickly or the passenger would have the same fate of the pilot.
I used the ax to chop away the top of the plane and was able to peel back the metal like opening a can of beans. I knocked the windows, that had caused her deep arm cuts, away on both sides. I was able to reach her seatbelt and

release it. I reached under the passengers armpits and was able to pull her free of the wreckage trying to keep her body is a straight alignment as I laid her on the snow.

I found a first aid kit in the plane. It was one of the large ones and had a lot of bandages and supplies. I unzipped her coat and managed to get her bleeding arms out of the tattered sleeves. I put pressure bandages on each arm and was able to slow, but not stop the bleeding. I did a quick body exam looking for broken bones and other cuts. Luckily she had no broken bones and the cuts were the ones I had already found on her arms and face.

She started to regain consciousness and wanted to sit up. I insisted that she lie still.

"What happened?"

"You were in a plane crash. You're going to be all right." I said.

"My head hurts and my arms do too. My god, I can't feel my hands!"

"You had a nasty bump on the head and you've been unconscious for a few minutes. Your arms have some very deep cuts. I bandaged both of them."

"Is Bill OK?" She asked.

"He died instantly on impact."

She began to cry and I did my best to comfort her. This was the part of first aid that I hated the most. I can handle the blood and getting in and doing the rescue, but comforting patients was not my bag.

"We were just gong out for a Sunday morning flight when we suddenly lost visibility." She sobbed. "Now Bill's dead. Where are we?"

"We're up Big River about two hundred miles. It took me a month to hike in."

"Oh my god." She replied. "Then we had been going the wrong way. I told Bill that he needed to get the compass fixed."

"Do you think you can walk if I help you. My cabin is about a hundred yards from here."

"I'll try." She replied.

She tried to stand. She became dizzy and passed out again. I picked her up and carried her to the cabin. She was light as a feather. I put a blanket on the kitchen table and laid her there. She started to come around again.

"Where am I?"

"You're on the kitchen table in my cabin." I said. "Lie still right there and I'll go back and get the first aid kit."

"OK. But don't leave me alone too long." She said. "I can't feel my hands. I'm scared."

"It'll be all right." I comforted.

I ran back and got the big first aid kit. I also found her very large purse. I was out of breath when I got back.

"I'm back." I said breathlessly. "Let me take a look at your arms."

"They don't hurt too bad, but my hands don't have any feeling."

"You're still losing blood." I said. "I'm going to rewrap both of your arms. What's your name?"

"Kelly." She replied. "What's yours?"

"Dave is what my friends call me." I replied

I removed the dressing from her right arm. The profuse bleeding started again. I cleaned out the wounds with some alcohol pads. I put several compress dressings on the wounds and wrapped them very tightly with a cling bandages. The bleeding seemed to slow a great deal on the upper wound and stop on the lower ones. I did the same with the left arm with the same results. I cleaned her facial cuts and put some butterfly closures on them.

"That's the best I can do for now." I said.

"Dave, how can we get me to a hospital?" She asked.

"We can't." I replied. "It would take a month to hike back out of here. You couldn't make the trip. The radio is broken in the plane and I don't have any way of communicating with the outside now. I only have a small potable radio to talk to the supply plane that will be here in two months. The radio only has a five mile range."

"So were stuck here?" She said.

"Until after spring flood and I can build a raft." I replied. "The only other hope, is that search planes will start looking when you are overdue from your flight plan. I could talk to one of them on the portable radio if they came this way."

"Bill didn't file a flight plan. He ask me to just go out for a Sunday morning sightseeing flight."

"Then you weren't related?" I asked.

"No Bill was just a casual acquaintance. I'd been out with him a couple of times, but no romantic sparks."

"Kelly, do you know if the plane had an emergency locator beacon?" I asked.

"I pretty sure he didn't because he was talking about getting one and also having the compass fixed. It wasn't working at all." Kelly replied.

"It looks like you're here for the duration then." I said. "I'm frankly worried about your arms. You've got some pretty heavy cuts and I'm having a hard time stopping the bleeding"

"I'm worried too." She replied. "I can't feel my hands or anything below those bandages."

"Make a fist with your right hand." I said.

"I'm trying." She said. "Nothing is happening."

"Try the left." I said.

"Same thing." She replied. "I'm trying but my hand isn't moving either. Dave, what's happened to me?"

"I had to put real tight bandages on your upper arms to control the bleeding." I said. "Maybe the bandages are cutting off the nerves. Just lie still so that we can get that bleeding stopped."

"Where did you learn first aid." She said. "You seem pretty knowledgeable."

"I used to be a volunteer fireman. We had to go through advanced first aid. Some of the guys went on to become EMT's, but first aid was not my bag. I wanted to squirt the water instead."

"Thank you for pulling me out of that plane wreck. I probably would have bled to death if you hadn't been here."

"You're stable for now but not out of the woods, so to speak." I said. "I really concerned about your lack of feeling in your hands and the bleeding in your upper arms. If you develop circulation problems then we really do have a problem."

"What happens if I have circulation problems?" She asked.

"Gangrene." I replied. "The tissue dies."

"Oh god, please don't let it happen." She said as she began to cry. "Dave, please you have to help me."

"Try and relax." I said. "It will help to stop the bleeding."

"I'll try."

"I'll be right over here." I said. "I want to see what all is in this first aid kit."

I took the first aid kit over to the kitchen counter. I went through it thoroughly. It was quite complete including suturing supplies. I read through the first aid book it too was quite complete, including a section on doing amputations. Something we both knew she was facing if gangrene set in.
I went back over to her. She had drifted off to sleep. I checked on the bandages. There was still a little seepage, but the bleeding seemed to be under control. Now if only we can maintain circulation she'll have a chance. I loosened the bandages a little. The bleeding seemed to stay under control.

I put another log on the fire, then went back out to the plane wreck. I was looking for anything that might be useful. The plane was pretty much bare. I had taken an old blanket with me. I pulled the dead pilot out of the wreckage. I wrapped him in the blanket and carried him over my shoulder to the cash. I managed to climb the ladder and get

147

him inside. He would soon freeze solid and the animals wouldn't get him there.

I went back in the cabin. Kelly was just waking. She tried to sit up. I helped her. Both of her arms dangled lifelessly at her side.

"I still don't have any feeling in my hands." She said.

"I loosened the bandages a little. I thought that might help."

"I think maybe that the nerves are severed." She said bravely.

"That's a possibility as deep as those cuts are." I said. "Both cuts are down to the bone."

"That's serious isn't it?" She asked.

"I'm afraid so, Kelly." I replied. "Would you like to sit in the chair by the fire?"

"I think I'd like to try." She said.

I helped her to her feet. She was unsteady and I held her firmly. She took a few tentative steps and made it to the chair. I helped her sit down. I put her lifeless arms on the arms of the chair. Her arms offered no resistance as I moved them

"How's that?" I asked.

"I would like it better if I could feel my hands and lower arms." She said. "Dave, I'm really scared."

"Just try and relax." I said. "I'll do everything I can for you."

"Thanks. You really are kind."

I went over and opened a can of soup and heated it up on the wood cook stove. I put part of it in a bowl and took it over to her.

"That smells good Dave." She said. "I'm afraid that you're going to have to feed me though. I still can't move my arms."

"I had planned on it." I replied.

When I was sure the soup was cool enough, I fed her the bowl full.

"Aren't you gong to have any?" Kelly asked.

"I'll have the other half of the can." I replied.

I went over to the wood cook stove and dished myself up the rest. I quickly devoured it.

"Dave, is Bill's body still in the plane?" She asked.

"While you were asleep, I got him out of the wreckage and put his body up in the cash." I said. "The body will freeze solid and the animals won't get it. We can bury him in the spring."

"Pour Bill." She said. "He was a nice man. He just wanted to take me for a ride in his new plane."

There was no conversation for while.

"Dave, what do you do out here all winter?" Kelly asked.

"I have a gold mine right out back. I work it and do some trapping too." I replied. "I planned on building a raft and taking some gold and furs out with me after the spring flood."

"What's going to happen to me?" She asked.

"I guess you'll have to stay here." I replied. "I'll take care of you and you can go out with me in the spring. If were lucky we can have the supply plane pilot send back a helicopter for you, but he won't be here for another two months."

"What about my arms?" She said. "I can't use them."

"We'll let them heal up and then cross that bridge." I said.

"What if I get gangrene?" She said.

"We'll deal with that if we have to." I said.

"You'll have to amputate them won't you." She said.

"Worst case scenario, yes." I replied. "I'll do all that I can to keep that from happening."

"God, I hope you can save them." She said as she started to cry. "I don't know what I would do without arms."

I put my arm around her shoulder to comfort her. She laid her head on my chest as she wept softly.

"Do you believe in god?" I asked.

"Yes, I used to go to Sunday school." Kelly replied. "I haven't prayed in a long time though."

I knelt beside her and offered a prayer for her healing and for the sole of Bill. She joined in the prayer asking god for guidance and wisdom for me. We both had tears in our eyes when we had finished.

"Why don't you sit here and I'll bring in the wood for the evening." I said.

"I'm not going to argue, even though I'd much rather have the use of my arms and be able to help." She said.

"Just sit here and try to regain as much strength as you can." I said.

"I will." She said. "I have a gut feeling before this is all over with that I'm going to need all the strength and courage that I can muster."

I went out to the wood pile and split enough wood to fill the wood box. It took me four trips with full armloads to adequately fill the wood box. I put another log on the fire. The weather had gotten a lot worse in the time that I was in the cabin with Kelly. I said another prayer for her when I was outside. I had a good idea what I was going to have to do to that poor woman. She probably knew it too. It was something that neither of us wanted me to have to do. If only a search helicopter would swoop down the valley she could get some decent help. The kind of help that she deserved to have, rather than the barbaric butchery help I had to offer.

I worked around the inside and outside of the cabin for the rest of the day. Kelly sat by the fire most of the time. I did help her up to go out to the outhouse. She was embarrassed when she asked me to pull down her pants and panties so she could go, but even more embarrassed when I needed to wipe her when she was finished. She was almost in tears when we came out and went back to the cabin.

"This is what I have to look forward to if my arms don't heal." She sobbed softly. "It will even be worse if you need to amputate my arms."

"Think positively." I said. "You are gong to get better."

I climbed up to the cash and got some meat for dinner. Bill's body was frozen now and was right where I had left it. I thawed the meat out and began to cook dinner.

"Is hamburger all right?" I asked.

"That will be great." She replied. "Almost anything sounds good now."

I fixed our dinner. I fed Kelly before I ate mine. She objected and said that I should eat first. After dinner we sat in front of the fire and talked. She was a beautiful person both outside and inside. I changed the dressing on her upper arms. The bleeding had stopped.

"What are we going to do for sleeping arrangements?" She asked.

"I thought that you could sleep in the bed and I would sleep in the chair."

"I would like you to share the bed with me." She said. "Not that I have a sexual encounter in mind. Far from it. I would feel more secure if you were sleeping beside me."

"If you insist." I said. "But that's only if you promise not to attack me."

"I'm in no shape to do any attacking. These arms just feel like I'm packing around dead weight."

I helped her get into bed. I stoked up the fire with couple of more logs then crawled in beside her. I moved close but was careful not to touch her suggestively.

"How's that?" I asked.

"You can put your arm around me I you want to." She replied.

I did as she suggested, but sleep came slowly. We both had her arms on our minds. I prayed that I wouldn't be forced to do the amputations. Once we were asleep we both slept soundly. I woke up in the middle of the night and put more logs on the fire. I looked at the lovely beauty lying there helplessly. I wish that I could do more to help her. I crawled back into bed next to her and drifted back off to sleep.

I awoke early. Kelly was still sleeping soundly. I slid quietly out of bed and started to the outhouse after I had put a log on the fire. When I opened the door to the cabin I was met by a snarling wolf. I quickly shut and bolted the door. I grabbed my rifle and jacked a round into the chamber. I opened the door again. The large wolf and several others were still there, snarling. I raised my rifle and squeezed off a round. Kelly screamed at the sound of the loud report. The big wolf dropped and the others quickly scattered. I closed the door and went over to Kelly.

"What were you shooting at?" She asked.

"I just shot a large wolf." I replied. "He and the rest of the pack were right outside the door."

"Are you OK?" She asked thoughtfully.

"I'm doing a lot better than the wolf." I replied. "Do you have a recipe for wolf stew?"

"I'm sorry I left my recipe books at home." She said. "We should be able to boil him somehow in a stew."

"How are your arms doing?" I asked.

"I still can't feel anything." She said. "I think they look a little darker than yesterday though."

"We'll have to see under a little better light." I replied. "I was just headed for the outhouse."

"Can I go with you?" She asked. "I'm about to burst."

I helped her get out of bed. She was a lot more steady on her feet than yesterday. I helped her slip her shoes on. I opened the door. The wolf was still laying in the same position. The others were gone. We both went into the outhouse. She went first and I went second. When we emerged from the outhouse. I picked up her hand and looked closely at it. It was much darker than yesterday and she still didn't have any feeling. I looked at her other arm. It was much darker as well.

"What's the verdict?" She asked. "They're a lot darker aren't they. I've developed circulation problems, havent I."

"I'm afraid so." I replied remorsefully.

"I need to be preparing myself mentally for my ordeal, don't I" She said.

"How you deal with what I'm afraid I'm going to have to do is critically important. You won't survive with a poor state of mind."

"Dave, help me to be strong." She said tearfully.

"We need to do some serious praying today. Unfortunately, I think that we are going to have to amputate tomorrow." I said.

"That soon?" She sniffed as we walked back into the cabin.

"If we wait too long we may lose you altogether." I said. "Poisons will seep through your body and I don't have any antibiotics to fight them."

"What would happen if we do it sooner, like right now?" She asked. "Will I have a better chance of surviving?"

"Yes you would." I replied. "I believe that you've adequately regained your strength. One little problem though."

"What's that?"

"I'm no surgeon. I only have a basic knowledge of first aid, not surgery." I replied.

"Why don't you practice on that dead wolf." She suggested. "You should be able to get a feel for what you'll be up against when you have to work on me."

"I suppose that will work." I replied.

She sat in the big chair by the fire. I got out the first aid book and reread the chapter on doing amputations. When I was finished I gathered all of the supplies that I would need. I would use plain black thread on the dead wolf and save the suturing material for Kelly's amputation. I retrieved the wolf and put it on the kitchen table. Kelly came over to watch.

I took the large scissors and cut a way the hair on part of the dead wolf's leg. Next I cut a large flap of skin using my hunting knife. I carefully cut into the wolf's leg and separated what would be the tricep and bicep muscle group. I got out the bone saw that I used for butchering and sawed the bone off. Next I took a coarse file and filed down the end of the bone to make it rounded. I used my knife to cut the bicep muscle. An artery was present so I tied it off with a length of thread and trimmed the edges with her manicure scissors. Next I cut the tricep muscle and tied the artery I found there. I used the needle and thread to suture the bicep to the tricep over the end of the rounded bone. I brought the flap of skin over the muscles I had sutured together. I used the needle and thread to suture the skin flap in place.

"Well what do you think?" I asked.

"You look like you know what you're doing." She said. "Why did you sew the two muscles together over the end of the bone?"

"If I don't those muscles won't have anything to pull against and they will shrink away quickly. This way they have each other to pull against. Beside the muscle will provide a padding for the end of the bone." I said. "You are probably going to want to get prosthetic arms. This way you will still have active muscle to activate a myoelectric arm."

"I've sometimes thought about artificial arms." Kelly said. "I'd think I'd look cool with hooks."

"You'll have all winter to think about that." I said.

"What do you have for an anesthesia?" She asked.

"I've been thinking about that too." I said. "The only thing I could think of is the two bottles of strong whisky that I brought along to celebrate if I really hit it in the mine."

"You mean, have me get drunk enough to pass out?" She asked.

"That's all that I could think of, unless you want to bite on a stick or have me punch you in the jaw." I replied.

"I think I'll get drunk." She said. "Are you ready to get this show on the road?"

"Are you sure you want me to do this?" I asked. "This is irreversible and we can't go back."

"I don't see as I have much of a choice." She said as tears started to form in her eyes. "If you don't cut my arms off, gangrene will set in and that will kill me for sure."

156

"There is no guarantee that gangrene still won't set in." I said.

"I know. I'm willing to take the chance." She sobbed. "Dave, I want you to cut my arms off. Please do it now while I have my courage up. Please."

I hauled the dead wolf with the freshly amputated leg out side and hung him in the butcher shed. I slit his throat and bled him out. I securely locked the heavy door. I went back in the house and thoroughly scrubbed the kitchen table.

I got out one of the bottles of whisky. I poured a water glass full. I held it up to her lips and she took a drink. By her reaction I could tell it was burning on the way down. I gave her another drink. She got it down without too much trouble. I stoked up the fire in the wood stove and pumped a large pan full of water. I set it on the stove to boil. I gave her another drink. She was getting pretty tipsy.

"Am I drunk yet." She slurred.

"Not yet." I said. "Your still awake. Here have another drink."

"Dave, I want you to do me a little favor." She said.

"What's that?"

"I want you to make both arms the same length, please." She said. "I don't want to be lopsided."

"I'll do my best." I replied.

I gave her a couple more drinks from the glass. I put all the utensils that I was going to need in the boiling water. I put a sheet on the table and helped her get up on it. I gave her another drink while she was sitting there with her feet dangling over the edge of the table. I removed her blouse that was badly blood stained. I left her bra on that nicely held her firm looking breasts.

"Do you want to play with those?" She slurred. "You can if you want to you know. I think I want you to play with my boobs."

"Thanks but I need to concentrate on what I have to do." I replied.

"Well you can play with them later then. Your not going to cut my boobs off to are you?" She slurred badly as her eyes fluttered opened and closed.

"No your boobs are fine." I comforted. "Here have another drink."

She finished off the water glass of whisky and I poured more in the glass. I gave her another drink. She slumped forward and I caught her. When I held her up her eyes fluttered open. I managed to get her to drink one more time. She passed out and I laid her out on the table. She was out like a light.

I washed my hands thoroughly. I used the tongs to pick the tools that I had to use out of the boiling water and put them on a clean towel. They consisted of two small hemostat clamps, my hunting knife, her manicure scissors, the bone saw, the coarse file and the needle. I opened one of the alcohol cleaning pads and I cleaned the area around where I was going to make the incision on her right arm. I poured some of the whisky over my hands.

I used a strip of cloth to make a tight constrictive band that I tied as tightly as I could just above the where my incisions would be. I picked up the hunting knife and made the large skin flap cut from the inside of her arm. I was able to make it about a quarter inch thick. I was able to separate the bicep muscles from the tricep. I found the brachial artery and tied it off with suture thread. I used the saw to cut through the bone. I made a rough cut with my hunting knife about two inches below the end of the bone all the way around her arm. As I finished the cut her arm was free from the elbow on down. I almost dropped it but caught it in time. I put her arm in the sink. I separated the bicep and tricep muscles even more. I spread out an alcohol wipe to try and catch the little bone chips that the coarse file to would make while I round off the end of the bone. When I had finished I used another wipe to clean off any contamination on the end of the bone that the file may have left. I began to trim her bicep carefully shorter than the bone. I spotted an artery before I cut it and tied it off with suture material. I found several more as I trimmed. I would put a hemostat clamp on them then tie them off just above the clamp. My procedure must have worked because they didn't bleed when I remove the clamp. Next was the tricep muscle. I pulled over the end of the bone and brought both muscles together to check length before I began trimming. I found several small arteries and was able to tie them off. I brought the two muscles into alignment on the top of her arm as she lie there. I poured some whiskey over them for antiseptic. I used the dissolving suture material to firmly tie the two muscles together. I brought the skin flap over the end of her arm. I trimmed away skin material where the flap would fit. I used regular thread to suture the skin into place. With the stitches exposed I could remove them in a couple of days when she began to heal. I released the constricting band. I finished by putting a dressing over the end of her now shortened arm and wrapped it tightly as I could with a cling bandage. One side was done.

I checked her carefully. Her breathing was fine and she was still passed out cold. I re-sterilized my tools and readied myself for Kelly's other arm. I took some careful measurements to be sure that I would carry out her wish to have both arms the same length.

I started on her other arm. I used the same procedure. I re-measured before I cut off the bone. The second arm procedure was like the first. After what seemed like an eternity I was finished. It had taken me a little over two hours to alter her permanently and irreversibly.

I checked her carotid pulse. It was strong and about the right speed for someone at rest. She was still passed out. She looked so frail there with arms that now terminated four inches above where her elbow used to be. I covered her with a warm blanket. I wrapped her arms in the sink and took them out to the cash. When I came back she was stirring. Her eyes fluttered open and she looked around the room trying to figure out where she was. She saw me.

"Hi there." She said with a week smile. " Did you do it."

"Yes." I replied. "You are now a double amputee."

"Thank you." She said as she started to cry softly.

"How do you feel." I asked.

"My arms hurt quite a bit, but my head feels like I was run over by a big truck." She said.

"I want you to take another drink and sleep some more." I said.

"I don't want any more whisky." She said. "I think I would make me sick. How about if I just lie still right here."

"OK." I said. "Try not to move. Especially your arms."

"I promise." She said. "What did you do with my hands."

"I put them in the cash. We can bury them in the spring when the ground thaws."

"I'm afraid you'll have to do it, I'm not going to be much help." She said trying to smile.

"You try and sleep some more." I said.

She closed her eyes and went to sleep. I sat in the big chair by the fire and contemplated the horrible thing that I had been required to do. I said a prayer for her recovery, then I nodded off for a while.

When I awoke Kelly was still asleep. I realized that I had not eaten all day. I fixed myself some lunch. I had my back to the table when Kelly said.

"When do we eat."

"I'm fixing myself a sandwich. Are you up to one, or would you like some soup?" I replied.

"A sandwich would be great." She said.

I made the sandwiches. I folded several blankets to form a wedge so that she could sit up a bit and still support her arms.

"I'm dying to see what you've done to me." She said.

I folded the blanket down to her waist.

"That's about what I expected." She said bravely.

"I'm sorry that I had to do such a horrible thing like that to you." I said as I stared to tear up.

"Dave, it's all right. You did it to save my life." She said firmly. "If you remember, I begged you to do it."

"Yes I know. But this is so permanent." I said.

"So is death." She said. "Not having any hands is not the way I wanted to finish my life, but I didn't want it to finish completely in two weeks when gangrene completely invaded my body. Dave, I owe you my life. Thank you for doing what you had to do."

I put the blanket back over her and fed her the sandwich. When she finished I gave her a glass of water. I took the blankets out from under her shoulders and she lie flat on the table. She closed her eyes and went back to sleep. I cleaned up the instruments and washed the bloody towels that I had used. She slept most of the day.

When she awoke in the evening it was dark outside. I helped her sit up on the edge of the table. She said she was a little dizzy when she first sat up. I put one of my flannel shirts on her and buttoned it up. I left the sleeves to dangle at the ends of her shortened arms. I helped her to the big chair and put more logs on the fire. I sat on the bed facing her.

"How are your arms feeling?" I asked.

"They hurt like hell." Kelly replied. "How long will I have to put up with the pain?"

"I'm not sure." I replied. "I think it will get less and less every day. Do you have any sensations like your hands are still there?"

"No it just hurts really bad near the ends." She said.

"That's where I did the skin flap and tied the muscles together. It's gong to be tender for a long time." I explained. "I made the flap on the outside of your arm so that you can pick things up with ends of your arms and not be pressing on the scar."

"You've thought of everything." She said.

162

"No that was a hint in the first aid book." I replied.

She looked tired and still very pale.

"Can I get you something to eat or drink?" I asked.

"I'm really thirsty." She said. "I would love a large glass of water."

I got up and pumped her some cold and fresh water. I held the glass while she drank.

"How about some dinner?" I asked.

"I really don't have much of an appetite." She said. "I would like a bowl of soup."

I got up and opened a can of soup and began heating it on the stove. I poured some in a bowl and sat down on a kitchen chair beside the big chair she was sitting in. It was still hot so I waited for it to cool. I fed her the first spoon full and waited for a reaction. It was just right so I fed her the rest of the bowl.

"Care for another?" I asked.

"That was just right." She said. "How about just before I go to bed. I would like another glass of water."

I got her another glass of water and held it for her while she drank.

"I don't know why I'm so thirsty." She said.

"Alcohol will dehydrate you badly." I said. "You had plenty of dehydration today."

"It's been years since I've had anything to drink. Getting drunk enough to pass out was a first."

"I'm glad that I brought the bottles on whim this time." I said.

"I'm glad you did too." She said. "I would have hated to see you sawing my arm off with that saw."

"I'd like to forget the details and concentrate on getting you healed up and getting your strength back."

"That sounds good to me." She said. "Will you pray for me?"

"I've been praying every since you crashed." I said

I knelt beside her and asked for healing.

When we were done praying we sat and talked for a long while. She was very intelligent and very interesting to talk to. Soon it was time for bed.

"Tell you what." I said. "I want to tape your arm stubs to your sides so that you won't move them during the night."

"Good idea." She said.

I helped her stand. She did much better this time and was quite steady on her feet. We walked over to the kitchen table.

"I hate to say this but I need to use the outhouse." She said.

"Are you up to walking that far." I said. "I could carry you."

"Let me try walking. You can pick me up if I need help."

I put a coat over her shoulders. I put a coat on too. I grabbed the big flashlight and the rifle. I opened the cabin door and shined the big light all around. It was clear. We started to walk slowly to the outhouse. We were about halfway there when she asked me to carry her. I picked her up and finished the first half of the journey. She went first and I helped her finish. She stood beside me while I also relieved myself. I opened the door and picked her up. We made it back to the cabin without incident. I set her down by the big chair and helped her sit down.

"I didn't realize I was that week." She said.

"You've done remarkably well considering I cut away almost a quarter of your body today. Are you ready for the rest of the soup?"

"That sounds great." She said. "Did you ever have dinner?"

"No we got talking and I guess I forgot." I said. "I'll make myself something while your soup is re-heating."

"You need to keep your strength up too." She said. "I'm depending on you."

I made myself some dinner and re-heated her soup. I fed her the soup and then I ate my dinner.

"Are you ready to have your arms taped?" I asked.

She nodded then got up and came over to the table where I was standing. I took my shirt that she was wearing off of her. She was standing there in her bra. I couldn't help but look at her nice breasts.

"Do I remember telling you to play with my breasts?" She asked.

"Yes. You asked me to play with them." I said.

Her face reddened and she said. "I really did mean that. I would like for you to touch them."

"Listen Kelly." I said. "You are a very attractive woman. I find that am very attracted to you. Its all I can do to keep my hands off of you. For both of our sake please don't tempt me like that until you are healed up."

"I'm sorry." She said. "I am so drawn to you. Maybe its because you saved my life. I just want to be close to you all the time."

"I'll be right here with you. Don't worry." I comforted.

I got out a roll of three inch wide tape and taped each of her stubs loosely to her sides. She could move them a little but not very far. I helped her get into bed and covered her up.

"Aren't you coming to bed now?" She asked.

"I'll sleep in the chair tonight." I replied.

"I want you to sleep next to me. Please." She begged.

"I don't think I should." I said as I saw tears forming in her eyes.

"Dave, please, I want you next to me." She said. "I fell safe if you're here where I can feel you."

I stoked up the fire and crawled in beside her. She snuggled next to me and soon was asleep. I didn't have any problem getting to sleep either.

The sun was streaming through the window when we woke up. I got up first and added some logs to the fire that was almost out. I got back in bed with her. She kissed me on the cheek. I faced her and kissed her on the lips. Our first encounter became a very passionate kiss. I broke it off.

"We're not ready for this." I said.

"I've been wanting to kiss you like that for three days now." She said.

"A little kissing is fine, but nothing more." I said.

We kissed again. This time longer and more passionate. I wanted to fondle her breasts in the worst way and I knew she wanted me to. I resisted the temptation, at least for now.

"OK, no more." I said. "One thing will lead to another and soon we'll both want to do things we shouldn't be doing. I'm concerned that we'll get fooling around and pull your sutures lose. You'd start bleeding again and I'd have to operate, and I sure as hell don't want to do that."

"I don't want that either." Kelly said. "Both for what I've put you through and for what I'd have to go through again. I'll behave, at least until I'm healed up."

"That will work out. We'll both know each other much, much better by then." I said. "I have some strong convictions about out of wedlock relationships."

"I won't tell you I'm a virgin, but I've developed them too." She replied. "I've only been with two guys. One when I was in high school and the other when I was a sophomore in college. I guess I finally believed that intimate relationships were for marriage."

"Good." I said. "We're thinking along the same lines. I've been intimate with three girls. One in high school, one as a freshman in college and one as a sophomore. I've been out of school three years now."

"Me too." She said. "Where did you go to college."

"It was a little school down south." I said. "I studied civil engineering, with a minor in geology. What about you?"

"I went to ESU. I majored in home economics." She replied. "With the geology background, I see why you're working the mine."

"It has all the signs of being close to pay dirt. This is my second year out here." I said. "We should change your dressings."

We got up. I put a blanket on the kitchen table and helped her sit up on it. She was not wearing a shirt, only her bra.

"How do you feel today?" I asked.

"I fell a lot stronger than yesterday." She said. "I didn't get lightheaded like I did before."

"That's a good sign." I said. "Your color looks much better."

I removed the tape that was holding her arms at her side. She shrugged her shoulders to try and get a little movement. I unwrapped her left arm stub first. It had bled a little and was still seeping a bit. I had Kelly lift her arm to see if it hurt too bad. She could only go about forty five degrees. I used an alcohol wipe to clean the dried blood from her incision where I had sewn the skin flap on.

"What do you think of my handiwork?" I asked.

"You did a good job. The incision is pretty straight." Kelly replied.

I messaged the end of the stump a little to encourage circulation. I stopped when tears began to form in her eyes. I put a clean dressing over the incision and wrapped tightly with a cling bandage. I did the right arm stump next. This one had bled a little more, but it had just about stopped. I

168

messaged it too and cleaned off the dried blood with the wipe before I put a clean dressing over the incision. I wrapped the dressing and the end of her arm stub with a cling bandage.

"That should do it." I said. "I think that you're going to heal OK. We'll need to message your stumps, sorry I meant arms, daily at least."

"Stumps is right." She said. "I don't have arms as people know them, just stumps."

"When we get back to civilization, you can have a plastic surgeon clean up the scars that I made on your stumps." I said.

"No way in hell." She said very defensively. "I want to proudly carry these scars to show the world what a wonderful man did with hunting knife to save my life. These scars are here for keeps."

"I'm speechless." I replied. "I don't know what to say. Is there anything else I can do for you?"

"I would love to lay in a bathtub for about an hour." She said. "I haven't seen a tub so how about a sponge bath?"

"You're right. We don't have a tub." I said. "I can give you a sponge bath if that's what you want."

I helped her down from the table. She went over and stood by the fireplace while I built a fire in the kitchen stove. Once the fire got gong I put on a large bucket of water on to heat. While the water was heating I went over and stood next to the fireplace with her. She put her head on my shoulder as we stood there. I put my arm around her soft shoulder.

169

When the water was ready. I removed her bra. I started washing her back and then around her neck and shoulders. She turned around and I washed under her chin and down to her breasts. I think she had as much enjoyment of me washing them as I did. I dried her upper half off. Next I took off her jeans and panties. She was standing there nude in front of me. It certainly didn't seem to bother her any. I cleaned her back side and then her front side. She squirmed like she was enjoying it when I washed her private parts. I dried her off. I found a clean pair of panties in her purse and put them on her, then her jeans. She didn't want to wear her bra. I turned the sleeves halfway inside out on the flannel shirt so that the cuffs were by her shoulders. I slipped the shirt over each of her arm stubs and over shoulders. I adjusted the sleeves by pulling them up until the end of the sleeve was tugging at the end of her arm stump. I buttoned the flannel shirt and tucked it in her jeans. I combed her hair. She walked over to the mirror.

"I don't look too bad like this, do I?" She asked

"No you look all right." I said.

"Just all right?" She pouted as she turned around.

"No you look better than all right. You are a real turn on." I said. "It's all I could do keep myself from throwing you down on the bed and going at it. Is that what you wanted to hear?"

"Only if you meant it." She countered.

"I meant it." I replied. "You seemed to enjoy me washing and looking at you."

"Isn't that the way a future wife is supposed to act? Show off for her intended." She said with a big smile.

"How do you know that I'll want to marry you?' I quizzed as she walked over to the fire by me.

"I don't for sure, but I have this gut feeling that you will." She said and gave me a kiss on the cheek. "We'll wait and see."

After that encounter I decided that I needed some breakfast. I made up enough oat meal and coffee for both of us. When it was ready and cool enough to eat we both sat at the table. I fed her first and then ate mine. I held her coffee cup so that she could have a drink.

When breakfast was over I decided to go out to the mine for a while. She decided that she wanted to read for a while and asked me for my bible. I set it on the table for her and asked her where she wanted to read. She said the Psalms. I turned to them for her. She sat down and started to read them, turning the page with her arm stump. I left her alone and went to the mine.

I worked in there the rest of the morning. The quartz vein that I was following was looking more promising all the time. When I went back to the cabin for lunch, Kelly was lying on the bed. She looked beautiful lying there sleeping, but so helpless without her arms. I started to fix lunch.

"Hi there." She said. "What are you doing?"

"I'm fixing lunch are you ready to eat?"

"Sure, I can eat anytime." She replied. "I felt tired so I laid down for a while."

"Good, listen to your body." I said. "Lunch is ready."

She got up and came over to the table. I fed her a sandwich and coffee, then I ate my lunch.

"How's the mine doing?" She asked.

171

"The quartz vein I've been following is looking more promising all the time."

"How do you know where to start the mine?" She asked.

"You look for just the right rock formation." I said. "What you are looking for triggers what the rock formation should look like. I'm looking for gold, so I'm following a quartz vein."

"That's the white streeks in the gray rocks." She said.

"You've got it." I said. "You usually find the gold with the quartz."

"Can I watch you work?" She asked.

"Not yet." I said. "Maybe in a few days when you get your strength back."

"Well OK." she pouted.

I went back out to the mine and finished the day. I came in and fixed dinner for us. Kelly had spent most of the day in the big chair by the fire recuperating.

I taped her arms before we went to bed.

The next morning we both got up. I stoked the fire and changed her dressings. The bleeding had stopped and her stumps didn't seem to be as painful when I massaged them. I worked in the mine while Kelly stayed in the cabin except when we made trips to the outhouse. The day was uneventful except that we used our time together to get to know each other better. She was indeed a beautiful person, internally and externally.

172

The next two days had the same routine. Kelly felt strong enough to go into the mine with me and watch me work. I was beginning to take some gold out of the vein.

The following morning I decided that here stitches through her skin should come out. She was healing nicely and her skin was starting to grow over the sutures. I used her manicure scissors to cut the sutures. I pulled them through with the forceps. There was just a few spots of blood. I cleaned them with an alcohol wipe before I put a clean dressing and cling bandage back on her stump.

"How much longer do my stumps have to stay bandaged? " She asked. "I have pretty good movement without pain."

"I'm not sure." I replied. "Maybe a few more days."

I butchered the wolf while she watched and gave me some suggestions on cuts. I wrapped the meat and put it up in the cash. She went with me to the mine for the rest of the afternoon. Even though she was unable to help, it was good to have her company.

A month passed. Kelly's arms had healed nicely even though they still had a few tender spots. I massaged her stumps twice a day to be sure that circulation was encouraged. She showed no sign of developing gangrene. My drastic action had paid off in her saved life.

Each day she went to the mine with me. She was wonderful company and tried her damnedest to try and move some of the rocks. The mine was paying off much better than I had expected. The vein had widened significantly and was producing a very high grade ore.

We prayed together each day and each day our comfort level with each other grew. As she had predicted I did ask her to become my wife. She accepted without hesitation. We decided to perform our own marriage ceremony out under the stars at midnight on new years eve. We found it hard to wait for the time to pass.

December thirty first finally came, our wedding evening. We had prepared a nice meal. I said we because Kelly had learned to a lot of things using her stub arms. When we sat down to eat I put the large rubber band on her right arm stub and slid a fork under it. She was able to eat most of her meal by herself.

As midnight approached I bundled her warmly then bundled myself. We went out side. It was a crisp clear night with no wind at all. The moon had not yet risen from behind the mountains. The sky appeared to be filled with a billion stars. At the stroke of midnight we began saying our vows and promises to each other. It was all from memory just the way each of us had planned our own. It was a beautiful thing to witness. It was almost to bad that no one else was there to be with us on this joyous occasion. After I pronounced us husband and wife, I kissed my bride. We both had tears in our eyes as we embraced. We had no sooner finished our kiss when the sky became totally ablaze with the northern lights. We had seen them before, but this light show paled anything we had seen before. It was like God approved of what we had done and was giving us his blessing. The magnificent show finally subsided and we went back to the cabin. I carried my wife across the threshold. We had a wonderful wedding night that lasted past noon the next day. We were both glad we had waited. It made our actions that night much more special.

We worked in the mine most of the next month, only taking time off to hunt for a deer for venison. Kelly was an excellent cook. We worked well together in the kitchen.

One morning we heard a plane. It was the supply plane bringing our staples just in time because we had been rationing ourselves. He made a pass over the cabin. I talked to the pilot on the radio and had him drop the chute on the frozen river in front of the cabin. The package landed right on target. The pilot spotted the plane wreckage. I told him what had happened and that Bill had been killed. He said he would contact the authorities. I also told him that Kelly was with me and to come back in one month rather than two because we were consuming more supplies than I had originally intended. He said he would and signaled a wigwag of his wings as he flew back down the river.

Suddenly we were alone again. We had discovered that Kelly could pull the sled using the shoulder harness that I had used to get the sled and supplies up here. We retrieved our supplies and took them to the cabin. They were stowed in their places. We could eat again.

Kelly and I fixed a fine meal to celebrate supplies. After dinner we relaxed in front of the fire. Life was good with her. I only wished that I hadn't needed to do the radical surgery on her and amputate both of her arms. She had adjusted well to her new ways of having to do things. Not once did she complain of her loss. I was proud to have her for a wife.

The vein in the mine had played out and we spent the days working in the shed using a small pick and hammer breaking the rocks that contained the quarts and gold. We were doing this manual ore concentration so that we could haul mostly gold out and minimize hauling out just rocks. The process seemed to be working. We had several boxes of concentrate when we finished. We had no idea what it was worth.

We were really done up here and had several months to go before breakup. All we had to do was wait it our now. We sent our days just fooling around outside on the nice days and inside on the stormy ones. One evening we were sitting around the fire after dinner, just talking.

"I've been thinking." She said. "When we get back, I think I want to get some prosthetic arms."

"I've always just assumed that." I replied.

"Some people never do get them." She said. "I would like to become able to do as much as I can without them, but to use them for going to work and social functions."

"What kind do you think you want to get." I asked.

"I think that I want to get hooks, rather than hands." She replied. "There was a girl in college that didn't have any hands and she wore them. I've always thought that they looked cool.

"What about social functions?" I asked.

"I'd probably wear the hooks, unless it was really fancy then I would wear prosthetic hands." She said.

"Well you have all winter to decide." I said.
One afternoon I was fooling around in the concentrator shed. I thought that Kelly was in the cabin. Suddenly I heard her scream. I rushed from the shed to see her on the ladder to the cash. Somewhere she had never been before. I raced over to her.

"What's the matter." I yelled.
She started to climb down the ladder. She turned to me and an her eyes were filled with tears. She was sobbing uncontrollably.

"What's wrong?" I asked softly.

"I wanted to surprise you and get down a venison roast." She sobbed. "I forgot that my arms were up there. I moved a tarp and saw my arms laying there. It was just awful. I'm sorry."

"I knew they were there and I've always kept them covered, just like Bill's body." I said.

"I knew it too." She sniffed, "I just wasn't ready for it. I'm sorry I went to pieces."

We went back in the house. I had her sit down by the fire in the big chair for a chat while I sat on the bed.

"It was just a shock. I wasn't expecting to see them. I knew they were there."

"We've never really talked that much about how you felt about loosing your arms." I said. "Maybe now would be a good time to get it all out."

"It was kind of strange." She said. "it wasn't until I saw them there and think about it, that I realize that I'm happier now than I was with arms."

"Could you elaborate?"
"Since I was a little girl I've been fascinated by people with missing limbs. I often wondered what it would be like to be an amputee, ether arm or leg. Sometimes I wished that I were one, not that I would do something as drastic as going out to purposely have a limb amputated or anything like that. I just wanted to be one. That's why when I started to show the signs of gangrene, that I didn't have a problem with you needing to amputee my arms. Now I'm the way that I wanted to be. Do you understand?"

"I think I do." I said. "I remember talking about this in a psychology class in college. They said in some people the drive is so great that they actually go out and cause an accident to cause the amputations to be done. In others the drive was not that great, but those people would spend there life wishing."

"I was in the second group, I was spending my life wishing that I was and amputee." She said. "Dave can you forgive me for the way I feel about this."

"Kelly, there's nothing to forgive. You feel the way you do. In your case you got lucky." I said.

"Dave thank you for being so understanding." She said. "I feel much better now that I've told you. It was becoming quite a burden on me. I never want to have any secrets from you."

"Thank you for sharing that with me. I know it was difficult for you." I said. "Kelly, I love you more than anything in this world."

"Oh Dave, I do love you too." She replied with tears of joy in her eyes. "You are so understanding and tender with me."

We embraced and kissed for a long time. I had a little better insight as to what make her tick. We bundled up and went for a walk out on the frozen river and enjoyed the rest of the afternoon together.

About two weeks later the piece and quiet of our valley was broken by the sounds of a helicopter. It was a government helicopter and landed near the plane crash sight. Kelly and I went out to greet them. When the helicopter engine stopped the pilot and a trouper got out. They came over and talked to us. They told us that the supply plane pilot had told them about the crash and that I had everything under control. They said they needed to do an official investigation. We all walked around the crash sight. Kelly told them that they had been out for just a fun flight when they got caught in the fast moving storm and that the compass was not operational. She told them that she had been badly hurt, but didn't tell them the extent of her injuries. I told them about Bill's body and how I had removed it. I invited them into the cabin for some coffee.
We all walked up to the cabin. I helped Kelly off with the long sleeved coat that she was wearing. You should have seen the looks on their faces when they saw Kelly the way she really is.

"Both of my arms were severely cut during the crash." She explained to her now dumbfounded audience. "The both had deep gashes down to the bone. I had no feeling below the gashes. Dave was able to get the bleeding stopped, but I

178

developed circulation problems. Dave amputated my arms just as gangrene was setting in."

"He probably saved your life then." The trouper said.

"I have no doubt in my mind that he did." Kelly replied. "I asked him to do it."

"What did you use to perform the operations?" He asked.

"My hunting knife mostly. I have a bone saw for butchering. She had some manicure scissors and the first aid kit had some dissolving sutures and a needle. It also had two small hemostat clamps and an ample supply of dressings and bandages. Luckily it was a big first aid kit. I used alcohol wipes and whisky for antiseptic."

"That's absolutely amazing." The trouper said. "What did you use for anesthesia?"

"Dave fed me straight whisky until I passed out." Kelly said.

"How did it work?" He asked.

"I didn't feel a thing during the operation." Kelly said. "But I had one hell of a hangover when I woke up. My head hurt worse than my arms."

"Dave, what did you do with the pilots body?" The trouper asked.

"I wrapped him in a blanket and put him up in the cash. I didn't want the animals getting him." I said. "I was planning on burying him in the spring when the ground thawed."

"His family would like to bury him in the family plot." The trouper said. "We can take him back with us. We can take the both of you too."

"I'm going to stay with Dave." Kelly said very emphatically. "My place is with him now."

"I have heavy load to bring out." I said. "I'm sure that we would be beyond your weight limits. Do you know Don Hanson?"

"I do." The pilot said. "I usually have coffee with him every morning."

"Could you send him back out for us with his big helicopter. I'm guessing we have about ten tons to haul out." I said.

"Sure. It'll take him a few days though, he's working a pipeline job." The pilot said. "That's quite a load."

"The mine has been good to us this year." I said.

"It sounds like it." The trouper replied. "If you can show us the body, we can get out of here."

"Kelly why don't you stay in here while we do this." I said.

She looked at me and nodded. The three of us went out to the cash. I helped them take the body down and put him in a body bag. I also asked him to take Kelly's arms and dispose of them properly. They said they would. We packed Bills body to the helicopter and loaded it. They got n and took off. I went back in the cabin.
Kelly was sitting on the bed crying. I sat beside her and put my arm around her.

"Poor Bill, all he wanted to do is to take me for a ride in his airplane." She sniffed.

"He'll be properly taken care of now." I said.

She sat up and looked me straight in the eye and said. "Did you have them take my arms too?"

180

"Yes." I replied sheepishly.

"Good." She said. "They're gone for good and now we won't have to deal with them. I'm the way I wanted to be and I'm with the man I love."

We embraced.

Susan

By Albert Tall

How often had she asked herself this question: "Why did I go to that party, why did I listen to his smooth talk, why didn't I leave when I still had the chance?" But she had gone, she had listened to the nice looking boy who sat next to her and she hadn't left. And because of that terrible things had happened to her, were still happening.....

She had accepted the invitation of her friend Deirdre to come to her graduation party. The party had been quite dull and she had been on the verge of leaving early, when a boy sat down next to her and struck up a conversation. He asked if she knew the hostess, and got her to talk about her friendship with Deirdre.

They had a pleasant time and at the end of the party he offered to bring her home. She had accepted and was awed when she saw his car: it was a brand new Mercedes. He was polite, gave her a peck on the cheek and asked her to go out with him. They dated a few times and soon they fell in love.

Susan was a very friendly, tall girl. She had beautiful blonde hair, a wide mass of curls and a nice body. She was a history teacher and taught in a small school in the West.

She was mesmerised by her new boyfriend. Andrew was a very young man, from East European ancestry. He called himself a businessman, but Susan never saw him do business. His father was very rich and apparently gave his son as much money as he needed.

The young couple led a life of luxury and after a few months Susan gave up her job. She had not really wanted to, but Andrew had insisted and finally she had given in.

Andrew could be very convincing and had the habit of starting to sulk whenever he didn't get what he wanted. This was, according to Susan, his only weak point. Without realising it, she always gave in when Andrew wanted something. But he was very generous and took Susan everywhere, all over the United States, often in his own private jet plane.

She had a wonderful time, and loved Andrew very much. Soon she left her own little flat and went to live with Andrew in his enormous bungalow.

The first sign of things going the wrong way was the tattoo. Whenever Andrew had the chance he brought up the subject of Susan having a tattoo. Susan disliked the idea and had always refused to be tattooed. She thought it was vulgar and didn't like her body to be permanently marked.

But Andrew kept nagging and one evening, when she had drunk a bit too much she had given in. As if he had known that she would relent, within an hour Andrew had a tattoo artist with his equipment come to his house. Susan had fallen asleep and woke up by the sound of the tattoo instrument and the sharp pricks of the needle. She tried to pull back, but Andrew held her firmly and after a while the tattoo artist was finished: Susan had on her shoulder the picture of a colourful butterfly. The ink was indelible, and she would never be able to get rid of it.

Susan had awoken the next morning with a burning pain in her shoulder and had cried. She was very angry with Andrew: she had been drunk and he had forced her to go through with everything.

This had been the moment to run away, she knew now what sort of a person her boyfriend was, what he was capable of

183

and at that moment the damage was minimal. But she had let him soothe her, promising it would never happen again and she had stayed...

He gave her lots of expensive presents and complimented her with her tattoo every time he saw her naked.

When she found magazines with pictures of bigbreasted girls, casually thrown at the back seat of the car, she felt very disappointed. She couldn't believe that her boyfriend enjoyed that kind of thing and asked herself why he had been so careless as to leave the magazines in plain view for her to find.

She soon found out what he was after. When she confronted him with the pornographic material he laughed and made nothing of it. He said that it was normal for a guy to read such magazines. She had asked if he was dissatisfied with her body: her breasts were the average size.

He pretended to think her question over and then told her that she could use "a bit extra in the upper regions" and mentioned a friend who was a plastic surgeon who did fantastic jobs with silicones.

Susan was horrified and had fled the room. Andrew came after her and acted as if he was very surprised. He stroked her hair, said nice words and finally she looked up. She had planned to leave him for good, but he used his smart tongue and against her better judgement, she stayed..

During the next month, their old life resumed and Susan almost forgot about the incident. But she was to be reminded of it in the worst possible way.

One evening after dinner she felt nauseous and told Andrew that she was going to bed early. As soon as her head hit the pillow she fell asleep. When she woke up she had a terrible headache and a very strange sensation in her chest. She opened her eyes and didn't recognise her surroundings. She appeared to be in a hospital, because everything around her was white. She started to panic, because she couldn't remember how she had come here. Had she had an accident? Was she ill? The last thing she remembered was going to bed in their own house. And now this strange pain in her chest, what had they done to her? She must have screamed, because a nurse ran into her room and tried to calm her. Susan lay back and closed her eyes. Everything went black and she slept again.

The second time she woke up she had a clear mind. A nurse was standing next to her, feeling her pulse. When the nurse saw her eyes open, she said that she would call her boyfriend, he was in the room next to hers.

Before Susan could say anything she had left and the next instant Andrew came in, carrying an enormous bunch of roses. He gave them to Susan and asked how she felt. Her mouth was very dry and she found it difficult to speak. She managed to croak: "What happened?"

Andrew shifted in his chair and started to speak: "We're in the family's private clinic. Now don't get angry with me, okay? Remember the plastic surgeon I mentioned the other day, he offered to make your tits a bit larger. I know that you were opposed to it, so I took the liberty of deciding for you. I know that you can't make up your mind, so I decided to go ahead with it. Honey, they will be magnificent! That surgeon is the best!"

Susan could not believe her ears. Was it really true, had Andrew taken her to the hospital, against her will and had they operated on her? She took a deep breath and pulled down the blanket that covered her breast. Where her modest breasts used to be, her night-gown now bulged with twin mountains. She gasped, tore away the gown that was fastened around her neck and looked at her bandaged front. She couldn't see her breasts, they were covered by bandages, but it was clear that they were now at least twice as big as they used to be. With trembling hands, she tried to cover her body again. Silently, she sank back into her pillow, pulled the blankets up and closed her eyes. Tears welled up from under her eyelids.

Andrew stood next to the bed and looked at her, uncertain

what to do. He stretched out his hand to touch hers, but she drew her hand away violently and ignored him. Andrew decided he'd better leave.

In the following days Susan had to learn to face the fact that she now had enormous breasts. Every time she tried to sit up she felt their heavy weight pulling down. All day long she thought of how people would react when she would leave the hospital. She envisaged all the men looking lecherously at her, people turning their head when she walked past, women despising her or making fun of her. She pulled the blankets over her face and cried.

Andrew came by regularly, but every time he showed his face, Susan shouted at the top of her lungs that he had to leave, so he retreated without a word. He had a nurse put enormous bunches of flowers in her room, but she told the staff that she didn't want them, so they were removed.

After two weeks a doctor came to remove the bandages and now Susan was for the first time able to see clearly what had been done to her. She stood up and stepped into the bathroom. In front of the mirror she tore away her night-gown and looked at her body. She saw two enormous breasts, with equally big nipples. Her knees felt weak and she almost fell. The nurse, who stood behind her helped her to keep her balance. Slowly Susan turned to the left and to the right. The mounds of flesh (or should she say: silicones?) danced with every movement. Susan turned around comple-tely and looked over her shoulder. She lifted her arms to gather her hair and saw her new breasts bulge out to the left and right of her slender back.

Slowly she walked back to her bed and sat down, crying. The doctor gathered the used bandages and left the room. He knew perfectly well that the girl he had operated on had not consented, but Andrew had offered so much money that he very conveniently had forgotten his Hippocratic oath. Andrew had assured him that it was her secret wish to have very big breasts. This had soothed his conscience, but now he saw that she was obviously very unhappy with what had

186

been done to her. He decided not to visit her anymore and went away to scrub in for a facelift operation. Soon he was completely engrossed in his work and had completely forgotten about the poor girl whom he had disfigured for life.

Andrew now resorted to notes, which he had a nurse bring to her. In the notes he apologised, told her how much he loved her and how beautiful she now was. He even had the guts to refer to her tattoo: she had accepted that too, hadn't she? He promised her all kinds of things, but she refused to see him. He also made it clear that Susan needn't try to complain to the staff about what had happened to her, the staff was well-paid and completely loyal to the Steltin family. They would also prevent her from leaving the clinic without Andrew's permission.

Susan's wounds had healed, the scars barely visible and she became used to the enormous weight of her new breasts. One of the nurses had bought her a new bra, her old one did not fit anymore. It was huge: when Susan saw her new bra for the first time, she sat with it in her lap and cried. But she needed support for her breasts, because having to carry their weight caused a permanent backache.

She took a deep breath and fastened the bra in front of her, then turned it around so that the giant cups were on the front side. One by one she laid her enormous soft melons in the cups and adjusted the straps. Her breasts seemed even larger now that they were encased in the strong fabric of the bra. She felt the straps on her shoulders biting into her flesh, although they were broad and padded. Susan realised that from now on she would feel this pain every moment of the day. Susan reached for her T-shirt and pulled it over her head. There it became stuck: it was impossible to pull her T-shirt over her gigantic breasts.

Slowly Susan pulled it over her head again and reached for her night-gown. She thought for a long time. She hated it to depend on someone who was affiliated with Andrew, she didn't want any favours. But she could hardly walk around in her night-gown for the rest of her life, so she called for the nurse and asked her to buy some new clothes. She asked for very large t-shirts and wide sweaters in order to mask the size of her new breasts. The nurse went away, but did not come back with the clothes she had asked for.

Later that afternoon, Susan sat near the window reading a book. She had to hold the book at a considerable distance, because her vision was limited by her gigantic melons. There was a knock on the door and an elderly lady stepped into her room. For an instant, Susan wanted to turn around, or hide because she was very ashamed. She didn't want anyone to see her. But it was no use, the lady had already entered. She introduced herself, she was sent by a famous fashion house, to take measurements in order to supply Susan with a completely new wardrobe. She said nothing with regard to Susan's disproportionate measurements. Apparently she had been instructed in advance what to expect.

Susan was puzzled and said that she just wanted some t-shirts and sweaters. She had her jeans (those still fitted) and didn't need anything else.

The lady explained that she had no permission to issue that kind of clothes. She was to take Susan's measurements in order to fit her with a number of tailored dresses, that would show off her figure to the full advantage. Susan was allowed to state her preference with regard to fabric and colour.

Susan sat down and sagged. So this was what Andrew had in mind for her. She was not allowed to hide or mask her enormous breasts. She was to wear tight dresses in which her bosom would seem even bigger. She started to cry.

Mrs Brick appeared not to notice and took out a measuring tape. She pulled Susan to her feet and started to measure her body. Susan had no energy left and allowed the lady to do what she had come for. Mrs Brick hummed and made notes in a small book. When she had finished she urged Susan gently to sit down again and said that she wanted to know a few things more. What colour did Susan prefer?

188

What fabric? And what was the size of her shoes? Susan wanted to shout at her, wanted to kick her, but she felt drained and answered the questions. She thought of telling the lady what had happened to her, to ask her to get the police but she had the feeling that it would be of no use. This lady was not going to help her. Mrs Brick closed her little book and stood up. She promised that Susan's new clothes would be ready in two days. She said goodbye and left the room.

Two days later Susan's clothes arrived.

She opened the large box and put its contents out on the bed. There were three dresses, all made of velvet, silk underwear, two new bras and two pair of high heeled shoes. She was used to Andrew's generousness, and was not in the least impressed. If Andrew thought that he could make it up to her by giving her clothes she didn't want he was mistaken!

What Susan didn't know: there were to hidden cameras in her room. In the adjacent room was a VCR that recorded every movement in her room and in her bathroom. Andrew had spent many hours watching the tapes. He sat hunched in his chair, watching everything Susan did, even the most intimate actions. He watched the swaying of her enormous breasts as Susan moved awkwardly, not used to the impairment of two soft mountains of flesh on her chest. He bit his lip whenever he saw her cry and asked himself again and again how he could win her back.

Now he sat watching Susan while she unpacked her clothes. He hoped, against better judge-ment, that these expensive clothes would soften her heart. But Susan turned away from the clothes on her bed and sat down, dressed in her night-gown, with her book.

Andrew beat with his fist on the television in frustration.

Almost against her will, Susan went back to the bed and picked up one of the dresses. The material it was made of felt wonderful to the touch and the colour was beautiful: a rich gold, which would match her hair beautifully.

Susan hesitated and then dropped her night-gown on the floor: she had walked around in it for weeks now and she wanted desperately to wear something beautiful for a change. In the room next-door Andrew drew in his breath. There was Susan in all her glory, naked. He had his nose almost against the television set. Susan stretched her body and picked up a pair of silken panties. She bent forward to put them on and her big heavy breasts almost pulled her down. She had to grip the bed for support. Then she put on the enormous bra and wriggled the soft flesh until it felt reasonably comfortable.

Next came the golden dress. Susan noticed that it was very narrow at the waist and very wide at the top. It must have been quite a challenge to make such a dress. But once she had pulled up the zipper at the back, she found out that the new dress fitted perfectly. She whirled around in front of the mirror and was astonished by the sight. People who would look at her would not see her beautiful dress, nor her golden hair or nice face. All attention would be drawn to her enormous tits, even more pronounced by her tightfitting dress. Susan was desperate. How could a man find such monstrous proportions attractive? These colossal swaying mountains of flesh did not belong to *her*, she found them vulgar and repulsive. No one would ever see her or approach her as a woman, as a person. People would only see those massive tits, which she ostensibly was very proud of, judged by the way she dressed.

Susan cried and walked slowly back to her chair. She didn't know what to do and thought of the moment that she would have to face other people. She imagined the way they would look at her, their scorn, their lewd jokes and their disapproval.

In the room next to hers, Andrew sat watching the monitor, moaning softly, while his swift moving hand pumped his erection.

The next day Andrew tried a different approach. Hiding

190

behind a bunch of pink roses he came into the room, on his knees. He thought that the sight of this would soften Susan's heart, but this was not the case. Susan threw everything she could lay her hands on at him. A heavy glass, filled with water struck his forehead. It started to bleed profusely and Andrew retreated yelping. One of the nurses put four stitches in.

What does a spoiled little boy do when he doesn't get what he wants? He goes to his daddy. This was exactly what Andrew did. He got into his fast car and drove to his father's house.

He was greeted by his father's two Dobermans. He followed them into the sittingroom, where his father sat watching television. After having used the remote control to switch off the television he approached his son and embraced him.

The old S. was a self-made millionaire who had worked himself up from the gutters of Moscow. He had got rich through ruthless dealings in the Mafia. He had moved to America and had been trying to gain American citizenship ever since, but not succeeding although he had enormous influence and was backed by the best lawyers of the country.

"What happened to your head?" he asked when he saw his son's bandaged head. His son started to cry and was led to the couch by his father. "Come on, tell me what is wrong, I'll help you, as I've always done" said his father. Andrew told the whole story and his father shook his head angrily. "How dares she! After all the things you did for her! Just leave it to me, son, I'll take care of it" he said angrily. Andrew looked at him and said: "But I don't want you to kill her! Please, promise me you will not do that! I still love her!"

The father tried to persuade the son to let him handle things, which meant: kill the girl, but Andrew made his father swear not to kill her. "But she has to be punished," said S. "Look what she did to you, a member of the S. family. We cannot let this happen without severe punishment!"

Andrew agreed, but repeated that he was still in love with her.

S. consoled his son and told him not to worry. He would think of something and he promised his son not to kill the girl.

In good spirits Andrew left his father's house, confident that he would find a solution.

That evening Susan was visited by one of S's lawyers who offered her a lot of money if she was to stay with Andrew. She spit in his face and told him that she would rather die than have anything more to do with Andrew.

The lawyer reported to S. and they made another plan. Naturally, S. wanted foremost to kill the girl, and have her body disappear. But he had sworn to his son that he wouldn't do that.

That same night two male nurses entered Susan's room. While one held her tight, the other injected a heavy sedative into her arm. She cried once, and then went limp. She was vaguely aware of the men stripping her down and fondling one by one her enormous breasts. They put her on a trolley and made rude jokes about her while they moved her away to the operating theatre. It was three o'clock in the morning and it was very quiet. There was only one nurse attending, and the two only other patients were fast asleep.

In the operation theatre everything was ready for a major operation. The anaesthetist was ready, the surgeon had on his gloves and the assistant hovered over the tray with shining, sterilised instruments.

Susan was put on the operating table and the anaesthetist put a rubber cap on her nose. For a little while Susan tried to fight the effect of the gas, but to no avail.

The surgeon adjusted the light over the poor naked girl, lying helpless on the operating table and asked for the knife....

After the operation Susan was wheeled back to her room.

There she was put on a monitor and a nurse sat next to her to wait for the moment that she would recover from the anaesthetic.

For Susan, waking up was a far bigger nightmare than the last time: then she had not known what had happened to her. Now she immediately knew that something terrible had happened. She felt her heart beating very fast and bit on her lip to stifle a scream. What had they done to her? Obviously she had had another operation, but her body felt numb, she had no sensation at all. She had a terrible headache from the drugs that had been used to sedate her, and she was relieved to feel sleep washing over her again.

The next time she woke up was in the middle of the night, the nurse at her bedside was sleeping, with her chin on her chest. Susan was very thirsty and tried to wake her up. She was unable to produce a sound and tried to clear her dry throat. She was too weak to move and tried again. A faint croaking sound was enough to wake the nurse. Susan was given a bit of water, but the nurse refused to talk to her.

Exhausted, Susan fell asleep again.

The periods that she was able to remain awake got longer and she started to get back the sensation in her body. Her left leg seemed to be on fire. She tried feebly to shift her leg in order to alleviate the pain, but her leg didn't respond to her commands. Suddenly she had a terrible premonition. With all her strength she removed the sheet from her legs. She saw that her left leg ended in a bandaged stump, twenty centimetres from her hip. Susan fell back into her pillows and lost consciousness.

In the next five days she regained her strength. She ate her meals without thinking and sat in her bed, staring out of the window. She refused to talk to anyone and they left her alone.

On the sixth day, the same lawyer who had spoken to her a few days ago, sat by her bed when she awoke. Susan was still very weak, but was able to listen to the terrible things the man

had to say.

" First of all, don't get angry with me, alright? I'm just the messenger. I had nothing to do with what's been done to you. I'm very sorry, but I think you will get over it. The surgeon says that you are very strong."

Susan looked at the man with such contempt that it made him shift uneasily in his chair. The man averted his eyes and looked at the papers in his lap. He continued: "The S. family decided that you had to be punished. They feel terribly insulted and first wanted to have you killed. But you owe your life to young Andrew: he absolutely forbade that you be killed. So they decided that you couldn't get away unpunished. They had surgery performed on you to teach you a lesson. With every step you make during the rest of your life you will be reminded of the things you did. Do you understand me so far?" Susan had sneered when she heard about Andrew's noble stand, but had remained silent since.

"We will bring you to a small town in the West of the country and there you will stay. We will pay the rent and we will give you a small allowance. You will have to find a job to earn a living. Andrew will not know where you are and the two of you are never to see each other. We will keep an eye on you, you know that we can do that, don't you?" Susan nodded. She knew that Andrew's father employed a number of private investigators who were able to lay hands on whatever information they needed. They had "checked her out" when she first met Andrew. The family had wanted to know everything about her, especially that she was no police spy. They had dug up the most obscure information about her.

"I don't need to warn you that you should never, never tell anyone what happened. Nobody will believe you and even if so, there is no proof. And you know the family owns the best lawyers in the country. We can win any lawsuit easily. And after that, there will be revenge, you know that! The family hurt you once and can easily hurt you twice."

194

The lawyer looked smug. He knew that Susan was terrified and believed every word he said. He went on. "I'm almost finished. In a week or so, when you are strong enough, you will be given a pair of crutches. You can use them to walk around. Then they will measure the size of your stump and they will fit you with a pegleg. Now listen carefully: you are not allowed to use any other aid than those crutches or the pegleg. You will be watched and you are not allowed to use a wheel-chair, elbow crutches or a prosthetic leg. You wear the peg or nothing. People will try to convince you to wear a cosmetic leg but you will refuse. Is that clear?"

Susan was frozen. During the last few days she had looked at what remained of her leg and had had visions of a beautiful, modern prosthesis. She had fantasised that as soon as she got away, she would get a leg like that and continue with her life. But now her hopes were shattered. They wanted to punish her and they knew exactly how to do that. But she also knew that she would obey...

"We're almost there," said the lawyer. "One more thing: your clothes. You are forbidden to wear anything but a skirt or a dress. No jeans or trousers, never. Not even in the house. If they ever spot you wearing those you will be punished." The lawyer put away the papers in his bag and stood up. "Young lady, you have been very lucky! You have insulted some very powerful people and you might easily have been crushed. If only you had shown a little bit more consideration with young Andrew, nothing would have happened. But you paid the price of your stubbornness. I hope that you have learnt your lesson and advise you to stay low. Get on with the rest of your life and stick to the rules." Susan was unable to react. When he was almost at the door he turned round and said: "I almost forgot. I hope it is clear that you should not try to reverse the operation of your bosom. It was Andrew's gift to you, and we would very much object against it if you were to try to have it removed. Farewell." He closed the door softly and left Susan sitting in her bed. She looked down at the covers. There was only one foot that pushed them up at the foot-end. Her tears fell down and made two large spots on her night-gown where her enormous breasts jutted out.

The next two weeks Susan learnt to walk with the aid of two wooden crutches which she had to put under her armpits. She put the ends of the crutches down in front of her and then swung her leg forward and put it down. With every step she felt the stump of her left leg swing gently under her night-gown. She even put on one of her new dresses and stood a long time in front of the mirror. She saw a pale girl with lots of blonde curls on crutches. The padded supports under her armpits pushed her enormous boobs even more in view. Between the two crutches only one leg was visible. There was no leg coming from under the left side of her dress. She turned around slowly and crutched to the chair. She longed to get away from this hospital, but every time she thought of going out she visualised the people who would stare at her. She would die of shame!

Her stump had healed well, and after two weeks the swelling had gone. An old man had measured its size and when she had been in the clinic for 18 days he came back with a cardboard box. In the box was her pegleg, the leg that she would have to wear for the rest of her life.

Some people might have lost all their hopes, all their energy when something as terrible as the things that happened to Susan happened to them. They might escape in a dark depression, from which they never would surface or they might consider committing suicide.

Susan had thought of suicide, many times. What kind of future lay in store for her? A girl with ridiculously big breasts, with only one leg? People would stare at her, at her slow, ponderous way of walking in her tight dress with her large breasts swinging wildly from left to right. She would be so ashamed and of course no man would ever feel attracted to her. She would die a crippled, maimed spinster.

It had probably been the smug, righteous approach of the lawyer that had made her clench her teeth and had caused her to get angry and resolved to get revenge. She decided not to take her own life, to survive and to show that they could not break her.

It was in this spirit that Susan confronted the man with her new leg. She wanted to get used to it as soon as possible and then she wanted out, she wanted to get away from this terrible place, these terrible people.

But her spirits were put to a severe test when she saw the object that the old man presented her with.

It was a shining black wooden peg, about a meter in length. On one end there was a rubber tip, the other end was attached to a black leather bucket. The bucket had eyelets through which a shoestring was laced. The back end had a stiff lip, which protruded for about 5 centimetres. Its purpose was probably to limit the stride of the wearer: her buttock would arrest the movement, so that the wooden stick would not disappear behind the wearer. She had to put her stump into the bucket. The front had to be laced in, in order to fit.

Susan swallowed. It was so ugly, and so big! How could she possibly walk with such a thing attached to her?

The old man gave her a couple of white stockings, and told her always to wear one because her stump would be tender for a long time and would hurt if a blister or a wound would occur.

Susan hesitated. Should she try it on in front of this man? The old man stood waiting patiently, so Susan decided to go ahead. She pulled up the hem of her night-gown, revealing her stump and pulled the white stocking over it. It fitted perfectly. The old man handed her the peg and she almost dropped it, it was so heavy.

With awkward movements, hampered by her enormous breasts whose size restricted her sight, she pulled the leather shaft of the pegleg over her stump. When it wouldn't go any further she started to lace it tight. The wooden shaft of her pegleg stood out horizontally.

At last she was finished and she was helped to stand up.

Very carefully she put some weight on her wooden leg. Her stump hurt, but not as much as she had thought it would. Her weight was not put on the bottom part of her stump, but rather on the whole surface. She gathered her courage and tried a little step. She had to lift up the left part of her body in order to swing the pegleg around in an arc. She put the peg down and tried to take a step with her remaining leg. It was very difficult: she had to throw her weight forward and take care at the same time that she didn't stray to the right while all her weight rested on the rubber tip of the peg. She kept trying, watched by the old man and soon she got the hang of it. The wooden peg and her foot made alternating sounds: tack, thud, tack thud. During this first hour she developed the typical swaying walking gate of a pegleguser. It would always remain like that.

The act of walking with a pegleg involved so many body movements, that her enormous breasts were shifting position constantly. She was aware of the effect this was going to have on everyone that watched. She realised that this was part of the punishment.

When, finally, she sat down on the bed again, her peg sticking out in full view, the old man announced his departure. "One more thing," he said. "Ordinarily a peg like yours would have a knee joint. You can secure it in place when you are walking, you can unlock it when you sit down. That way it doesn't stick out the way it does now. But I was ordered not to make a knee joint. Instead I made a click-and-turn mechanism at the top of your peg." He reached under Susan's dress, she heard a clicking sound and the man emerged with the wooden shaft of her pegleg in his hand. The leather bucket was still attached to her. "You can put this part under your chair", said the old man. Then people will not trip over your leg." Susan looked at the sudden flatness of her dress and was amazed of the cruel refinement of this punishment. Either her ugly artificial leg would be in full view or it would be clearly visible that she had no left leg. The old man handed her back the wooden

198

shaft, but now Susan was presented with a real problem: she was not able to see the socket in which the wooden shaft had to be put. Her gigantic breasts made it impossible to see what she was doing. Feeling for the metal socket on the leather of the bucket, she was able to put the end of the peg in. She would need the help of a mirror to see how the thing worked.

In the next few days, Susan learned to walk with and without the aid of the crutches. She got accustomed to the fact that she needed her whole body and a lot of energy to perform the simple act of walking. She pulled the straps of her enormous bra as tight as possible in order to minimise the swaying, but it didn't help much. She would have to get used to the fact that her breasts were living a life of their own while she moved her body ponderously from one place to another.

She forced herself to practice as long as possible, because there was only one glimmer of hope in her desperate situation: they had promised not to kill her and to set her free. She was not going to give them a reason to keep her longer than necessary.

She learned the difficulties of walking with a pegleg: because she had no feeling, she had to watch out for possible snags all the time. The rubber tip could get caught in the carpet, it could slip on a wet floor, if she took too large a step the stiff leather lip at the back of her pegleg bit into her buttock. Many times she fell, often because she lost her balance. And, of course, she was not helped at all by the heavy weight of her enormous tits. Her body ached, her stump was sore, but she learned.

They kept their promise. After 82 days of imprisonment and two major operations they told her to pack her bags. Two burly men came into Susan's room and told her to come with them.

Susan didn't have much to pack: she could leave her old clothes behind, because they didn't fit her anymore. So she put her two dresses (she wore one), some underwear and stumpsocks in a linen bag, took her crutches and put them under her armpits.

There were no goodbyes. The staff were invisible as Susan crutched in the direction of the door that had been kept closed for her so long. One of the men held open the door for her while the other went to fetch the car.

Passers-by saw a tall girl with a large bosom in a tight dress walking towards a car, one of her feet shod in a brown shoe, the other foot missing, a wooden shaft ending in a rubber tip in its place.

They could hear the "thud" sound every time the wooden pegleg hit the street and saw her enormous breasts swaying in time with her effort to walk properly. They saw one of her compani-ons put her crutches in the trunk and, maybe, if they were bold enough to slow down, they saw the girl sitting down in the front seat of the car, her wooden peg sticking out sideways. She fumbled under her dress, unable to see what she was doing and retrieved the wooden peg from under her dress. She swung her remaining leg into the car, put the wooden peg in the back and closed the door.

They brought her to an airfield and accompanied her in the plane. They flew for a number of hours and when their plane had landed, the took her by rented car to a small town in the middle of the country.

There they showed her her new house, a small, old house. They gave her the keys, told her that from now on she had a different name and that her boyfriend did not know where she lived. She shivered at the mentioning of that word. They repeated the rules one more time and indicated that they would return from time to time to check up on her. Then they left.

The next couple of days Susan spent exploring her little house. It was furnished, but everything was old or cheap. There were some supplies in the refrigerator, but she would have to leave the house soon to do some shopping. She dreaded that day, when she would have to expose herself to the neighbours. They would gape at her wooden leg, her swaying gait and her enormous breasts.

She postponed leaving the house, until she was almost starving. When she had been in her new house for seven days she knew that she had to go outside, otherwise she would become too weak. So, on a sunny afternoon, she gathered all her courage and went out.

Susan managed to settle in the small community. At first she kept her head down whenever someone spoke to her, terribly ashamed about her appearance. But the people were kind and she soon dared to look at them.

She found a job in the town library. She enjoyed working there, but hated the fact that in order to gain entrance to the library, one had to climb high marble stairs. Susan knew only one way to climb stairs: she had her hand on the banister and hopped one tread at the time with her sound leg. She had to trail her pegleg behind, the leather lip at the back biting in her buttock.

She loved it when she had reached her workplace, that she could remove the wooden part of the peg and hide it behind her chair. People who came in would just see an ordinary girl in a dress, not a cripple. They would of course see her gigantic breasts, and boys in particular would snigger, but they wouldn't know that she had only one leg.

How does a human being recuperate after having been treated so brutally? We never really know.

In Susan's case she watched television a lot, tried to make a real home of her little house by adding small things like a pretty vase with flowers. She had very little money and had to economise even on food. She seldomly ventured out of the house. After her work she quickly went home and locked the door. Every once in a while she saw a familiar face: someone sent by Andrew's father to keep an eye on her.

In the first week she had found an envelope on her doormat. In it was an anonymous note. It reminded her of her obligations. She was not allowed to wear bulky clothes, her ample forms must be visible at all times, or jeans. She was to speak to no one about what happened to her. They would watch her and punish her immediately if she were to disobey.

Susan was terrified of Andrew's father and was resolved to do exactly as she was told.

Summer came and Susan decided to buy a bicycle. The trips to the library were very tiresome for her, and she would travel much faster if she had a bike. She had come upon the idea when she saw an elderly man rolling a bicycle out of a shed. Susan immediately noticed the fact that his right leg was missing and that he wore a pegleg just like hers. She stopped and stared. She was surprised to see someone else wearing an old fashioned pegleg. To her surprise she saw the man climbing on the bicycle and the ride away. She was stunned: how could a one-legged person ride a bicycle? Would she be able to do it? It would give her much more freedom of movement and she knew that she could afford a bike, if it was not too expensive a model.

She was excited and thought about what to do next.

When she got home from work she sat down to think. Soon she had a plan. The little town she now lived in had only one bicycle repairshop. She passed it every day on her way to the library. The owner was a friendly young man her age, who often greeted her cordially while standing in the doorway of his shop. He never stared at her swaying breasts as she passed or at her leg. She was almost sure that the old man she had seen must have had his bike altered at this shop to enable him to ride it. She would go to the shop and ask the young man to make her a special bike as well.

It took a lot of nerves for her to enter the shop that Saturday. She had made sure that she was the only customer and she proceeded to the back of the shop, where the owner was mending a child's bicycle. He stood up and faced his new customer. He had heard the "thud - tack" sound of her foot and peg on the floor.

Susan blushed, looked at the floor and started to speak in a rush. The shopowner tried to hear what she said, but couldn't. So he interrupted her and asked if she wanted to sit down. Susan shot a quick glance at his friendly face, saw that he was looking at her in a neutral, natural way and lost some of her apprehension. "I came here to ask if you can make me a special bicycle, like you did for an old man I saw the other day. Can You?" She looked up anxiously and waited for his reply. The shopowner looked puzzled, but then his face brightened. "Oh, you mean mister Pendergast, the guy with the wooden leg, yes I remember! Is he still at it?" Susan nodded. "I saw him on his bike and I wondered if you could make one for me as well, because I have a ..." at this point she faltered. She had never spoken out loud about her handicap. But she continued: "I have a wooden leg also, as you can see."

The owner was very kind and understanding. He customised a second hand bicycle for Susan. The left footpedal was fixed in the lowest position. He welded a round metal cup on it to receive the rubber tip of Susan's peg. A craftily designed system of clogs enabled her to use only her right leg to propel herself forwards.

Susan was delighted and was soon able to get up and off the bicycle by herself. Bicycling remained a tricky thing to do, because her left side was immobile. People stared at this blonde haired girl on the bicycle, her right leg pumping like mad. The wind would blow up her dress every once in a while and people would see one hard working leg and one immobile leather-covered stump.

Susan enjoyed her new freedom and her trips became longer and longer. Fortunately the accident happened in town, not somewhere else in a remote place. Susan didn't pay attention to an iron post and crashed into it with the fixed left pedal of her bike. The pedal broke, her pegleg snapped off at the joint and Susan fell hard.

Susan had been out for a few seconds. When she was conscious again, she felt terribly ashamed. She was lying in the street, her bicycle behind her, heavily damaged and a few feet away lay the black wooden part of her peg leg. She knew that the click-on snap off mechanis-m must have given way.

People were watching her and there was only one thing she wanted to do: get away, become invisible! She knew that she wasn't hurt badly, maybe her skin had some bruises, but definitely nothing broken. With the help of a bystander she stood up. Awkwardly she stood standing on her one remaining leg. She had never felt so ashamed. She remembered another time she had fallen with her bicycle, but at that time she had not been an invalid and had been able to jump quickly on her bike, make herself scarce. She had driven a few blocks before she took the time to examine the damage. She hurt all over but at least no one was watching her.

She knew it was impossible to jump on her bike now, and she saw a rising number of specta-tors, watching her standing there on her one leg, hopping a little bit to maintain her balance. The man who had helped her stand up obviously didn't know what to do. At that moment the crowd parted and she recognised Peter, the owner of the bicycle shop. Peter quickly put her bicycle against a lamppost, picked up her peg and offered her his arm. That way, hopping while she leaned on Peter's arm she left the scene. It cost her a lot of energy to move in this fashion, and she cursed her large breasts because they jumped up and down like crazy while she hopped, but she felt relieved that she could escape the stares of the bystanders. Soon the crowd disappeared.

Peter's shop was not far away and soon she was able to sit down at the back of his shop. She was exhausted and her body hurt all over. Peter turned the sign on the door, which indicated that the shop was closed and joined her. "I'm so glad you came to help me" Susan said. "How did you know I needed help?" "I saw it happen" answered Peter. "I saw you swaying and then you hit the post. It happens all the time you know. They should remove the thing. Are you hurt?"

Susan told him that at the moment she hurt all over, but that she was sure that it was not serious. "I'm more concerned about...". She didn't know what word to use for her pegleg. She had never talked to anyone about it. She indicated it with a movement of her head. Peter was still holding her broken pegleg in his hand. Apparently Peter had forgotten all about it, because he seemed not to understand what she meant. Then suddenly he said: "Oh you mean this?" and he lifted her pegleg into the air. Susan blushed and nodded.

Peter examined the top part and said that he would probably be able to fix it. "Can I see the other part where it's supposed to fit in?" he asked. Susan blushed even more and didn't know what to do. She felt terribly ashamed, and thought frenetically what to do: lift her dress and show him the leather part that was fixed to her stump? He would be able to see her panties as well. Or should she quickly untie the laces and remove the leather bucket? But then he would be able to see her panties *and* her stump! Peter smiled at her and made the decision easy for her by offering to leave her alone for awhile. He walked away to the front and Susan quickly unlaced the leather shaft and pulled it from her stump. She had it in her hands when Peter returned and she handed it to him without looking. She was sure that this intimate leather object, that was not to be seen by any other person, still felt warm to the touch. "It may even smell of me," she thought miserably. She looked down and hid her face between the curtains of her hair. Warm tears stained the golden velvet that covered her enormous breasts. She now felt acutely how refined the punishment was that Andrew's father had devised for her. Here she was, in one room with an attractive young man, whom she liked very much and now she felt terribly humiliated. She couldn't exchange little jokes, she couldn't flirt. All she could do was sit there, feeling terribly embarrassed while the young man was studying the old-fashioned object that she had been forced to wear but needed so badly.

Peter saw that she was crying and sat beside her. He

stroked her hair and said soothing words, reassuring her that everything would be alright. Susan didn't hear a word of what he was saying. All she could think of was the small distance between his healthy, strong and hairy right leg and the stump of her left leg.

One thing led to the other. Peter was a real gentleman. He fixed her leg in the repairshop and left her alone to attach everything to her body again. She tried the click-on system and it worked perfectly. She felt a bit more relaxed now that she had regained her mobility and even said yes to his invitation to join him eating a pizza. It was delivered to them and they ate it in the backroom of the shop. Peter seemed completely relaxed and told all kinds of funny stories. Not once did he mention her handicap or the size of her breasts and Susan felt very grateful.

He picked up her bicycle and brought her home with his old car, because her bicycle had to be repaired. When she was alone her mood constantly changed: now she had the familiar feeling of butterflies in her stomach then she told herself not to be a fool. How could a handsome boy like Peter ever feel attracted to a one-legged girl with preposterous big breasts? And even if he liked her: how could she enter into a relationship with Andrew's guards around? They would certainly report to Andrew's father and he was certain to punish her. She was not to have a relation with anybody else but Andrew! She had blown her chances and was to remain single for the rest of her life. Susan didn't sleep that night.

Matters were taken out of her hands. Peter stopped by the next day, with her bicycle that he had fixed and asked her to join him for a little ride. He had been so generous that she couldn't refuse. She hoped that no one was watching her, climbed awkwardly on her bike and together they drove off.

It felt very good to be able to move in such an easy way. Her single leg turned the pedal round and she had no problem keeping up with Peter. Peter had a nice tenspeed racing bike, but he adjusted his speed to his companion.

They talked about a lot of things and on several occasions Susan caught herself feeling elated.

But she knew it couldn't last.

Peter had the patience of a lion. He felt very much attracted to this strange handicapped girl. He knew that she had come to live in his town only recently and wondered about her history. Every time the conversation tended to go in that direction she clamped shut. Obviously she was terrified to talk about her past. Peter loved this strange girl with the enormous breasts and the strange old-fashioned artificial limb. Had she always had such big breasts? It was almost impossible, because she was very slim in other regions. How had she lost her leg? And why didn't she wear a modern cosmetic prosthesis? Peter knew that nowadays people could be fitted with very realistic looking limbs, with which they were able to walk a lot better than with a pegleg such as Susan's. Every time he saw her lumbering on her stiff pegleg he wanted to hug her and help her find a better prosthesis. But he knew that she didn't want to talk about it. He had once brought up the subject and she had put a finger on his lips, and begged him not to ask. She had looked so miserably then, that he had agreed. But he was determined to find the truth and decided that patience and kindness were the best way to act.

His love for her became deeper and deeper and he dreamed of kissing her enormous breasts, and of burying his head between them. He also dreamed of holding the stump of her leg in his hand, caressing it and imagined how it would feel if she pushed it hard against his prick...

Maybe, if Susan had told everything, the terrible things that were about to happen wouldn't have occurred. But she hadn't. She had hoped that they would leave her alone and that she would be allowed to lead her own life.

Her relationship with Peter was reported to Andrew's father, who decided that it was time to put an end to this story. He was afraid that Susan might tell her lover everything about his family. This might lead to an investigation by the police and he didn't fancy that. He ordered one of his hitmen to kill Susan....

The bell rang in Susan's little house and she made her way to the door. A deliveryvan stood in front of her house and a large box sat on her porch. From the corner of her eye she saw the van speeding away, which surprised her mildly. Most delivery services waited for the recipients to sign for a package. She bent over and picked up the parcel. It was quite heavy and she carried it to the table. She wondered whom it was from and looked for an address. She only found her own and started to unwrap the parcel. When she had removed the paper she tried to open the cardboard lid when suddenly she heard a loud ticking noise. Suddenly she realised what was in the box. There was only one thing that she could do. She lifted the box and carried it to the window. The tall windows reached from the ceiling till about 50 centimetres from the ground. Fortunately they were open to the fresh spring air. Maybe Susan would have made it in time, but the rubber tip of her pegleg snagged in the carpet and she started to fall when she was still two meters from the window. In a last effort she stretched her arms in the hope that the bomb would fall outside.

The bomb exploded at the moment her body hit the floor, her outstretched arms over the windowsill. Her head and body were protected from the impact by the low wall under the window, but her hands and arms were ripped to shreds by the force of the explosion.

There was glass everywhere and a big smoking crater just outside the window.

Inside lay the still body of Susan, blood oozing from the remnants of her arms.

Susan would have bled to death if Peter hadn't saved her. He was just about to ring the bell when the door was forced open by the shock wave. He ran inside and saw his love lying motionless on the floor. His ears still ringing, he did what was best under the circumstances: he used pieces of electric cord as a tourniquet to stop the flow of blood and dialled the emergency number. The ambulance and fire department were already on their way and Susan was brought to the local hospital.

Against all odds, Susan survived the explosion. She had saved her own life by putting the box outside, the low wall had protected her head and body. In any other case she would have been blown to pieces. The bomb had been very strong.

She lived, but her arms could not be saved. There was nothing for the surgeon to salvage. He had to remove the last shreds of dead flesh, and constructed two round stumps, ten centimetres below Susan's shoulders. The stumps were exactly the same in size. Susan was now a triple amputee.

It took a very long time for Susan to recover, but Peter visited her every day. The police had found it appropriate to declare her dead. This way, she would be protected against another attack and they could continue their investigation.

It was Peter's love that pulled her through. He helped her with everything, didn't make a fuss about anything and promised her that he would always love her, whatever her handicap.

So Susan's wounds healed, she was able to sit up in bed but she needed help for everything. It made her crazy to have to ask help for even the simplest things. If she wanted a bit of water: she needed someone to put the glass to her lips. Even if she had an itch, someone had to scratch. She lost track of the number of times she had stretched out one of her pathetic short stumps to perform a minor task, discovering that she was helpless. One of the things she found most humiliating was that she had to be helped on the toilet. She felt terribly embarrassed when strange hands cleaned her body.

The ritual of getting her clothed was another moment she hated. She closed her eyes while strange hands put her enormous breasts into her bra. She felt ashamed that people could see her maimed body and that she had to endure all this. Sometimes those insensitive hands did not fit her heavy breasts comfortably into the cups of her bra. She couldn't get herself to ask them to make her more comfortable. Instead she tried to shift the position of her big mammaries using the short stumps of her arms, but most of the time she didn't succeed.

There was one person with whom she didn't feel so utterly ashamed: Peter. Peter had endless patience and knew exactly what she wanted. He offered to help her even with the intimate things and finally she consented. The first time she was in pain because the nurse had neglected her and she hadn't peed for five hours. She needed to go so badly that she accepted Peter's offer to help her, although this meant that he would be able to see her private parts. But she almost burst and could only think of one thing: relieving her full bladder.

Peter pulled back the covers, gently pulled her panties down, put a urinal under her and finally she could let go. She averted her face while he kept her in balance. The stump of her left leg was in full view and she felt his hand around her shoulder touching her armstump.

She cried while the golden stream of urine clattered into the urinal.

She thought of how it could have been: Peter and her getting to know each other in normal circumstances, she with a whole body, able to flirt with him , able to make love to him and give him satisfaction.

But here she was, maimed, a cripple for the rest of her life, not even capable of performing the basics.

When she was finished Peter removed the urinal, used some tissue to gently clean her genitalia, pulled up her panties and made her comfortable again. She still averted his eyes and he had to call her twice before she looked up.

"Don't be ashamed", he said. "I don't mind helping you, I love it. I love you." He pulled her face around until she was able to look into her eyes and gently kissed her.

Susan began to cry harder.

Peter can convince Susan that he loves her but she can't believe it is really true. When she is being washed by a nurse she looks down at her maimed body and wonders how anyone could fall in love with an invalid like her.

But Peter really is and he proves it every day.

Finally Susan gives in and tells him the whole story. She knew of course who had been responsible for the bomb that almost killed her. Her only hope now was, that they would forget about her because they thought that she was dead.

Peter was astonished and trembled with anger. He knew that he wouldn't stand a chance against the family, so he made no promises, but in his heart he resolved to make that miserable creature Andrew pay. Sooner or later he would pay for what he had done to his love.

In the meantime the only sensible thing for him to do was to comfort Susan, to be there when she needed him, which was quite often: she was completely helpless.

His bicycle shop was failing because he was seldom there.

There was another problem: Susan did not dare to claim money from her old insurance company, because that might alert Andrew's family. If they knew that she was still alive they would certainly come after her to finish the job. There was no insurance in her new name.

This meant that Peter had to pay Susan's hospital bills. He had been able to pay quite a sum, but he didn't have nearly enough to pay the all the expensive bills. Without telling Susan he sold his shop and used the proceeds to pay most of her bills.

Three weeks after Susan had been admitted she was visited by a representative of a firm specialised in prosthetics. He showed her the newest fashion in myoelectric artificial arms and went as far as to measure the size of Susan's armstumps.

Peter heard about this and rang the number of the salesman. When he heard the prize of the artificial limbs he went pale. They were every expensive and he had no money left. He had barely enough to pay for Susan's last days in the hospital. When the salesman heard that there was no money he backed off immediately: they were no charitable organisation and he could do nothing without pay.

Peter racked his brain and tossed all night, but he couldn't find a solution. So Susan's last day in hospital he told her about the money. "I'm terribly sorry, but I can't afford the money involved with the artificial arms you saw." he said.

Susan leaned back and closed her eyes. Would it never end? The long and slow process of accepting her severe handicaps had only just started, she had spent hours of thinking how she would try to cope with her sophisticated artificial hands, and now this.

She assured Peter that she didn't blame him and that she was grateful that he had paid the rest of her bills but she was on the verge of panic. "I can't live like this", she said and lifted her pathetic short armstumps. "I cannot even put on my pegleg! I can't walk, I can't do anything if I don't get artificial arms. I will be completely helpless all day, I can't bare it!". Susan started to cry and Peter could only hug her and wipe the tears off her face.

The hospital staff learned about the financial problems and decided to collect money amongst the nurses and doctors to help Susan. They were able to raise quite a lot of money, but it was not nearly enough to pay for the expensive modern prostheses. One of the older doctors had an idea: "Why don't we ask Jones, the old orthopaedic worker, to make her a pair of old fashioned hooks? I know they are ugly and completely outdated, but at least she will be able to perform a number of simple tasks with them." They all agreed that under the circumstances this was probably best. They talked about their plan with Susan and Peter and they agreed. Jones visited Susan to take her measures and he

212

used his almost forgotten skills to make her a harness of leather straps that fitted around her upper body. Attached to the harness were two artificial arms, that ended in double hooks made of shiny steel. Susan would have to learn to operate the arms and hooks by flexing her shoulders. That way she could extend her arms and open and close the hooks.

It was Susan and Peter's last visit to the orthopaedic worker. Jones had been very kind and had done a very fast job. It had taken him only a day and a half to fix the artificial arms for Susan. She lumbered into his workshop. It was a sad sight to see a pretty young girl with huge breasts, the sleeves of her dress empty, a wooden leg sticking out under the hem.

Jones asked her to undress and Peter helped her to remove the dress. She was sitting on a stool, shivering in her bra and panties, the crude contraption on her left leg clearly visible, the short stumps of her arms still red and tender.

She looked on miserably while Jones affixed the harness to her upper body. He had to make some alterations to the leather straps, because they had to run free from her large bosom. Finally both artificial arms were in place and Jones Asked her to put on her dress again.

Peter did everything for her, her new arms still hung limp along her side.

Jones began instructing her in the use of her new arms and Susan did her best to follow his instructions.

It took Susan months learning to use her new arms. Often things she tried to manipulate with her hooks fell on the ground, sometimes she involuntary crushed them. In the beginning she could only do the simplest of jobs, but she learned quickly.

Peter and Susan moved to another city and got married. The justice of the peace who married them didn't know what to do with the ring. Should he put it on one of the bride's hooks? Peter suggested a string around her neck and this was arranged.

Susan still wears my ring around her neck, on a golden chain.

We have lived in the town of L. now for four years and we believe that there is no more threat of the family. I have a good job now and I've saved enough to pay for proper artificial limbs for Susan, but she refuses. She is accustomed to her old fashioned limbs and doesn't want to learn to use new ones. She accepts the fact that she will always be stared at. Her swaying gait, her enormous breasts and her steel hooks always draw attention. She feels miserable about that and often complains that nobody ever regards her as a *person*, they only see her handicaps.

She is always glad to be home again, in our safe haven.

I sit in my chair and I watch my wife. She sings while she is preparing our evening meal. Now and then she takes a tiny step. I see her hip rise and I see the rubber tip of her pegleg lift and come down with a soft thud. She does it without thinking and she is not aware of the tender feelings this awakens in me. It is astonishing to see how nimble she is with her steel hooks. Only rarely she has to ask for my help. She is able to perform even the most difficult tasks with her double hooks. She wants her sleeves always to be short, so they will not hamper her movements. I watch her preparing the meal and I am very much in love with her.

We have an evening ritual: we go to the bedroom and Susan undresses. She has no difficulty doing this and she walks to the bathroom naked. She feels no shame at all for me and I can't get enough of the sight. Her enormous breasts are free at last and swing wildly from left to right as she makes her way to the bathroom. The top of her left thigh emerges from the black leather bucket in which her stump rests. The wooden pegleg makes a small arch with every step it makes, and Susan lifts her left buttock and hip to get the peg off the ground. The leather lip at the back of the shaft around her stump bites in her soft flesh and has left a red mark. I will massage her later and put a little ointment on the tender

214

spot.

I see her deftly take the toothbrush between the steel hooks and brush her white, even teeth.

She comes back to the bed and I'm ready to help.

She has no problem removing her pegleg, she unfastens the strings in two seconds. She holds her pegleg between her two hooks and puts it on the floor against a chair. She removes the white stumpsock and uses her artificial arms to hold her large breasts while she hops the small distance to our bed on her one leg. I find the sight of the steel hooks on the soft, white flesh very erotic. My groin stirs.

She turns around, sits on the edge of the bed and swings her leg on the bed. She wriggles back until she sits against the headboard. All the time I have watched her, and she knows it. She looks at me and suddenly one of her steel hooks grabs my half erect penis. I gasp as the cold metal touches the tender spot. But of course she doesn't hurt me. She knows exactly what force to apply. My cock grows instantly in its circle of steel. She smiles and releases me.

Then it is time to undo the harness and to remove her arms. I unbuckle the straps and one by one I pull her arms from her stumps. I remove the white stumpsocks and caress her short arm-stumps. I see the red welds left behind by her bra and the straps of her harness and Slowly I kiss and massage everyone of them. Meanwhile her legstump is leading a life of its own and pushes insistently against my erect cock.

But I don't give up. I caress every part of her beautiful, maimed body and need a lot of time for her magnificent breasts. She told me often that she couldn't believe that a man could feel attracted to such grotesque breasts but every time I reassured her that for me they were wonderful. This is one of the reasons she doesn't want to be operated on to reduce the size of her breasts. She says that it is her gift to me. The other reason is, that she already lost so much, she refuses to lose more. And, understandably, she is very afraid of operating theatres.

You may think that Susan is only capable of a minimum of movement, but this is completely untrue. Her short armstumps are almost completely useless, especially because her big breasts are constantly in the way, but she manages to use them in an extraordinary way. She has learnt to make maximum use of her one remaining limb when she is not wearing her hooks.

She is capable of almost every movement. It takes her only a few seconds to sit upright or to get out of bed.

It is amazing to see how well-developed the muscles in her back are. Not only does she lack the use of her arms, she also has the tremendous weight of her breasts to cope with.

It gives me a warm feeling when I realise that she does not want her bosom to be made smaller because I am attracted by them.

If she wants to go to the toilet she needs no help: she wriggles out of bed, stands up in one fluent motion and hops to the bathroom and back. She even flushes the pan afterwards by pulling the handle with her teeth. She quickly returns and is back beside me in no time, pushing her enormous breasts against me. (This is her way of caressing me: her arm-stumps aren't long enough to reach me).

So our lovemaking is *not* a static activity! Susan wriggles and pushes and slides any direction she wants. If she wants to be on top I let her climb upon my outstretched body and when, finally she is sitting astride me, panting, I arrange a pillow under the stump of her leg, so that she is comfortable and then she deftly manoeuvres her body in order to get me inside. If my rigid member slides inside her she sighs and smiles in a heavenly fashion. She starts gyrating her lower body, her breasts swing in unison, and caresses the sides of her breasts with her short stumps. I touch every lovely part of her, trying to prevent coming too soon. I start with her lovely face, remove a few strands of hair that cling to her lips, massage her shoulders, move my hands to her armstumps and caress the perfectly round, smooth surface of the tips. Then my hands try to grasp her tits, but they are far too big to fit into my hands, so I want to bury my face in them and I gently pull her forward. Her eyes open in alarm: she is afraid to fall forward and she knows that she cannot break her fall. I hold her and lower her upper body gently on mine and bury my face in her bosom. Our lower bodies are still connected.

We kiss passionately and I feel Susan writhing harder and harder to gain maximum pleasure. I can't hold it much longer and I lift Susan's head because I want to look into her eyes. I see that she is trying to reach my face and I reach out to her. Her stump now strokes my face and then she gets rigid for a single second, then she thrashes around, her stumps flailing and while she cries out loudly, she comes. With a few strokes I feel my semen rise as well and grunting I push my body hard against Susan's.

We lie together, spent, and soon we fall asleep.

In the morning she nudges me with her nose: time to get up. I yawn, kiss my beautiful wife and

follow her while she hops to the bathroom. In our extra large shower cabin I wash her lovely body and when we are ready towel her off. I fetch a clean pair of stumpsocks from the wardrobe. I put them on her lovely stumps, and put her harness around her upper body followed by her hooks. I see her open and close her hooks a few times and then she grabs her pegleg to put it on.

She stands up and walks to the wardrobe to select a dress. Then my wife is ready to begin a new day.

SURPRISE ENCOUNTER
By Wolff Shmitterz

It was all very friendly and civilized. There was no bickering and no unloading of hostilities when Paula and I were divorced. It was her idea, she wanted to marry Ben Barton of the town's first family. I wasn't poverty-stricken, I had always managed to provide comfortable living for my brood, but I couldn't compete with the Barton money, and one advantage of it all was that I didn't have to mortgage my future for her support. Furthermore, I was on good terms with my kids-in fact the two older boys made no secret of their opinion that I had taken a screwing,. and their little sister was really shook up at the thought that I wasn't going to live with them any more. I was free to see them whenever I wanted to, and in fact Paula and Ben welcomed the weekends when I took the three of them with me and they could go wherever they chose.

Ben was a decent, nice guy, and I had nothing against him. He took a genuine interest in my kids and had sense enough to know that money wasn't going to buy their affection, so I felt quite comfortable about them. Paula was the one that was uptight about the whole business-- she was sort of the uptight kind anyhow, and she felt guilty about the way she had treated me, since I had been pretty good to her and had been a loyal husband. I put a good face on it, but the truth was it had shaken me up pretty badly. My boss, God bless his hard-boiled exterior, is a sensitive and perceptive guy on the inside, as I had reason to learn for the first time when he asked me to have lunch with him about ten months after we were divorced.

"Charlie," he began after we had our coffee. "Why don't you take off a couple of months and get yourself a change of scenery? I don't have any complaints about your work, but you know, you're my long - range thinker and I don't want you to be upset about something if I can help it. I think this divorce has hit you harder than you're letting on."

"Thanks, Max, for bringing it up. I've been thinking about the same thing lately, and I'm not so sure it would be good for me to cut any more mooring lines than have already been cut for me. This old place has been awfully good to me, and it's something I can still cling to. You know what I mean."

"Good, I was hoping you would say something like that, but I wanted to give you the opening. I have an assignment, and you might be interested in it. It would give you a change of scenery, but it would require you to spend enough time back here that you wouldn't feel that the mooring lines were cut. I grinned at him. "Let's hear more."

"You know the mess that Bill Lavery left Research in Newport." I nodded. We had been talking about it just about a week ago, and I had shot off my face about what I thought somebody should do." I want you to go out there and set them straight." I gasped. I was always long on thinking up ideas about how other people should do things, but I never visualized myself doing them. "You think I could do that?" I asked him.

"You're God damn right I do. I've been thinking about what you told me about that last week, and the more I think about it the surer I am that you're right. I don't know why I didn't think to look at it that way myself. I'm sure as hell you've got the answer. I always thought of Parker as just a kid, but you're absolutely right he's the man to put in there, young as he is. All he needs is somebody like you to shore him up for about six months until he gets used to the responsibility."

"But, gosh, Max, how will all those section heads take it if we jump a youngster like Parker up over their heads?"

"Damn it, Charlie, you gave me the answer to that question yourself. They don't any of them want any more responsibility, and if they had, the door has been wide open for six months for any one of them to walk in and take charge."

My first reaction was to be a little scared. Then I thought, my boy, if Max thinks you can do it you can do it. The more I thought about it the better I felt, and suddenly I felt a burst of self confidence.

"Sure, Max. I can do it. I'll get a couple of things lined up here and be ready to move out there on Monday. Maybe I'll have to come back and get another dose of self confidence from you now and then."

"That'll be easy, my boy. Thanks for taking a load off my mind."

"It's just dawning on me that you've taken a load off MY mind. Thanks, friend." We got up from the table and shook hands. Good old Max. He had perceived just what was eating me, better than I had. When Paula had deserted me for another guy she had taken a fair share of my self-confidence along with her. One of the things that shook me up was the fact that I thought rather well of my sexual abilities, and it was a blow to realize that they hadn't been enough to make Paula want to stay with me in spite of our personality conflicts. But, then, Paula was ambitious, if nothing else, and even though I was successful in a very highly-paid job I hadn't made a very conspicuous climb up the ladder of success, and I just wasn't interested in the social rat race.

I had been pretty lonely and sex-hungry. I had bedded down a few eager dames, and at first it had seemed fun to be on the prowl again. But I soon found that just screwing wasn't nourishment for my particular kind of hunger for female companionship. I wanted somebody to be with, to care about, and who would care about me. Somebody to go home to and to love. I hadn't found her yet.

And yet--there was Peggy. She was the cashier at the restaurant where I had taken to going for my meals, and I realized that one of the reasons I went back there so regularly was to see her, and to look at her while I ate my evening meal. By this time the hostess knew that I liked to sit where I could see the people coming in and out, and I had a hunch she knew what I really wanted to see. Peggy was a really good looking blonde, at least from the waist up, I had never seen her except behind that desk.

She had a wonderful warmth about her, and I enjoyed stopping for a little chat with her whenever she wasn't too busy with customers. She was a widow, I had learned, whose husband had bean killed in the very early days of the war in Viet Nam, childless and apparently quite unattached. It puzzled me a little why so attractive a woman wasn't spoken for, because I'd have gambled my last buck that she was completely female. My own marital status had come up for similar review during our little chats, but we had never gone past the casual type of conversation in passing.

The evening after I had had my conversation with Max I stayed quite late getting some last-minute details worked out, so I was one of the last customers into the restaurant before closing time. By that time I had two pretty sharp feelings of hunger, and I knew I was going to satisfy only one of them with food. Peggy was busy checking out her receipts and she looked up with obvious pleasure when I greeted her. She looked particularly lovely to me right then, anyhow, and the warmth of her greeting put a glow into me as I walked in and set down at my usual table. With my renewed sense of confidence had come a sense of buoyancy I hadn't felt for a long time, and I resolved I would ask Peggy tonight if we could have a date before I went away to the West Coast.

The thought tickled me, and I found myself impatiently waiting for my meal to be over. Somehow, I was recapturing a feeling I hadn't known since long before Paula and I were married, my resolved to outwait a large and somewhat noisy family party who seemed long since to have finished their meal, and were chattering over an after-dinner drink. So I toyed with my food, and killed time.

"What's wrong, Mr. Miller? Is there something wrong with your stew?" My waitress was concerned about my not eating.

"No, Kathy, it's just fine. I'm just not too hungry tonight. I've a lot of things on my mind, I guess."

Finally my party got up and took their noisy leave, and I finished up my meal and took my check up to Peggy's desk. When she smiled at me I became surer than ever that she had a special kind of warmth that she saved for me. It bolstered my confidence which I found I needed, as I was excited as a kid. After we had exchanged the usual greetings and she had counted out my change, I said, "Peggy, when are you through here?"

She smiled that nice smile and said, "In about twenty minutes, Mr. Miller. There's nobody else eating, and we're closed now. All I have to do is to get through checking things over and then see that everything is properly closed up. My partner took off tonight and closing is up to me."

I went on. "I don't know if you wear any man's collar or not, but if you don't, I thought you might like to go out with an old fossil like me for the rest of the evening."

She laughed, and I relaxed from my childish state of tension. Somehow she had made me feel as though we were lifelong friends and my request was the most natural thing in the world. "I don't wear any man's collar, or any women's either, and you don't look like an old fossil to me. I wouldn't guess your age to be much more than mine. I'm thirty five, and you can't be more than forty."

"The hell you are!" I exclaimed, in genuine surprise. "Not that I regard it as too much of a compliment, but I took you for more like twenty five."

"Well, thank you very much! But I'm afraid you might not want to take me out. I'm crippled, you know."
This was another surprise. "I didn't know, but do you suppose I'm the kind of a hairpin to whom it would make any difference? Because I'm not, and it doesn't."

She gave me a wry smile. "I haven't always been too good at telling one from the other," she said, "but I do appreciate your kind invitation, and I'd be glad to accept, thank you. What had you in mind?' "My name is Charlie, by the way, and I had in mind the late show at this Castle. "Oh my, I'm not dressed for any-thing like that. I'd have to go home and change, Would there be time?"

"It would be close, but you don't need to change, you look lovely the way you are."

"You're awfully nice to say that, but I'd really prefer to go home before I went out in public with you anywhere." "Just as you say. When and where should I pick you up?"

"Why don't you just follow me home, and wait in my place while I change. We're both grown up, and if you don't mind I don't."

I grinned at her. I was liking her more every minute. "I don't mind."

"Ok then, I'll just get out in the kitchen and see that everything is closed up, end I'll be with you."

I watched with some curiosity as she got up and turned back toward the little closet right behind the desk where she always sat. It was a sort of U-shaped thing, and she just rested her hands on the sides of the "U" and took a step

226

back. She opened the door to take out her coat and slipped into it, then pulled out a pair of crutches and slipped them under her arms. "I have one leg, so I can't move very far without these or my artificial leg." I could see she was watching for my reaction. "I don't wear that when I'm going to be sitting for so long." I just smiled at her, and she set out toward the kitchen, walking with the long, graceful strides of obviously long experience. Her rear view was gorgeous, and the walk struck me as extraordinarily sexy, and I felt the welcome stirring in my groin that foretold an interesting evening. When she came back at a pace that would hurry me to match, I was assured the front view was equally gorgeous.

As I joined her to walk out to the parking lot, I said, "It wouldn't occur to me to think of you as lame. You walk so gracefully and so fast, there's nothing lame about you, if you don't mind my commenting."

"You're nice to say that, but by the common definition, anybody who walks with crutches is lame. And also very conspicuous."

"Conspicuously lovely, I'll agree."

And lovely she was. The rest of her body was altogether up to the expectations raised by the top half that had been all I ever saw up until now, and I felt a stirring of the old juices as I looked at her striding along, matching my pace with such ease. She wore a short skirt, and her right leg was shapely and graceful, and it struck me that it was mare than ordinarily sexy just by virtue of holding the center of the stage all by itself. I'm a kind of leg man myself anyhow-- well, I don't know, I'm an ass man and a tit man too, and each of these enthusiasms found something to rejoice in as I looked at her, and not orgetting the face, for hers was lovely and oval, and topped with really golden hair, with a sort of ponytail that had been looped up in a loose bun at the back of her head. She wore a pump with a moderate heel, and her foot was no small ornament, but genuinely graceful and shapely. I had often watched her hands, and they were somehow sexy too. They weren't any small ornaments either, and as I watched her walking I realized that they had a lot of work to do.

She laughed. "I see I'm going to have to watch you. You're a flatterer."

"Not in this instance, I'm not. You are a genuinely beautiful woman, and I'm getting more interested in knowing you better."

"Thank you most kindly sir. I can say I share your interest in blocks, so we won't have any traffic problems."

We drove in the driveway of a rather handsome ranch house, set in a well-kept yard. "It's a double house," she explained as we went in through her garage and entered a back door. "And I rent out the other half. I hope you don't mind going in through the kitchen." I knew it was only a rhetorical question, and made no reply.

The most conspicuous object in the comfortable and tastefully furnished living room was a big Steinway grand piano, and it caught my eye at once.

"Oho! I see you are a Brahms lover. So am I."

She brightened. "Oh, really! Do you play?"

"I work on these pieces. They're to hard for me, but I love them and keep wishing I were good enough to play them right."

"Oh, Charlie! I can say we have a lot in common. Just wait a minute and I'll get my leg on and slip into a different dress."

228

"Hey, you don't have to get any leg on my account. I think you're just great the way you are, dress and all. I had a hunch that was what you had on your mind."

She hesitated a minute. "You know, I'd be crushed if you made this suggestion, but do you know what I'd rather do than go out tonight?"

We were getting along all right. I grinned at her, "Sure I know, and that was the only reason I didn't make the same suggestion myself. You'd rather stay here and play the piano, and so would I."

She looked at me with a funny expression. "I'm going to like you, she said.

I walked over to her as she looked at me with big eyes. "And I'm going to like you." I put my hand on her shoulders and looked into her eyes. She looked back at me and volumes passed between us. I leaned down and placed a restrained kiss on her cheek. "Go on now and get comfortable. I'll see the leg some other time. Meanwhile I'll get comfortable too, if you'll show me where the john is."

"No thanks, Peggy, I'm not much of a drinker, as you already know though, I expect you'd enjoy one, and I'll have a soft drink or something with you."

"I often have one when I get home. It helps me relax, but tonight I don't feel the Ned for one, and I can play better when I haven't had one."

She sat herself down on the couch. I looked at her again, and it came over me again what a truly beautiful woman she was. She certainly wasn't skinny, with the proper curves and padding in all the right places, but there was no suggestion of extra fat about her. Her face was classically beautiful, a serene oval with large, wide-spaced blue eyes and contrasting-black lashes and brows, even though there was no question about the naturalness of her blonde hair. She had a classic Greek nose, with a full bridge, good bones in her cheeks, and a mouth that was definitely more than just a little rosebud, mobile and expressive, and definitely sexy and kissable.

Her breasts were obviously supported but lightly, and they were full and high. The full negligee she was wearing dropped right down from her breasts and rather obscured the outlines of her body, but I had lready seen a trim waist and a belly with the smallest suggestion of fullness. Her hips were a little wide, and I had already relished the satisfyingly beautiful aspect of her rear view. How much more she seemed to me now than simply the pretty girl I had always seen behind the desk!

I could see the outline of the stump of her amputated left leg. It was about half the length of her full high, or a fraction more, and when she hitched herself over to reach the table beside her it raised up in a reflex action, and I could see that it was not as full as her thigh, but wasn't skinny by any means. I found I was stimulated at the sight of this truncated stub of leg, and in fact I was having a little trouble concealing the growing erection that resulted. Oh well, I thought, she can't hold it against me so long as I behave like a gentleman, and I was determined to do that.

We talked about our enthusiasm for the piano, and we were tickled to know that each of us loved so much of the same music. We got up and looked at some old books of music that she had, and again when I watched her rise up from the depths of the couch, I saw her stump raise itself up as she lifted herself up by her hands. I realized that without her leg she was unbalanced, and while I could depend on my legs to help counterbalance my weight, she had only one, and had to compensate with her hands. She wore a slipper not unlike the shoe she had worn when I first saw her, but I noticed that she had removed her stocking and her leg was bare. I had by this time a full-blown erection, and hoped I had concealed it under my jacket.

"Will you play for me?" she asked me.

So we played. She was bashful about being the first, so I played for her. I didn't do too well, but I wasn't ashamed. She played for me then, and she was better than I and didn't make so many mistakes. But with my big hands I could do Brahms' wrist-breaking left hands and wide spreads better than she could, so we both felt good about things. We reveled in Brahms, and then went in for a little Chopin, and she played a nice Mendelssohn prelude. It was intoxicating, but I was getting a hard on looking at her, and it was hard to keep my mind from sex.

"We'll play Bach another night, shall we?" she finally said.

"Let's talk for a little while. I'm going on my vacation next week, so I won't be around for a couple of weeks."

"Where are you going on your vacation?" I asked her. "I'm leaving here next week for six months on the West Coast. I'll be back here often, but I don't know whether that will satisfy my need to see you or not."

When she looked at me I could see that she knew what was forming in my mind. "I was going to drive East and visit a few of my friends, but I haven't made any very definite plans."

I swallowed a couple of times and took the plunge. "Peggy, we haven't known each other except in a very casual fashion, but I feel in many ways I've known you for a long time. Otherwise what I am about to propose would be an insult to you, but I think you already know me well enough to know that isn't my intention. Could we spend as much time together as possible between now and next week, so you could make up your mind whether or not you could consent to go along with me? Before you answer, I want to make clear that my intentions are honorable. I'm ten months divorced after fifteen years of marriage, the divorce was at my wife's request because she wanted to marry another man. I'm forty years old, gainfully employed, and I've never been so attracted to a woman as I find I am attracted to you."

I stopped out of breath. "Charlie," she said, "I've got the same feeling that you have, that you and I have known each other for a long time. I'm thrilled by what you suggest, and I'm scared too. I've got to remind you that you're saddling yourself with a cripple. I'm thirty five and I've been a widow for the years-- a lonely widow. I've met a lot of men. I know I've got psychological problems, every unattached woman my age, and every female amputee are very vulnerable to them. I couldn't stand being rejected again."

"Peggy, I know you're one-legged, and it doesn't make any difference to me. There's no way in which I can think of you as a cripple, but that's beside the point, anyway it's just a play on words. I'm a loving kind of guy, and I'm not afraid of your problems. Everybody has problems, and the people who realize it are far ahead of those who don't. I need somebody to love, and I want to be loved by somebody.

"Peggy, I know you're one-legged, and it doesn't make any difference to me. There's no way in which I can think of you as a cripple, but that's beside the point, anyway--it's just a play on words. I'm not afraid of your problems, everybody has problems, and the people who realize it are far ahead of those who don't. I need somebody to love, and I want to be loved by somebody. What's more, I'm sex-hungry as hell, and I'll have to get out of here pretty soon or I'll forget that you're a lady."

"Charlie, I'm not a lady, I'm a sex-starved broad at this point, and if you're feeling the same way, the best thing we can do is to make sure we're sexually compatible, and that I'm not repulsive to you."

My answer was to take her in my arms and crush her body to mine. "You lovely, beautiful girl, that's the last thing that could happen. Peggy, dear, I love you!"

She clung to me. "Oh, dear God!" she said.

"May I undress you?" I asked, and not waiting for an answer I unzipped her negligee, but she panicked, and looked at me with pleading eyes. "Oh, Charlie, please-" while she held the gown tightly about her.

"Peggy, dear! Are you changing your mind, or are you just being uptight? "tight?"

Still with those pleading eyes, she looked at me and whispered, "I'm so repulsive looking."

"Peggy, I can't believe it. You may as well take the plunge now, we've got to that point, and if you don't now we've got to go through all this agony some time again."

She nodded dumbly, and I uncovered her beautiful body. I undid her bra and cherished those rich, gorgeous breasts, savoring them in my hands and kissing both of them. When I pulled off her brief little panties and looked at her stump, I could hear her sharp intake of breath. I had to admit, it wasn't pretty. For a third of its length to the end of it, along the outer surface it was terribly scarred, furrowed and disfigured, with a deep, ugly, irregular scar running down to the very tip of it. I wasn't repelled, it wrung my heart with a deep, loving sense of compassion for her, and it seemed to emphasize the perfection of her beauty. I looked back in her eyes. They were wide and agonized; she had one hand to her mouth, and disaster was written in big letters on that lovely face. I sat down beside her, took her hand in mine, and looked into those stricken eyes.

233

"Dearest Peggy," I told her, "I love you. Do you suppose that any stump could turn me away from such a beautiful woman as you are? Please believe it doesn't, and it won't.

I felt her tense body relax, and the blue eyes clouded over and the tears came. She put her head on my shoulder and clung to me and sobbed deeply, and I stroked her hair and let the storm play itself out. "My poor, sweet, lovely darling," I murmured. Soon she straightened herself up, and I handed her my handkerchief and she wiped her eyes and blew her nose. "Charlie," she said, "Take me, and take me hard, and then we'll talk. It's been eight awful years, and I need it."

I stripped off my clothes and left them in a heap in nothing flat. She looked at my rod, a good sight if I do say so, gave a funny little grin and a shrug, and looked up at me. "Oh, boy!" she said.

I wasn't going to short-change her, or me either, for that matter. Not our first time out, I wasn't. She was still sitting up, and I was glad she hadn't done a spread-eagle for me. I began by sitting beside her and kissing her deeply, while my free hand went over her body and her thigh and her stump, end caressed her breasts. Then I laid her gently back on the couch and suckled her while I spread her stump and thigh with my hand, and gently stroked their inner surfaces up toward her genitals. She put her arms around me and pressed me to her breast and stroked my hair, and gave little sounds of pleasure.

After a while doing that, I put my head down and began to eat her.

"Oh!" she gasped. "That feels so good! Nobody ever did that to me before."

All the while her hands were busy in my hair, and I grabbed one of them and held it tight, and we eemed to be loving

234

each other with our hands, it felt so soft, yet strong and alive in my grasp. Her breath began to come faster, and her body began to ripple.

"Take me now," she said, "I want it so-- oh, fuck me! fuck me!" and, oh boy! I did.

"Oh God, O God!" she wailed, I'm going to come-- it's been-- so-- long-- Oh God, I love you, Oh, Oh, Oh, God it's still coming-- I never-- Oh, Charlie, hold me dearest, hold me tight." Then she went limp.

That was fine, but I had girded myself for a long run, and I still hadn't come. I eased up and raised myself up to look at her and to see our mated bodies together. I kept moving gently within her, and all the while her eyes were closed and her breath was coming in deep drafts. I began to caress her breasts, and to dwell on their still enlarged nipples. Soon she opened her eyes and looked into mine. "My love, my dearest, dearest love!" she murmured. Then her eyes opened wider, and she humped her body a couple of times. "Still got more?"

My reply was to start in on her again, gently this time, but with long strokes that took me all the way in and nearly all the way out, straining upward all the while against our union. We certainly matched each other well-- I had had a certain amount of trouble with small women not having the length to swallow my equipment all the way, but while I could feel the end of the road, and it was stimulating, I couldn't have reached any more deeply. "Oh, it feels so good!" she said, and then started to move herself to augment our motion, and I speeded up, and soon it came to me in a big explosion, and I crushed her to me while the fireworks let go inside me, and I spilled my seed within her. Just as I was coming to the end of that climactic outburst she took off again, and wailed and squirmed under me.

We lay quietly for a while and then mopped ourselves dry and sat up. "Peggy, dearest, you are wonderful! I can't thank you enough for what you have done for me. You are a dear, beautiful, sweet, sexy darling!"

She gave me an adoring look. "Charlie, however wonderful it might have been for you, it couldn't have equaled what it did for me. I'm sorry I made so much noise-- thank heaven our neighbors are away! Darling, what I have to do now is to tell you again and again how much I love you, and to talk about what you have done for me, and just get a long accumulation of frustration and hopelessness cleared out of my mind. Will you be my shrink for a while?"

"Be my guest. We'll make it mutual. Except I can't think of the word "shrink" when I look at you. Look what's happening already." And indeed it was, the old tool was getting set up for business again. "You know, it's not cricket for shrinks to do that with lovely lady patients."

She looked at it, and raised her eyebrows with a cute little smile.

"You'll just have to wait for a little while. I'm wrung out. I thought women were always able to outlast men, but I'll revive. I just have to talk for a while, now."

She went on. "You've got to know what tonight has done for me. Dan was killed just 10 years ago, and I waited for ten years before I could be comfortable with a man. Then I met a nice man who paid a lot of attention to me and took me out on dates, and in due time-- not as quick as with you!-- it came to the point of making love, and when he laid eyes on my hideous stump he just folded up like a pricked balloon. When he couldn't get it up he was terribly embarrassed, and the more he made excuses trying to save his feelings and mine, the more dreadful it became. He finally just rushed out. It hurt me terribly. I went to see my dear old surgeon friend, and begged him to re-amputate my stump, or to do

236

some plastic surgery, or anything to get that awful albatross off me that I could never get away from. He refused. He said his conscience wouldn't let him make my stump any shorter, and that I should talk to some of his patients who had to live with short stumps with artificial legs. He said, "I could do some plastic surgery and make it look better, but no way will it ever be beautiful. Let me suggest looking at it another way. Just look on it as a safety device to help you tell the men from the boys. Any man who is turned away from as lovely a woman as

you by such a thing is a guy you're better off without, because something would turn him against you eventually anyhow. When the right man comes along, he won't accept or reject you on the basis of how cute your stump is. You're lucky to eliminate that kind before you get hooked with them."

"He must be a wonderful man, and I praise God for him, and hope I can meet him some time. You were lucky to have that kind of advice." "You will meet him, all right. I'll take you to him, and say, "Here's the man you predicted would come to me. Damn it all, why did you have to make it take so long?" It's funny, I have hoped for a long time that you were going to be my fairy prince that I had dreamed about for so many years. When you said what you did to me, --you know-- I knew at last you were, and the dam broke right then, and what had been dammed up for eight years just let go. Men are always asking me for dates, but I can always tell the kind that are looking for a quick lay, I was asked by a man I'd have enjoyed going out with, but all of them said they'd call me later, or that they'd forgotten an important engagement, when I told them I was lame, or when they found I was one-legged. Something told me from the beginning that you were going to be different, and except at that last panicky moment, I kept my faith. You can see maybe, why I broke down all over you. I'm not given to that kind of thing."

"I'll credit myself with a good bust-up on your shoulder some time. You've done me the same kind of good, I was pretty bruised by being deserted by my wife of 15 years-- that's tough for a guy's ego. I owe you some tears, my dear, for what you've done for me. But remember, I'm still your shrink, and we're not through with the catharsis on your stump."

The alarm showed up in her eyes again for an instant. "What are you going to do?"

"I'm going to look at it, and get to know it, and you're going to tell me how it got that way."

She looked at me uncertainly, and then swallowed. "All right, doctor. I was ten years old, and I was playing in our front yard when a truck came through the fence and ran over my left leg. The surgeon, our old family friend, had to do the amputation-- yes, the same one I begged to amputate it again-- and he told me about it. The skin on the side of my thigh was terribly lacerated, but the bone and muscle were still there, and he explained how a surgeon tries to sacrifice as little of the human body as he can, and how important for an amputee to have a stump that is long enough to wear an artificial leg. So, he patiently patched up the lacerated skin and saved the stump."

I looked at it with new eyes, and I could see the patient work that had gone into it. It suddenly came over to me how this good man must have felt having that unhappy task to do on the pretty little girl, the daughter of his good friend. The tears came into my eyes when I visualized myself in that spot, and I wanted more than ever to meet him.

"I'll bet he cried when he saw what he had to do."

"Yes, that's just what he told me. I didn't tell you that, you're very perceptive."

"Your much-hated stump told me that. Now that it has performed just the function that your surgeon friend predicted for it, I would think you might feel differently toward it. If you hadn't had it, you would have got that first guy you told me about instead of getting me. And it's already a good friend of mine."

She looked at me. "Well," she said, "I must admit I no longer want to have it amputated, but I'd as soon have a good meat leg instead."

"I know, I can't blame you for that. But, you are so perfect in your beauty except for that, I'd be likely to be uncomfortable with you if you didn't have that, or some other flaaw. I'm just very comfortable with you, and it right now, the way you are." We were sitting on the side of the bed, and my penis was standing right up, patiently waiting. I stood up and took her stump in my hand, and put the end of my penis against it, and moved it around into the deep scar at the end. The sensation blew my mind.

Peggy began to move the stump around while I moved my body around to keep the two of them pressed together. Peggy gave an uncertain sort of giggle. "It feels kind of good," she said, and moved it a little more vigorously.

"That's a real surprise."

"It blows my mind," I said, and I leaned down to hug her stump, stroking up and down the inner surface of it meanwhile. Then I stroked the same smooth surface with the tip of my penis, and she grabbed my faithful prong and leaned down and pressed her face against it, with much the same gesture I had used with her stump. "They don't look too different, do they?" I said.

"My God, they don't," she replied, "and your penis is absolutely beautiful!"

239

I laughed, "O.K. my dear, therapy is over for today. We'll finish up with another roll in the hay, if you don't mind."

Peggy looked up at me, "Oh, Charlie, aren't you wonderful! See, I have an erection, too. I'm going to rape you! She sprang to her foot, and hopped after me, with her stump pointed toward me, her arms flapping and her breasts bouncing wildly. Her golden hair was flying in all directions, and her lovely blue eyes were laughing. I straddled her stump, and crushed her to me and kissed her passionately while she took little hops to keep her balance as we swayed around. I clamped her stump between my thighs, and reached around behind my leg and rubbed the end of it.

"Oh!" she exclaimed, "That's wonderful!" I was simply beside myself with excitement, I had never known anything like it.

We moved toward the bed in a kind of waddling movement, and when we got to the side of it we tumbled on it, with me on top of her. I was wild with excitement by this time, and she was soaking wet, and I spread her thigh and stump apart, and rubbed the inner surface of both of them, then entered her violently. She gasped, and then responded, humping her body and making little unconscious grunts. I drew my foot up under her, sat up and rolled over on my back with her on top of me, and she tried to make it, but failed, her stump wasn't long enough, so she lay down on top of me and humped her body violently, and I rolled back over with her underneath, and really worked out on her. This time I came first. I had been so excited and while I was still pumping it into her she came with a cry and a funny gagging sound, and she really had a good one, her back was arched and she was totally possessed by her passion, trembling and gasping.

We were both pretty much pooped, and just panted for a while. Then I rose up and started to get off her, but she said, "Oh, don't take it away! It feels so good!" So I laid

240

down on her again, and loved her and relished the feel of her beautiful soft body against mine.

When we finally got up, she said, "It's nearly one o'clock, and we'd better get to bed. I have a pair of pajamas that will fit you, and a toothbrush." I raised my eyebrows, and then she blushed furiously. "They used to belong to Dan, and I just kept them-- you know, in case."

I hugged her. "You dear girl - I love you so!" "Oh, Charlie, just think how our lives have changed in just a few hours."

"You've got lots of plans to make tomorrow. Is there any reason we can't be married, the first thing, or would you rather wait until we can plan something that we can invite some of our friends to come to. I must admit I'd sort of like to have my kids be there, but that wouldn't require much of a delay."

"You're absolutely sure, are you? - you know-"

I stood up and pulled her up to her foot, and put my hands on her shoulders and put my face close to hers, and looked in her eyes. "Are you sure?"

"Oh! Yes!"

"I'm sure, too. I'm sure because I know that I love you, and because you are a lovely, beautiful woman, beautiful on the inside and the outside, and because you are grown-up and mature in spite of your youthful appearance, and because we both love the same kind of music, and because you are the sexiest female I ever had anything to do with, and because I need you desperately and can't live without you."

"Oh, Charlie, you're making me cry. You don't mind having a cripple for a wife, then?"

"Damn it, Peggy, you aren't a cripple, you are one of the most graceful females I know. Didn't my therapy do you any more good than that, or did you say that just to hear me say what I did."

"Oh, you saw right through me, didn't you? I can see I'll have to be very careful with you. You might have said that I'm the only woman you know that can have an erection." "That's right, and give me one in record time, too. That's what you're doing right now, waving that stump of yours around."

"Charlie! you're insatiable! I've got to see that you save your strength. I'll get something on right now." She gave a cute little giggle. "It's nice to have that power over you, though. I'll use it with discretion after this."

"It really is something. You've got a lot more control over that than I have over my dong."

"I'll try to use it wisely," she said demurely. She leaned over to pick up her gown, and casually putting her stump on the arm of the couch to keep her balance, slipped it on. I picked up her crutches and handed them to her, and she took them in her left hand while she leaned over for her slipper.

"I'll bring these," I said, holding up her bra and panties. "Maybe I'll steal them to hide away somewhere."

"That could get to be a pretty expensive habit, if my plans go the way I expect them to."

"No, I'll just steal the first ones. I don't have a very big collection of trophies."

"I'm glad for that, my darling. I don't have, either."

I kissed her, and then, before I gathered up my own clothes I watched her swing herself gracefully across the room and

242

down the hall. She was mine, bless her! I called after her, "I forgot to ask you what your last name is."

"Smith." she said, "but that will change in a couple of days."

The Mall
By Ricardo Gonzales

The sound of the trash cans being tossed on the pavement outside her window woke Ginny up. The trash collectors were very early this morning she thought as she turned towards the window. She lay in bed, awake now, thinking about the things she had to attend to that day. It was about 6am in the morning and the sun was shining off her beautiful long blond hair that lay on her pillow. Well,she thought, I guess I can lay here all day or get up and get to the things that needed to be done. As she pulled herself up to a sitting position on the bed, Ginny leaned over to push the blankets off of her helpless legs and then she scooted over to the edge of the bed and leaned out to pull the wheelchair in position so that she could transfer from the bed to the chair.

Ginny had been a cripple now for more then ten years every since she got polio when she was a senior in high school. She had been a promising gymnast and a weight trainer but the polio put an end to her dreams of competing in the olympic games.

Ginny pulled herself into her chair carefully placing her feet in the footrests on the wheelchair. She did this with her hands because she had very little muscle control in her legs. She then wheeled herself into the bathroom. The room had been specially fitted out to accomadate her disability. There were handrails on the wall by the toilet and the bathtub and the wash basin had an opening under it that allowed her to wheel her chair under it so she could be close to the lowered sink. She thought, as she pulled herself out of her wheelchair and on to the toilet to relieve herself, how lucky she was to have an uncle who owned the apartment building she lived in and was also a general contractor and thus could make the necessary modifications to the apartment to make her life easier.

After she finished on the toilet she was able to pull herself over to a sitting position on the side of the bathtub and turn on the water. It was early Auguest and it was already getting warm so the coldness of the bathtub was not uncomfortable at all , it actually felt good. Because she was a polio victim rather then a true paraplegic she could feel even though she was paralyzed for the most part from just below the bottom of her hips down. Polio affects people in different ways. In Ginny's case she was only affected in the legs wheras other people can be affected in any part of their bodies. She first lifted one lifeless leg over into the bathtub from the bathroom floor and then with her left hand leaning across the bathtub to grab the handrail she lifted her other helpless leg over the side of the tub into the warm water that was slowly rising in the tub. She then lowered herself into the water using the handrail and the side of the tub for support. The warm water felt soothing to her and as always it felt sexy on her body as the water swirled while the tub was being filled. She laid back in the tub and brought her left crippled foot up to her left buttock and gently leaned her limp knee against the side of the tub and then she did the same with her right leg so that now both legs were leaning against their respective sides of the tub. She closed her eyes and began to rub her clitoris very gently fantacizing some of the things that really aroused her. As she felt the tightness well up in her and the itch in her genitals become more intense she could feel even her lifeless legs take on a life of their own and start to spasm. More and more she stroked her clit until, like a volcano that erupts after threatening to for a long time, she climaxed. God was that the best feeling. Even when she masturbated before the polio struck she could'nt remember it being as good as it was now. She used to tighten up her legs so they we're like two steel cords when she climaxed in the past but now since having polio she had almost no control over her legs and thus they did what they were going to do which was for the most part go into spasms when she came. It was a very erotic sensation. Well ,she thought, that was one of the few benifits of having polio.

After Ginny finished her bath she pulled herself up and on to the side of the tub and grabbed the towel hanging from the towel rack near by. She dried herself off and slowly rocking from one buttock to the other, she was able to dry her bottom. After she was finished drying herself she pulled herself into her wheel chair and very carefully placed her

246

withered legs and feet in the proper place on the footrests. She then wheeled herself over to the bathroom sink and got out her hair blower and finished drying her hair. She put it up into a ponytail. She then brushed her teeth with her electric toothbrush. Ginny always had beautiful teeth that were very white and perfectly formed. Even though she needed braces on her legs, she never had to have them on her teeth. She then put on the little makeup that she used. Light lipstick and very little eyeshadow and eyebrow pencil. You almost could'nt tell she had any makeup on. Thats how she liked it. She then wheeled over to her closet and picked out the outfit she was going to wear that day. She was going to meet her friend Eleanor for breakfast and then they were going to meet a couple of other friends and go shopping at the mall that day. She chose a short skirt and a blouse that snapped inside the skirt. She had most of her skirts and blouses made that way so that her blouses would'nt pull out of her skirts as she swung along on her crutchs. This was one of the little secrets you learned about dressing if you had to use crutchs. Another one was to have zippers sewn into the inside seam of your pants legs so you could get your pants over your braces with out to much difficulty.. That way you could wear very tight pants and look good and tailored, eventhough you wore braces. Ginny laid out the short pleated black skirt and the dark blue satin blouse on her bed and then wheeled over to the dresser to get out her panties and her nylons. She put her panties on by reaching down to her feet and putting each foot through the respective leg opening in the panties and pulled them up over her knees. She then rocked back and forth in her chair as she worked them up over her hips first with one hand and then the other. She could feel the thong of the panties slide in between her buttocks. She got a very pleasant feeling of sexuality as the thong caressed her anus. She pulled the sides of her panties up high to and she arched her back which enhanced the feeling. She sure was horny today, she thought. After she got her panties on she put on her nylons by reaching down and with one hand holding her leg up and the other hand putting the nylon over the foot, she would then pull the nylon up her leg until she got it over her knee and then she would lift that leg with one hand and pull the nylon all the way up with the other hand. Ginny wore her nylons as high as possible because she wore her legbraces very high and she liked to have the nylons act as barrier between the braces and her legs. Without nylons her legs would perspire under the leather of her braces. Ginny wheeled over to her braces and crutchs and started to put her legbraces on. Ginny lifted first her left leg and swung the foot rest of the wheelchair out from under her foot and then she gently lowered her foot to the floor. The wood floor felt cool on her foot. It brought back memories of before she got polio and how she loved to go around barefoot. Well, she thought, that will never be again. A slight wave of sadness surrounded her for a moment until she shook it off. She did the same thing with her right foot. She was now ready to put on her braces. She took the left brace into her right hand and by lifting her left leg up with her left hand she was able to slip the brace under her leg. She now reached over and placed her foot into the shoe attached to the brace. Since she would probably be walking alot today she had picked a pump with a strap across the instep and with a wide 2inch heel. She had various shoes of different styles and heels. She had put these shoes on her braces the previous evening before she went to bed. That way she would'nt have to worry about it this morning. She also had three pairs of wooden crutchs that were different lengths for each   heel heighth. After Ginny got her braces positioned properly she started to lace them up. She had full thigh cuffs from her hips to just above her knees. She had knee pads with straps that snapped on four protruding rivets so she did'nt have to buckle them up and she had a 3inch calf cuff that had a strap and buckle that held it in place. She liked her braces to fit her legs very tightly because they felt more supportive that way but the final tightening of the thigh cuffs came after she stood up in her braces. She had gone as far as she could go without standing up so she pushed hers hips to the edge of her wheelchair seat and twisted her body so that part of her right buttock and leg was off the chair. She then straightened out her right leg until she could feel the spring -loaded French lock on her brace click into place. She then pushed her self up by placing both hands on the arms of the wheelchair and swinging her hips back and up until she had pulled the right leg under her for support. She then swung herself to the left until she felt the left leg - lock snap into place. She always enjoyed this maneuver when she had on the thong panties because she could feel the thong dig into her bum. She really enjoyed that. She then quickly grabbed a crutch and put it under har left arm pit and then the right one. She could feel her legs settle in the braces and she felt the tops of her braces push her buttocks up as she settled in them. This was always a comforting feeling for her, almost like somebody taking her lower buttocks into their two hands. It felt sexy to her. She swung herself over to the wall on her crutchs and leaning against the wall with her back she put the crutchs aside for a moment and finished tighting the laces,first on her left thigh cuff then the right. She also knew that by doing this there was no way her nylons would sag. She then grabbed her crutchs and swung to the bed where her skirt and blouse was. She was a beautiful sight in her black leather and aluminum braces, black nylons, red thong panties and no bra. Ginny very seldom wore a bra because her breasts were not very large but they were very firm. Ginnys rear was beautiful as it hung ever so slightly over the tops of her braces. She ,thru lots of exercise, had a very firm butt which she was immensley proud of. It was an erogenous part of her body and she liked to have it fondled. She reached down with one hand on the bed and twisted herself around as she unlocked her left brace. She ended up sitting on the bed with one leg bent and the other locked straight. She laid her crutchs on the bed and put on her blouse. She then took her skirt and put it over her head and lowered it to her waist and zipped it up in the back. She then positioned her crutchs under one arm and pulled herself up on the locked leg and moved her hips so the other leg would lock. Then she moved one crutch under her other arm. She crutched back to the wall and again leaned against it with her back. She then partially unzipped the skirt and snapped the six snaps that would hold her blouse in place. After zipping her skirt back up and getting her pocketbook with the shoulder strap, she was ready to go out. She looked in the mirror and what she saw pleased her. There she stood, 5ft 7inchs tall, a beautiful blond girl of 29yrs. Old with a gorgeous smile. She observed her strong broad shoulders and her muscular arms, holding on to the dark wooden crutchs with the leather sling tops, that were still very feminine. She liked the way her body tapered down to a very small waist and narrow hips. Her skirt was about mid-thigh in length and she could see the laced black leather of her thigh cuffs peak out the bottom of her skirt down to the large black leather pads that covered her knees but gave her braces so much more reinforcement. The shoes she had put on her braces were very attractive as well as comfortable for a long walk in the mall. She turned sideways in the mirror and saw a very nice view of her small firm breasts pushing out the front of her tight blouse and how cute she thought her rear was as it protruded out in the back. Even though she was crippled by polio she thought of herself as reasonably attractive. Of course being as humble as she was by nature she would never reveal that emotion to anybody but herself. She was looking forward to this day with her friends.

Ginny swung out the front door of her apartment , carefully down the wheelchair ramp, and down the side of her apartment to the garage where her van was. Being partial to dark colors in her clothes didn't follow thru with her van. The van was a bright red Chevy Astro. She had a wheelchair lift in the van and usually kept a separate chair in the van from the one in the house. She hit the button and the sliding door on the side opened and the lift unfolded itself. She reached in and pulled the chair onto the lift and pressed the button to lower it. When the lift was ground level she sat down in the chair and pressed the button that lifted her, the chair and the crutchs she was holding up to the entrance of the van. She put her crutchs in a special rack that held them and then she wheeled herself to the steering wheel and reached down on each side of her chair to lock it in place. Ginny could drive her van from her wheelchair with hand controls which was alot more convenient then trying to transfer to the drivers seat. Since Ginny earned a good living this had been one of the luxuries that she had afforded herself. She started the van, carefully backed out of her garage and started towards Eleanors place.

Ginny had made and kept some close friends when she was in rehab and every one of them had been affected differently by the dreaded virus. For example, Ginny could walk very easily with full legbraces and crutchs wheras some of her friends would never even stand again. In that case I guess you could call her very lucky compared to them. Her very best friend Eleanor would use a wheelchair more often then Ginny because her back had been affected as well as her legs and she could'nt support herself on the crutchs and braces without alot more effort then Ginny. Eleanor had very acute scoliosis that gave her an abnormally prounounced sway back. Eleanor preferred walking on her braces more then using her wheelchair but sometimes she got to tired and thats when her chair came in handy. Because Eleanor's back was so affected by the polio she had to wear a very tight corset with metal stays that went from the top of her hips to just the bottom of her bust. She preferred black and so she had them custom made by a friendly orthotist out of a very soft black leather that was lined with a white horsehide. The corset laced up the front and she wore it very tight so that she had good support for her middle and her back. This gave her an hour-glass figure that turned alot of heads as she pulled herself along on her crutchs. Especially when she wore tight slacks. Because of her scoliosis it was easier for Eleanor to walk in her braces with her legs slightly bent. She had dial-a-locks on her braces which allowed her to set her braces at any position when they locked. She had them adjusted so that when she walked she looked like she was just getting ready to sit down . Walking like this gave her more balance then if she was walking with her braces straight. Although this made her appear slightly shorter and it made her look like she was having a harder time walking on her braces it was actually much easier for her to walk that way. She also wore her braces very high on her legs like Ginny, so she would sit on the tops of her braces and this enhanced her buttocks even more. Eleanors wheel chairs had also been fitted out with very prominent lumbar supports that supported her twisted back.

Eleanor had been amply endowed by the creator and because she had developed very powerful upper arms, shoulders,and chest muscles from walking on her crutchs and using her wheel chair she had a large bust. Eleanor was also blessed with a lovely face and beautiful long black hair that she almost always wore in either a ponytail or pulled back tightly in a bun. Eventhough Eleanor was much more severly affected by the polio then Ginny was, she got alot more male attention then Ginny because of her flirtatious ways and her sunny disposition. Ginny was more shy and the guys thought she was a little stand offish when in fact she ached to be as sought after as Eleanor was. She would never admit that to anyone though; not even to Eleanor.

Eleanor never let the polio get in the way of her social life like Ginny did. Ginny became very introverted after the polio struck not that she was a social butterfly before the big "P". It's just that she was very serious about her gymnastics, weight training, and getting good grades in school so she could go to college and become a physical education teacher. If Ginny had any social life it was because of Eleanor.

Ginny met Eleanor when she was in rehab. Eleanor had been through it three years before and would visit the new kids that contracted polio and help cheer them up and motivate them to try hard to get well and not let the disease get them down. Ginny was one of those kids who had fallen into a kind of depression because of what had happened to her and if it had'nt been for Eleanor working with her and becoming her friend, who knows what would have happened to Ginny. Because of Eleanor, Ginny got on her feet, finished high school only one semester behind, went on to college and although did'nt major in physical education, she did get a degree in microbiology and was now enjoying her work in one of the best medical research companys in the country as a laboratory supervisor. It never would have happened if it had'nt been for Eleanors support and friendship. Ginny loved Eleanor for what she had done for her. Eleanor had become the closest person in Ginnys life eventhough Eleanor was four years her senior. Eleanor had grown to feel the same way about Ginny.

Eleanor had a good job as a receptionist and all around girl Friday in her older brothers law offices. She got to meet alot of people who would come to the office on business of one kind or another. I guess that I should tell you more about Ginny and Eleanor and some of their disabled and able-bodied friends before I go on with the rest of my story.

Let me go back and give you a little bit more of a description of Ginny. Ginny was about 5'7" and about 140lbs of very well developed body. Like Eleanor she had developed very powerful arms, shoulders, back and stomach muscles from walking on crutchs for the last ten years. Although Eleanor did'nt have the very strong stomach muscles and lower back muscles that Ginny had ,the "Merry Widow" corset that she wore made up for any weakness she had in those areas. Ginny was much faster on her crutchs then Eleanor but when she and Eleanor were walking together she made it a point to not leave Eleanor behind.

Ginny was like that. She was a very thoughtful and compassionate women. When you walked behind Ginny and she was swinging along on her crutchs with her long blond hair blowing in the wind it was a joy to behold because she glided along so gracefully. Wheras Ginny made walking on crutchs easy, you could see the strain on Eleanor as she pulled herself along on her crutchs. Like Eleanor, Ginny had a very appealing behind. She had very narrow hips compared to Eleanor but when you looked at her from the side her buttocks protruded out almost to much. Sitting on the tops of her braces accentuated her rear as it did Eleanors. They both had very prominent rears,especially Eleanor who was 2inchs shorter then Ginny and a good

10lbs. heavier. From the back Eleanors hips were much fuller and more sensuous then Ginnys.

Unlike Eleanor, Ginny had a small bust but enough that made it interesting. I guess I should tell you something about there legs. Like I said earlier, Ginny had been a gymnast and a weight-trainer. She was in prime physical condition when the polio struck. She had had very developed calf and thigh muscles. The polio only affected her from just below her hips down so her legs looked ,although thinner because of the polio, almost normal in size even though they were very flaccid as far as muscle tone was concerned. Eleanors body was much more ravaged by the polio.

Eleanor had been in her first year of college when she got polio. She was in great physical shape because she had been naturally born that way and had taken alot of ballet in school since she was ten years old. However the polio had hit her so hard that she had absolutly no muscle control in her legs. Because her legs had been full when she got the polio they didntly outwardly show as much atrophy as had actually occured. If you held one of Eleanors legs in your hand it would have felt very soft and mushy. If you held one of Ginnys legs in your hand it would be firmer yet still much softer then a normal well developed leg.   Ginny could actually walk without braces if she held on to something and lifted each of her legs high with her arm with each step so as to kick out her paralyzed feet. It was'nt very graceful but it would work if she did'nt have her braces on and her chair was out of reach. However she could'nt support her weight very long without her braces. Eleanor could only stand if she had on her braces.

Eleanor had awakened about an hour before Ginny. She lay in bed clearing her head after the frequent dream that she just had. At least once a month she would dream that she was walking without aids and that she was totally whole in body. This time she had been going to the movies with a high school friend and they were seeing the movie "The Other Side Of The Mountain". This was the story of Jill Kinmont the famous skier in the '60's who had become a quadraplegic from a skiing accident. In her dream, Eleanor was feeling the emotion of how sad she felt for Jill but how glad she was that it was'nt her, only to wake up and realize that she too was crippled albeit from a different cause and that she was'nt as severly disabled as Jill Kinmont. Like Ginny, Eleanor kept her wheelchair close to her bed at night and so she rolled over with great difficulty on her stomach and reached out to pull it over closer to the bed so that she could transfer to it. Being much more disabled then Ginny, she would have to do things slower then Ginny. As I said before, she was very strong in her shoulders, chest, and arms. She reached down to her legs and pulled them over so that the force of them turning would allow her to turn her whole body back so that she was on her back again. She now slowly maneuvered her night shirt off by pulling it up as she wigglrd around on the bed. After getting it off by finally pulling it over her head she lay there naked on the bed feeling the coolness of the air on her moist body. After a couple of minutes she reached over to the nightstand and grabbed her corset. She maneuvered it in place and while lying on her back, she laced it up very tightly. Thats better she thought as she raised herself first on her elbows then all the way up to a sitting position. She then kind of fell towards the wheelchair and with first one hand on the seat of the chair and the other on the bed she scooted her bare rear over to the edge of the bed and finally into the seat of the wheelchair. There she sat in the wheelchair with only her corset on and with her feet and most of her legs still on the bed. She rested for a moment and then using her strong muscular arms, she backed the chair up enough to where she had enough room to lift her legs off the bed and put her feet into the footrests of the wheelchair. She was very careful doing this. A few times she had pulled the chair to far back and her feet fell to the floor which really hurt and could cause some damage. She had absolutly no control over her legs or feet. They were lifeless except that she could feel them. I guess you could equate that with knowing your ears are there and that you can feel them but no matter how hard you try you can't move them on their own.

Like Ginny's apartment, Eleanors condo was adapted to

her needs. She had deliberatly purchased the one story condo because it was in a special condo development for people with disabilities. The builders wife had been born with Spina Bifida and thus he was sensitive to the needs of the disabled. It was a big gamble on his part to build the development but it had paid off. He had sold all 36 units within a year of completion and he had made a reasonable profit financially. I think the real profit he made was the gratitude of 36 disabled buyers who appreciated the risk he took and the compassion he showed in modifying each unit to fit their special needs. Some had two bedrooms for those who did'nt need a caregiver and others had three bedrooms for the people who needed a full time live in caregiver.

Each unit had its own 2 car garage with extra high doors to accomadate a large van if needed. This was great for alot of the tenants because, like Eleanor and Ginny, most of the people in the development got around in large vans with wheelchair lifts.

Eleanor, after finishing going to the bathroom, wheeled herself up to the bathroom sink and brushed her teeth and washed her face. She had taken her bath just before bed time the night before so she did'nt need one this morning. She then brushed out her long raven colored hair and then she pulled it back into a severe bun so it would stay out of her way as she went thru the mall. She was really looking forward to the little shopping trip at the mall today. It was considered one of the finest shopping malls in the U. S. Eleanor wanted to find a good leather handbag that she could hold alot of stuff in but could wear over her shoulder when walking on her crutchs. She was also looking forward to seeing Ginny and sharing with her what had taken place two nights ago with one of the guys who lived in her condo development. Unlike Ginny, Eleanor liked to confide in Ginny and describe almost blow for blow what her sex life was about. Ginny knew that this made Eleanor feel attractive and like a normal girl eventhough she was crippled. Ginny also appreciated the storys because they would make her horny and she would fantacize about them when she masturbated.

After Eleanor had finished with her makeup she wheeled

over to her closet and pulled out the outfit she would wear to go shopping. She really liked Scottish plaid pleated skirts. She had them in all colors. She pulled a green one from her closet and laid it out on her unmade bed. She then pulled out a tan, button down collar, long sleeve blouse/shirt to wear with the skirt. She also laid that on the bed. She then wheeled over to her bureau and pulled out a pair of white satin panties, a matching bra and a pair of medium brown hip length stockings. She put the panties on pretty much how I described the way Ginny did it. Next came the bra to support her 38D bust and then she pulled on her nylons by first lifting one leg over the other one and manipulating the stocking first on one foot and then reversing her legs ,the other foot. She then wheeled over to get her legbraces and put them on.

The pair of legbraces that Eleanor picked today were the ones with the dark brown lace up leather cuffs on the thighs and the kneepads that buckled on and that also had the 4inch cuff s that laced up on the calf. She had brown lace - up oxford shoes attached to the braces that had built up heels to offset the slightly bent way she locked her braces. If the heels had'nt been built up they would have almost always been off the ground and would not have given her feet good support. She would always be on the balls of her feet without the built up heels. Like Ginny, Eleanor felt safest walking in braces when they fit real tight. With that in mind she did what Ginny had done, namely standing in her braces for the final adjustment on the thigh laces. She laced them loosely until she stood up on them and then as she settled comfortably into her legbraces she finished tightening the laces on her cuffs. Like Ginny, she also got a sexual rush from the tops of her braces pushing up her ample rear. When Eleanor stood on her braces she looked like somebody with their legs tied together who was slightly crouched and was going to jump with their legs that way. Her rear rode high because of her arched back and she basically hung on the tops of her leather topped crutchs. Eventhough it was tedious for her to walk that way, she would rather walk then sit in that wheelchair that really made her feel crippled. She also felt sexier walking then in the chair. I guess she was right because she got alot of male attention.

She crutched herself over to the bed and kind of sat on it without unlocking her braces. She pulled the skirt over her head and then put on the blouse. Like Ginnys skirts, all of Eleanors skirts and blouses had the snaps that kept them in place so the blouse would'nt pull out as she pulled herself along on her crutchs. After putting the skirt and blouse on she dragged herself over to the long mirror that hung on her door and gazed at herself. Not bad she thought but she also reminded herself that she did'nt want to get any heavier because she was already voluptuous enough. The muscle tone in Eleanors hips and lower stomach was'nt as good as Ginnys but she was apparently firm enough for most of the guys who had been lucky enough to be there. She turned towards the window when she heard Ginnys horn announce that she had arrived. She quickly looked one more time in the mirror, crutched over to get her shoulder bag and go to the front door and wave to Ginny that she would be right out. She then went back to her bedroom and got into her wheelchair, put her crutchs in the crutch holder attached to the chair, and wheeled herself out to the waiting van. Ginny had already lowered the lift and Eleanor wheeled on to it and Ginny lifted her into the van. After she secured her chair to the chair locks on the floor of the van she transferred to the passenger side front bucket seat. The seat swiveled and locked so that she could, with very little difficulty, slide from the secured wheelchair into the seat and the power swivel turned the chair so she was facing forward in the van. She turned to Ginny and smiled. She then reached over and took Ginnys hand and kissed it and told her how good it was to see her. Ginny kissed Eleanors hand and squeezed it also telling Eleanor how much she had missed her and that they had to catch up on what was going on since it had been almost two weeks since they had seen each other. Ginny started the engine of the van and put it into gear. They were off to meet Jeri and Donna at the mall.

Jeri had already been up for about an hour when she

heard Donna stirring in her room. Jeri had awakened and slid off her bed to the floor where her exercise equipment was. She liked to work out with no clothes on so she slipped out of her teddy and threw it on the bed before getting on the floor. Jeri was a very early riser because she felt that she had to work out for at least 45 min. every day if she wanted to keep her figure and stay very strong. She swung herself over to the workout mat by sitting on her bottom and using her powerful arms to swing herself along. Since she only had 6inch stumps for legs, she could sucessfully perform this maneuver by holding her stumps together and in the air as she swung herself along.

Her favorite exercise was to do arm curls with free weights and to lay on her stomach and attach her stumps to the two straps attached to her workout board and do back archs. She felt very sexy when she did this exercise because her clit rubbed against the soft leather that covered the workout board and this gave her a sexual rush. A couple of times the dynamics had been so perfect between her arching her back and squeezing her beautiful hard buttocks together that she came while doing the exercise. She loved the feel of the tightness that she felt in her buttocks every time she arched her back. She also loved to reverse the process and to do stomach crunchs. She had a stomach that looked like a washboard. If Jeri had had her legs back she could have easily competed in some of those women bodybuilding contests and she probably would have won.

After Jeri finished her exercises she swung herself over to the bathroom and pulled herself up on the toilet to relieve herself. She then swung herself up to the side of the bathtub and turned on the water. After her bath she swung herself over to the stool that she sat on in front of the bathroom pullman. She pulled herself up on the stool using both arms to pull up her body. She dried her hair with a blow-dryer and then she brushed her teeth and put on her makeup. Like Ginny, Jeri did'nt need alot of makeup to look glamorous. It was about this time she heard Donna stirring in her bedroom. Each bedroom in the house had its own private bathroom. The rooms were overly large to accomodate moving around in a wheel chair. Jeri swung over to her bureau and pulled out some purple thong panties and a matching bra. She put them on as she sat on the floor with her stumps straight out in front of her. She then swung herself over to the closet and got out her stump boots. For those of you who don'nt know what they are, I'll describe them for you. Jeri's were a soft black leather on the outside lined with bleached white sheepskin on the inside. They were cylindrical and as wide at the bottom as they were at the top. The inside had been form fitted to Jeri's stumps and were very comfortable. The bottoms had a leather round sole that gave her stability as she stood in them. The sole was about 2inchs wider in diameter then the boot itself. They laced from almost the bottom all the way up to the top. The boots were a couple of inchs longer then Jeri's stumps and thus were heavily padded at the bottom so as not to irritate Jeri's stumps when she walked in them. It also added 2 inchs to her heighth which she liked. The boots went all the way up Jeri's stumps to her butt. Like Ginny and Eleanor with their braces, Jeri sat on the tops of her stump boots just as she sat on the tops of her prosthesis.

Jeri grabbed her short underarm crutchs from the closet and leaned them against the wall. She then laid down on her back and rolled over on her stomach. She then pushed herself up so that she was standing up in the boots. She grabbed her crutchs and crutched over to Donnas room. When Jeri was standing in her stump boots she was about 4 feet tall. Jeri was only in her panties, bra, and boots. She knocked on Donnas bedroom door and Donna yelled out to come in. She was in her bathtub. Jeri came in and swung herself over to the open bathroom door and went in. She stood by the tub and looked at Donnas naked crippled body lying in the tub partially covered with soapy water. Donna was very pale and her legs were extremely atrophied and thus very skinny. Her stomach was flaccid although the skin was tight. She did have a beautiful set of breasts that were perfectly formed with small pink hard nipples. Her arms and

260

her upper back had some muscle tone although not a great deal. She did have very broad muscular shoulders which had not been affected by the polio. She used her shoulders alot to compensate for the other parts of her upper body that did'nt work so well. Because she was sitting in the tub, Jeri could'nt see Donnas rear but she knew what it looked like. She had almost no muscle control in her buttocks but it was beautifully formed when she lay on her stomach. It was ,however, very soft. She used a special cushion in her wheelchair so she would'nt develop pressure sores on it. Donna and Jeri were going to meet Ginny and Eleanor at a restaurant at the mall about 11:30 AM for an early lunch. Since they had plenty of time there was no rush. Donna took the straps for her lift and fitted them under her rear. She aked Jeri to hit the button that would lift her out of the bath tub and into the plastic upholstered wheelchair that she used when bathing. Jeri pushed the button and Donna was lifted out of her bath tub and Jeri helped guide her down and into the chair. Donna undid the lift straps and grabbed a towel and started to dry herself off. Jeri loved to watch Donna move because she was so ingenious the way every move was thought out to accomplish something so she did'nt waste any energy. After Donna was dry she wheeled over to her other chair and transferred into it. Because the polio had so ravaged Donnas body, moves like this were very difficult. With a great deal of strain she made the transfer and was instantly more comfortable bacause of the extra cushion in this chair.

Unknown to most people, Jeri and Donna were lovers when one or the other did'nt have male companionship to satisfy them sexually. This was one of those times. Jeri could feel the desire swell up in her for Donna as she watched Donna struggling thru her morning routine. Down deep Jeri enjoyed women sexually as much as men. Donna preferred men more then women but she was very turned on to the muscular body that Jeri posessed as well as the tenderness and thoughtfulness she showed when they made love. She loved to run her hands over Jeri's hard butt and feel the ripples in her stomach. She loved the sweet smell of Jeris clit when she tongued her. She loved it when Jeri would wrap her strong arms around her and kiss her. Conversly, Jeri loved the helplessness of Donna. She loved the pained expressions on Donna's face as she dragged her crippled body up and on to the bed from her wheelchair. She loved the squeals of pleasure that Donna made when Jeri ran her tongue into her clit and her anus. She loved to cradle Donna in her arms and hold her gently. She loved the way Donna put so much emotion into her lovemaking. If Jeri was really truthful to her self she would probably admit that she loved Donna a little bit. Many a night they fell asleep in each others arms. The beautiful, muscular legless girl with the slightly olive complexion and the pale crippled plain looking girl.

Donna knew when Jeri wanted her. The flattering comments, the stroking of Donnas hair, the gentle kiss on the neck, the wonderful touch of her hand on her lifeless but very sensitive legs. Conversley, Donna could feel desire well up in her as she watched Jeri crutch around the house in her stump boots with only her panties on. Sometimes she would'nt even wear panties and this really aroused Donna quickly. She really liked to watch Jeris very round butt as the boots struggled to push it up with each swing she took on her crutchs. Jeri knew this turned Donna on and she would walk around as if Donna was'nt there but really accenting each swing on her crutchs. When she did this Donna would get so wet that she had to wash the cushion of her wheelchair after they made love.

This morning Jeri took Donnas blow dryer and started to blow dry Donnas hair. At the same time she started to caress her neck with her lips. Jeri loved the smell of Donna right after she had had a bath. Donna started to respond and Jeri put down the blow-dryer and kissed Donna passionatly forcing her tongue into Donnas mouth. Donna returned her advances just as hungarally by reaching behind Jeri and feeling her hot tight butt as it ever so slightly hung over the tops of her stump boots. Donna forced her tongue into Jeris mouth and with her other hand she massaged Jeris firm breasts. Jeri moved around to the front of Donnas wheelchair and put on the locks. She then leaned on the arms of the chair and started to kiss Donnas breasts. She worked her way down to Donnas stomach then , leaning against the front of the chair she first raised one of Donnas withered legs up and had Donna hold it. She then reached down for the other leg and had Donna hold that one to. Donna now sat spread-eagle in her wheelchair as Jeri bent down and started to tongue her clit. When Jeri put her mouth on Donnas clit she could hear the rush of air as Donna sucked in her stomach. Donna had great difficulty moving her hips but when Jeri did this to her they took on a life of their own and she could move them slightly. She felt herself pumping her hips as best as she could as Jeris hot tongue caressed the lips of her vagina and rubbed over her clitoris. Jeri could feel Donnas body tensing up and moving in rythum with the stroking she was doing on Donna. Jeri could feel her clit getting very wet and starting to run out of her on to the tops of her boots. She could feel the fever growing in Donna as she inserted one of her fingers into Donnas anus as she continued to suck Donnas clit. Low animal sounds were coming from deep inside Donna and they started to get louder. Jeri knew she was close to cumming because the sounds were getting louder and she could feel the spasms starting in Donnas rear where she had inserted her finger. Then Donna let out a loud grunt and started to shake all over for about thirty seconds.as she climaxed. After Donna came, Jeri gently put her feet back in the footrests of the wheelchair. She then pushed Donnas wheelchair over to the bed and helped Donna up on to the bed. This was difficult because Donna was sapped of all energy. Jeri got Donna onto the bed and then she crawled up on to the bed and took Donna into her arms. She held Donna very close and then she started to caress her body and then she kissed her gently on the mouth. After a few minutes Donna got her strength back and this time she wanted to satisfy Jeri. It was hard for Donna to move around the bed so she guided Jeris moves as she kissed her. Finally she got Jeri on her back and she had Jeri put a pillow under her butt which lifted her pubic area up. Donna, with great difficulty, pulled herself up to where her mouth was over Jeris clit. She commanded Jeri to hold her boot clad stumps wide apart and in the air. Jeri complied because she knew what pleasure Donna was going to inflict on her as she started to tongue Jeris clit and vagina. Jeri could feel her hips moving strongly as she got closer and closer to the big "C". Finally she hit and it was magnificant. Donna knew exactly how to satisfy Jeri. They then took the 69 position after about 20 minutes and delivered again to each other the wonderful gift of sexual orgasm.. In this position, Jeri was usually on top because it was easier for Donna to stay on the bottom.

A half hour went by and it was time to get ready to go out. Jeri lowered herself to the floor and holding on to the bed and then the wall she made her way stiff-legged over to the bathroom sink. She ran hot water over a wash rag and cleaned herself up. She wet the washrag again and made her way back to the bed and she washed Donna down. They did'nt have time to take baths again so this would have to do , Jeri thought.

She then helped Donna get into her wheelchair and then she got her crutchs and swung on them back to her bedroom to get dressed. Jeri liked to wear light weight solid color sleeveless sundresses. She had different length clothes depending on whether she was going to use her wheelchair, wear her prothesis, or go out in her stump boots. Today she was going to wear her boots so she picked a light burgundy sundress that was cut very short so that it would'nt touch the ground if she wore her boots. She liked dresses that were tight in the bodice and had a slight flair at the hips. She pulled this dress over her head and let it fall over her body. She crutched to the full length mirror in the bedroom and admired herself. She stood there and saw a handsome woman with high cheekbones and reddish brown hair that she would wear in a pagebow today. She observed the large 36C bust as the dress stretched over it. She saw the very small waist that the tight bodice of the dress revealed. She turned sideways in the mirror and saw her heavily muscled left arm holding on to her crutch. The back of her dress was cut so that you could see her tan shoulders and strong upper back. She followed the dress down and observed how it tightly hugged the top of her rear and then dropped loosely to about 2inchs below the bottom of her hips. She saw the boots peeking out about 6inchs below the dress. At that moment she had a feeling of angst wishing that she had her legs back and had nice boots on instead of these straight formless leather cylinders that allowed her to walk on her stumps without pain. The momentary desire for her long lost legs swept her up in such a wave of depression that she could feel her eyes moisten. The feeling passed quickly as she realized that she had to hurry so that she would have time to help Donna finish getting ready. With that she grabbed her crutchs and started to swing over to Donnas bedroom.

After Jeri had gotten Donna into her wheelchair, Jeri left her alone to finish cleaning herself up from the sex they had just had. Donna wheeled herself over to the bathroom sink and finished sponging herself off and wiping her love parts. After she finished she put on a light coat of makeup and then wheeled over to get her legbraces and attached corset. This is where Jeri was a blessing. Almost every morning, Jeri would help Donna get into her braces. Jeri swung into the room and came over to Donna. Donna wheeled over to the bed and Jeri followed. She helped Donna get on the bed and lay flat on her back. Donna had carried her braces with her to the bed and now Jeri took them and laid them out on the bed next to Donna. Now Donna had to scoot in position so that she lay on top of the braces so that she could buckle and lace herself in. Once Donna got to that position she could get herself in the braces with relative ease. First she would get back up to a sitting position and get her feet into the flat heeled oxfords. She would lace them up and then she would buckle up the narrow calf cuffs of her braces. After that she would tighten the buckles on the two narrow thigh cuffs. She would then lay down in the corset and laying there she would lace it up as tightly as she could and tie the laces. Jeri would then help her sit back up and help her get back into her wheelchair. Once that was done Jeri would tighten the laces on the corset so Donnas body would have good support. This would prevent her back from sagging and create the usual problems of scoliosis and breathing difficulties. Now the next step was to pick out her outfit for the day. She wheeled to her closet and picked out a simple flowered pattern dress that had a slight waist. Jeri helped her get it over her head and got it laying nicely on her as she sat in the chair. Donna went back to the bathroom and combed out her long pale blond hair and let it hang below her shoulders. She decided to take a few minutes and do a special job on her makeup because, after all, she might meet a nice guy today. When she was finished she turned to Jeri and asked how she looked. Jeri thought she looked great and she told her that. Jeri thought she was great but not just her looks but her whole being. Jeri could get very emotional about Donna. They were ready to go meet Ginny and Eleanor.

Ginny pulled the van into a handicapped parking space at the mall. This was the closest they could get to the restaurant where they were going to meet Jeri and Donna. To get out of the van, Eleanor had to transfer back to her wheelchair which she did. She then opened the van door and the lift unfolded. Wheeling on to the lift she hit the button and was lowered to the ground. She then sent the lift back up to Ginny who did the same thing. They had both brought their crutchs down with them. After getting on their feet and on to the crutchs they lifted their chairs, with the help of the lift, back up into the van and locked it. They both started swinging themselves along on their crutchs towards the mall entrance. Ginny moved along in a graceful effortless manner with her legs straight. The skirt she wore hugged her rear when she would put her crutchs out in front of her as her pelvis jutted out while she started the next swinging arc as she moved along. You could make out the tops of her braces pushing against the lower part of her buttocks. This in turn pushed her rear out and looked very sexy.

Eleanor, on the other hand, had her legs slightly bent in her braces and thus hung on the tops of her crutchs while her powerful arms pulled her crippled body along. Her blouse strained against her large beautiful breasts and her small waist that was pinched by the corset enhanced her already ample rear as she pulled herself quickly to keep up with Ginny. Ginny, realizing that Eleanor was struggling to keep up, slowed down so Eleanor would.nt have to work so hard. After they had gone a few yards they heard a horn blow. Turning around they saw Jeri and Donna pulling into the handicapped space next to their van. Jeri also had a van but today they were in Donnas car. Donna had a 2 door Buick that had a very large back seat to accomadate her wheelchair. If Jeri had brought her chair they would have gone in Jeri's van but Donna felt it was her turn to drive so they went in her car. Jeri opened the passenger side and slipped out of the seat and then she grabbed her crutchs and closed the door. She swung her body on the crutchs over to the drivers side and helped Donna get out of the car. Donna would stand with her braces holding her upright while she held on to the side of the car. Jeri, in the meantime, took her wheelchair out from behind the drivers seat and put it behind Donna making sure she locked the brakes. Donna reached behind her right leg and unlocked the French lock on her brace and felt herself fall into the wheelchair. She unlocked her left leg and then she lifted it up and swung the footrest of the wheelchair under it and then carefully put her foot into it. She did the same thing with her right foot. They were then already to go eat. With Jeri, Ginny, and Eleanor pulling themselves along on their crutchs, Donna wheeled herself slowly beside them towards the entrance of the mall. Jeri hurried to get ahead of them a little bit so that she could hold the door for the rest of them. Once they were inside the mall they could see the restaurant entrance ahead of them. They made their way to the restaurant, ignoring the stares of the shoppers that they passed along the way.

Over the years each of them had to fight their own internal battle of how to put up with those who showed them attention by staring at them and/or asking them personal questions when they would come across them. Ginny would be cool and just look forward and not acknowledge the stares or the questions. If somebody was especially obnoxious she would tell them to mind there own business. This was totally out of character for Ginny because of all of the girls, she was probably the most compassionate and the kindest. Ginny had a hard time revealing her inner feelings with anyone and this was just another example of that. Eleanor, with her extroverted ways, would smile and say hello. She would even stop and talk to the person staring so as to put them at ease. Alot of times she would field questions of what happened to her; why she walked in her braces the way she did; did it hurt to be crippled; could she feel below the waist; etc. She would always answer and offer additional information about her condition if she thought the other person was interested. The people she would try to get away from the quickest were those who kept telling her how sorry they were for her. She found them to be very patronizing and she did'nt believe for one minute that they cared as much as they put on. Jeri's handicap was much more obvious. She did'nt have legs. The stares she got did'nt bother her because she was very confident in her feelings of being attractive and desirable, which she was. She would get questions mainly revolving around whether she was born that way or was she in an accident. She would politley answer the questions with short comments and try to get away as quickly as possible. Donna was more like Eleanor with people who approached her. Of all of them, Donna was the most debilitated by her handicap. She very seldom attempted to walk with her crutchs and braces. She almost always used the wheelchair and thus could get away very quickly from those she found obnoxious. When your on crutchs you don'nt move nearly as fast as you can in a wheelchair. The only reason the others did'nt use their chairs more is they all thought that they would lose some independance by relying on their wheelchairs to much.

Well maybe it's time I told you a little bit about me. I'm going to tell you the real truth about me rather then the story that I've told all of the people in our circle of friends.

As I mentioned earlier, I'm 36 years old. I moved to Los Angeles about 7 years ago with some money saved up and quite a nice inheritance from my folks estate and not much else. My folks had passed away within a year of each other and I was all alone in the world so moving to a new place across the country allowed me to do what I had fantacized doing since I was a little kid, namely to live my life as a cripple. Why, you ask, would I want to do that. Hell, I wish I knew. Every since I could remember, I've wanted to walk with long legbraces and crutchs. In Chicago I had found an orthotist who made me a very nice pair of long legbraces for about 50% more then I would have paid if I had been a legitimate "crip", all cash thankyou. I bought a Ford van and had it outfitted with handcontrols and drove to California. Out here the weather is good most of the year and frankly it's easier to get around on crutchs and/or a wheelchair then in the east, especially in the winter. Frankly, another reason is that I heard the girls were more interesting and adventurous when they meet somebody like me. I have'nt been disappointed.

Well let me describe myself to you. I'm about 5ft 10inchs tall. I have dark brown hair that I wear kind of longish, blue eyes and am built more on the slender side except I have deliberatly built my arms, chest, and back muscles up alot. I also have a very defined buttocks and a very small waist . I've walked only with legbraces and crutchs for the past 7 years so my legs have atrophied to such a state that I look like I could have had polio. Which is exactly what everybody I know out here thinks and what I want them to think.

To earn a living and still have some freedom to come and go as I please, I turned my hobby into a source of income. I now trade the commoditys market to earn my living. I've been so good at it that I could probably quit and still live a very comfortable life. Until I met Jeri and her friends I still had a longing for something else in my life. After meeting Jeri,Ginny, Eleanor and Donna I feel more complete. They have become the most important people in my life.

I've dated alot of girls (I'll tell you a few stories about some of them later on) but those four are the ones that give me the most satisfaction. You know, I've described all of us to you but it's still hard to understand what we really look like so I guess the best way to describe us is to compare us to people in public life. Ginny looks alot like Jamie Leigh Curtis with long hair.   Eleanor resembles a cross between Adrienne Barbeaux and Paula Abdul. Donna has a strong resemblence to Meryl Streep. Jeri looks alot like Madonna and I guess you could say that I (if you stretch your imagination far enough) look like Robert Urich.

Since moving to LA I've acquired a number of pairs of legbraces, crutchs, and a couple of wheelchairs. All my braces go right up to my butt. I like to sit on the top of them because it makes me feel more helpless and makes my butt protrude. I think thats very sexy on a woman and I've been told by women, including the "fab four" that my rear is one of my best "ASSets" if you know what I mean. Besides it feels very sexy to have your butt pushed up by your braces when you swing along on your crutchs. It's kind of like somebody fondling it which I thoroughly enjoy. Anyway, back to my braces. All but one pair have wide leather thigh cuffs that go from my butt to the tops of my knees. They lace up on the thigh. I wear leather knee pads on all my braces and on all of them but one pair they have a 3inch cuff about midcalf that has a strap and a buckle. They are all black leather except the ones that have an 8inch cuff on the calf that laces up.   These braces are a rawhide colored leather . I use underarm wooden crutchs. They are a dark colored wood and they have dark colored leather saddles at the top. The rawhide colored braces are made of steel rather then aluminum and are much stronger and heavier. I keep my cowboy boots attached to these and wear them when I wear tight jeans. I like to wear the braces outside my jeans to see how women react to them. I've had alot of interesting comments as well as some interesting encounters. I'll relate to you later on some of my adventures in a few western bars.

Besides wearing jeans I like to go out in spandex leotards with my braces on the outside of the leotard. I usually wear this outfit when I go to the gymn. When I'm dressed this way I get alot of attention which pleases me to no end. You can see all of the braces right up to where my butt hangs over the top and you can see all of my manhood right out in front. After working out I like to hit the malls and watch some of the reactions I get when I crutch around the different stores. I'll relate one experience to you that I found kind of interesting. One day this lady comes up to me in the mall and practically panting asks if she could call me. Since she was very good looking and had a good but slightly overly voluptious figure, I gave her my number. We have gotten together a number of times in hotel rooms. She is married but she and her husband are seperated and will probably get divorced. Thats why we meet in a hotel. I don't know when I've ever met a more horny able-bodied woman. I qualify her as able-bodied because she dos'nt come close to the intensity of sexual desire that I have found in some of the dis-abled women I've known. She is about 10 years older then me. She related to me that she had'nt had sex in the last seven years except when she masturbated. That was the main reason she was getting divorced. Her husband had lost all interest in sex.

I asked her why she picked me. She told me that she had had a fantasy for years of making love to a helpless man who looked real good and had alot of upper body definition. She said that when she saw me, She felt she could at last live out her fantasy. To help her along I really played the "crippled" role. I'd take off my braces and drag myself around the floor and up on to the bed without using my legs and it would drive her crazy. She liked to take off my braces and to put them back on me after we had sex and were getting ready to leave. She had told me that after meeting me that she fantacized getting some braces for herself and seeing what it would be like to have to use them. She asked me not to think poorly of her for those thoughts because she knew that I, being disabled, probably thought she was a little weird. I of course comforted her and told her that I felt that those thoughts were natural and that I could understand her curiosity after her having seen what I go through.

THE RANCH
By Ed Carlson

"Morning Hank."

"Morning Miss Josey." Hank replied.

"Are we all set to drive the herd up to the north range?" I asked.

"Just as soon as we get Dandy saddled and Cookie gets the rest of his stuff loaded. I'd like to pull out by nine."

"Why don't I ride that new paint that you broke last week?"

"Are you sure Miss Josey. He's still got a lot of spunk in him. Bucked George off yesterday."

"Good. It'll be another challenge for me. Go ahead and saddle him for me."

"OK. Don't say I didn't warn you." Hank said as he walked back to the coral.

I turned and walked back into the ranch house. I stopped at the door for a moment to allow my eyes to adjust to the dim light of large living room. In a moment I continued on up the stairs. I had packed most of the things I would be needing. I finished by putting a clean bra in the saddle bag. I was quite proud of myself for being able to pack a weeks worth of clothes in saddle bags.

I struggled with the straps the way I always do. I can do most things with these damn hooks, but sometimes I have trouble with straps and buckles. I finally won the small battle and slung the saddle bag over my shoulder. The weight of the saddle bag pressed down on my over the shoulder strap that held my left arm in place. It was part of a bilateral harness and identical to the right arm.

I admired myself in the mirror. I was wearing my tight blue jeans and my western boots complete with spurs that made my long legs look even longer. I had a tight western shirt that shown off my nicely developed breasts. The shinny steel hooks were showing from the cuffs of my shirt that were snapped around my prosthetic wrists. My blond hair was pulled back in a pony tail. I thought I really looked sharp.

With my saddle bags slung smartly over my shoulder, I walked out onto the balcony and pulled my door shut with my hook. I thought briefly how much easier things were once I had them install the lever hardware everywhere on the ranch. Doorknobs were a thing of the past here on J-Double-Hook ranch. I continued on down the stairs and then into the kitchen. Cookie was gone. I looked out the window and saw him putting the last of the supplies in the back of the old pickup.

"Mariah, lock up before you leave."

She answered from the other end of the house and I walked out the back door then down the steps. "Are you about ready?" I asked.

"That's the last of it. I'm set." Cookie replied.

"Good. I'll tell Hank. See you at the lunch stop." I said as I started for the corral.

They were just finishing putting the saddle on the paint when I got there.

"Is he ready?"

"The question is are you ready, Miss Josey." One of the wranglers said as he took my saddle bag and tied it to the saddle of the freshly broken paint horse.

"No time like the present. Hold his head." I said as I put a foot up into the stirrup. With a hook around the saddle horn,

274

I tried to pull myself up but couldn't get the leverage I needed . "Need a little boost." I said.

With my foot still in the stirrup, I gave a hop with the foot still on the ground. The wrangler caught my boot in midair and continued my upward movement. They were use to helping me. It was almost like it was part of their job. In fact it is part of their job. They all work for me and I pay them for what I want them to do. If I want to get on a horse then it's their job to see that I get on the horse.

I swung my leg over and was seated firmly in the saddle when I put my free foot in the stirrup. The wrangler held the colt's head a little longer to let him settle down and to be sure that I had the reigns grasped firmly in my hooks. As soon as he released the bridle, the young horse reared and then settled down as I spoke softly to him. He raced around the corral a couple of times and reared again when I pulled back on the reigns. He quickly settled down and it became apparent that he and I would become good friends. We walked around the corral a couple of times before I signaled for one of the boys to open the gate. The young paint remained calm as we walked slowly out of the corral. Hank and the rest of the crew followed as my new friend and I headed for the herd.

Hank joined me and we led the way as we started up the road. After we had gone a little way I let the young paint have his head. He increased his walk to a trot and eventually broke into a gallop. I let him go about a half mile before I reigned him in. Which was no easy task for a girl with two artificial arms that terminate in shinny steel hooks. Because my little arm stumps are so short, less than three inches, I have a difficult time getting much leverage. We waited for Hank and the rest of the hands to catch up.

"That young paint really likes to run." Hank observed as he rode up beside me.

"He's a spirited one all right." I replied as I worked at controlling the horse. With the rest of the hands trailing along we were soon at the herd.

Hank gathered the hands around and made their assignments. We would rotate positions every hour. Each of the hands knew what needed to be done. I started by riding point with Hank.

The rest of the hands moved into position as we began to bunch and move the herd northward. Leading the way and riding point is probably the best position to be on a cattle drive. That is if you know where you're going and what you're doing. This is my fifteenth drive. My first on was when I was ten. I got to ride with Cookie in the chuck wagon then.

Hank dropped back and I was left alone leading the herd. We came up over a bluff. The huge sky was magnificent. It was a deep blue with white billowy clouds. The prairie seemed to stretch indefinitely. The tall grass waved in the breeze like waves on the ocean. I remember seeing the ocean once. It was when I was three and just getting out of the hospital. I remember that I was wearing my new arms with the shinny steel hooks. My mind wandered as I continued to lead the herd slowly across the vast open spaces. Following the track that Cookie had made with the pickup. An old sickle bar hay mower lying in the middle of a field flashed back my memory to the accident so many years ago.

I was three at the time. I loved to watch the hands put up hay. Especially the way, with two of them working together, would pick up almost and entire shock of hay and pitch it onto the hay wagon. I loved to watch my father cut hay. I had been following along while my father cut the hay the sickle mower. A team of two white horses pulled the mowing machine. I was walking close behind when I stumbled over a rock and fell forward across the sickle bar. Instinctively I stuck my arms out to break my fall. I still clearly remember my father yelling 'whoa' just as the freshly sharpened sickle bar sliced both of my arms off almost right at the shoulder. I remember him yelling for help and seeing blood all over the freshly mown hay. My blood. I don't remember much after that. I barely remember being in Doc Nelson's office before they moved me to the hospital in the city. I remember my mom crying a lot as she sat by me in the hospital. I remember how much my arms hurt, or what was left of them. I remember how frustrated I was because I couldn't do things, I still am as far as that goes. I remember the look on my fathers face when he realized what had happened. He had a hard time being around me after that and soon left mom and me to run the ranch. I saw him a couple of times before he died. He asked my forgiveness on his death bed. It was a forgiveness that I never had to give because I had never held him responsible for my accident. After all it wasn't his fault I tripped. Mom's life wasn't much fun either, I guess. She raised me by herself, out here in the wide open spaces. She helped me get use to my new arms and always found the money to buy me new ones as I grew. Because I've always worn artificial arms, I'm really quite helpless with them off. I can't pick things up with my toes the way that some double arm amputees can. I use my teeth a little, but not much. I rely on these hooks a lot more than I like to admit. The kids at school started to tease me about my arms. I put a stop to that by hitting the bully along side the head with a hook. Mom died two years ago. I inherited the spread and changed the name. Kind of fitting I thought. Strange the way your mind wanders.

"Time to switch." Hank said as he rode up and snapped me back to the present. "How's that young paint doing?"

"He's doing fine. He's going to be a good horse."

"Why don't you put him through his paces and pick up strays." Hank said.

"OK." I said as I wheeled off to the side. I sure am lucky to have Hank. He knows what he's doing and because the hands all respect him they work hard for him.

The herd continued on by as I sat there on my new paint horse. When they had passed I fell in behind and began searching the little draws and pockets for strays. I found a couple and worked them back into the herd. I followed along behind and soon we were stopping the herd by the lake while we took a lunch break.

One of the wranglers tied my horse to Cookies truck for me and I swung down. It felt good to stretch. Soon Cookie had sandwiches and coffee served to everyone. As was our custom Hank and I were the last ones to get our food. As I sat there eating I felt as though someone was watching. I looked up to see one of our new wranglers looking at me. He quickly looked away when we made eye contact. I continued to look at him and smiled broadly at him when he turned back to me. He smiled back, shyly. I finished eating my lunch and had another cup of Cookies coffee. Then I got up I walked over to the wrangler. "How are doing?" I asked.

"Just fine Miss Josey. That grub sure tasted good."

"I noticed you staring at my hooks. Have you ever seen things like these up close before?"

"I'm awfully sorry about the staring mam." He stammered apologetically. "It's just that I've never seen a girl with a hook arm before, let alone two of them."

"Here take a good look." I said as I raised an arm and held the hook where he could watch as I opened and closed it. "These are manual hooks and operate by cables that I operate by pulling with my opposite shoulder. See."

"I wondered what made them work. You sure do use them good." He said, dumbfounded that I would be so brave as to show him my hooks.

"I should by now. I've been wearing arms like this for twenty two years now. Lost real arms when I was only three. These arms are really the only arms I ever remember using." I said as we walked over to the horses. "I'll need a boost up. Because I have only very short arm stubs I can't very much leverage."

"I'll be glad to help you Miss Josey." He said.

I put my foot in the stirrup and one hook around the saddle horn. I gave a hop and he caught my boot and continued my upward direction. I settled down in the saddle and he untied the new paint horse then handed me the reigns. I opened a hook and took them from him then let the hook close. "What's your name?" I asked.

"It's Ralph, Mam."

"Ralph, thanks for the boost. See you around."

He smiled and tipped his broad brimmed hat.

As I sat back in the saddle I could feel the beginning of my monthly occurrence. Something I had not prepared for. I wheeled the horse around and rode over to Hank who had just mounted up.

"Who's your new friend?" Hank asked

"Oh, Ralph was looking at my hooks so I gave him a little demonstration. How long has he been with us?"

"Two months now. I've had him mostly working line fence. That's why you haven't seen him around much."

"Is he a good worker?"

"He sure is. I wish all of my hands were that good. He's a bit on the shy side. I don't think he's been around girls that much."

"How old is he?"

"He just turned twenty one. Why the interest?"

"He just seemed like a nice young fellow. You know me always looking. Where do you want me?"

"Why don't you hang back and watch for strays until we get back away from the canyon here." Hank said.

"OK, then I need to go back to the ranch and pick up some things I forgot. I'll catch up in the morning." I replied.

"Let me send one of the boys back with you. There's no one back there."

"Thanks, but I'll be all right by myself."

I helped the wranglers get the herd moving. A couple of cows strayed from the herd and I was quickly able to get them back in line.

The herd was well out of the canyon when I dropped back to check out one of the little draws near the lake to see if any strays had ventured there. The new paint horse and I made a sweep of the canyon and determined that none of the strays had ventured in there. The canyon was deserted and none of the herd was in there. It was kind of an eerie place as the wind whistled through the sticker brush.

I decided to try and go up the steep side of the canyon rather than going back and all the way around. I urged the young paint horse up the steep side of the canyon wall. I had one hook clamped firmly around the saddle horn and the other holding the reigns. He had gone over halfway up when he hesitated. I urged him on with my spur. This was the first time he had been spurred and he reared, then lunged forward. His actions suppressed me. My feet came out of the stirrups and I began sliding backwards over his rear. As I slid the reigns tightened even more which made him rear again. This action had me hanging by my hook that was still clamped firmly to saddle horn. As my arm came up over my head I could feel the artificial arm coming out of the socket and separating from my little arm stub. My western shirt was becoming tighter around my neck as the arm pulled further. I began gasping for air as I struggled to get out of my predicament. Suddenly the snap buttons on my shirt began to pop and I slid further away from the arm that was completely clear the socket by this time, being held in proximity by the bilateral harness and the shirt. He jumped again. My shirt came off completely as did my other arm still attached to the bilateral harness. I fell to the steeply sloping ground. The horse turned and bolted down the canyon with my arms still attached to the saddle and flopping wildly around as he continued to run and buck. With no arms and unable to stop myself I began to tumble and roll down the steep canyon side. I rolled and tumbled for what seemed and eternity until I came to rest in a sticker bush.

I was dazed as I lie there. My stump-socks were snared by the bush and remained with the bush when I struggled to my feet. It felt strange to be standing all alone in only my bra with no prosthetic arms that were so much a part of me. The arms that were the first thing that I put on each morning and the arms that I removed as I was getting into bed. It felt almost as if I were naked. I started to walk back down the canyon toward the lake. I was amazed how much lighter I felt without the weight of the arms that I always wore and were so much a part of me.

I considered going back up the canyon wall now that I was on foot. I quickly dismissed the idea when I thought of slipping and rolling back down the hillside again. My way out had to be by backtracking to the end of the canyon down by the lake. I started my long walk. My spurs jingled with each step and I soon wish that I could be rid of them. After a good half hour of walking I finally made it back to the little lake. The afternoon sun beat down on me and the reflection in the lake made it even brighter. I could feel my untanned shoulders start to sunburn. Suddenly I was extremely thirsty and dying for a drink of water. I walked along the edge of the lake until I came to a spot where I thought I could get a drink. The grassy bank sloped steeply right to the waters edge. If I only had hands I could just reach down and scoop up several handful's of water and be on my way.

I lie down on my stomach close to the water with my feet up hill. I used the toes of my boots to propel me ahead slowly. My arm stubs are so short that they don't touch the ground when I lie on my breasts. I continued to inch myself slowly to the point where my face was out over the shallow water. I reached our and bent my face down in the water and took a good drink. I came up for air and went back for another. With my thirst quenched I tried to wiggle my way back up the hill. As I wiggled I only slid further down the bank until soon my breasts were in the water and stirring up the mud bottom. The more that I struggled the further I slid until I was soon having difficulty keeping my head above water. I screamed for help to no avail. My nearest assistance must have been at least ten miles away by now. I gave a large push forward with my boot and slid all the way into the water. I was able to get my feet under me and now thoroughly drenched, stand up. I must have been a site standing there in the shallows of the lake dripping wet with in muddy water, with no arms, in my bra, blue jeans and cowboy boots.

I took a couple of steps up the slippery grassy bank and slipped. I landed hard on my breasts with no arms to break my fall. As I tried to get up I slid back into the lake. I got to my feet and waded along the shallow water until the bank flattened out where the cattle had drunk. I slipped again. This time in the mud. I slipped several times as struggled to my feet. By the time I was able to get out and back to the trail I was thoroughly covered with mud. Mud that had less than a pleasant odor. With my boots full of water and my spurs jingling I started back down the trail for home.

I came to a large rock. The rock also had a sharp edge. I was able to work the straps of the spur on my right foot enough to make it fall off. I was equally successful with the left. I was also able to lie on my back to elevate my feet and drain the water out of my boots. With my tight blue jeans freshly wet I continued my hike. The warm afternoon sun and the ever present wind soon dried my clothing that was now thoroughly caked with mud. The trail worked it's way up from the lake and back up to the broader trail. I kept going and soon I was in an area where the herd apparently milled around a lot. By the tracks I couldn't determine which way the trail went. As I looked around I saw several trails going every which way from this point. There was no sign of the tracks that Cookies truck made. Becoming quite concerned I decided to started in the direction of what I believed to be the ranch house.

I had walked about an hour when all the time looking for a familiar landmark. I found none. What seemed to be such a simple task as gong back the way I came had turned into a nightmare. I was beginning to panic. I left the trail that I was following and struggled to the top of the hill. The view from the top of the hill was commanding. I felt much relieved when I spotted the ranch house a long way off in the distance. It was about ninety degrees from the direction that I had been traveling. Noting the sun's position securely in my mind, started down the rolling hills toward the house. High clouds were building. There would be no stars tonight.

The hike was long and I reached the ranch house complex quite a while after sundown. The twilight was about to turn to darkness when I walked up on the large verandah porch.

The motion sensor turned the light on. I instinctively tried to reach for the door handle with my nonexistent hook. I felt kind of silly when I realized what I had done. I stepped back and pushed the lever down with my boot. Nothing happened. Then I remember telling Mariah to lock up before she left. The key is kept over the door on the trim piece. Without arms there is no way that I could reach it. I had given Mariah the rest of the week off and she was going to town to visit her sister. The place was completely deserted and had a strange silence. I turned and started back down the stairs from the verandah. When I was half way down the light went out. I stumbled when I reached the bottom step. This time when I fell I was able to roll and break my fall.

I struggled to my feet and started for the barn. It was moon-less night and now with the high overcast, pitch black. I couldn't have seen my hand in front of my face even if I had one. After much wandering around in the dark, I finally found the barn. It was as dark inside as it was outside. We had never installed electricity in the barn or any yard lights. I managed to feel the wall with my right short arm stub. I found a horse stall and went inside. Luckily the stalls had all been cleaned and new bedding hay put down before the hands left to move the herd. My luck was still running when I brushed what I believed to be a horse blanket with my breasts. It smelled like one as I got my face close to it. Using a arm stub and my breasts I managed to locate the end. I used my teeth to pull it down to the floor of the stall. I got to my knees and using my teeth straightened the blanket out. I found what I believed to be the middle and wiggled under it for warmth during the night. I must have been more tired than I thought and fell right to sleep.

I awoke the next morning with sun streaming in the open barn door and shining on me. The warmth of the sun felt good after the cold of the high desert night. It took me a moment to figure out where I was. I thought for a moment and then did a full recall of the previous days adventure. I rolled over and got on my knees. The horse blanket slid off when I sat up and back on my heels. The crotch of my blue jeans was badly stained a bright crimson. I struggled to my feet and made my way outside into the bright morning sunlight.

I walked over to the house. I tried the front door again with no success of entry. I walked around to the back. The back door was secured as well. I walked around the house looking for a open window. The only one I found open was the window to my bedroom on the second floor. If only I had arms and hands I could climb up the lattice work that the roses climbed. Being almost completely armless it was out of the question. If only I was inside, I could put on my old arms and be able to manage. Being almost totally dependent on prosthetics to function is the pits.

I walked around the house again looking for some means of entry. I was in luck an old ladder was leaning up the against the side of the house. I was going up to the verandah roof. The same roof that was under my window. I hate high places and I'd never climbed a ladder before, but there is always a first time for every thing. I started slowly up the rickety old ladder by leaning way forward and resting my breasts on the wrungs. I was on the fifth wrung when it broke and I fell with one leg on each side of the fourth wrung. My inside leg had also wrapped around the lower wrung while my outside leg dangled free. I couldn't maneuver it to touch anything solid. I couldn't go up and I couldn't go down. I was stuck there on that ladder. If I had arms and hands, I simply could have pulled myself up, but being armless I was stuck there on the ladder.

I sat there contemplating my fate and having visions of buzzards circling the ranch house. I heard a rider coming. When the sound became louder I began to scream for help.

Ralph came running around the corner. "I heard you yelling and came as fast as I could Miss Josey."

"Oh Ralph, thank god it's you. Please help me down."

He walked up three wrungs of the ladder and put his arm around my waist. He Lifted me clear of the ladder wrung and then carried me down unceremoniously under his arm. He gently put me on the ground and said. "Are you all right, Mam?"

"I'm fine now that you're here. Why did you come back?"

"The night rider spotted your paint horse running around without you. Hank sent me back to see if you were in trouble."

"You're a godsend. Remind me to thank him for sending you. I had visions of staying that way until the whole bunch of you came back. I lost my artificial arms when I fell off the horse, I'm going to need your help before we ride back to the herd." I said as we started to walk back around the house. We walked up on the big verandah porch and I said. "The key to the door is up there on the trim. I need you to unlock the door."

He reached up and retrieved the key. With a quick twist of the wrist we were inside. I had him follow me inside.

"This is the first time I've been in the big house." He said.

"Use this phone. Call the cell phone in Cookie's truck. The number is right there. Tell that I'm OK and that your at the ranch house with me. Also tell them that we should catch up by nightfall"

He picked up the phone and made the call. The way he talked when Cookie answered reminded me of an old movie where the fellow was shouting into phone. He finished the call and hung up.

"Cookie said that they caught your horse. It had only one of your hook arms on the saddle. They also have your saddle bags."

"Good. Please follow me Out back. I need your help some more." I said as I led the way to the back porch and had him unlock the back door. We went our by the hose bib.

"Turn the water on and hose the mud off of me."

He turned the water on and began hosing me off. The water in the hose was warm at first and I let out a scream when it turned cold. He immediately quit spraying me when I let out the scream.

"That's OK Ralph keep going. I'll get use to it."

"You startled me when you screamed Mam."

"The water just turned cold keep going."

He reluctantly did as he was instructed. He looked like he could almost feel how cold the well water was that he was spraying me with.

"That was real cleaver of you Mam. Getting yourself all covered with mud that way."

"What do you mean Ralph?"

"The way you covered yourself with mud like that to keep from getting sunburn. I don't think I would have thought to do it that way."

"Well the mud wasn't my idea. It happened while I was trying to get out of the lake. OK that's good." I said when he had gotten most of the mud off my upper body. "I need to take a shower badly. Mariah usually helps me but she's not here. You'll have to do it."

"I don't know if I can Mam. I've never seen a girl naked except in a magazine."

"Ralph, relax I'll tell you what to do. Because I haven't had arms since I was only three, people have always helped me baths and showers. It will be OK."

"Well all right Mam. What do I do first."

"Lets start by pulling my boots off." I said as I sat on the bench and raised a leg.

He pulled my right, then my left boot off before he removed my socks.

"Bra is next." I said as I stood up and turned away from him. "Undo the snap." I felt his hands tugging at the back strap. "Just push the little hooks together." Soon the bra strap was loose. I turned to face him. "Now take the bra off."

His face turned beet red when he removed my bra and stared at my well developed breasts with my very erect nipples.

"Do you like what you see?" I teased.

Ralph's face got even redder at my comment. "Y.. y.. yes Mam."

"Good, you'll have a chance to touch them when I'm in the shower. Now undo my blue jeans and take them off."

He gingerly reached down and undid the top button and unzipped my blue jeans. He then slid them down around my knees. I know that he noticed the crimson color of the crotch, but didn't say anything. I sat on the bench. I held up a foot and he pulled my right pant leg off. I held up my other foot and he removed them completely and just stood there holding them.

"Just throw them over there." I instructed and pointed with my chin as I stood up. "OK. Now my underwear."

He carefully reached over and pulled my soaked panties down around my ankles. I stepped out of them and he picked them up. Again he just stood there, holding the panties without comment.

"Just throw them on top of the blue jeans."

He threw the panties on the blue jeans and just stood there looking like he wanted to run away screaming.

"Come one follow me." I said as I walked Back into the house. He followed me. I had him lock the back door again. He followed me into the front entry, up the stairs and into my bedroom. He paused when I went into my bathroom.

"Were not done yet. You need to wash me up. It's OK. Come on in here."

He sheepishly walked into the bathroom where I stood totally nude.

"Turn on the water in the shower, please. I'll get in and then you rinse me down with the hand shower head."

I stepped in the shower stall and he reached in and got the hand shower head then carefully began to wet me down. His face turned even redder as I spread my legs so that he could rinse my most private parts.

"OK now put the shower head in the holder. Good. Now get a washcloth and soap and lather me up."

He dutifully did as he was instructed. I held out my little arm stubs for him to do first and then told him to start at my shoulders and work down. He followed my instructions. I bent backward and stuck out my breasts further when it was time for him to wash them. I could tell by the big grin on his face that he was enjoying his task.

"Well do you like touching them?"

"I sure do Mam. I ain't never touched a woman's breast before. They are a lot firmer than I thought a breast might be."

"All women's breasts are a different. Mine are probably firmer than most."

He didn't say any thing as he continued to wash my body. He appeared to be very intent on his work.

I spread my legs as he began washing my pubic hair. I jumped a little when he hit my spot. His hand was cupped around my crotch when I said. "Do you like touching that."

He didn't say anything at first but the pressure he was applying increased. "I never imagined that you would want me to touch you there Mam."

"I enjoy your gentle touch. Have you ever thought about having sex with me?"

"Oh no Mam! I wouldn't think of such a thing. No Mam."

"What's the matter. Don't you like girls?"

"Oh Mam, I do like girls. It...it...it's just that your the boss Mam."

"OK I won't embarrass you any more. Please finish washing me and then rinse again."

He quickly finished and rinsed me off again.

"OK now wash my hair please. Undo the rubber band. The shampoo is on the shelf beside you."

He removed the rubber band. I shook my head and my hair fell down around my shoulders. He wet it down then lathered it up with the shampoo. He rinsed it and I had him lather it a second time. He thoroughly rinsed it when he was finished.

"Now turn off the water and dry me off please."

He reached in and turned off the water. I stepped out on the bath mat and he began to gently dry me off with a big fluffy towel. I really did enjoy his touch. I had him dry and comb my hair. When he finished I walked into the bedroom. Ralph followed.

"Ralph. In the top drawer there is a clean bra. Could you please put it on me?"

He opened the drawer and took one out. "This one Mam."

"That will do just fine. Now put the cups under my breasts and the straps over my shoulders. Good now fasten the strap in the back when I turn around."

He did as he was instructed and I was wearing a clean bra. It felt good to have clean clothing next to my body after my ordeal with the hillside and the lake.

"OK were doing just fine." I said as I turned to face him. His face reddened when I gave him a peck on the cheek. "Now also in the top drawer are stump socks. Here on this end."

He reached in and pulled out one of the stump socks that I wear.

"Now put one end around this arm. Good. Now flatten out the cloth across my back and put the other end over my other arm. Good." I said as I stretched and moved to get the stump socks into just the right position. "Now you're going to help me put on some arms."

"OK Mam. What do I do?"

"Get the arms down from the shelf there. These are my old ones. The ones that I lost are only two months old. Good. Lay them on the bed. OK now turn them over so the straps are on top. Give the right one a full twist so that the straps aren't twisted. Great. Now grab each arm by the upper part. Good. Now pick them up and slide the left one down my left arm when I lift it up. Good. Now the right one. Were doing just fine. Now help me lower them forward as I let my arms down. Fine. Now please straighten out the straps. Good going we did it."

I flexed my shoulders and both hooks opened and closed properly.

"Good job. Ralph, thank you so much." I said as I rewarded him with a kiss. As shy as he was he didn't kiss me back much.

"Your... your...your welcome Mam." He stammered.

"I can finish dressing now. Could you saddle Dandy for me please. I think he's is the south pasture."

"OK Mam. Be glad to." He said before he turned and walked quickly out the door like a man that had just been freed from prison.

I went in the bathroom and attended to my monthly occurrence. The cold steel of my hooks touching my most private parts is one thing that has always seemed strange.

With the task accomplished, I walked backing to the bedroom. I put on panties and clean socks. I got a clean pair of blue jeans out of the drawer and put them up but I didn't fasten them. I got out a clean western shirt and put it on. As always I struggled with the snaps and my hooks. I finally got the front snaps done. I heard Ralph come back into the house as I was pulling on my boots.

"Dandy's all saddled up."

"Ralph, could you come up and help me a minute, please."

I heard him coming up the stairs.

"Yes, Miss Josey?"

I held my arms out and he snapped the cuff buttons around my prosthetic wrists.

"Could you please do my top button on my jeans?"

He reached down and gently buttoned the top button and zipped up my blue jeans.

I put my arms around him and pulled him close. I gave him a passionate kiss. This time he kissed me back. I wanted him right then but knew it was not the time. When the kiss broke off I said, "That's for saving me and all of your help."

"Your welcome. I sure wasn't expecting a reward like that."

"I'll be down in a minute."

He turned and left the bedroom. I grabbed a small purse size duffel and put in some feminine products and was able to zip it up. It felt great to have arms and hooks on again.

I took the small duffel and went down stairs. We walked out on the verandah. I had Ralph lock the door and put the key

293

on top of the trim piece. We walked out to the hitching post. I put one foot up in the stirrup of Dandy's saddle and one hook around the saddle horn. "I'm going to need a boost." I said. I gave a hop. Ralph caught my boot in mid air and continued my momentum. I put my other foot in the stirrup. I opened my hook and Ralph smiled up at me as he put the reigns in it.

He got on his horse and we started out toward the herd. We gave the horses their head and soon they were going at a moderate gallop.

I reigned up when we could see the dust cloud of the herd ahead. We dismounted and sat by the little stream while the horses drank. As we sat there we kissed a couple of more times. This time he touched my breasts.

When the horses were rested he helped me remount. He mounted and was sitting beside me. I stuck our a hook and he held it in his hand.

"Ralph, I have a favor to ask."

"Sure Miss Josey what is it?"

"I'd like to keep what has happened today our little secret. OK."

"OK. I can keep a secret."

"I just don't want the whole crew looking at me and wishing they could give me a bath too. If you know what I mean."

"OH yes. I know how the hands do talk. My lips are sealed."

"I knew I could count on you." I said. "I would like to go out with you on a date sometime."

"That would be fine with me too, Mam." He said as we gave each other a wink and started walking the horses slowly toward the herd, still holding on to my hook just as the afternoon sun began to set.

A SAILOR'S HOMECOMING
By J. N. Deere

I really began to believe that this cruise would never end. We had left Norfolk in July, and the six months of deployment that had become so routine for me in the past, now seemed like an eternity. My wife Rhonda, had seemed to handle the separation well up to about two and a half months ago. Letters came for me each day there was mail call, and the e-mail to the ship flowed like water. Then suddenly it fizzled out, and I only received short messages and hardly any letter mail. I became worried, scared is more the word, as I had never loved anyone like I loved Rhonda. I called the house for almost three weeks straight, and when anyone answered the phone at all, it was her Mom. When I would speak to her and ask for Rhonda, all I would get for response was "John, she is not in right now, and I 'm not sure when she will be home." Being the typical sailor, I began to think that maybe this Navy life was destroying my marriage and that the love of my life had sought refuge in the arms of another.

Then we pulled into Rota, Spain and I called home and she finally answered the phone. I was so thankful to hear her wonderful voice, but something was different. Her voice and manner on the phone was not the warm, sexy and reassuring personality I was used to. I would ask her repeatedly if everything was OK, but all I would get in response was "Yeah" and that was all. All of the bells and whistles in the back of my mind were going off as loud as the aircraft crash alarm on the Ship I was riding. I knew there was something was seriously wrong at home, and I was helpless to do anything about it until I returned. My nights became sleepless and my mind was doing mach 3. I really felt like my whole world was caving in on me.

The night before a navy ship returns from a six-month deployment is referred to as "Channel Fever." I had no interest in the festivities up on the ship, I just stayed on my Landing Craft in my stateroom, and packed. I had a thousand thoughts running at a hundred miles per hour through my mind. Would she be there at the Unit when I pulled in? Would there even be a home for me to go home to? Would she meet me at the pier with another man? Who knew? I damn sure didn't.

0515 the well-deck of the ship is flooded and the four Landing Craft from my detachment came alive one last time as we backed out of mother and into the darkness. Thirty-five minutes away in the silence of the bay was the entrance to Little Creek Harbor and ten minutes beyond that was the unit piers where our families were anxiously awaiting our return. I put my Dress Blues on and took the con from my Chief. He went below to change, and all I could think of was "Will she be on the pier, or not?" We rounded the bend to the unit and we could see the big tent that our unit had set up as reception area for us. All of the families were standing as close to the piers as possible, trying to get a glimpse of their husband or son. I grabbed the binoculars and began to search the parking lot for my wife's red Intrepid. My heart sank when I failed to spot it. Just as I started to drop my spyglasses, I caught sight of my mother-in-law. "This is not a good sign" I thought out loud. After an eternity we finally got tied up and shut down. I immediately climbed on to the pier and quickly made my way through the crowd to my wife's mother. She grabbed me tightly and hugged me, tears were streaming down her cheeks as she said " I know you must be confused but Rhonda is here." "Why isn't she standing here with you!" I demanded. I spotted my Mother-in-law's van parked across the compound, and stepped quickly toward it. My Mother-in-law was almost running to keep up with my four-foot stride, saying "John there is something you must know." I paid her no heed as I finally saw the lovely face of my Rhonda. She was smiling at me through the windshield, but as I approached the passenger side door, I could see her always perfect makeup was tear stained.

I pulled the passenger door open and immediately took her in my arms and held her close to me as she held me back. My eyes were shut as I held her to me and repeated over and over again "I love you and I missed you!" Rhonda finally gained her composure and said softly "Are you sure you can love me like this, as a cripple." "A cripple?" I said confused and stunned. Her eyes turned from mine and looked toward the floor. Mine followed and then I realized what she was referring to. It took a second to register that only her left leg was showing from the hem of her lovely blue skirt, and there was only an empty space where her right leg used to be. I held her close once more and told her again that I loved her and that she was not a cripple to me, nor would she ever be.

My heart was pounding so hard that I thought I was going to have a heart attack right there. I had always found one-legged women attractive and collected quite a menagerie of devotee material while deployed, but never in a million years did I ever imagine that my lovely Rhonda would ever become an amputee. I again reaffirmed my love for her in front of my Mother-in-law, who was in tears saying "She was so sure you were going to come home and see her condition that you would immediately leave her." I took my Mother-in-law in my arms and hugged her and kissed her also saying " I couldn't love her any less, only more."

The ride home was kind of quiet. Rhonda and I sat in the back seat of the van and just held each other. I couldn't help wanting to steal glances at her beautiful nylon-clad left leg. She had worn my favorite blue skirt with the slit up the left side, and the white silk blouse I had sent her from France. She was wearing dark taupe nylons, I wasn't sure if it was a garter stocking, or tailored pantyhose, but it didn't matter to me she looked awesome! On her sexy petite foot, was a three-inch pump with a bow at the back of the shoe. We finally pulled up to our house in the country and my Mother-in-law parked along the front walk. I was the first out of the van, and held out my arms to help my lovely wife from the vehicle. Rhonda reached down to the floor and retrieved a pair of what appeared to be custom-made rosewood underarm crutches and handed them to me. They were Very light in my hands, and beautifully crafted, with soft leather saddles and brass fittings. Rhonda gracefully slid from her seat, and carefully placed her high-heeled foot on the drive and stood. I stand six feet six inches flat foot, and Rhonda is five foot eleven inches without her heels, but with this three-inch heel, she was an impressive six foot two. She reached for her crutches and I gently handed them to her. She mounted them and looked up into my eyes and said " So what do you think of your one-legged wife?" I looked deep into her eyes and said "I think she is absolutely the most beautiful woman I have ever beheld." I saw a tear form in the corner of her eye as she smiled at me and said "God I am sure glad you are home, these past two and a half months have been hell for me."

I began to unload my gear from the van while Rhonda and her mom talked on the walkway. Rhonda kissed her mom and said she would call her later. My Mother-in-law came over and kissed and hugged me, then climbed into her van and drove away. My eyes were riveted on her as I watched her crutch down the walk to our front steps. I almost drooled at the way her sexy behind swayed gently as she swung her crutches forward and then stepped through with her left leg. It was some of the most graceful crutch walking I have ever witnessed. She carefully mounted the front steps, her high-heeled foot first, then her crutches. When she reached the porch, she turned and looked to me as if seeking approval , and all I could do was smile, and make sure that my eyes showed love and support.

She waited as I climbed the stairs with my sea bag, and then I gently set it down, and scooped her up in my arms, crutches and all and opened the door and carried her across the threshold just like newly weds. I gently set her down and allowed her to regain her balance and then took her in my arms and kissed her deeply, our tongues wrestling for position, as the six long months of sexual abstinence began to surface as a stiff, throbbing erection. I felt her strong hands begin to undo the13 buttons of my dress blue uniform pants. I wanted to rub her sexy ass, but I was holding her up while she was undoing my pants and freeing my throbbing organ. Finally I could take no more, and locked the front door, and carried her upstairs leaving my pants and her crutches at the door. It was now her turn, She was breathing heavily, and I was working my way

300

to her skirt zipper when she stopped me and said " You need to see me now for what I am before we go any further." She kicked off her pump, and hopped to the bathroom and closed the door. Two minutes later she emerged wearing an elegant white bustier with a long, dark taupe reinforced heel and toe stocking on her left leg and a tailored stocking on her short but full stump. Rhonda had always worn a garter belt and stockings since we met and only on occasion pantyhose, and those only when her outfit absolutely warranted it. She was now using a pair of well-polished aluminum forearm crutches and was wearing a short-heeled bedroom slipper that I had bought her from Frederick's a long time ago. She looked incredible to say the least, and I told her so in no uncertain terms. She crutched up to me as I sat on the edge of our king size bed, her hot sex only inches from my nose, and said, "What do you think?" I was speechless. Her stump was very short, only about seven inches, and all I could do was take it's little bulk into my hands and kiss it. I could feel her tears of joy drip on the back of my neck as I planted a series of kisses across the scar line that ran like a smile across the bottom of what remained her right leg.

She hopped back and laid her crutches on the floor, and then hopped to the edge of the bed and sat down beside me. She looked deeply into my eyes and said, " I have wanted you so bad since you left and since the accident I was sure you would reject me like I was some kind of freak." "Sweetheart", I said, "I could never reject you, and you definitely are not a freak, in fact you are more beautiful now than ever before!" "Are you sure you will not be embarrassed to go places with me since I will have use crutches for the rest of my life?" she asked. "Of course not sweetness, in fact I would be honored to be seen anywhere and at anytime with you, because you are the love of my life, my friend and above all my wife."

I was horny as hell, but I had to know what happened, so I took her hand into mine, and said "Please tell me sweetheart what happened to your leg". She stared at me for a brief second and took a deep breath as if trying to muster the courage to raise a painful memory and share it in the easiest way possible. Finally she said very softly "Three months ago while you were off of the coast of Bosnia, I went out with Beverly and Amy for dinner. I thought it would just be a fun night out, little did I know that it would change all of our lives forever. I had a couple of glasses of wine, and Amy was feeling pretty tipsy, so I let Bev drive our car home. We had just crossed the Ware River Bridge, and we were approaching the wye at Hartfield, when suddenly Bev slumped in the driver's seat and we careened out of control and into the path of an oncoming pickup. The last thing I remember was Amy screaming from the back seat." I could tell this was almost unbearable for her and the tears were forming in the corners of her eyes, as she reached for a tissue. I held her hand tighter as she continued. "The next thing I remember is waking up in a hospital room, with my mom beside my bed holding my hand and looking as if she hadn't slept in a week. My whole body felt like a lead weight had been dropped on me and I was sore from head to toe. My lower body was extremely sore, and my right leg felt like somebody was trying to burn it in half with a torch. My mom kept saying, "Everything is going to be fine" until she began to sound like a broken record.

Finally the doctor came in to the room, picked up my chart and made a few notes. She sat down on the edge of the bed and with a calm voice asked, "How are you feeling?" "Sore is an understatement, but if I could just put out this fire in my right foot, I wouldn't feel all that bad" I said. "Rhonda" the doctor said, " I did everything I could to save your right leg. But when the truck collided with your car, it crushed the bones to just fragments and you were on the verge of bleeding to death." "If we didn't amputate your right leg immediately you would have died right there in the emergency room." "I refused to believe her", Rhonda said. I knew my leg was there, it just hurt like hell. "No Rhonda," the doctor said, the compassion in her eyes and tone of voice told me this was real, "The burning sensation in what remains of your right leg is known as phantom pain." She went on to say that after the muscle groups began to heal the pain would ease, but I wasn't really listening. "John, my mind was spinning, all I could think of was that I was now a woman with only one leg. No longer a complete woman, the complete, beautiful two-legged woman you married. I was now a one-legged cripple who would never be able to wear a pair of nylons for you, wear two high-heels for you, or go dancing with you." " John, I was so devastated", she said. And to add to that the doctor told me since my injuries were so severe, they had to amputate high up my thigh and I would probably have to use crutches the rest of my life because I would not have enough residual limb to propel a prosthesis.

I finally gathered up the courage to look under the covers and all I saw was a small bandaged lump where my right leg used to be. I knew right then and there for sure that when you discovered what had happened John, you would leave me. How could I blame you? Who would want to be married to an incomplete woman. I once again took Rhonda in my arms, held her close and assured her that nothing could be further from the truth. She wept softly for a moment and then continued. "Mom stayed at the house, and hoped to catch your calls, and I told her specifically not to tell you about any of this, because I couldn't handle anything else especially the possibility of losing us.

Finally I was released from the hospital, and Mom brought me home. I was so depressed when you did call I couldn't construct a clear sentence. Each time I would write or attempt to e-mail you, my missing leg kept coming out on paper, so I didn't write much and prayed for nights on end that you would still love me when you returned. "I was so scared that I was losing you Rhonda, when the mail stopped, and only receiving short, strange e-mail's." "Frankly honey I felt like I was losing my mind", I gently said. " I didn't want to mislead you John, but I just didn't know how to tell you that I only had one leg." "I was so afraid of your reaction." I took her other hand, and looked deep into her eyes once again, and told her that she had nothing to fear. She softly said "John, make love to me." I was more than ready to oblige, and slid to the center of our king-size bed, where we began to slowly explore each other's bodies. We broke into a long, deep French kiss, my hands were carressing her full breasts through the silky material of her bustier. Her hands had moved down to my aching dick, and the strong but soft grip of her fingers around me, was pure heaven. As her breathing became more rapid, she whispered, "I want to feel your tongue inside of me!" I was glad to oblige. I kissed my way down between her breasts, leaving little baby kisses all the way to the bottom hem of her bustier. Then I slowly dragged my tongue along her garter straps kissing all along the tops of her nylons. I could smell her womanly scent as I kissed every inch of her lovely little stump. "Oh god, your lips feel so good on my stump!", She said. " I have got to feel your tongue in my pussy. Please honey, I am so hot!" Rhonda's white, silk panties were completely soaked as I pushed them aside and began to lick at her steaming love nest. She was almost completely shaved down there and my tongue immediately found her clit and began to lick it like there was no tomorrow. She pulled her left leg back almost to her head, and her stump was shaking uncontrollably as she rocked her hips in time to my roving tongue. Suddenly her breathing stopped, her back arched, and as she cried out in orgasm, she grabbed my head pulled it further into her love mound. I continued to lick her until her breathing returned to normal. She guided my face back to hers and kissed me saying, "I have needed that for so long. Now it is you turn, and I want to feel you inside of me!" "I want to get on top of you John", she said. So I rolled onto my back as she maneuvered herself on her hands and one knee to position her pussy over my rock-hard cock. She swung her stump over my waist, and I almost shredded her panties taking them off of her waist. I placed my hands on her waist to support her as she grabbed my manhood, and guided it slowly into her hot, wet pussy. As she lowered herself onto me, and placed her hands on the bed to maintain balance, I once again began to massage her nylon encased stump. "Mmmmmmmmmm, honey, I love the way you are touching my stump", She moaned. "Does my stump turn you on baby?" Rhonda didn't even have to move, because as she said those words, my balls went so tight, I thought they were in a vise and pumped a load of hot cum into her that seemed to last for ever. She also came again and collapsed onto me in a heap of hot sweaty bodies.

We must have dozed off to sleep because the next thing we knew it was late afternoon. Rhonda was still asleep in my arms when I woke up. I gently kissed her forehead, and her beautiful green eyes opened. "I love you", I said. "I love you too", Rhonda said. It was definitely shower time, and Rhonda stood up from the bed, balanced on her one leg, and asked me to grab her crutches. I gladly did so and followed her to the bathroom. Watching her on crutches had to be probably the most erotic experience of my life. She glanced over her shoulder as we made our way to the walk-in closet, and I smiled back at her and said, "That has got to be the sexiest walk I have ever seen in all my life!" "You think so huh?!", she grinned back. "Do you think you will be able to adjust to me having to use crutches for the rest of my life?" Rhonda asked. I stepped up to her and kissed her gently on the lips and said, "I already have."

After a long shower and helping my wife dry off, I suggested we go out for a bite to eat. "How about the Blue fin", I suggested. "Sounds great to me", she replied. "What should I wear", she asked. "Surprise me", I said. She beckoned me to join her in the closet. I came into our walk-in dressing area and she said "You can help me pick out something." She pointed toward a dressing stool, and said, "Please be seated, sir." Rhonda placed her crutches against the wall, and took a short hop to her hutch and opened the drawer. Smiling at me she said, "Our first display this evening sir is hosiery." She pulled out a pair of Hanes Silk Reflections Silver Smoke Pantyhose with Reinforced Toes and Control Top. She hopped over to the stool and sat down beside me. I have always been turned on watching Rhonda slide on a pair of nylons, and this time was no exception. "We amputee ladies have special ways of managing our hosiery selections, sir", she said. Rhonda was

305

smiling at my growing erection as she gathered the sheer leg of the pantyhose and inserted her foot. She paused and adjusted the reinforced toe, so it was even across her red-painted toenails. Rhonda then gently tugged the hose up her long, left leg, raising her sexy foot close enough for me kiss. She put her foot on the floor, stood and balanced on her single leg. She continued to pull the glimmering nylon up her left thigh until it was slightly above her right stump. "I will now demonstrate how an amputee woman should properly manage the remaining leg of her pantyhose." She carefully slid her hand through the right leg of the pantyhose until she reached the toe. She gently pulled the leg back through itself, until a small pouch that was slightly smaller than her stump hung from the panty portion of the hose. Rhonda then carefully slid the nylon pouch over her stump and then finished pulling the panty over her beautiful, naked bottom. I almost came right on the spot. She smiled again and said, "What do you think, sir?" All I could say was "Incredible!" She made some adjustments to the remaining leg of the pantyhose, so it would ride up the back of her stump in the panty, then hopped to her dress rack and took down a gray, pin-striped skirt and jacket combo. I nodded approvingly as she put her luscious 36d's into a lacy black bra, and then into a black silk blouse. All of this was done while she was perfectly balanced on her left leg. Rhonda took the skirt and hopped back to the stool where I was still sitting. She sat down again, and took my rock-hard penis and stroked it slowly saying, "We will just have to do something with this later won't we?" I could only nod in agreement. She slid into the skirt and made the comment that this was one of the things she had to get used to, and that was sitting down to get dressed. She took out a 2½ inch patent leather pump and slid her pretty foot into it. She stood and grabbed her rosewood underarm crutches and pirouetted in front of me saying "What do you think, babe?" I stood and walked over to her and kissed her gently saying "You are an absolute goddess!" "Great, I'm glad you like it, now get dressed so we can eat, I'm starving."

I finally got dressed and we headed for the garage. Rhonda grabbed the door before I could reach it and stopped me saying, "I guess you have figured out that our car was destroyed in the accident, but Beverly's mom and Dad bought us a new one, take a look." When I opened the door that led to the garage sitting next to my Dodge truck was a new 2000 Lincoln Towncar. All I could say was "Wow!" Beyond that, I was pretty much speechless. Rhonda crutched to the passenger side, and I followed to get the door for her. She turned around and sat down on the seat, then neatly stowed her crutches behind our seat in the back. She then lifted her leg and turned in the seat as I closed the door.

We began to catch up on the six months of news as we drove to the restaurant. Not much had happened prior to the accident, but the aftermath of that night was a delicate subject and I approached it as such. "What happened to Amy and Bev?" I asked. There was a long pause and Rhonda stared out the window. She finally turned back to me and softly said "Beverly died at the hospital the night of the accident of massive head and internal injuries. Amy was pinned in the back seat of the car for over 30 minutes as the fire and rescue crews worked to extricate her. I was flown off on the Nightingale, and a second unit was brought in for Amy. Her left arm was crushed between the shell of the car and the front seat. She was flown to Norfolk, and I was flown to Richmond. Her left arm was amputated through the shoulder two hours after she arrived at the hospital. Rhonda held my hand tightly as she shared the events of that awful night with me. I held hers right back in support of the tremendous effort it was taking to express those thoughts. I told her again I was glad she was ok that I loved with my whole heart and soul, and that I would be by her side for all eternity to come. She then leaned over and kissed me saying, "I am so glad, because I don't know what I would have done if you had said otherwise."

We arrived at the Blue Fin Restaurant, and parked in the handicapped area. I immediately went to the passenger side of the car and opened the door for Rhonda. She swung around in the seat and as she did so, she gave me a real show of her gorgeous nylon-clad leg and stump. Her skirt had ridden up rather high, and she caught me staring at her. She grinned and said, "Do you like the view, sailor?" I just smiled and took her crutches from the back seat, and offered her my hand. She took it and pulled herself up to a standing position and took a few tentative hops to get her balance. She took her crutches and mounted them. Rhonda knew exactly what I was thinking, and as I followed her to the door of the restaurant, she once again gave me an awesome display of crutch walking. I held the door for her and she swung through. When we passed through the second door into the lobby, the whole place came to a stop, and we immediately became the center of attention. As we proceeded to the hostess, the conversation and surroundings returned to normal. As we sat waiting for our table Rhonda turned to me and whispered, "I guess I will never truly get used to being stared at, or being the topic of conversation, but as long as I have you by my side John, nothing could bother me." I leaned over and kissed her and told her once more that I would never leave her.

After a romantic, candlelit dinner we headed for home. Rhonda was sitting in the middle cuddled next to me, holding my hand and showing lots of nylon-clad leg. She would also wiggle her little stump under her skirt, and before long her skirt was riding high on her thighs. "Take me home and make love to me, sailor," she whispered in my ear. We couldn't get home fast enough. During the whole trip, she was rubbing my crotch, and I was still hard from the little fashion show earlier at the house. By the time we pulled into the garage, my dick was hard enough to cut steel. I quickly exited the car, and helped Rhonda out, and before I knew it she was flying on her crutches into the house. She was calling out teasingly, "Come and catch me sailor boy". Man, she was quick on those crutches. By the time I caught her, she was halfway up the stairs to our room. I slipped up behind her and as she mounted each step, I slid my hand up her skirt and gently caressed her nylon-clad stump. As I rubbed her little nub, I could feel the dampness in her pantyhose crotch. "No fair", she said. "I have to use both my hands to climb the stairs, and yours are busy up my skirt bud", she commented teasingly.

I followed her into our vanity area, where she quickly turned. I took her into my arms and her crutches clattered to the floor. We fell into a deep passionate kiss. Rhonda was undoing my zipper in an attempt to free my stiff rod as I was working the clasp and zipper to her skirt. My pants and her skirt fell almost at the same time. We were still kissing deeply as I was rubbing her nylon encased crotch, and she was stroking my manhood. She broke the kiss saying, "I want you to take me from behind right here like we used to". This was always one of my favorite sexual positions, but I was always concerned with my lover's satisfaction, so I never forced this position on her. Rhonda turned around and placed both hands on the vanity for support. I was rubbing her nylon-clad bottom when she said, "Pull my pantyhose down and just fuck me with your big dick!" I carefully slid down her hose until they just cleared the tip of her stump, she lifted the little bulk up as if she were resting an imaginary foot on the vanity counter and I could see the wetness glistening between her leg and stump. I grabbed my prick, and began to rub it in the moistness of her labia, as she moaned, "Stop teasing me with it and give it to me, PLEASE"! I pressed my way into her tight cunt and as I did so, she cried out in orgasm. "Just fuck me, John, fill me full please!" I couldn't hold back and after a few short, tentative strokes, I exploded deep inside her filling her to overflowing with my love juices. As I came, Rhonda climaxed a second time, hopping on her left foot with her stump waving helplessly in the air, as I held on to her voluptuous hips. We finally regained our breathing control, and I prepared a warm washcloth, and helped my darling wife clean up. We finished undressing and I carried her in my arms to our bed, where I gently laid her down and crawled in beside her. I reached over and kissed her sweet lips once more and took her into my arms. "I Love you,

John and I am so glad you are home and accept for who I am now. I can't imagine my life without you." She said. I looked into her beautiful green eyes and replied, "I love you Rhonda with my whole heart and soul, and nothing will ever keep us apart". She laid her head upon my chest and was soon fast asleep. I laid in the darkness with my beautiful one-legged wife in my arms and realized this was the best homecoming ever.

THE ZIGGURAT

By R. Kalbfuss

Fate is so strange. I constantly run into people I knew in high school or college. I had gone to Middletown High in the suburbs of New York City. The students were typically suburban freshly scrubbed kids. We never got into trouble. The kids always went to college and we quickly lost touch with our classmates.

I had always had an interest in history which ultimately led to law school. It was spring and I had just graduated from law school and landed the "first big job," with a big New York City law firm.. To celebrate my new job I went out on the town to go pub crawling with a couple of my new associates.

We went to a well known bar in the east village called the Ziggarat. It was named for a planted area near the door that had really exotic plants, and it was beautifully lighted. There were a lot of bikers in the bar but this was not a "Hells Angels" hang-out so we didn't feel that we were invading anybody's terri☐tory or turf. By now we were pretty sloshed, but I could still walk or stagger a little. Then, I al☐most instantly sobered up. . .

The bar maid was one of the most unusual people I had seen in the East Village. She was extremely slender, with small breasts. She was wearing a lycra body suit that magni☐fied every glistening curve. She had beautiful long straight black hair, and beautiful white alabaster complexion, very little of which you could see because of the almost solid tattoo coverage.. But then it was all marred by mis☐sing teeth. There were extensive "biker" tat☐toos. She was missing all of the index finger, middle finger and ring finger on her left hand. I watched her as she moved back and forth behind the bar, and I noticed that she had a strange stiff walk. As I looked down, to my sorrow, I noticed a peg leg. She was a 25 year old "hag." I had never seen anybody in such bad shape at such a young age. Then as she lisped and slurred her words, I recognized her voice--I KNEW HER! She was one of my classmates from Middletown High. It was Marilyn!

"Hey Marilyn! I haven't seen you since high school--It's me Jeff. We ought to get toge☐ther sometime and we'll tell each other of the 7-year plagues. She laughed,

"My god Jeff! I haven't sheen you shince we finished high shkool.!" She lisped.

Yeah, if you can wait around til I finish we can go out and I will share my plagues with you.but it won't be pretty." and I thought--she must have been through hell. . .

We went to another bar after she finis☐hed for the night. As we walked along, a lot of guys and even some women in the village said hi, and we stopped to talk often on the way to the Next Whiskey Bar, which was the name of the place where we ended up.

"When we finished high shkool inshtead of going off to college like you did, my parentsh had shplit up, and my father wouldn't shpring for college so I ended up working in a word-prochessing pool for a law firm. The work was very tedioush, and I wor☐ked the four-to-mid shift.After work to relieve my boredom, I ushed to go to the Ziggerat to unwind. I wash alwaysh kind of virtuoush, lord knows I shaw a lot of marital battling between my own parentsh.

"I musht have learned all the wrong techniquesh for getting along with guysh from my mother. The firsht guy I got involved with wash a biker I met at the Ziggerat. He washa tattoo artist and naturally I got quite a few tatsh. Shince I worked at a law firm, they shaid, I could get as many tattoos as I wanted as long as they didn't show, so I always wore a sweater at work, but my armsh got pretty sho☐lid pretty quickly, and thighsh and lower legsh and pretty shoon after a year, I was pretty well covered with tatsh. Alright that explainsh the tattoosh. . . .

"Breaking up is shch shweet shrrow. Well after he covered my body with tattoosh, we had an acshident on his bike. He got killed and my leg got mangled. So I was on crut□chesh for montsh wish my leg full of pins. It jusht wouldn't heal. Then I caught shtaph and the bonesh in my lower leg rotted away within a month or two, and they amputated my leg just above the knee, along with over twenty tattooesh.. It jusht could not be repaired.

"I went through the whole rehab bit, with the artificial leg. I tried to go to work, and they tolerated a lot.

"Then I met a "dealer," Tom-Tom and moved in with him. that wash my down-fall. He got me hooked on ecstasy and I was always high, eventually I made too many mishtakes at work, and got fired. Shomeone broke into the apartment and shtole the artificial leg. Luckily, shome of the guys at the Ziggerat knew a guy on the Bowery who could make me a peg leg, cheap! He was an old man, and had been making peg-legsh for the beggarsh on the Bowery. What's funny, I was by no meansh the firsht woman to get a peg from him. God itsh sure crude, but damn it it worksh! Sho I started working at the Zhigarat.. Tommy wash OK ash long as I didn't flirt with any guys. He wash, of courshe very shuspicioush and very jealoush. Naturally, the guysh in the bar went wild with the peg leg. I made great tipsh The more meshed up I got the better the tipsh.

Everything went OK, but I did have an acshident putting the chain back on Tom'sh motorcycle. We were both high on ectashy and shouldn't have been fooling with the bike, it wouldn't shtart and he started it as I was putting the chain back on. In a she□cond the chain had grabbed my left hand pulled it into the shprocket and the figersh were inshstantly lying on the ground. all chewed up and like red pulp or mashed potatoes with some bones shticking out here and there. There wash not☐hing they could do with the mess so there wash nothing left to be reattached. Sho now I have a thumb and little finger and a beautifully shculpted left hand with nice neat stitches inbetween the thumb and little finger. The damn chain actually chewed up shome of my hand, sho I don't even have all the bonesh out to where the fingers should begin.

"Then I noticed that the guys were going wild over my hand as well as my peg and tattooes. Working in a bar, I got lots of chances to show off my newly mangled left hand. This showing off drove Tom crazy -- Literally crazy. One night after work he was completely stoned and he hit me in the face with a hammer and knocked out some of my teeth. That is the story of my life--"it could not be repaired." The mouth could not be repaired unless I had cash which had gone for ecstacy, The fingersh could not be repaired and the leg could not be repaired or at leasht it died trying to get well. Of courshe Tom got shent up for ashault, but look at me, The guysh at the bar have shympathy for me but my romantic life is zilch-nada zero. . ."

By this time, I was almost crying over Marilyn's sad tale. "Yeah, you got mangled, but you still have a really beauti☐ful bod." and I reached over and gently rubbed her back. Marilyn smiled a toothless smile and then we kissed at the bar.

"Do you want to come over to my apartment--it is nothing like Middletown." . . .

Marilyn had kept Tom's apartment, which, because of his dealing, was nicely fur☐nished. When we arrived, Marilyn said excuse me, I want to get more comfortable. Now wea☐ring a body suit, and a peg-leg what was there to get more comfortable about. . . .

After a few minutes she came out wearing a micro tennis skirt that showed her streamlined and abbrievated

316

thigh stump, and her remaining beautifully scultpted leg, a halter top, and a thong bikini. By now it was about six in the morning so we put on a video and al☐though we were exhausted we kissed and I really woke up and became very excited. She gently undressed me and and massaged me with her two fingered hand. Now I had never been massaged with such a sculptured hand. She placed my erect member between her thumb and little finger on her left hand and as she rubbed back and forth, WOW!!!

As I undressed Marilyn, slowly, it was like uncovering a piece of painted scultpture. Her remaining figure was perfectly carved, the colorful tattoos gave the turning of a three-dimen☐sional object excitement. She had kept what remained in great shape--there was hardly an ounce of fat on that bod. I gently rubbed the curves--the stump required its own exploration, the touch had to be very delicate. lWe kissed, carressed, and finally coupled. We assembled two bodies into one beautiful sculpture. . .

CATHY

By Cathy Coine

I was born in Genoa, Nebraska and was put up for adoption. My biologocal mother was 18 and my father was in the service in 1964. Her family lived on a farm in Genoa and I am sure she thought I would be better off somewhere else, and that her age was a factor in her decision. I was one month old when the adoption went through. My parents had really wanted a girl, and they had 4 sons at that time, PJ, Brian, Tom, & Jim.

My grandfather had called the house and my brother Tom had gotten on the phone and told him, „we just brought home a girl with 1 and half legs". He almost had heart failure and my grandmother Nana grabbed the phone as my mother did and asked what did Tom tell him. Well my mother explained that she had adopted a baby girl, partially against her parents wishes.

My mother wanted her parents to accept me as one of their own. So one day when there were visiting, my mother had her hands full and handed me to Grandpa and went along with her business. He was then forced to look at me and love filled his eyes because as my mother told me later, I didn't cry and he saw that I was a happy child. The next thing my mother knew is that they left the house and went shopping to buy their first grandaughter some gifts.

I did not recieve my first prosthesis until I was 14 months. So I had learned to hop before I had learned to walk, and to keep up with 4 older brothers I had to hop quickly. Since I had maneuvered around without my leg for a few years, my parents had difficulty keeping me attached to it. I used to hide it in closets and other hiding spots around the house. My mother had to rig up a hanger and rope to keep me in one location until I got used to the prosthesis.

My mother had wanted to adopt another little girl, when she had found out that she was pregnant once again. 2 ¾ years after I was born, I had another brother. So I had to learn to deal with 5 brothers as well as my disability. I would never change   a   thing.

My doctor had told mom to not treat me any different than any of the boys. Otherwise I would become lazy and expect them to do everything for me. She had days that I would cry to be carried and the public thought that she was torturing me. Any other child they would think she was disciplining them as to making them walk, but since I was handicpped she was torturing me. To this day I am glad that the Doctor told her to do that, because it has helped me learn to deal with the handicap. On visits to the Prosthetic/Orthepedic Center, I used to play with other amputees in the waiting area but I was too young to ask questions or understand. I loved talking to other people, and enjoyed meeting others in the   same   boat   as   I.

My mother had fought to get me into a normal school and succeeded. They had told her that I would do better in a special school, but she saw the way I was with the boys and had known better. So I walked a mile to school just like the other   boys   had.

At age 6 my father had a job in Ithica, New York, so we transferred there temporarily. When my leg had broken, my mother had used duct tape to repair it. When we returned to Lincoln, we went to the bracemaker, and he laughed his head off to the conditional way we repaired the leg.

At age 8, my mother had decided it would be good for me to go to a camp with other children who had disabilities. To see that I wasn't the only one, and to learn how other people deal with their handicaps. I was a camper for 6 years, and I used to cry when my mother came to pick me up, cause I loved the friendships I had made and I wasn't in the brother/sister role of conflicts.

At age 9 I had an operation to keep the bone from growing through the skin. I had missed some school, where we were learning cursive handwriting, but I caught on quickly when I returned. I had to use crutches and the boys at school used to say they were cootie guns. So I chased them all around the playground on crutches.

The elementary PE teacher used to take me by his side and I liked being treated special. He once called me to his side, when I was doing the daily run around the backstops with crutches, and had told me I didn't have to run, when I was on crutches. I was a little disappointed that he kept me from participating, but I liked the attention. On days when we played war ball, I would stand by him, and when most of the kids were out, I would jump in and the boys would say that isn't fair. But they soon caught on and would strike me out in the beginning. We had a three legged race once on a field day and I happened to be on crutches and one team made it tough to win and they sure screamed that it wasn't right that I got to use my pair of crutches.

In Jr. High, my mother had talked to the PE instructor and told her not to keep me from any activities. So we had a high jump and I kept moving to the end of the line and she saw that and said I was next. I ran and jumped and knocked the bar over. She then said I had to go again, cause I had missed two jumps. They had raised the bar and I jumped and made it.
The whole class cheered. I was terribly embarrassed.

There was another incident in PE in Jr High, where we got to choose the gym for Gymnastics, and me being female chose the male gym. Also with my arm strength I could achieve a lot more there. I was really shy about my leg at this time of my life and wore sweat pants that covered the leg. It was also broken at that time and I had used duct tape to repair it, so I could continue using it, instead of going without the leg. I was on the rings doing a parallel dismount when my leg weight pulled the joint out of the tape. The spotter saw the leg come out of joint and said „hold on I'll catch you". And so I let go of the rings and fell into his arms and he set me down and replied „Dam I forgot". I then decided it was time to fix the leg and was on cruches for a day or two.

Over the summer of '79 I got the opportunity to volunteer at the Easter Seals camp, that I adored as a child. The previous summer a counselor told me how I could go about trying to volunteer and I jumped at the chance to be there all summer. In the interview I was very shy and the Director said he would let me try a week, but I couldn't go to the training. So I showed up for the first week at camp and my shyness left and he liked how I worked with everyone and had let me stay the whole summer. At camp I had some difficulty transferring people from their chairs to the bed/commode/pool/etc. because I didn't have the training. But   I   helped   when   I   could.

This summer I had the experience of a first love, even though it was short lived. He was good friends with another girl, Brenda, she told him he knew her first and that he had to make a choice and he chose her. She was overweight and acted as my friend also. He still talked to me, but made her feel more important. One weekend we all went to Lincoln, Doug, Brenda, Bob, Amy and I. Brenda had tried to lose me and I found Doug and she had gotten lost while we were in the   mall.

After camp I had called Doug on his Birthday, he was from out of town, and Mom told me to write down what I wanted to say so the phone call would be short and to the point. I was so scared. I had mailed him a bracelet with his name on it,   and   just   asked   if   he   had   recieved   it.

In 9th grade we didn't get the choice of gyms for gymnastics, and I was forced to do the routines as any normal child. This had made me mad, because I couldn't do some of the events easily. I chose floor exercises, cause I could tumble, and I chose the vault cause I could jump, and do a straddle jump. As for the third choice, I always liked the balance beam, but it was a bad choice. She told me I had to do a summersault or some form of acrobatic move, or I would recieve an F. So I decided the pretzel could be the closest move, and not too dangerous. This is where you lie on your back on the beam and bring your legs over your head, and touch the bar with your feet and then bring the knees to either side of your head. Of course I fell off, and failed that event. The balance is uneven weight, and I fell because my sense   of   balance   was   off.

My second summer of camp '80 as a volunteer went better because I knew people, and got to go through the training. This summer was a good year because there were more staff at my age, and I had developed closer realtionships. I am   still   great   friends   to   one   counselor,   Jeff.

Well my brother Brian went to Cornell, Ithica New York. I had missed him very much, because he was the brother that kept us kids in line. He thought all the situations through, before giving his advice. Also he offered to teach me to drive, and I was jealous that he was so far away, and other girls were taking up his time. I still look for his advice today.

After camp I started high School, 10th grade. Jim, my brother went to a different Jr. High, so it was different to be back in school with him. On the first day, he came up from behind me and banged my head with his books, but I was glad to see him, cause I couldn't find the D-wing for driver's Ed. This year I had an operation for tightening the ligaments in my leg, because I had a trick knee, it would dislocate when I fell. So in December, I went to the hospital. I had a male nurse, and he enjoyed chatting with me on his breaks, and I enjoyed his company. He would come in and give me back rubs, and once he walked in when I was changing night gowns, and I jumped when I saw him. He had apologized, but I had said he was a nurse, and had seen this a hundred times over. After I was back on my feet I went to visit him, and he was transferred to another area. So I didn't get to see him. I had one teacher in 10th grade, which she taught about Family Living. We had to keep a notebook during the class and turn it in at the end of the semester. One day after school, she asked me why I limped and I replied, „I have a wooden leg" and the next day she winked at me and tried to do all of my work, but I told her no that I could do it. That is one of the reasons I didn't want to attend the University of Nebraska where my parents taught. I knew too many professors through my parentsand didn't want it easier or tougher on me for that reason.

I had joined a class, where it was Volunteers In Action, and could recieve credit hours for volunteering, so I took advantage of the chance. We got to go camping, with blind and deaf students in Nebraska City. Well one weekend, my leg needed reapir, but I had to go hiking/camping, and knew I'd need it, so I talked to the brace maker into making minor repairs, so I could go. That weekend, we had deaf students, which were our peers. The first night we played a game called murder, where you look across the table at other

325

people, and try to guess whose winking at people (murdering) and also did night hikes. The next day I was talking and jumping, and the next thing I knew I was a foot shorter. My ankle had broken off. So the kids ran to Ivan to go get some sticks to splint a broken leg. Ivan had come back with wood, and saw me holding my foot, and his eyes almost popped out of his head. He had no clue that I had a wooden leg. We tried to brace the leg with the sticks, and it didn't work. On of the leaders had a bendable shovel, and so we taped the foot to it, and most of the weekend I stayed by the tent. But when we had to hike back to the van, I had two   nice   guys   to   use   as   crutches.

This was Jim's senior year. And he wanted to keep his friends away from me.

Because we were so close in age I often had crushes on his friends and he hated the thought of seeing me around his friends. So he had told his friends that I was a bitch, so they would stay away from me. I believe that was his way to protect his little sister, cause he knew what his friends were like.

Well he ran track/Cross Sountry and had a party at our house, and one of his friends did like me, and told me so at the party. He said, „If you weren't Jim's brother, I would take you to the sack right now". So I could see why Jim had wanted to protect me, but did I miss out on relationships, because of his protection. Of course that wasn't the way to go.

After Jim went away to college, I had to find my identity on my own at school. This year was unbearable. The kids that paid attention to me were the „smokers", „delayed grade students", not the kids I wanted to be around when I myself was considering college, so I decided to transfer to another high school, for the senior year. I tried out for Choir at my old high school, and had made it. I was torn in between leaving and staying, because I tried out the year before and didn't make it. I wanted to be in that choir desparately. But the director said when you make a decision you should stick with it. So I did.

This year at camp, summer '82, the art director quit and I was asked to replace her duties, and would get paid for it. So I jumped at the chance. I set up arts and crafts to help counselors get the time to make banners for activities and boutineers/coursauges for the banquet dance.

Now that I started a new school my senior year, I had joined up with friends that I knew in Jr. High, especially a good friend Margarita. They were achievers, and thus my grades had improved immensely. I was automatically enrolled for the choir because I had made choir at the other high school. While in choir, Ivan came to visit me, he had joined the marines and was back visiting, and he went to school there, previously.

That drove most of the girls wild, to see that a georgious guy had paid attention to me. He went to the director and asked if he could speak to me, so I went to meet him and he gave me a picture. The whole class of girls wanted to know how I rated to get a chance to meet with him. It sure boosted my ego.

In my senior year, I took advantage of saving up all my allowed days to be absent for the last 2 weeks of school. I volunteered with special olympics which took me out for 2 days of school, and just laying back and riding out the two weeks of school. I did still go to choir, to practice for the graduation songs. While in the class I got a pass to go see the principal and I was scared to death that he caught me. He had told me that I knew his son, because his son also had volunteered to help with Special Olympics and he then gave me an award from the United Way for volunteering more than 100 hours my senior year. How lucky could I be.

During the Spring semester , 1983, Jim had offered to have me go to Northwest and explore my choices of college, and I revelled in the chance to see what college life was like. It was senior weekend, and he didn't sign me up for any of the activities. I went on a thursday night and he had a floor party, and so we went. I was supposed to stay with his girlfriend, but she was sick and went home early. So Jim had to sneak me into his dormroom at midnight, so we walked up 7 flights of stairs. The next morniing his alarm went of each hour for classes. I had to go to the bathroom, but didn't want to wake him, finally at 10 I couldn't wait any longer, and he said I could roam the halls so I went downstairs and a janitor showed me where to go. He knew I had spent the night there, but didn't know why. I know what went through his mind. Friday night, I was with his girlfriend and her firiends. we went to a flick and back to the dorms. Saturday, I went to get Jim some lunch, and walked across campus to the deli. People said hi to me left and right, and I knew then that this was the place for me. Saturday night he took me to his fraternity for a party, and I enjoyed meeting his   friends.

After graduation, I was asked to volunteer on a few trips. We took mentally challenged people to the Ozarks and Texas. It was a chance to see the world before college and before camp started. This year at camp, 1983, I was a head counselor, until we fired a counselor, and then I became the head counselor/cabin leader. It was too much responsibility. I was stretched too far. I had to be two places at once, and I   wasn't   paid   enough   for   two   jobs.

Well then I started my first year at college, Fall 1983, at Northwest Missouri State University. My first career choice

328

was „Nursing", because I wanted to show others how they had cared for me. Then I was interested in Occupational Theraphy, then Accounting and finally Computer Management Systems. I became involved with ROTC in college, as a way to meet people, and BE ALL THAT I CAN BE. I was an assistant instructor for a rapelling course, and joined Rangers, which I earned a beret. I had to pass a skills test, a written test, a survival weekend, go to Ranger meetings, and complete a training course. I swam instead of running 2 miles, a ½ mile in the pool, after sit-ups and push ups skills test. They had formals twice a year, and the staff gave me an award for outstanding student, the war of 1812. Other times I recieved other awards. One year I got the snag award. I was rapelling and had caught my shirt between the rope and the snap link. They had to cut me out of my shirt, and lower me to the ground. My brother Jim had heard of this and said „I know you needed a date for the ROTC formal, but didn't need to advertise it".

There was a performer named Barber & Seville that was a vantriloquist and his act was where the doll was holding him. He had come to Northwest to perform his act and I went to him after the performance. I asked him if I could use his dummy for a date to the ROTC formal, because my leg seemed to have an attraction for it. He laughed, and Betty my friend and I talked with him until about 1 am in the morning. He had told me the next time he comes to perform at Northwest he would like me to do a comedy act. He said my first line should be, „My name used to be Cathy Dollar, but it had lost interest—Cathy Coyne".

Well in between dropping out of college and returning, changing degrees, I finally graduated in May of 1992. I talked to my parents about coming to Kansas City, where there was more opportunity for jobs and still keep the independence. Finally in December 1992 I landed a job as Programmer Analyst 1 at the County Corthouse in

Downtown Kansas City, if I hadn't gotten that job, I would have had to move back to Lincoln.

Now I am still employed at the courthouse and my health insurance bought a new leg, before the court transferred to another carrier of insurance. The new insurance will not pay for any repairs or new legs, so I was very lucky. I started working for DST June 5, 1995 and am learning more and more every day about programming. I still try to BE ALL THAT I CAN BE.

ALL IN THE FAMILY
By Roger Tigers

I was pretty nervous by the time I drove up to the house. Well, wouldn't you be when you're about to meet your new girlfriend's family for the first time? And the fact that my new girlfriend was a special lady didn't exactly help to put my nerves at ease either.

I had met her two weeks before in the lobby of a cinema. It was intermission time and everyone was queuing to get something to drink. Except for this good looking brunette that was standing slightly offside to the crowd. She immediately caught my attention, since she was leaning on two fore-arm crutches. The reason for the crutches was quite obvious. There was no left leg to be seen.

Despite a racing heart and a freshly broken out sweat I managed to control myself and inconspicuously joined the queue to try and get hold of a coke. After I got one I more or less casually drifted nearer to where she was standing, and I noticed that she had been joined by another girl, this one a pretty blonde, with no apparent lack of any limbs. A quietly observed the pair, and before I knew it the signal went off indicating that the movie was about to continue.

After enjoying the rest of the movie I started to move towards the exit, and by some weird stroke of luck bumped into the one-legged brunette, who promptly fell over. It goes without saying that I apologised sincerely, and then a thought struck me: I invited the girl for a drink, their choice of place, to make up for my lack of attention. To my surprise they accepted.

They directed me to a quiet little bar, where they apparently were regular customers, because the bartender greeted them by their first names. We talked and laughed, and I learned that Lisa - that's her name - had lost her leg in a car crash. In fact, her left leg had been so badly mangled that they had to perform what is called a disarticulation at the hip. Also, a small part of her hip bone had been removed.

332

Her type of amputation made it very difficult for her to use an artificial leg, and she had discarded that possibility very soon. She always went on crutches after that.

The other girl, Amanda, had been Lisa's friend ever since the two of them were two years old, and - as Lisa explained - was almost like a sister. You know how those relationships work.

So that's how it started. The next two weeks were heaven. Lisa, the one-legged girl, accepted my diner invitation for the next day, and we did see each other every day for the next two weeks. I was falling in love. And so was she, apparently, because she asked if I would come over for the weekend to meet her family. She made it very clear, by normal and by body language, that she wanted to be steady with me, as the expression goes.

So one early Friday evening I found myself sitting in my car that I had just parked in front of Lisa's house, gathering courage to get out, walk to the front door, and ring the bell. Lisa had told me to be there around six o'clock, because that's when the whole family would gradually be coming in for their monthly get-together. Lisa was still living with her parents, and her mother had at one time established a tradition to have all children and their partners (if any) over for the weekend. It would be an ideal time to meet them all, so Lisa explained.

When I had finally gathered enough courage, I walked to the house and pressed the door bell. After a couple of seconds the door was opened by a middle aged man:
"Hi! Come in, come in! You must be Thomas. I'm Lisa's dad. Lisa told me to expect you. She's upstairs and will be down in a minute." He ushered me in, told me to sit down and to call him Harold, and asked me if I would like something to drink.
Harold was the prototype of a genuinely nice man, and he still is, by the way. He didn't look at all like the fifty-three

year old man that he actually is. He looks far more youthful, in fact I have seen men in their thirties who older. And more depressed. If anything, Harold was definitely not depressed.

The definition of a minute, as in "down in a minute" is of course "close to a quarter of an hour". So naturally Harold and I got into conversation. What I did for a living, what he did for a living, stuff like that, but never did he give the impression that he was checking me out. He was just genuinely interested.

After about ten minutes the sound of a car horn came from outside the house. "Ah, excuse me, Thomas, that'll be the wife with the groceries. I have to give her a hand with that. Be right back."

He got up opened the door and went out, presumably to get the groceries out of his wife's car. Meanwhile his wife came in. I was flabbergasted. In strode the most stunningly beautiful late-fortyish/early-fiftyish women I had ever seen. Ah, but what exactly is beauty? In this case a very pretty face, very elegant clothing, but above all a missing right arm and right leg! The sweater that she wore had no right sleeve, the right shoulder being neatly sewn up. The jeans had no right leg but snugly fit the stumpless hip. It appeared to me as a disarticulation as well, both at the hip and at the shoulder.

The way she moved with only her one crutch defies any description. I had stood up when she arrived, but now stood nailed to the floor. She approached me.

"Hello. You must be Thomas, right?" She extended her left hand, which I took as in a dream.

"Lisa has already told us a lot about you. She's made us curious to get to know you. You two seem to have it on, so to speak."

"Err....yes....errrr"

"Well, well, and very eloquent, too!" she said, smiling. "I'm sorry, Thomas, but I can't help myself. I just love to surprise people with my appearance. And I seem to have succeeded again."

"I'm sorry, ma'am, it's just, well, I hadn't expected...."

"Well, how could you have? Come on, sit down, have a sip of whatever you're drinking, and relax. I won't bite."

I sagged back down onto the couch. I was just about to carefully formulate my next sound, when she said:

"To cut a long story short: same car crash that Lisa lost her leg in. My arm was gone on the spot, my leg was badly crushed, but still attached to my body. They 'saved' it, so to speak. But after two years of horrible pains and lots of other trouble, I decided to have it removed. Now I am as you see me, one-legged and one-armed and as happy as you can imagine."

"Yes, ma'am", was all that came out of the orifice in the front of my head.

"Whoa, strong reply!" she laughed.

"Mother, stop teasing him!" That was Lisa's voice coming from the top of the stairs. Stairs!? Only now did I realise that this house had stairs! Now, wouldn't you want to move, having a disabled wife and daughter? Strange....

Lisa came hopping down the stairs, using one crutch and the hand rail for balance. I noticed that her other crutch was waiting for her at the bottom of the staircase.

"OK, time for me to leave you for a couple of minutes. I have to change anyway. Be right back." Lisa's mother hopped towards the stairs and in a most amazing way started to climb them!

"Aren't those stairs a bit of a bother for the two of you?" I asked Lisa.

"No, not at all. Keeps us in shape."

We sat on the couch.

"Look, Thomas, I'm sorry if my mother surprised you, but that's how she is. Very soon after the amputation of her leg she decided that the best way to confront people in her new condition was, well, to confront them. Don't give them a chance to stare surreptitiously, only give them a chance to look you straight in the eye. It works, most of the time anyway. I'm beginning to adopt her approach myself, and I must admit, it helps me."

"Well, it's not only her missing limbs that surprised me. She is a very pretty lady anyway. And what's more, I think she's nice, too. So is your dad, by the way."

"Well, that's my family for you, a great bunch of nice guys and gals. Wait till you meet my sisters and brother. I did tell you I have two sisters and one brother, didn't I?"

"Yep, you did. Let me think...Laura, she's older than you are. Then there's Lucille, she's two years younger, and your brother's name is Charles. He's the youngest."

Lisa laughed. "Well, well, you've done your homework!" Then she became serious.

"Look, Tom, I have to tell you something. The reason I wanted to see more of you in the past two weeks is because I think I'm starting to love you. I have feelings about you that I have never had before. Anyway, we talked about that already. But there's a second reason, which is also the reason I invited you over to meet my folks. I think you secretly hold special feeling towards people like me and my mum. You know, amputees."

This remarks immediately put me in the red face league. Lisa was absolutely right, of course, and apparently had caught on to me way before I was ready to confess to her. Well, what's there to confess? It's not "bad", is it? Lisa continued.

"Anyway, you seem to be the kind of guy I'd like to spend the rest of my life with. That's how I feel right this moment."

"Lisa, I am ashamed that I haven't yet had the guts to tell you, but yes, the fact that you're missing a leg was the main reason for my interest in you. But in the meantime I have gotten to know you, and so far, I haven't found anything, neither physically nor emotionally, to change my mind. God, that sounds analytic, doesn't it!? What I mean is, I like you. A lot. A great big enormous lot." And by way of exclamation mark I kissed her.

336

"Silly!" she exclaimed. "You're nuts! But as long as you're nuts about me, it's okay."

After Lisa's dad had come back in and her mother had come back down, now dressed in a casual armless dress, showing her equally armless shoulder we got into a lively talk. The second and third round of drink sure helped to loosen nerves and tongues.

After about an hour another car drove up to the house. "Ah, that'll be Laura and her husband," Lisa's mother explained as she got up to open the door (her hopping absolutely drives me nuts!). And again I got a shock! In came Laura, who was completely armless! My God, what kind of a family was this!? Fortunately Lisa succeeded in drawing my attention, otherwise I would still be staring at Laura.

"Thomas, meet Laura, my older sister, Laura, this is Thomas I told you about. Oh, and Tom, this is Fred, Laura's husband."

Laura, it turned out had been born that way. There were no shoulders either. She was a thalidomide victim, although seeing how she used her legs and feet as we would our arms and feet certainly made me redefine the word 'victim'. I was told that Laura and Fred had two children, but they were staying at Fred parents' for the weekend. Fred's dad had a sailing boat and their kids were absolutely crazy about sailing.

When I think about it now, I realise that having an armless daughter, and sister, must have made these people so much more at easy with the idea of missing limbs. I think it must have helped Lisa and her mother overcome their accident. Anyway, I couldn't believe my luck. Here I was, a devotee, right in the middle of a family with three amputees, and quite in love with one of them.

Lisa and her mother and sister went to the kitchen to prepare dinner. I wondered just how they would manage, but I was supposed to stay in the living room and wait, together with Lisa's dad, who didn't hesitate to drop the bombshell.

"So, Thomas, you're one of the uniquely interested, aren't you? Don't worry, I am one myself, and you can imagine I am one of the happiest men alive right now."

"Well, yes, you're right, Harold. There's no reason to deny it, not here anyway. I guess Lisa caught on to me right away."

"You bet! She's very perceptive. Takes after her mother in that respect. But I have a confession to make. She told us about you last week and that she intended to invite you some time. It was me and my wife who came up with the idea to invite this weekend so that we had the chance to confront you with both Lisa's mum and sister."

This statement didn't really take me by surprise. It was just the sort of thing these people would do, without any malice intent, by the way.

Before our conversation could continue, the door bell rang. Harold got up.

"That's probably Charlie with his new girlfriend."

I stood up again to meet the new arrivals. And then nearly fell over from the surprise I got. Charlie's "new girlfriend" wheeled herself in, immediately followed by a good look young man, presumably Charlie. The girlfriend had no legs, only two equally long stumps, neatly enclosed in tight fitting jeans. Good Lord, would these surprises ever stop!? What kind of family had I got into?

The girl, Tina, wheeled herself over to where I was standing and introduced herself. "Hi, I'm Tina. You must be the Thomas Lisa has been blabbering on about."

I took her hand and managed to utter a weak "Yeah, that's me."

"Hi, I am Charles, Lisa's brother," the young man interrupted. I shook his hand, too. Boy, this was some lucky guy!

Harold and I settled back into our seats, while Charles pulled up another chair after having poured himself and Tina a drink. Tina manoeuvred her wheelchair right alongside where I was sitting.

In hindsight it was pretty logical for Charles to get involved with an amputee. Due to Laura's armless state and after the accident in which Lisa and her mother had lost their limbs, the family had very often been around other amputees, in rehab centres, in support groups, you name it. Charles and Lucille, both having a full set of limbs were in contact with amputees from that moment on. Especially Charles had made it a point to accompany Lisa of his mother as often as possible to such gatherings as possible. He naturally developed a keen interest in the female amputee. And so it was only logical that his girlfriends were amputees, too. His latest conquest, Tina, appeared to be the true "special one"; they were planning to get married in three months.

So, the family was almost complete. The only one not present yet was the youngest sister, Lucille (who preferred to be called Lucy, so I was told). I was starting to wonder if yet another surprise was in store for me. What would Lucy be like? What surprise could she probably have? Most of the permutations were already present: missing one leg in Lisa's case, missing one arm and one leg in her mother's case, Laura was missing both arms, and Tina was missing both legs. What else could there be? Missing all limbs, perhaps?

I caught myself in this mathematical analysis just in time. What was I thinking!? These are people, damn it!

At that moment Lisa's mother hopped in from the kitchen. What a sight!

"Thomas, Lisa asks if you could please join her in the kitchen. She's got something to tell you," she said. "You better refill your glass first."

Charles got up and took my tumbler. "The same, Tom?" he asked on his way to the drinks cabinet.

"Yes, please."

Charles handed my glass sat down again. An eerie silence suddenly hung over our little group, and I decided to get to the kitchen before this silence became uncomfortable. "Well, if you'll excuse me."

I went into the kitchen, where Lisa sat at the kitchen bar. She pointed at a stool opposite hers, and I sat down. She had a very serious look on her face.

"Thomas, I think this is when we ought to prepare you for the next bombshell this family is about to drop on you. It's about Lucille...."

Oh, God, it was going to get worse! Or better!?

"You may not understand this, but we're going to have to tell you. You're reaction towards what I'm about to tell you is crucial. If you'll feel that you'd have to get out of here, like a good number of other guys have done before you, please don't hesitate. Most people just can't take it."

I stared at her blankly. "Errr...what...."

Lisa went on. "We discussed this, my family and I. Sooner or later you will find out, and we thought that instead of letting find out by yourself, like we did with former boyfriends of me or my sisters, we decided to tell you today. It will tell you a lot about us. And your reaction will tell us a lot about you. Since you're my guy, or rather, since I would like you to be my guy, I volunteered to be the one to tell you."

Silence. I stared at Lisa, and just when I started to open my mouth, Lisa continued.

"As I said, it's about Lucille. Or rather, it's about all of us, because we more or less share Lucille's ideas."

I broke in: "What the hell is this about!? You are making me awfully curious and not a little nervous, I might add. What is it about Lucille, and about you, that is supposed to scare me away? Because, that's the point, isn't it? You're gonna see how I react to something and find out if I'll get scared or not."

"Calm down, Thomas, calm down, and hear me out."

Silence followed, as if she was still trying to find the right approach to tell me whatever it was she was going to tell me.

I looked back at Lisa. "Well?"

"OK. The fact that Laura was born without arms, that mum lost two limbs in the car crash, and that I also lost a leg, has put some pretty strong ideas in Lucille's mind. So over the past couple of years she more and more wanted to become like her mother and sisters: an amputee. At the same time, my dad and Charlie developed a, shall we say, preference for ladies who are minus a limb. Or two. Daddy has always had this interest, so he claims, so my mothers new condition only helped to deepen his feelings for her. Charlie has been interested in amputee girls he came into contact with some of mum's and my friends. I think you know what I'm talking about, because I think you share such feelings."
It wasn't a question and no answer was expected. But she was right, of course. She went on.

"Lucille developed strong wannabe feelings over the years. Above anything else, she wanted to become like her mother or one of her sisters. When we were out, *we* always got the stares and the attention. Nobody saw Lucille. At first my parents didn't think much of her simulating having one leg, using a pair of my crutches to move about the house. And that was the big mistake; she was never taken seriously."

The rest of the family was utterly silent. They had the attitude of an audience who had heard this story before, more than once. Not the bored attitude of people listening to the umpteenth repetition, however. It got the uncomfortable feeling that it was all building up to something. Lisa, sensing my apprehension, decided to delay no longer.

"So, one day Lucille went out, just as she always did, to go to school. An hour later we got a call from one of her school teachers. She was in hospital. To cut the story short, she had gone to the rail road track nearby, had lied down with one over the rails and waited for the freight train that passed by every morning. The driver had seen her - he was the one who had alerted the rescuers - but had been unable to stop the train. Her leg was gone at the knee, but due to the damage they had to amputate just below her hip."

I must have gone a little pale. "You okay, Tom?"

"Yeah....well....umm...." I was lost for words, and took another sip of my drink. I barely managed to suppress a coughing fit. Lisa touched my hand.

"I realise that this must be a bombshell for you, Tom, but we do feel that it's better to tell you now than have you find out on your own later."

"Uhhh, yeah, you're right. I do appreciate your telling me this. But I don't think it is relevant to what we feel for each other. Is it?"

342

"No, well, at least, not as far as *I* am concerned. But you just wait a while, Tom, because there's more."

Good Lord! What could possibly top this?

"Lucille recovered and returned home. Things returned to normal, or what goes for normal in this household. Two months later Lucille repeated her stunt. In hindsight we know we shouldn't have let her go out on her own, but she was only going to visit her school friend about a block from here. When her friend called why she hadn't arrived yet, we immediately became very suspicious. And we were right. Lucille had managed to get her other leg damaged to a point where they could do nothing else but remove it. She had planned it all very carefully. She had even applied a tourniquet to minimise blood loss. She had told her rescuers that she had had the presence of mind to tie off her leg after having been run over by the train, but we knew better. She had tied it off, and *then* had put her leg over the tracks. That was three years ago. And six months ago, shortly after she had left the house in her wheelchair to go to the mall with two of her friends, one of these friends called to say that they had lost sight of her. The girl was rather distressed, because she knew of Lucille's previous two 'accidents'. Her fears were justified. While her friends had been waiting in a queue to get some ice cream, Lucille had made her escape. She had wheeled into the park opposite the mall, where she had noticed some guys grinding chopped wood into small splinters using some awful machine. She had waited for the men to move off and had somehow managed to turn on the machine. She had then put her left arm into it. It is still not clear how she managed to circumvent the safety catch, but she did. Her arm was gone to the elbow, but they couldn't save that. She now has an eight inch stump."

I was absolutely speechless. Could this possibly be true. Could someone do this to himself? Or herself? I did know about people who more than anything else wanted to loose a limb, some of them even wanted to get rid of two. But to actually go so far as to stage three accidents in order to have your legs and an arm removed, and at the same time putting yourself into mortal danger, that was something unheard of. At least by me.

"Where is she now? Is she being treated for her psychological condition?" I asked, and at the same moment realised my mistake. That was not the kind of question Lisa had wanted to hear.

"Do you think it might make a difference!?" she snapped. "Will it get her her limbs back!?"

"No, of course not, I'm sorry. What I mean is, isn't her wish to loose limbs something similar to the death wish of someone who is suicidal? Shouldn't she have counselling, or something like that? Maybe I'm wrong, but her problem is in her head, isn't it?"

"Well, yes, when your older sisters always get all the attention, you're bound to try to emulate them. But the problem isn't hers alone. It's ours, as a family."

She was close to tears. Well, I could understand that. Slowly I was getting an idea of how this family was put together. It was the most intriguing mixture of amputees, wannabees and devotees, and that was probably a cause for a lot of mixed feelings among the family members. I myself, I could only begin to imagine how Harold and Charles were feeling. I too have a strong fascination with the female figure who is missing one or more limbs. But at times, I also felt horribly guilty about this interest. How could one possibly be attracted to someone else's misery?

Furthermore, I found it highly unlikely that they hadn't taken any steps to avoid a second, and even a third attempt at voluntary amputation, as in Lucille's case. Could it just possibly be that the family had agreed with what had

344

happened? Or, even worse, that they had, consciously or unconsciously, driven Lucille to her acts?

I caught myself; my thoughts were going in a direction that wasn't very pretty. It must have registered on my face, for at that very moment Lisa interrupted my line of thinking.

"Thomas. Listen carefully. After Lucille's second accident we decided to go talk to a family therapist. He confronted us with his conclusion that we wanted Lucille to become an amputee all along. And it is true, of course."

Bingo! My thinking was right on the mark! It didn't make me feel better at all, however.

"The question now is, Tom, will you fit in? Will you *want* to fit in? If not, please go now, and forget about me and my family."

"Ah, no, Lisa," I replied. "I won't go for that kind of choice. My choice is, do I want to be with you or not. The answer to that is 'yes', and if your family comes with the package, that's all right with me. I mean, I haven't had much chance yet to get to know them, but they seem to be a genuinely nice bunch of people. Hell, I haven't even got to know you! It's been only two weeks. But so far, I like what I see. Very, very much."

I paused to have another sip of my drink, a very good quality whiskey. Irish, by the taste of it. I put my glass back down, rather firmly.

"OK, since it's confession time, I'll reciprocate. You know very well that you having only one leg was the first reason for me to notice you. Meanwhile, I have gotten to know the person 'behind the stump' a bit better, and I can only repeat, I like you a lot. Now, you and your family already suspect that I'm a devotee, and to this I say 'Yes, indeed I am'. I couldn't have found a better woman. You are exactly

345

right. And as far as your family goes, I couldn't have found a better bunch of in-laws. Your mum and sisters, as well as Charles girlfriend, are to me, shall we say, 'fascinating' women. And your dad and brother are guys just like me, fascinated. Who could ask for more? But apart from all this, my fascination and devotion are towards you. I want you."

Half an hour later, Lucille arrived home. She was the most amazing young woman I have ever seen. If she would still have had all her limbs, she might have been a strong contender in any miss competition. A face as a goddess, framed by the most beautiful red hear I had ever seen, smile that would melt the polar ice caps, breast that would make any woman envious, and a perfect body. However, there were no legs and no left arm. Her clothes made the absence of these limbs all the more clear; she wore a pair of jeans that fitted tighter than a surgeon's glove and a sleeveless top. None of these garments did anything to hide her defects. On the contrary, they only drew more attention to the stumps. Which was of course exactly what Lucille wanted.

When she came in she was using an electric wheelchair, which she controlled with her right hand. But after having greeted everyone in the living room - including me - she slid out of the chair and move on the floor toward the couch. This, and the way she managed to get onto the couch were one of the most amazing sights things a man can ever witness; I certainly won't forget it, no matter how long I live.

DOORS
By Leon Dewolf

Martin was sitting in his car again and reading a magazine. Every now and then he looked up and watched the doors of the building, in front of which he had waited so often. Not the magazine, but those doors, and what was behind them, was the reason why he had parked his car here.

Rolf eased his Volkswagen around the corner into the side street, looking out for a parking space. He had left in time and could take his time searching. He had promised Marianne to fetch her, and as always, he kept his word.

If this went on any longer, she would be late. Marianne looked at the clock and slowly began to lose her temper. Of course, she had been late, and she wasn't the only customer. But she had already been waiting for almost an hour without being helped any further. It would take only a small adjustment, they said; that should have been ready by now.

Every parking space was taken, even the ones for the disabled. Rolf decided to make a couple of laps around the block; a space was bound to be vacated. In one of the parked cars a man was sitting, reading a magazine. Is he also waiting for someone? He could inherit a space here soon, surely.

"You must excuse us for taking so long. We had to lathe some of the material away from the top, and replace a part down at this side. Want to try it?" The apprentice looked at Marianne with a smile. She stood up and said: "About time. Let's see."

This was the best spot. From here Martin couldn't only see the doors of the workshop, and the short stair case leading up to them, but also the parking lot for customers, next to the building. All space were occupied today. "Promising," he thought. "Luckily I could leave the office early today." Afternoons, between four and five thirty always was the best time. Hopefully, something could be seen.

Marianne looked into the socket and fumed: "I can't wear it like this; without the coating I'll get a rash!" Before she could sit down again, the apprentice ensured her that the coating couldn't be applied until after they had made sure that the socket would fit. Doubtfully, Marianne looked at the young man. "I sure hope it fits. My boy friend is picking me up in five minutes, and I don't want to let him wait." Embarrassed the apprentice remarked that that wouldn't be enough time. "The coating will have to dry. Even if it fits right away, the leg can't be worn for another hour."

From the corner of his eyes Martin noticed the doors opening. An old man came out of the building and went down the stairs, slowly, step by step. "Nothing. Oh well, there's still time." Martin went back to his magazine.

"There, that old guy will probably take off in his car." Rolf drove his red Volkswagen towards the customer's lot and indeed saw the man enter a car. At that moment a woman left the building and walked toward an other car. He immediately started the engine and backed up to the workshop entrance. Rolf parked his car in the free space and mumbled: "Marianne should come out any moment now."

They had taken their time, but on the other hand had done a good job. Even without the coating the leg fitted like a glove. Marianne had left her booth and now walked up and down the practice area. In the large mirror she watched herself and decided that it went well. A young girl, who was just putting on her jacket, said admiringly: "Great, the way you're walking! One can hardly notice. A blind man can see that I limp around on a wooden leg." She took a few steps toward Marianne, and went on: "I suppose you have a long stump, the way you're controlling your prosthesis. I don't have one at all, they took my leg at the hip." Marianne had noticed immediately that the girl had to be disarticulated at the hip joint, and recently as well. She could only walk very slowly and with great effort. "Thanks, but my stump is short as well," she answered. "Practice makes perfect. I'm sure

349

you'll do better in time." Marianne looked at the girl encouragingly. She lifted her shoulders: "Don't think so. Actually, I prefer to go without the damned leg, but my mother insists that I wear it." She turned around, took a pair of crutches under one arm, and limped towards the exit. "Bye, gotta go. My mum is waiting."

Martin was mad. Why did this woman had to stop her car exactly in front of the entrance? She totally obstructed his view! He could just see the doors opening again and a pretty young girl exiting. She had to be about sixteen years old, with long, loose, blond hair. Once more, Martin noticed this debilitating feeling, the butterflies in his stomach, as he stared towards the doors. Yes! The girl was about to descend the stairs. She held the railing with one hand, and carefully took one step after another, right leg first, stiff, without flexing the knee, moved only by the hip. Far too quickly, she disappeared behind the waiting car.

"Marianne is late again," Rolf thought. He hated it to get his gril friend to and from the orthopedist's. He had first met Marianne about four years ago, while jogging. She was a sportive, attractive young woman with almost black hair, fashionably short. They had met regularly, had fallen inlove, and were soon living together. What a happy time that had been; unfortunately, too short. Only three weeks after getting into their new home, it had happened. He had gotten a call at the office, from the hospital. Marianne had been in an accident and was operated on that very moment. He had dropped everything and rushed to the hospital, where a head nurse had intercepted him. "Your girl friend came out of OR just a couple of minutes ago. She's in her room now. The chief surgeon wants to see you before you go to her." A tired, overworked man had come towards him. "Miller," he introduced himself. "We've had a serious rail accident, lots of wounded. We've just operated on your girl friend; she's going to live. Serious leg injuries, fortunately left side only, but we had to amputate. Go see her, support her. I'm afraid I'll have to go back to OR." He turned abruptly and left. Rolf had followed the head nurse in a trance, into the ward. Marianne was in bed, pale. "Be brave," he had thought, "be brave."

Back in her booth Marianne opened the valve in the socket of her prosthesis. She pulled the leg off her stump and gave it to the apprentice. With both hands she massaged the short stump of her left thigh. The soft flesh around the bone remnant relaxed under her kneading movements. "The socket is a bit too narrow; I'll have to have some more material removed." Marianne laughed, and then, more seriously told the apprentice: "No, it's all right. Just the coating." The apprentice disappeared with the prosthesis and Marianne took another look at the clock. Rolf had already been waiting for fifteen minutes, now. She had to go out and tell him it was going to take longer.

"A hip disarticulate! And not just any!" Martin hadn't been this excited since a long time. He had never seen her before -- did she live here in town? She must have lost her leg recently, because he had never noticed her before. But she wasn't for him, much too young, he couldn't hold any hopes there. He didn't even bother to write down the licence plate of the car that drove off with his new discovery. In his mind he pictured her, how this young beauty would remove her prosthesis at home and how she would move around on crutches, around the house, in the garden, perhaps even in the street. He pictured her in a mini skirt, only one slender but strong leg, between the crutches. The image of the difficultly limping girl in jeans and jacket, that he had seen just now, was replaced by his ideal image. Martin was still dreaming when he noticed the doors opening yet again.

He had supported her as much as he could. Himself listless and confused, Rolf had tried to stand by Marianne. Shortly after the accident they had both been depressed. Nothing was as it used to be. Every daily chore tired Marianne, she had refused to leave the house, had allowed herself to sink deeper and deeper. During that time he had worried about her a lot, and had taken as much off her mind as possible. He had also felt sorry for her, this poor disabled woman who had been so horribly mutilated. He had never been able to endure the view of her amputated leg, he had hated to see her move on crutches. Soon the pity had changed into feeling sorry for himself, he had felt betrayed and denied a mutual future, doomed to give up his own interests and to always 'be there' for Marianne. After eventually getting her prosthesis, as well as a job quite close to home, things had become a bit better. He still feared the moments when her disability was all too clear to him: at the beach, or while skiing, these trips to the orthopedic workshop, and especially at night, when she took off her leg and hopped into bed. How tragic that this had to happen to him, no, to his girl friend. During the almost three years since the amputation they had hardly made love; he was too repulsed by her appearance, and she seemed much too uncertain. But he couldn't leave Marianne, in her condition. Rolf sighed and looked at his watch again. Almost twenty minutes late!

A young woman appeared in the door frame and held the door for a sportingly dressed man who was following her. He or she? The question was soon answered. Martin saw how the young woman quickly descended the stairs and approached a car. The man stayed behind at the top of the stairs and then began to descend as well, slowly and with some effort. "Nope! But I've been lucky today," Martin told himself, and he thought about driving off to go home. "OK, five more minutes... who knows..."

"Rolf doesn't like to wait, especially not here at the workshop," Marianne though. He was always so tense, and at the same time overly friendly, when he had to, no, wanted to pick her up here. She had often told him that she could go alone, but he had always said that he didn't mind, that it was it was 'on his way anyway'. But she knew damn well that he did mind. He had changed so much since her amputation, always nice and considerate, but he protected her, didn't take her for full. Always these questions: You all right? Can I help? Can you manage on your own? Can you manage? Of course she could! She had become used to being one-legged in the past three years, and she hardly felt disabled anymore. The only thing that made her feel disabled were these questions and remarks from Rolf, always accompanied by a forced smile. Why couldn't he just get to grips with the situation and live with her like before? Marianne took her skirt, that she had taken off for trying the leg, and pulled it up over her one leg. "Well, granted, the situation isn't quite like before, but our relationship could use a boost," she thought while buttening up the skirt. Marianne took two old wooden crutches from the corner, meant to be used by customers. She positioned the crutches under her arm pits and carefully took a step. "I haven't used antiques like these for years. Feels funny." Marianne opened the curtain of the booth and swang through the practice area toward the exit. "No problem, height is just about right," she thought. She told a passing employee: "Be right back, I have to tell someone I'll be delayed."

There, the doors opened again. Martin peered over the edge of his magazine and wished himself luck. "Marianne Reitel! On crutches!" He hardly believed his eyes. He had seen this young woman often, here in town. He had followed her on occasions and he had even succeeded in finding out her name. She was by far the most beautiful, most attractive amputee he had ever seen. But she had always used a prosthesis. How gracefully she went down the stairs and across the parking lot. With every step her knee-length skirt stretched around her single leg and clearly revealed the contours of a short thigh stump. Martin had never thought that Marianne had such a short stump, well as she went on her prosthesis. What a woman! Unfortunately Martin had also found out that she lived with a man, so he had never had the courage to speak to her. What he would give to be in that guy's place...

Rolf saw Marianne round the corner and move towards his car. He paled. "No leg! Why isn't she wearing the prosthesis? She know I don't like that." A wave of pity struck him, but above all, self-pity: "Of all people, why did my girl friend have to be crippled? How awful she looks on those crutches." As always Rolf forced his smile and opened the car door. "Come, my dear, good thing you're ready so soon. I didn't even have to wait."

Marianne had reached the car and bent over inside the open door. "Hi, Rolf, of course you had to wait, don't be silly!" Marianne watched Rolf -- and there it was again, this forced smile. "And stop the act, I can tell it's very inconvenient for you, waiting here" she went on. "But, no! I like to do it, for you. I'm always there for you", Rolf countered. Now she was really mad. Here he was again, with his eternal protectionism. "Oh, cut that out! I can manage very well by myself! Go home, I'll have to stay another half hour, and will follow you. Alone."

Rolf looked at Marianne with amazement. Why did she react so strange? He only wanted to help. "No, no, I can wait. It's too much effort for you to get home by bus."

"Too much effort? Yes, I know, the poor cripple, unable to do anything herself, always depending on help!" Seething, she lifted the hem of her skirt, and raised her leg stump toward Rolf. "Here, look, this makes me a cripple. Repulses you, right? But despite this I am an independent woman, don't you forget." She dropped the skirt, slammed the car door and yelled: "Go home! I don't need you like this." Skillfully she turned on her crutches and quickly moved back into the building.

Martin had watched the scene. They were obviously having a row. With fascination he had seen Marianne lift her skirt. And he hadn't failed to notice that she had held up her stump towards the young man, with an angry look on her face. Anger became her, Martin decided. What had the row been about? Now Martin saw Marianne go back up the stairs and disappear behind the doors. At the same time he noticed that the red Volkswagen maneuvered out of the parking space and drove off. So, she was staying a while longer. He, too, saw no immediate reason to leave right away...

He had never seen Marianne like that before. What did she mean, anyway? He spent all his spare time with her, was always there for her -- and she blamed he for it! Now, Rolf had gotten angry as well. "She'll find out how far she'll get without me. Even if she can't help being disabled, she could be a little more grateful!" Roughly, he had started the car and was now on his way home.

"It's got to stop", Marianne told herself as she went back into the booth. "Rolf treats me like a child! I'm his partner, his wife, with everything that comes with that. He won't have me like I am, not anymore, anyway. He finds me repulsive, with my appearance -- and I can't change that." She took off her skirt again and watched herself. There she was, standing on her lonely right leg, a single, dainty foot, a single, strong calf, a single, well formed knee, and a single, long thigh. The stump of her left leg began shortly below her tight knickers, a half-round hanging from her hip. When she moved it slightly, the flesh underneath the tight skin rippled. "Looks like a breast," she thought, "it's not half as terrible as Rolf finds it. Well... bit of a strange place for a breast!" She laughed inwardly and lifted the stump a little to get a better look at the scar. The doctors had done a good job. Only a pale line was visible, the severed muscles had not contracted; a perfect, smooth semi-sphere. "I'm not ugly, just because of this. If Rolf really loved me, he could get over this. He used to always tell me how good I looked -- and now I'm suddenly no longer attractive to him. I'm still a woman, aren't I, a good looking woman." Marianne felt the anger rise again. "Sex, yes exactly, that's the problem. We're living together like brother and sister, sexually there's nothing going on between us anymore. I need a man, a real man, who loves me, who can satisfy me. It'll never work out with Rolf." She had tried to talk about this with Rolf, but he had never answered her attempts. "This can't go on," she thought again. "I've gotten used to Rolf, but that's about it. We're not in love anymore, haven't been for a long time." She sat down and unconsciously went over her right thigh with her hand. "I want to be caressed and loved, smooching and fucking -- I need that..." Her hand went up along the inside of her thight, until she felt the stump, lying flat on the chair. Marianne spread the short stump slightly to the side and brought her hand further up. She put her left hand on the cool skin of her stump and carefully stroked the scar. She followed the line, ending close to her pussy. She stopped abruptly and moved her hands away. "No, Marianne, this can't go on. You don't want to satisfy yourself all the time, you need a man, one that not only shares a table, but also the bed."

Rolf had calmed down a bit. He was waiting at a red light and in his mind went over what had happened. Never before had he seen Marianne so angry -- and never before had she reacted so strongly. Why did she resist his help all of a sudden? What had he done wrong? Sure, their relationship was far from ideal, but that wasn't his fault! "Marianne's amputation has destroyed everything," he thought bitterly.

In his car, Martin returned to his magazine and observed the doors every now and then. Nothing happened.

"I'm sorry, I've bungled it." The apprentice stood in the booth, embarrassed, and looked at Marianne. "To mucg of the coating was applied, and I had to remove it again. A new layer will certainly not dry before closing time. Could you return tomorrow morning so that I can get you a new coating?" Marianne saw how embarrassed the situation made him, and avoided to sneer at him. "Oh, God, why did I agree to be helped by this beginner," she thought. But she didn't want to sit around here for hours again tomorrow. With a steady voice she answered: "No, finish the leg now; I'll come and pick it up tomorrow morning, when the coating is dry. But first, fetch me a pair of decent crutches; I can't go home on these ancient wooden things." This startled the apprentice. "You want to go home without a prosthesis? But..."

"I have to!" Marianne interrupted, "go on -- and call me a taxi!"

His decision made, Rolf touched the indicator switch, went into a side street, and turned the car. He couldn't just leave the situation: "I'll drive back and wait for Marianne anyway. We dp belong together and I won't just let myself be shoved aside. I'll tell her she insulted me; this fight has to end."

Marianne had put on her skirt and jacket again. With two, three hops she had left the booth and was now leaning against the wall, waiting for her crutches. The practice area was now empty; only a woman of about forty was moving slowly and unsurely on a still undressed tubular prosthesis, observed by a prosthetist. She too had lost her left leg, but she had a much longer stump than Marianne's. The mechanical knee was attached directly to the plastic socket that fitted the thigh stump. Marianne had also used a leg with a similar socket, but had had to discard it; the plastic material irritated her sensitive skin. "May I ask you something?" Marianne addressed the woman, who now stopped and turned. "Sure. I'm Caroline". Marianne introduced herself, and asked: "Don't you have any problems with the plastic? I always get a rash from this stuff." Caroline looked down at her prosthesis and said: "I don't know, this is my first prosthesis. But the people here tell me that this plastic is OK for the skin." The prosthetist, who had now approached the two women, confirmed that the socket was made of a new, skin-friendly plastic. "You must try it on your next leg, Marianne. This socket is much lighter that a wooden one." He looked beneath Marianne and only then noticed that she was standing on one leg. "Why don't you have a prosthesis? Should've been ready by now." Marianne told him of the apprentice's error. The prosthetist lifted his shoulders and apologised: "He's still got a lot to learn! But it's good to leave your leg here overnight;

that way the coating can really dry well. Did you order a taxi yet?" After confirming this, he turned to Caroline again. "Look, you won't be the only woman travelling through town on one leg. Take off the prosthesis and let's continue tomorrow."

"What takes Marianne so long?" Martin wondered. He knew the workshop always closed at five thirty; it couldn't be long now. Again he looked at the closed doors. The red Volkswagen had not returned. Would Marianne go home by herself, now? "That would be my chance," Martin thought, "I could offer her a lift into the city." But how would he address her? He had often pondered these possibilities. He was rather shy towards amputees, although - or perhaps just because - he found them so attractive. As long as he could remember, he had always had a weak spot for such special girls and women. He didn't know where this interest came from; it simply was there and he couldn't shake it.

As always around this time, traffic into the city center had become chaos. Rolf was in a jam and was sorry for not returning earlier. He would now miss Marianne and she'd have to go through this chaos all by herself. "She'll have pressure spots on her stump again and hop around without her prosthesis all evening. What an unnecessary shame!"

The apprentice had brought her a pair of fore arm crutches, already adjusted to her height. "Thanks. A good choice." Marianne positioned the aluminium crutches, that had a reddish shine. "They match my skirt perfectly - this looks quite passable, doesn't it?" The apprentice blushed. "I never thought of that," he stuttered. Marianne laughed. "It's all right, you still have a lot to learn!" The prosthetist, who stood nearby, now chuckled as well. "Sure, you look good, Marianne, but it's not the crutches that cause that." Now it was Marianne's turn to blush. Embarrassed she looked down. If only Rolf could look upon her this way. She quickly look at the mirror and saw a slim young woman in a short leather jacket and a red skirt, leaning easily on two reddishly gleaming crutches. "Only one leg, but apart from that not at all bad," Marianne confirmed. She smiled and the prosthetist for his compliment. "Well, I did look better four years ago," she went on, indicating her lonely right leg with one of the crutches. "Not better, different," the prosthetist replied. "Those who are repulsed by your appearance are beyond help. But enough; your taxi will be here by now."

Martin had put down his magazine. He feverishly pondered how to proceed. He simply had to find the courage to speak to Marianne! He definitely wanted to get to know this woman. Even if she was half as nice as she appeared, perhaps his dreams could suddenly come true. But how?

After saying goodbye Marianne swung easily toward the exit. She felt lighter now, more free. Without realising it, the prosthetist had confirmed it to her; Rolf was beyond help. He was the problem, not she. The time had come to separate from him and become independent.

Rolf looked at his watch. "Almost half past five, I'll never make it..." Annoyed he stepped on the accelerator to proceed another couple of yards.

There, the doors opened. It was her, and still without prosthesis! "Now is the time to get out and go to her," he ordered himself, "now, or never!" But Martin remained seated, paralysed by shame to have longed for this unique woman, imprisoned by his special feelings. Once again, he didn't trust himself to do that which all other men did again and again; approach a good looking woman. Martin picked up the magazine again.

The taxi hadn't arrived yet. Marianne closed the doors behind her, carefully descended the steps and moved toward the customers parking lot, swinging between her crutches. The red Volkswagen was no longer there. "Good," she thought. "Rolf has gone." She turned and now went towards the street. She scanned along the parked cars; no red VW there either. But no trace of the taxi, for that matter. She'd have to wait. While scanning the street she noticed a young man in a BMW, reading a magazine. Apparently, he was also waiting.

From the corner of his eye he noticed that Marianne watched him. He heart skipped a beat. "Keep low," he calmed himself.

She should've waited inside. At least she would have had something to read. Marianne slowly became impatient, although she knew quite well that you'd have to wait a long time for a taxi at this hour.

At last Rolf had a free road before him, at least until the next red light. In front of him was only a taxi, which he'd been following for a while. Two crossings, then to the left, and he'd be back at the workshop.

And what if she recognised him? Martin had followed Marianne on a number of occasions; she would put him in his place, mock him and perhaps tell him to go to hell. He should leave. He put away his magazine, grabbed the car keys, and just when he wanted to start the car, he saw Marianne approach him.

The man in the BMW had put his magazine away and apparently was about to drive off. Should she ask him? Perhaps he could take her downtown, that taxi wouldn't be here for some time, anyway. Her decision made, she began to cross the street. The man looked at her, immediately looked away again. "Oh well, the leg," Marianne thought, "he'll be embarrassed, but what the heck, he won't refuse a cripple a small favor!" A wicked smile on her face, she knocked on the window of the car.

Martin froze. No, that couldn't be. What should he say? Mechanically he pushed the button to lower the electric window. With a dry mouth and a flat voice he asked: "Yes?"

360

"Excuse me, I saw you are about to leave. I'm waiting for a taxi, but it hasn't shown up. Could you please take me downtown with you?" Marianne had bent forward and smiled at the man. "If it's on your way, to the station would be fine."

"Sure, no problem. It's on my way." It was as if a stone had been lifted from Martin's chest. She hadn't sneered at him, but rather, had been friendly. He smiled back and said: "Get in, and let's go." Martin bent over the passenger seat and opened the door. Still smiled he watched how the pretty young woman moved in front of the radiator, stepped on to the pedestrian walkway and reached the passenger door.

The taxi in front of him also prepared to go left. "I'll still be on time," Rolf thought, "that must be the taxi that Marianne ordered."

Marianne noticed how the man observed her. His eyes followed her when she moved around the car. But there was no repulsion in his eyes, like she was used to in Rolf's, neither sympathy, like she had seen so often. He smiled and didn't seem to be disturbed by her appearance. "He look at me, like the old days..." went through Marianne's mind. She had reached the open door, turned around easily, and sat down in the passenger seat, her crutches and her right leg still on the pavement. She looked over her shoulder and asked the man if he could take her crutches.

"Glad to. Is it OK to put them on the back seat?" He took the aluminium crutches from her and stored the in the back. "Sure, they'll be out of the way there," Marianne replied, while swinging her leg into the car. She closed the door and turned towards the man. This movement caused the fabric of her skirt to get caught under her thigh so that it tightened around her stump.

"Thanks a lot for your help," Marianne went on, "and... oh, sorry." She saw that he looked down and only now noticed how clearly outlined her stump was. Marianne straightened her skirt and explained: "I had an accident a couple of years ago, and as you can see, I lost my leg. It's not as bad as you might think, I've gotten used to it quite well. No reason for sympathy."

At last there was a hole in the oncoming trafic and Rolf could go left. Behind the taxi he drove down the street, watching to see if Marianne was waiting outside, so that he wouldn't have to inside to all those cripples. Rolf had only gone in with his girlfriend once, and that had been enough for him. The memory of all the prosthetists in their white coats and their customers, moving with great effort on half-finished prostheses, still made him uncomfortable. And his Marianne had been among them, one of these disabled, a cripple for life. "Yes," Rolf sighed, "what kind of a life is there for us?"

Never before had Martin been so close to a woma amputee. Never before had he seen a stump so clearly. His excitement grew. "I can't let her notice, be cool," he told himself. He started the car and drove off. "Must've been dreadful, becoming disabled suddenly." Martin looked at Marianne inquisitively, but avoided looking at her stump again.

"Sure," Marianne answered, "there are a few things that you can't do anymore, but most things are still OK. I normally wear a prosthesis; I can get about pretty well with that. If I wouldn't have had to leave it at the workshop today, you wouldn't even have noticed."

O yes I would, Martin thought, I always do. He smiled and said: "Probably. I wouldn't have noticed *it*, but I would have noticed *you*! A pretty woman like you is always noticed!"

362

Marianne could hardly believe her ears. This total stranger made her a compliment! She looked at him. There was a sparkle in his eyes. However, he seemed to be serious, it wasn't one of those inevitable plattitudes. Was it a pick-up line? They didn't even know each other. "I'm not going to be that easy," it went through Marianne's mind. And yet she somehow felt flattered. With mixed feelings she countered: "Thanks for the flowers, but pretty, that was in the past, I guess. You should see how people stare at me when I go swimming for instance. Not because I'm pretty, but because I'm a freak, as they put it. You have heard of freak shows, haven't you? In the circus? Disabled people, exhibited like exotic animals."

The taxi did indeed stop in front of the workshop, the driver got out and rushed up the stairs. Rolf turned his volkswagen into the reserved parking space again, and got out. No sign of Marianne anywhere; she'd probably come out together with the taxi driver. Indeed, the doord opened almost immediately and the taxi driver appeared. He held the doors open with one hand and waited. But to Rolf's disappointment it wasn't Marianne who came out, but an older lady, followed by one of the prosthetists. Ashamed, Rolf looked away, for this lady, too, was on crutches and only one leg could be seen coming out from under her knee-length skirt. "Is this becoming a fashion?" Rolf wondered. "First Marianne without prosthesis and now that woman too! How terrible! They should hide their disability!" He overcame his repulsion and went toward these people, who were just about to descend the stairs. "Excuse me, is Marianne Reitel still here? I'm supposed to pick her up." The prosthetist shook his head. "No, she just left five minutes ago, I'm sorry." "Damn," Rolf mumbled to himself, going back to the car, "too late."

Martin concentrated on the road and didn't dare look at Marianne again. Had he been too bold? Had he insulted her? "I don't want to sound cheeky," he replied, without taking his eyes off the road, "but, believe me, you're no freak to me. You really look good and you seem... sympathetic,... open. You're an attractive woman, even if you are minus one leg." He shot her a quick look and noticed that she watched him with large eyes. He had to try now: "I like you. A lot. The amputation really makes you into a very special woman. My name is Martin, by the way."

"Hello, Martin," she stammered, surprised, "I'm Marianne." She mustered the young man from head to toe. He had stopped the car at a red light and looked into her eyes with his sparkling eyes. Doubtfully Marianne asked: "You like me? Despite my disability?" She straightened the fabric over her stump again, so that her one-leggedness became more apparent. "Despite the fact that I'm an amputee and only have a short stump here?"

His heart raced, the excitement constricted his throat. Martin pulled himself together and earnestly looked Marianne in the eyes. "Yes, I like you. I find you beautiful -- not despite the disability, but rather because you're an amputee." It was out now. Martin lowered his eyes and admiringly observed the small, rounded stump, clearly outlined under the red fabric. He smiled and look into Marianne's eyes again. "That stump makes you into something quite special -- and I like things special. It underlines your beauty, this deviation from the perfect, and its tragedy is exciting, makes you attractive." The lights changed to green, but Martin did not react and didn't let his eyes stray from Marianne, which made her very uncertain. Martin inhaled deeply. He had to say it: "I fall for amputated women; and you are the most beautiful I've ever seen."

"What did you say!? You like amputees? That's... unheard of!" Marianne felt a wave of antipathy well up in her. "You've got a real kink. Look at this!" She took the hem of her skirt and revealed her stump. "There's nothing beautiful about this. If I'd want to be found attractive, then surely not because of this." She raised the short thigh stump a little so that Martin couldn't help but notice the thin scar.

364

"Oh, yes!" Martin replied, and he watched the round stump that she held up to him, smiling. "I do have a kink, but who can call himself normal? I know other men who the same way I do -- not many, but a few. I like amputee women, I can't help it." Behind the car a horn concert had started and it was only then that Martin noticed the green light.

Suddenly, Marianne saw the comedy of the situation. She laughed out loud and told Martin: "I think you're supposed to drive on. This is not a good time for revelations and confessions." She covered her stump and observed Martin as he concentrated on the road again. "Weird", it went through her mind, "he really gets off on my amputation. Rolf finds it horrible and Martin finds it attractive. Not all that bad, really, that not everybody is like Rolf... and this Martin type is really sympathetic. Doesn't look too bad, either. I'd like to know more about him, to understand more about his remarkable... preference."

Rolf had steered his car back into the slow trafic. Nothing would come of the meal he had planned for them together. He had wanted to surprise Marianne and had reserved a table at her favourite restaurant a while back. But after this sequence of events... In reality Rolf was quite happy he couldn't take her out tonight, so cross was he with Marianne.

In silence Martin steered the car through the evening rush hour. He had taken the plunge, at last he had taken the plunge... "Hopefully my words haven't disgusted Marianne. Why doesn't she say anything? Did I frighten her that much?" he wondered. He shot her a glance. She was in deep thought and seemed not to notice him at all. His fear grew and after a while the silence seemed almost impossible to break. Martin gathered all his courage: "I apologise, Marianne, I didn't mean to hurt you, but I..."

That was as far as he got. Marianne interrupted him and said soothingly: "You shouldn't apologise, Martin. You didn't hurt me, you just confused me. What you just said is completely new to me -- so different from everything I've heard from other men so far, about my disability." She looked out the window, and added: "Even my boy friend finds my body repulsive -- and now... your confession." She turned towards Martin and said in an upbeat manner: "You're interested in me, I'm interested in your interest; tell me about yourself."

Martin relaxed. He looked at Marianne: "Marianne, I can't describe how happy I am that you don't loathe me. I'll gladly tell you about me, and I'd like to know a lot about you. Can I buy you a cup of coffee?"

Marianne looked at her watch. "No, out of the question", she replied forcefully, and after a short pause she added: "By this time you're supposed to invite me to dinner. I know an excellent Italian just two blocks from here. Not one with pizzas and pastas, but with a real Toscany kitchen." She didn't want to go back to Rolf right now...

An evening with Marianne! Martin couldn't believe his luck. "Hey, great, making time for me like that! I'll very gladly invite you: Please be my guest, beautiful lady!" he went on. "What about a little aperitif to get going? There's a new bar right up there, very trendy." Without waiting for Marianne's answer Martin steered his BMW in the first free parking space; by this time there were enough of them available. He switched off the engine, got out and hurried around the car to assist Marianne getting out. Martin was too late. Marianne had already opened the door and gotten out of the car. She stood on her single leg and bent forward to take the crutches from the back seat. Under her skirt her round buttocks and short stump were clearly outlined; she had to stretch the stump backwards in order to keep her balance. Martin sighed. When Marianne stood straight again she turned around with two or three short hops and then leaned lightly on her crutches. "All set?" she asked, smiling. Martin locked the car. "Sure. It's down there."

Without talking they moved towards the bar. Marianne was surprised about herself. She didn't feel at all apprehensive, being among people, without a prosthesis. No, she actually liked to be noticed and draw attention. But nobody watched her as Martin did, who obviously enjoyed it to walk next to her and who occasionally cast a look at her leg. She grinned inwardly: "If only Rolf could see me now! He'd have a heart attack!"

"She moves very elegantly on those crutches," Martin thought. "No limping on a prosthesis; she almost floats. And before, the view of her taking the crutches from the car..." He had always dreamt of such situations, wondered how to behave -- and now, actually experiencing it, everything was different, simpler. He felt good, somehow liberated. Everything went naturally, he could just be himself.

Rolf thought miserably that it was going to be another boring television evening, without him working up the courage to speak about their fight. It was about time, anyway, to have a talk about not only today's row, but also about their relationship as a whole. It couldn't go on like this.

They reached the crowded bar, and Martin went in first to hold the door for Marianne. Some people watched them and cast a look at the pretty one-legged woman, who graciously moved through the entrance. For only a moment the noise died down in the establishment, only the jukebox could be heard. But only a fraction of a second later the room was noisy as before. Martin weaved his way through the crowd, Marianne directly behind him, hopping rather than crutching. Martin looked back over his shoulder and asked through the noise: "Shall we sit at the bar? Perhaps I can conquer a stool for you."

"I can't hear you! What was that?" Marianne shouted. Martin repeated the question, louder this time. Marianne bent forward and said in his ear: "Let me go in front; I think I'll have a better chance!" She almost lost her balance and made one hop towards Martin, who wanted to let her pass.

For the first time he touched her. He noticed her firm breasts, pressed against him. Instinctively he caught her around her waist. Marianne looked at him with surprise and they briefly looked into each other's eyes. He wanted to pull back his hand, when Marianne held both crutches under her right arm and placed her left on his shoulder. "Yes," he heard her say, "in this crowd I won't get far on crutches. Hold me, and lead me." Martin felt Marianne press closer to him, and held her a bit stronger. He supported her easily, both struggling their way through the crowd. With every tiny step he could take Marianne made a short hop, holding on to him, pressed closely to him. "Your stump, it's your little stubbie!" With every hop she took, her short thigh stump pressed against his leg. Martin blushed, his heart raced. "Stay cool," he commanded himself, "the night's still young."

When at last they reached the bar, Marianne let go of her escort and shot him a wicked glance. She tapped one of the young men, who were sitting at the bar, on his shoulder and asked: "How about giving up your seat for me?" The man hardly turned his head and went: "Women's lib, huh? Go find someone dumber." At that, Marianne bent forward and leaned her crutches against the bar, right in front of the youngster, who turned, and said: "Skiing is an acquired skill, oldie." Marianne grinned from ear to ear and replied: "Oh yes, I learned it again, babyface." She hopped a few times as if descending a slope. The young man turned pale. Only now he noticed why Marianne had her crutches with her. Without another word he stood and disappeared in the crowd. "Thanks!" Marianne called after him, and then broke into loud laughter. Turning towards Martin, she said: "See? There are advantages!" She easily lifted her stump and sat with her left hip on the stool. "Come, there's room enough

368

for you here." On their way towards the bar, Marianne hadn't failed to notice how she excited Martin. Would he dare to share the stool with her, to feel the touch of her stump directly against his thigh? "I am behaving really frivolous, like an adolescent," she mumbled, but secretly she hoped he would sit next to her.

Martin, too, felt like being back in his puberty. He was embarrassed by his quite obvious erection and hoped that Marianne wouldn't notice his excitement. At the same time, he lusted for this one-legged woman, so badly that he wanted nothing more than take her on the spot. How exciting she was, sitting there, using the bar stool almost like a prosthesis, and how innocently she laughed and invited him next to her. "Martin," he told himself, "grow up and behave yourself."

Rolf approached their home and noticed with surprise that there were no lights on inside the house. Wasn't Marianne there? She had left before him, hadn't she? He drove the car into the parking garage and rode the elevator up.

"Well, are you going to stand there?" Marianne asked when she noticed Martin's indecision. Encouragingly, she added: "Come to me..." At last Martin conquered himself and sat down on the edge of the stool, almost as if he didn't want to touch her. "How timid he suddenly is," she thought, and added: "... next to me, come on!" Marianne put her arm around his waist and pulled him closer. She lifted her stump slightly and rubbed it against Martin's thigh. He must like that, after all that he had told her. She whispered in his ear: "So, you say I appeal to you -- I, a one-legged cripple? Why would I believe you? I need proof!" With a wicked smile on her face she pressed her stump even harder against Martin.

Martin now let go of all inhibitions and stroked her short hair, her neck, her back, until he reached her waist. He looked deeply into her eyes, bent forward and carefully placed a kiss on her lips.

Indeed, the door was locked. So, where was Marianne? She should've been home a long time ago! He quickly unlocked the door and opened it. "Marianne, are you there?" No reply. "You don't care a thing about what I do for you, do you!?" he yelled into the empty house, and angrily slammed the door behind him.

Marianne reciprocated the kiss, at first holding back a little, then more surely. Yes, this was the man she wanted, this was the one she wanted to seduce, and to be seduce by. She felt how Martin put his other arm around her and held her closer to him. In a tight embrace they sat on the stool, the kiss refusing to come to an end. Her eyes closed, carried by her feelings, Marianne stroked Martin's back, and then noticed his hands starting to wander over her body. Tenderly he directed them from her waist to her hips, and after a short hesitation, to her thigh. He took her stump in his right hand and squeezed ever so slightly. Slowly, Marianne freed herself from his embrace and said, beaming: "The prosecution rests! All doors are open to you."

TERRI & JANET
By Andreio Higgins

Terri smiled widely. "How about a little 'gee-I've-missed-you' greeting? ... You can re-do my lipstick before we go." Our deep, wet kiss was accompanied by Terri rubbing her incredible breasts back and forth across my chest. When we got tired of trying to suck each others' tongues out, Terri stepped back and motioned me in. "You haven't seen my new place before. How do you think it looks? More to the point, how do I look?"

Wearing nylons and 5-1/2 inch heels, and with a short dressing robe, Terri looked just fine, and I said so. She's about five feet tall, and her perfect figure is flawed by only one thing: a pair of breasts that would be in proportion only if she were larger framed and six inches taller. I don't consider her arms to be a flaw. The right one ends seven inches below the elbow, the left one four inches above. Terri lost her hand when she was seven. The stump, which is very slender, is nearly without scar. Her left arm was amputated three years ago, the result of infection. I tend to think of the remaining stump as that of a miniature thigh, because it's full and soft and has a fairly dramatic scar where they sewed it closed.

During the week, Terri uses a forearm hook and an artificial arm. The hook simply slips on her stump, is held in place by suction and is self-contained. That is, the hooks are articulated by means of a tiny motor that gets its signals from the nerves inside her stump. Terri has used a hook ever since the beginning, and after 24 years of practice, she's extremely competent.

Her artificial arm is really for appearances. It's amazingly authentic looking, with a skin-like texture which includes the proper creases. The slightly curved (relaxed) fingers have polished nails, and she usually wears a bracelet and a ring or two. But the man made limb, although it does articulate, is not especially useful, at least not compared to her hook. Perhaps because she's had one nearly all her life, Terri prefers a hook; besides, she says it looks erotic, especially compared to a fake hand. So, come after work and on the weekends, she puts her artificial arm on the shelf and replaces it with her "old arm" or, "robot" or, not infrequently, she replaces it with nothing. In any case, she wears a variety of things, sometimes with long sleeves, sometimes it's short sleeves, and sometimes it's a blouse or dress that's sleeveless. It's pretty dramatic when all that shows past the cuffs of a nice dress's long sleeves area is a (mismatched) pair of man made wrists and steel hooks. Then again, it's not a dull sight when the sleeves are short, and you can see where one hook's stump sleeve ends, but not the other. And I don't find it boring with a sleeveless garment, when you can see her robot arm completely, as well as the slight bulge, just barely below the shoulder, where her stump disappears into the aluminum.

When Terri elects to not use a long hook in public, I prefer sleeves long enough to hide her four inch arm (elbow length is best). It's not that I don't like to see her "short stump", I do; it's just that I guess I don't want others to do so. Besides, her right arm and its hook are accentuated by the way the empty portion of the left sleeve flops around at random.

Terri sat down on the couch and motioned toward the kitchen. "Want a drink and something to nibble? or should we just go?" I smiled and said that I wouldn't mind nibbling her breasts ... and "some other things." Terri grinned, "Thought you might feel that way. That's why I didn't bother to finish dressing."

With that, Terri shrugged the robe off her shoulders, revealing crotchless panty hose and no bra. Still smiling, she poked her breasts with the end of her handless right arm and, at the same time, waved her four inch stump. "I trust these will suffice for appetizers." I said I was sure they would. But I was glancing elsewhere. Terri noticed, moved her thighs apart, dropped her forearm stump between them and deliberately played with herself. "Not now," she laughed, "This is for dessert ... later. First you've got to nibble on breasts ... and 'some other things'." Terri held up both her stumps.

I sat, leaned over and "nibbled". I also let my hands roam, across her breasts and up and down her amputated arms. During all this, Terri occasionally interrupted her sighs, asking me to "bite a little harder", and by doing a thorough job on my ear with her tongue. After about 10 minutes of this, Terri whispered, "Let's go to dinner, so we can have dessert." Before getting up, I took a final try at sucking the rock hard nipple in my mouth down my throat. Then I followed Terri to the bedroom where a dress was already laying out.

"Touch up my lipstick," Terri smiled. "And then a quick massage before you help me finish dressing." Terri remained standing while I applied lipstick. Then I took a seat on the stool in front of the three-way, full-length mirror and waited for Terri to sit on my lap. We were both facing the mirror. Terri's legs were spread just enough for her knees to be outside mine. She drew back her feet and pointed the shoes' toes outward enough so the heels' reflection was clear to see. Then she held her stumps out slightly and smiled at me in the mirror. "A good one please."

I did a bit of massaging around her neck and across her shoulders before I let my fingers drop dawn her back and then go forward to cup a hard nippled breast in each hand. I kneaded and squeezed, making the soft flesh bulge between my fingers. Then I moved my left hand back and up and ran it along the under side of her short stump. I treated the four inch remainder of her arm, including the end, just as I had her breast. I then did the same to the comparatively long, slender stump of her right arm. Next I used both hands on a single item, alternating between her breasts and stumps. Believe me, there is no better position for what I was doing; furthermore, I can't think of a better location in which to do it. In the first instance, your hands, as well as the objects

374

they're to message, are positioned perfectly; in the second instance, the clear view afforded by a well lit room and a mirror such as Terri's is, well, rather exciting.

Terri finally said I'd done an "adequate job", and we prepared to go. "Red bra, black trim, top drawer," Terri said as she went to the dressing table and sat. I had no trouble finding the bra, nor did I have any trouble getting her still hard nippled breasts into the severely shaped cups and it finally fastened. Terri said I must be out of practice, it took so long. I said I was just making sure I did a proper job and would she have rather done it herself.

Terri stood and reviewed in the mirror. "Don't be a brat," she said, shaking her shoulders. "You know perfectly well there's no way in hell I could put it on by myself." Terri motioned to the dress on the bed. "It's got a fitted bodice and short sleeves." She paused for a moment. "So," Terri waved her stumps, "what's your pleasure as far as these are concerned?" I said that, having seen her stumps for the last half hour, they were beginning to bore me, and that I thought she ought to use two hooks. Terri laughed, "You lie. You never tire of my stumps. The only reason you want me to use one of my long hooks is because you want to put it on. She smiled, sat down and pointed with her short stump. "They're in the closet. Either one's fine with me, but if you decide on robot, I'll change shoes. There's a pair of pumps on the top shelf, black with silver heels .... after all, I wouldn't want shoes that didn't match my outfit, would I?"

In the closet, I pondered her long hooks. I always have difficulty deciding which I'd rather see. The old arm (it really is an antique) is made of wood. The blemished surface, the oversized elbow hinge pins and the old-fashioned control lever and wire, not to mention the hooks themselves (which are original, somewhat poorly shaped, and tarnished) create a false impression. Hidden by the old, crude-looking artificial limb, state of the art innards flex the elbow, articulate the hooks and even rotate the wrist. Terri's robot arm is at the other end of the spectrum as far as appearance is concerned. Above the elbow, it's a combination of a short, blunt-ended stump sleeve that gives way to an equally short piece of inch-diameter tube. All in all, it looks more like a miniature peg leg than an upper arm. The elbow, which is a ball joint, is an elaborate assembly of precision machined parts. A pair of slender rods form the forearm; the wrist, like the elbow, is precision made, and the hooks, which have a marvelous shape and taper, are bright and shiny and without the slightest blemish. The primary parts are aluminum, the working parts, stainless steel. In both cases, the metal is in its natural state and well polished.

Of course, the thing looks nothing like an arm. It appears to have been designed by someone who knew what an arm was supposed to do, but had no idea what one looked like . This is especially true when Terri uses the machine-like thing to pick up and inspect a piece of jewelry or grab an appetizer. In either case it's quite a sight when the wrist silently (and smoothly) rotates, bringing the treasure that's clamped between the flashing steel fingers into proper position. Terri says she prefers to think of it as though some unknown robot decided to make a gesture of affection by having an arm amputated and giving it to her.

I grabbed Terri's old arm; I could always ask her to change when we go back. Besides, I thought it would go well with her barebacked platformed clogs, which were made of wood and had a dramatic grain pattern just like the antique arm. While Terri sat at the dressing table, I slipped the hollow, miniature, tree-trunk-like upper arm over her stump and fastened the strips in place. Then I slipped her short hook on and helped with her dress. The previous comment about a "fitted bodice" had been an understatement.

Terri went to the mirror for an appraisal. As she turned to review all angles, She articulated her hooks, checking that they were working properly. "I know you've got reservations at 'The Steak-Out', but let's cancel and go to 'Big Al's' and have fried chicken. I feel like finger food. Besides, I'll be able to feed you,"

Terri grinned and clicked her hooks. "If, that is, you promise to make sure you lick my fingers clean."

The meal was great and, yes, I made sure Terri's fingers were clean. We decided on an after dinner drink. In the lounge, I slipped the rubber tubes on her forearm hook. With her "gloves" on Terri can pick up a stemmed glass with no worry of it slipping. When the second drink was gone, we caught each other's eyes and, without saying anything, got up.

Back at Terri's place, she turned and smiled. "Let's undress each other here ... and then make-out on the couch ... and finally, do it on the floor. Make us a couple of cognacs while I get a bed-spread. Carpet burns are such a drag." When she returned, I smoothed out the thick, quilted bedspread and joined her on the couch. We clinked our glasses, took a sip and then, before swallowing, clamped our mouths together and mixed the tangy liquid.

Terri stood. I removed her dress and tossed it aside, then she stepped out of the panties after I pulled them down her shimmering legs. When I finished, she slowly unbuttoned my shirt and got it off. Then she knelt and began on my pants, working the belt free and the zipper open. When she drug my pants and shorts down, the steel fingers of her old arm's ungloved hooks were still cool as they ran along my legs. Before she stood, Terri ran her hooks back up my legs, gently played with me for a moment and took me in her mouth for just a second.

Back on the couch, we finished the brandy, and I took off her "gloves". During the kisses that followed, I massaged her still housed breasts and investigated the warm dampness at the top of her thighs. For her part, Terri's short hook constantly explored between my legs. During a

377

breather, I decided it was time to expose her hard nippled breasts. As I reached around to undo her bra, Terri tongued my ear and whispered, "Take off my arm, too. One hook is enough; besides, I want to feel you .... with more than just my mouth. I tossed her bra and antique artificial arm on top of the dress at the far end of the couch. As I mouthed first one and then the other of her oversized breasts, including their full, rock-hard nipples, Terri probed between my legs with her hook and rubbed my neck and ear with the four-inch stump of her left arm.

On the floor, we rolled around on the bedspread, groping, feeling and using our mouths on each other. During these preliminaries, I ate her twice (she came the first time), and she swallowed me more than once. When Terri smiled and nodded at the foot stool, I knew she was ready for what she calls "a proper 69".

I'm on my back, with my right knee pulled back so my thigh is out to the side. The padded foot stool (which is only 10 inches high) is just to the left of my head. Terri, who is facing the opposite way, is on my right. She is laying on her right side, using my thigh as a pillow. Her left knee is resting on the foot stool, her thigh crossing only inches from my face. Her mouth is ideally located to swallow me and, with her right shoulder resting on my thigh, her short hook is in perfect position to help. Her four inch stump moves back and forth, alternating between rubbing my belly and helping her hook and mouth. With her right thigh next to my head and the left one held up and out of the way, my ..ah.. access to her is similarly excellent. Just before we start, I generally reach down with my left hand and fill it with her soft, naked left breast.

We got into position and began ... slowly. As her warm mouth worked on me, I licked and sucked, concentrating on her erect clitoris. I couldn't see what her hook was doing, but feel was enough. Our reserved beginning quickly moved on to a more intense stage, where she interrupted her mouth to rub and poke at me with her short stump. I responded by increasing the rhythm of my flattering tongue and by using more muscle to squeeze the soft blob that filled my hand. Before long we were grunting, both from lack of breath and from simple passion. A little later, I heard a thumping on the carpet as Terri knocked her hook free. I interrupted my feast just long enough to glance up and see it roll across the floor. By the time my mouth was back in position, I could feel the slim, firm stump of Terri's handless forearm as it rubbed my thighs and probed between them.

The first few times, after we'd devised this arrangement, I was the first to climax. Then, I would get her to do the same, frantically licking and sucking as I relaxed, still in her mouth. But Terri decided she wanted it the other way around: she wanted to climax first. It was amazing how she seemed to be able to tell even better than I, that split second just before I reached the point of no return. And when she does, she pulls her mouth away (1) to forestall my climax and (2) as a signal that she is ready. I redouble my efforts, which is no mean feat, considering what they've been up to that at point and taking into account my aching tongue. (I think, and Terri agrees, that tongues should be stronger and, like some other parts of the body, they should get erect). At that point Terri puts her now unfilled mouth to a new use: she talks. Although, I must say the delivery, as well as the dialogue, are hardly every day. The voice is husky and interrupted by gasps and cries; the dialogue is not composed of sentences, but consists of short phrases and single words, sometimes sounding like a whispered plea, other times like an urgent command.

Terri slowly drew her tight lips up along me until I came out of her mouth and then wiggled so she could reach me with both her stumps. She shifted a bit on her side, slightly widening her thighs. " Suck harder." (It was the whispered plea). Terri was ready. I sucked harder and, as always, waited for the next words. I followed each request as she made them. "Lick it ... suck it ... Oh God, yes, yes ... suck and lick ... at the same time ... harder ... please, harder ... yes, yes, yes ... God, I love it ... Ahhhh ... yeeee ... suckkkk ... harder ... faster ....." Terri's breathing was labored and her upheld thigh was beginning to shake and quiver. I drew her nipple-like clitoris into my mouth as deep as I could, and I urged my tongue to attack it. "Yessss, ARGGhhhh ... Ohhh ... YEEEeeee ARRrr-CCCHHhhhhhh ... STUMP ... Stump ... STUMP . ...

Terri's four inch arm was nearly a blur as it frantically pawed the air and furiously pounded my belly. I let go of Terri's breast and grabbed the short, flipper-like thing that seemed to have gone mad. I squeeze and kneaded the soft flesh to the point I could clearly feel the remaining piece of bone as it moved around inside. Terri was unable to utter an intelligible word: her efforts at communication being reduced to guttural moans and gasping cries. When she climaxed, her short stump was wrenched from my tight grasp and a hot ooze greeted my desperately flattering tongue.

Terri finally managed to gasp, "Your turn ... I want you ... I want you to come in my mouth." With that, she threw her head down, and I plunged in to the point I could feel the back of her throat. Terri worked on me with her mouth and stumps, urgently, as though she wanted me to climax quickly. I tried to forestall it by continuing to gently lick her, concentrating on the incredible softness of what my tongue was slowly exploring. But, of course, Terri and nature won, and I involuntarily erupted in her mouth with a rapid series of forceful bursts that felt like hot lava as they ran through me. I could see Terri's throat work as she drank me. She kept her head in place and continued to gently work her lips and tongue long after my climax had run its all too short course.

With breaths regained, we got back on the couch. "Let's have another drink," Terri smiled, "while we recoup and get ready for scene two." got some more cognac and returned. "I guess you'll have to feed it to me," Terri grinned, waving her naked stumps. As we relaxed and talked I occasionally brushed a hand across her semi hard nipples or caressed one of her stumps; Terri similarly petted me with her handless arm. During all this, I would take a sip of brandy and then share it with her. Sometimes I forced a portion into Terri's mouth, other times she would swirl the tangy liquid around inside my mouth with her tongue before sucking out more than her fair share. Half an hour later, we were back on the floor. Terri retrieved her short hook and used it, and her mouth, to revitalize me. Her ministrations were successful and, although I was far from as hard as I'd been previously, I managed to preform adequately. Terri isn't quite as vocal while making love she is when she's being eaten, but she still gets the point across.

The following morning, Terri decided she felt like being "pampered for a while". "A while" can be an hour or nearly all day. Once it lasted clear on through the evening until we went to bed. The basic idea is simple: Terri leaves her hook, off. The result is that I have to do "all the work". I suppose making the bed, doing something about breakfast, along with its clean up, and so forth could be classified work, but it's not what you'd call taxing. The other "work" consisted of helping Terri to shower and get dressed, feeding her and doing any other little items she happens to desire, but is unable to accomplish by herself because "rather than arms and hands, the poor thing has nothing more than a pair of ugly, useless stumps." (Terri rarely gets that out without losing her somber look).

She may want me to rub sun tan lotion all over her naked body on the back porch ("Be sure and do a good job on my stumps ... you know how easily they burn") : or perhaps she'll decide she needs to try on most of her high heels, intimate underthings and most severe bras, the excuse being, "I think I've got a few things that don't fit right anymore." Usually when this happens, Terri will pick the most sexy combination for last and then leave it on for a while because "It's fun to walk around like this sometimes. I mean, there's something kind of exciting about being dressed so inappropriately. I hope you don't mind."

I hardly mind; still, it's sort of difficult to keep track of yardage and first downs when your girl friend is meandering back and forth wearing gleaming black nylons and platformed high heels, along with an extreme corset or bra that does incredible things for her already incredible tits, and leaves her shoulders and the stumps of her arms naked and bare. Needless to say, I usually (read always) seem to miss a play or two, unless it's a whale of a series.

Another thing Terri likes when she's in this mood is for me to make various snacks. Some, I have to feed to her, sandwiches and the like; others she can do with no help. One of her favorites is a fairly thick onion dip and chips. Terri pokes the end of her handless forearm into the bowl until there's a blob of dip on the end, then, using that as glue, she goes to the second bowl and gets a chip. It's really quite an enjoyable sight, but the best part about chips 'n dip is that Terri also feeds me. I always make sure I get every bit of dip off the end of her stump.

I pampered her until about 4 o'clock when Terri said we ought to make love, take a nap, go out to dinner and then, "following too many after dinner drinks", come back and "do things to each other". I had no problem with the schedule. And considering Terri was wearing nothing but a pair of thigh high, platformed boots when she made the suggestion. I was anxious to get on with the first item on the agenda.

Returning to her bedroom, following a delightful shower together, Terri said, "I think I'll skip my hooks tonight."

On the comparatively rare occasions that Terri feels like going out sans hooks, she always wears the shiniest of nylons, very high heels and something that fits ..ah.. well. Her favorite combination is her lizard pumps and a green cocktail dress. The green shoes are platformed 1-3/4 inches and have seven inch heels; the dress, with a slightly flared skirt that's hemmed just above the knee, has a wide belt, fitted bodice, deeply V-ed, and sleeves. Between her overly shiny nylons and extreme heels, Terri's shapely calves are shown off quite well, and the cleavage display is certainly an eye-catcher. But the dress' sleeves are the real show. Both are slim and tailored and are not cuffed or trimmed with any decorations. But they are different lengths, each ending about an inch past the end of its respective stump.

As Terri moves, the mismatched sleeves' open ends flop nicely, accentuating that the unseen remains of her arms are just barely hidden. Hidden, that is, until Terri begins talking, at which time the end of first one and then the other of her stumps pop in and out of view as she gesticulates and/or points.

Other attire, when she's using no hooks include:

A long sleeved dress worn with a cape. The left sleeve is folded across her short stump and sewn in place. The idea is that until the cape comes off, no one notices anything unusual. Removing the cape is accomplished by my taking it off her right shoulder first. After everyone who happens to be looking has absorbed the fact that the poor girl has a hook instead of a hand, I remove the cape the rest of the way, bringing into view her clearly defined short stump.

Sometimes Terri reverses things and uses just a long hook. On such occasions, Terri almost always wears something sleeveless (or tantamount to) because "It looks better when you can see more." With one of her arms being soft and smooth, but with its hand amputated, and the other looking as though it belongs to a robot, the sight is pretty dramatic.

Another of her show off tricks is to use a hook (usually a forearm one) and bandage her other stump. Again, it's important that the sleeves are the proper length. When it's her four inch arm that's bandaged, this means short sleeves.

I'm sure you can "see" it for yourself. I mean, when the cape comes free and her bandaged stump comes into view, it doesn't take any great effort to imagine that the poor thing has very recently undergone her second amputation. Only this time, rather than losing just a part of an arm, the doctors changed sides and cut off the whole thing.

Since we were still in pampered mode and Terri was going to ignore her looks. I had to do her hair and make-up and help her dress. Believe me, those are fun tasks. At the restaurant (we went to a place Terri said was "marvelous"), Terri as usual ordered an up martini ("One of the best drinks around to drink through a straw," is her comment). I, of course. have to feed her the olive, as I have to feed her dinner.

The place was small and intimate, and the owner seemed delighted to see Terri. He beamed at her, said he was pleased to meet me and them, with a smile and a nod at the empty ends of Terri's sleeves, whispered, "I'll give you that small booth in the corner and have one of the place settings removed." When we were seated, I commented that Terri had apparently been here before ... with a date, but without her hooks. She grinned. "Once or twice. After all, I couldn't sit around doing nothing, waiting for you to come back from Germany or Holland or wherever it was. Besides, I've met a couple of guys who think I'm really quite nice. In fact one of them, Charlie, can do a massage nearly as well as you. And another one, Edgar, takes even longer than you to put on a bra." Terri smiled, waiting for my reaction.

I'd been gone for 9 months. And I certainly didn't have a special claim on Terri. Besides, she'd got wants, just like anyone. I understood that. Actually, the thought of her in bed with someone else didn't bother me all that much. And if you had gotten intimate enough to take Terri to bed, you'd obviously have ..ah.. discovered her arms. But the thought of Charlie massaging her stumps and the vision of Edgar helping her dress got me. I wondered which one she'd come here with: which one had sat with her in this intimate booth, with thighs touching and, using his knife, fork and spoon had fed both himself and Terri from their common plate. Hell, it could have been both of them.

I smiled and said I was glad to hear that Charlie gave a message that was "almost" as good as I did, and I sincerely hoped Edgar's technique wasn't quite up to mine. And, by the way, I asked, "Do either of them or any of your stable of admirers, for that matter, think that in addition to being 'quite nice,' that you're the sexiest thing alive ... like I do?"

Terri laughed. "Well not exactly. They're all a little embarrassed... no, that's not right, it's self conscious, when we're out. And most are ..ah.. solicitous in a way that creates the impression they think I'm... oh, I don't know, helpless and/or am due some amount of pity or special sympathy. Sort of a big brother kind of thing."

Terri smiled and dropped her long stump to my lap and forced it between my legs. I tightened my thighs to hold it in place and reached across her shoulders and closed my hand on her four inch arm. Terri twisted slightly back and forth, making both her stumps move. "Not to worry, Dear. When it comes to the perfect gentleman friend, one who can appreciate the special features and fulfill the particular desires of this poor armless girl, you're the one for me.

"Here comes the salad: better get ready to feed me. And when we're through here I trust you'll feed me," Terri's mouth opened and she ran her tongue around her glistening red lips, "a treat for dessert. I just love to eat something special after dinner ... don't you?"

We rubbed knees and thighs, and Terri scratched my shin with a high heel as I fed her. We sat close together and shared single bowls and plates, as well as coffee.

Back at her place, Terri said, "Get comfortable and fix us a drink while I change." By the time I'd put on some music, fixed a large brandy and settled on the couch, Terri returned. She'd removed all her clothes and donned a pair of hooks. Other than her artificial arms, the only other items of ..ah.. attire were white, high heeled boots. But they weren't a pair: the left one, with a five inch heel, went nearly to her knee; the other had a one inch platform and six inch heel, and the gleaming white leather went up to the middle of her thigh. The unclothed remainder of her body accentuated the ..ah.. mechanicalness of her hooks. As Terri crossed the room her breasts bounced in time to her uneven gait, and she kept her arms in motion, their two-finger claw hands clicking like castanets. "Thought the different boots would look good ... mismatched, like my arms. I hope you don't mind how they make me limp. Also," she smiled, "you've been such a dear, doing things for me all day, I thought I ought to put my hooks on so I could return the favor. If you'd be so kind as to come over here, I'll fumble your clothes off."

To the accompaniment of numerous clicks and the feel of her steel fingers frequently brushing my skin, I had my clothes removed. On the couch, Terri said, "I need some mouth to mouth resuscitation empty she stood and walked around the room once. Then she got to the floor, spread her legs and, using her hooks, pulled her boots back until they were nearly touching her hips. When the slender heels were securely jammed in the carpet, she raised her hooks and opened them both. "It's time for dessert. Let's eat."

I crawled over her head and we enjoyed a full serving of each other. After a little while, I reversed my position and slid into her hot dampness. I began slowly, wanting to build to a proper crescendo. As I pumped into her, Terri's artificial arm, laying on the floor, jerked occasionally. Her other hook was playing with a rock hard nipple, poking and pinching it.

Just as I was getting ready to increase my rhythm, Terri whispered, "When we're done I want to just drop off to sleep. Let's finish in bed."

After we'd pulled down the bedspread and covers all the way, Terri motioned for me to lay down. She went to each side of the bed and turned on the bedside lamps, then crossed the room and flipped the switch for the overhead light. Back in the center of the room, she stopped and smiled at me. Slowly and with deliberation she took off her hooks. When she had the fastenings undone she wiggled her shoulders, and her artificial arm dropped to the dresser. Then she held her short hook's sleeve under her four inch stump and pulled her handless forearm free. As a final touch, Terri arranged her hooks so they were both clearly visible from where I was laying. She turned and looked closely at each of her stumps as though examining them for imperfections. Her breasts went into bounce mode as she limped across the room and to the other side of the bed. She rolled over close and smiled. "They're a hassle to take off; besides, I think it's fun to wear boots to bed."

A high heel made its way along my calf. "You don't mind, do you?" Before I could answer, a warm, handless forearm worked its way between my legs, and Terri covered my mouth with hers.

"Make us a drink while I take my legs off." As I headed toward the small bar, I glanced back across the room. Janet was on the regular couch, her dress pulled up and her left leg already laying on the floor. By the time I returned, the right one had joined it, and Janet was waiting with an outstretched hand. We clicked our glasses and took a sip. Janet handed me her drink and turned so she was leaning against the arm rest. She ooched back till she was sitting up straight and then arranged her dress, being careful to smooth the light fabric along or over the ends of her legless thighs. When the material was wrinkle-free across her lap, Janet spread her stumps ever so slightly and then ran her finger along the dress, making a small, but distinct valley between them. "There," Janet smiled, taking her drink back. "The better for you to see, my dear." I smiled and nodded approval. Janet spoke as though reading from some invisible book.

"Ah, yes, the legless lovely turns on the couch and, facing her gentleman companion, meticulously arranges her skirt to emphasize the size and shape of her stumps. He, of course, is spellbound and rudely stares at her oddly shaped, truncated lap. Every now and then his eyes flick to where the mechanical limbs that take the place of her nonexistent legs are laying uselessly on the floor. However, these glances are but momentary. His real attention is focused on her and the way the carefully arranged dress accentuates the remains of her amputated legs. At one point, as though unable to control himself, he reaches out. His fingers quiver as they touch one of her legless thighs, tracing its length in what seems to be wonderment."

As I conformed to the verbal script, Janet sipped her drink and continued. "The disabled damsel doesn't seem to mind. In fact, her look is one of satisfaction. Then, as though getting more comfortable, she shifts her position and, in doing so, the hem of her dress creeps up slightly, exposing the end of her left stump. But she makes no move to hide it. In fact, she lifts it slightly and pulls her dress back even further, exposing first the blunt, scarred end of her legless thigh, then the full, smooth flesh above.

"Her gentleman friend hesitates and then moves his hand. The first touch of her naked stump seems to paralyze him, but only momentarily. For he immediately begins to caress and squeeze with an urgency born of desire. The legless girl sets her drink aside and moves again, sliding down and forward on the couch. She holds her dress, the hem of which ends up at her hips, exposing black lace panties. Her companion doesn't hesitate this time. His other hand moves quickly, and as it embraces her second stump, the girl sighs. Not a sigh of resignation but one of longing.

"Her partner seems to lose all reserve, because he drops his hands to her legless thighs and, when they reach the lace undergarment, he quickly pulls it off and casts it aside. The girl raises what's left of her legs and spreads them slightly, as though making an offering. He pauses not at all before taking a stump in each hand and lowering his head between them.

"The girl's sighs are clearly ones of relish, and before long, they're replaced by gasps and grunts of ecstasy. And as her sounds of passion increase, his head works its way deeper. Alternating with her animal like utterances, there are brief periods when she's quiet. But during these, there are other sounds to be heard... wet, lapping sounds that emanate from deep between her upheld stumps. There are also periodic grunts and gasps from him. At one point she cries, 'Oh God. Suck it harder ... please suck it harder.' Another gasp is followed by another urgent plea. 'Lick it faster! Faster! ... and .. OOhhhh ... MMmmm ... squeeze ... OOooHHhhhh ... squeeze my stumps.'

"The girl is writhing: the man's head is bobbing and moving with urgency; his hands are cupping the end of her stumps, holding the legless things wide apart and kneading the naked flesh. Her hands are active, but she can't seem to make up her mind: One minute they're on his head, pulling it deeper, the next they're on her breasts, rubbing and with the fingers digging in. Her head is thrown back, eyes closed. The gasps and sharp cries of ecstasy become nearly continuous.

"Then there's is a slight pause: the girl's head stops, her eyes open and she looks intently, first at each of her legless thighs, and then at the head buried between them. It begins as a low moan, increases to a loud cry and finally, with eyes again closed and head flung back, she lets forth with a long, guttural shriek. It's a scream of desperation, of release, and of such a sensual nature there is no question but that the legless girl has climaxed...."

Janet's third person monologue ceased and was replaced by a series of moans uttered in the first person. She was delicious, and her stumps felt lovely beneath my squeezing fingers. Janet caught her breath, and I could feel her hand on my neck. "Oh dear God. How I love it ... I love to be eaten ... I love it ... suck it harder ... lick it faster ... yes, yes, yes ... that's it ... and my stumps ... squeeze my stumps ... play with them .... rub them ... do things to my stumps ... aahhh ... oohhhh ... AAHHhhhhhh ... OOhhhYYiiii ... AARRggg ... AARRggg ... FLAHHRRGGHHhihhhhhhhhhhgggggggYYlllllliiiiiiii...."

Her stumps quivered, as though she were trying to shake the legs that were no longer there. And midway through her final cry, a warm, sweet ooze came forth to greet my frantic tongue.

As we caught our breaths, we worked on our drinks. "Get my plastic boots, will you?" Janet said when her glass was empty. I got up and went to the bedroom. By the time I returned, Janet had turned around. I knelt and slipped the rigid plastic cones on her stumps, which Janet had positioned so they were sticking out over the edge of the cushion.

She has four sets of stump boots, which Janet simply calls her boots. One set is plastic, much like the buckets of her artificial legs, the other three are leather, one black, one white and one burgundy. The black and white ones lace up, the burgundy boots fasten with buckles. The boots extend past the ends of the stumps about four inches, tapering until they end with a rubber tip a little bigger than a hockey puck. It is amazing (not to mention exciting) to watch Janet as she goes hither and yon around the place. Of course each short step lands with a notice-able jolt, and her upper body tips from side to side as she alternately moves each of her short, stiff legs. But she doesn't need a cane and, despite the awkwardness of it all, Janet appears to be well in control. In fact, it's not unusual for her to carry a pair of half full drinks.

The boots look good with shorts; they look more than mildly interesting when she doesn't bother (like this time) to change from her normal, knee-length dress or skirt; and they look marvelous when she's naked wearing a short robe. But naturally the bizarre boots (and Janet herself) look by far the best when she's dressed in bedroom attire or is not dressed at all. In either case, as her jolting limp takes her across the room, to merely say that her breasts are active would be totally misleading.

Janet says her boots are comfortable as well as functional; hence, she virtually never uses her legs at home. This accounts for the interior decorating of her place, which is ..ah.. unusual. But with her money Janet can easily afford what she wants.

At first it appears to be a strange movie set. The ceilings are regular height, and the doors are standard, except for the knobs being about a foot lower than normal. Throughout the rest of the place all the furniture and fixtures are duplicated. One set of normal proportions and another that is small. At first, the small items look miniature, but then you notice that they really aren't undersize; they are merely low. The full kitchen has a set of counters 18 inches high. Numerous chairs, even a couch, are low, and sitting you're only four or five inches off the floor. They have tables to match, with their surfaces at 12 to 18 inches. Even the bathroom has special fixtures, including a low sink and toilet, a shower with the head at 4 feet and a sunken tub. The bedroom is appointed similarly, with a low dressing table and a king-sized bed that is actually just a specially made mattress, six inches thick. Close to the bed there is a trapeze-like bar which hangs about 5 feet off the floor. "My idea," Janet had smiled when I'd first seen it. "To help me stand up after I've put my legs on. Then I hang on to it while my stumps settle in."

In addition to not using her legs at home, Janet also prefers not to use them when we go out. That is to say, rather than using both she will use just the right one. Janet says that for some unknown reason it seems to be the better of the two. It's not more comfortable, it simply seems to work better than the left one. The leg, which is cosmetic masterpiece, tends to look significantly more real when it's by itself. It's obvious that there's something wrong with it, but it simply doesn't occur to anyone that it could be artificial. This is especially true when its every-day foot has been replaced with an angled one that's wearing a severe high heel. If Janet's wearing pants, the ruse is virtually undetectable. The other substitute for her artificial limbs is a single peg leg. When she's in the mood for this, Janet accentuates it even more by wearing a skirt that's hemmed above the knee (but just below the peg's stump bucket) and is very tight. She's got a couple like this, but I think the dark burgundy one (suede) is the best. Below the slim waist, there is a lovely flare of hips, then the more-than-normal reverse taper as the snug leather hugs her thighs. (Keep in mind there's no need for the skirt to have any . . ah. . slack for knee movement).

Rather than a pair of legs, or even one leg protruding from under the skirt, there is only a dark, fluted piece of wood jutting out below the overly narrow and otherwise empty hem.

In either case crutches are obviously required, and, considering the problems posed by sitting down and getting up (forget stairs!), they are far from the norm. They look rather ordinary, except for being slightly bigger in diameter. They're also heavier than "normal" forearm crutches, but this isn't apparent. Inside the staffs there a small, but strong mechanism, consisting of a battery, a motor, a strong spring, an hydraulic piston and various miscellaneous smaller parts. When it's time to sit down, Janet positions herself so her foot (or the tip of her single peg leg) is about 30 inches in front of the intended seat. She then places the crutch tips back even with the front of the chair or car seat. When she's happy with her tripod stance and the location of each of her supports, Janet presses a button on the end of the crutch's handle(s) and, supported better than 90 percent by her arms, her crutches lower her to the edge of the seat. Janet then puts her crutches aside, moves back on the seat and, finally, releases the knee lock if she's got an artificial leg. Getting up is simply the reverse: lock leg straight, ooch out to edge of seat, drop foot or peg leg tip to the floor, get crutches in place and press the buttons. Seemingly by magic, her crutches hoist her upright.

The way it works is this. Going down, the button press activates the various parts required to let hydraulic fluid escape slowly from one chamber to another. This allows the telescoping crutch staff to become shorter, in a smooth, controlled manner. Not all that tricky, really. It's the converse that's so ingenious. While Janet is sitting, there activity going on inside in her idle crutches. A check valve opens, which allows the hydraulic fluid to return to its "normal" location, when the time comes. The small motor starts, and a tiny hydraulic pump activates another ram that's on top of the spring, compressing it. When this is accomplished, a keeper holds the spring, the motor automatically shuts off, and the crutch is "cocked". When it's time to stand, Janet moves well forward on the chair, gets her crutches (or, in the case of a peg leg, arm and crutch) in position and, as before, presses the button. This opens a check valve, and the hydraulic fluid that is holding the spring tightly compressed begins flow back to its storage chamber, allowing the spring to extend, and a controlled manner, Janet's crutches magically lengthen themselves and smoothly hoist her upright.

Naturally there's a wheelchair, and it gets same use at home, particularly when Janet is by herself. She'll also use it for occasions such as all day at the zoo or a long evening of Christmas shopping. But other than that, Janet rarely uses it out of the house. Janet's comment was, "Regular legs or just one or a peg leg with crutches, there's no doubt but that I'm far from normal in the leg department, and a lot of people realize or guess that they've both been cut off. But a wheelchair makes one look so helpless."

Then there are her two "carts"; one low, the other high. The low one is practically identical to a moving dolly; simply a square platform (padded) with four wheels, two of which swivel. Janet just bends a bit at the waist and, using her hands, propels herself where ever she wants to go. The other cart was Janet's idea. It's motorized, and the platform, which has a pair of upright stump buckets in which Janet "stands", looks as though its origin was in the mind of some futuristic author or bizarre mechanical engineer. Here again, Janet's money meant that obliging herself was no problem. The only problem was getting it made the way she wanted it.

When her boots were in place, Janet thumped to the kitchen to get a couple of hors d'oeuvres. Following that we bathed together and I carried her back to the bedroom. Janet decided it was a "dress up evening" and choose a dark maroon dress to go with her hand carved peg leg. Before we left, she sat and got up a few times, making sure her crutches were working right and as a treat for me.

Back home, Janet headed for the bedroom while I poured a pair of brandies. I took a seat on the low couch and had enjoyed a couple of sips by the time she returned. I knew at first glance what she had in mind.

Janet likes all kinds of attention, and she likes it in various ways. But she has a favorite, and I could tell that that was what she had in mind. It begins as follows:

She changes to some seductive clothes, sometimes a leather half bra and crotchless panties, or perhaps a black satin corset, with cutouts for her nipples and garters to hold up her "amputated nylons", as she calls them. This time it was the latter.

The gloves, which reach well past the elbow are of various colors but black leather, lace-up boots.

She always wears her black leather, lace-up boots.

We have a brandy on the couch, where Janet tends to occasionally finger one of her semi-hard nipples and frequently changes position, drawing attention of her booted stumps as they stiffly move around.

Then she stands up and goes around the room, making no effort to reduce the effects of what her short, rigid legs do to her breasts.

When Janet thinks I've had enough of that treat, she comes over, I stand, and she undresses me.

Following a couple of kisses and brief sucks (which Janet says is to make sure I'm adequately excited -- completely unnecessary) she gets on her back and slowly raises her booted stumps high and wide. The voice is always raspy, "Please fuck me."

I do. It's an urgent mating, with little in the way of preliminaries, and Janet climaxes almost immediately. It's a short-lived one that doesn't reach the heights it could. Janet's theory is that such a quickie, which is less than fully rewarding, is the best base for some prolonged foreplay and that the real fuck or, better yet, fucks, that follow have their climaxes much improved.

I should add that Janet has an amazing ability to climax.

So, when Janet returned wearing her black leather stump boots, gartered nylons and a short, waist-cinching corset that supported her breasts on a pair of little black satin shelves, I knew what she had in mind. Following the preliminary quickie, Janet limped off to the bathroom to use the specially made bidet, while I got two more drinks.

Back on the couch, the full-size one this time, we talked for a while, before Janet wiggled her stumps, indicating that I should take off the boots. After I unlaced them and pulled the leather cones off her stumps, I undid the garters where they fasten to the corset (Janet says that although a useless, dangling pant leg might be attractive, dangling garters aren't). When I finally pulled the custom-made, sock-like nylons off her legless thighs, Janet smiled and put down her empty glass.

I sat near the edge of the couch and helped her get into position, sitting astride my thigh (right, this time) like it were a saddle. As I do a thorough job on her breasts and lipsticked nipples, Janet rides my thigh. As she thrusts her hips, her stumps (which are hanging down) jerk back and forth as though their amputated legs are searching for nonexistent stirrups. Just before it's time to go on to the next phase, Janet ooches back, nearly to my knee, brings the stump that's between my legs up and uses the legless thing to play with me. After a bit of that, I straighten my leg and Janet slides down to the floor, where I join her.

We're both on our backs, Janet with a pillow under her head. I'm in front of her, with my head resting on her belly. Janet's stumps are raised and resting on my shoulders, close enough that I can feel the soft flesh of her inner thighs against my ears. I begin massaging her stumps. This is not a series of casual squeezes and gentle caresses, but a real massage. I always begin by running my hands from naked hips along her thighs. I let my fingers flex along the way, but when I get the legless ends cupped in my hands, I squeeze and knead as though they were a pair of breasts.

396

Janet sort of purrs and makes little comments as she absently tousles my hair.

Following those preliminaries, I get down to business. Concentrating on one stump and then the other, I use both hands. Near my face, the soft flesh bulges between my gripping fingers. For the last three or four inches and at the ends, even though the flesh is firmer and more dense, the my massage is forceful enough that I can feel the severed bone moving around inside. Janet says that the sensations are neither those of simple relaxation or those of sexual arousal, but an interesting combination that feels "incredible" (especially before my hands and fingers begin to get tired) and that she could enjoy it "for hours". (My arms, hands and fingers would never last even one hour, but I do pretty well for 15 or 20 minutes, considering the effort it takes to massage Janet's stumps to her satisfaction.)

Shortly after my hands and fingers began to tire, Janet sort of grunted and twisted my head: a signal for me to turn over. By the time I was on my stomach, Janet had worked a pillow under her hips and was waiting. I moved up between her legless thighs and, as I did so, I took an end in each hand. When I was in position, which included holding the stumps of her legs back past vertical and spread wide, I dropped my head and buried my face deep between them. She was warm and damp and there was a slight scent of some delightful perfume. As always when she's being eaten, Janet delivered her fragmented dialogue. About the time my neck and tongue began to tire, Janet gasped, "Me, me!", indicating that she wanted something in her mouth, too. I quickly changed my position until I was facing the other way, straddling her.

As I went back to my feast, Janet slid another pillow under her head and I slid into her soft, warm mouth. Before too long, Janet was writhing and, although my neck was tired, I certainly didn't want to stop what we were doing.

"Put ... my boots ... back on ... please." Janet had pulled her mouth back in order to gasp out the request. I slipped them over her stumps and tightened the buckles, snugging the top one until the soft flesh bulged slightly above the gleaming black leather. Janet got upright and limped across the room toward the far corner, where she pulled a chair out of the way. Hidden beneath the chair are a pair of chocks fastened to the floor. The chocks, which are L-shaped, are about five inches on a side and about two inches high; they are placed about 30 inches apart. Janet went past the chocks slightly and bent forward to rest her hand on the floor. Then she backed up and worked her boots wide apart, until the ends were tight against the restraining chocks. She bent her elbows and dropped her chest down until she was resting on her forearms. Finally, Janet violently moved her hips back and forth few times, making certain that her booted stumps were properly and securely held by the chocks. "Please ... fuck me!" It sounded more like an order than a request.

I grabbed the blanket and knee walked over to her. When I had the blanket spread out, I worked myself up next to her, made sure I was in her (but just barely) and reached around to grab both her breasts. Then, following a desperate "Hurry!" from Janet, I tightened my hands on her breasts, and, as the soft flesh dimpled beneath my fingers, I drove into her snug dampness as deep as I could.

In addition to the fact that they look good, Janet's gloves are worn specifically to avoid carpet burns on her elbows during this arrangement. And it's a good thing, too, because, before long, we were in a frenzy, grunting and gasping with passionate abandon. For my part, I tried and coordinate my forceful pulling on her breasts to coincide with the near violent thrusts of my hips. All the while, Janet jerked from side to side and lunging back and forth as best as her restrained stumps would allow. I invariably climax first, and just before I do, Janet will pause, waiting for my eruption. When it arrives, she thumps the floor with her hands and groans a groan of infinite pleasure. Janet's climax followed almost immediately, and when it did, it was accompanied by a cry of desperation, coupled with body spasm that jarred one of her boots free of its check. Janet lurched sideways. Despite her stump's desperate efforts to maintain position, she began to topple. I pulled my hands back to her belly and, like a mad man, pulled her to me so we would not come uncoupled. I was successful in holding her up until she managed to once again get her 'footing'. But until she did, Janet's stiff, booted stump feverishly probed and stabbed as it blindly searched for the security of its chock. Needless to say, this extra bit of ..ah.. activity added a touch of spice to our lovemaking.

We lay sprawled on the floor. Janet had rolled over, and I had remove her boots. As I stroked one of her stumps, Janet gently played with herself. After we caught our breaths, Janet said, "Clean me up and then let's go to bed." I got the bottle and soft towel from the end table drawer.

While I was playing human bidet, I commented that the perfumed scent was new. Janet smiled and said she hoped I liked it. When I returned from putting things away, Janet sat up. She spread her stumps and raised her hands. "How about carrying me off to bed," she smiled. I reached down and got my hands on her waist. She put her arms around my neck, and I straightened up, bringing Janet right along with me. Janet nodded, indicating that she had hold of herself and then, when she raised and spread her stumps, I slid my hands off her waist and down under her hips, where I locked my fingers "Take me for a little walk," she whispered wetly in my ear. As I started off Janet wiggled, and by the time we'd gone around the room twice I could feel the warmth between her thighs on my belly. "Let's go to the guest room." Again, a wet active tongue slightly distorted Janet's words.

I went down the hall and smiled when I went through the door. There were two piles of pillows laid out on the bed.

The lower had two pillows, behind that was a stack of five. "Before or after dinner," I asked, referring to the layout. Janet did the tongue thing again.

"Oh, yesterday, my dear. I like to plan ahead." At the foot of the bed I turned around and sat down. When I was seated, I slid my hands up past Janet's waist and took both her breasts. The nipples were already hard, and she purred as I fingered them.

"Lay back!" Janet said in a husky voice and took her arms from around my neck. When I did, my head landed on the pair of perfectly positioned pillows. I put my arms up, over my head and waited. Janet let out a sigh of anticipation and then began to move. She used her hands on my chest and then shoulders. Walking on her stumps, and bobbing from side to side, Janet worked her way up my chest. I watched her stumps change shape, becoming fuller and dimpled near the end as they alternately took her weight. Finally one and then the other legless thigh passed my shoulders. Janet put her forearms on the high pile of pillows, and I reached up. When my hands were full of her hard-nippled breasts, Janet thrust her hips forward and down. "Devour me. Consume me. Eat me. Oh, God .... EAT ME!"

To the accompaniment of Janet's constant verbal urgings I did indeed try to devour her. As I licked, sucked and nibbled, the soft, velvet flesh became more warm and damp, her pulsing clitoris frequently twitched, and it occurred to me (and not for the first time) that whoever said, "You can't have your cake and eat it too," had never feasted on Janet. When it was over, Janet ooched back down; I sat up and then stood, lifting her with me.

In her bed, Janet moved down until she could drop her head and take me in her mouth. Laying on her stomach, the ends of her legless thighs were just past my feet. As she brought me back to life with her mouth and hands, I bent my knees slightly and used my feet, toes and ankles to massage her stumps. (God, that room should have a mirrored ceiling!) Her efforts were successful and when she deemed me ready, Janet pulled herself up to sit astride me. "Help me," she said in the husky voice as she put her hands on my chest. I cupped the ends of her stumps in my hands and helped her raise up. It took a few seconds for us to get aligned. And when I finally began to slide into her we stopped and waited for a moment. Then Janet nodded and we both relaxed. She literally fell. It was as though I had impaled her.

When she came to rest she stayed motionless for a moment looking me in the eye and spoke in a tone of need. "Fuck me!"

I bucked and thrust my hips. Janet writhed and squirmed, varying her position between sitting up straight with back arched and laying forward until her breasts were touching me. I alternated between squeezing and kneading her stumps and doing the same to her breasts. In the former case I gave equal time to the soft, full thighs and to their firmer, dimpled ends; in the latter, I frequently pinched and rolled the rock hard nipples between thumb and forefinger. It took a while for my juices to come to a boil, and I think Janet held herself in check, because when it finally happened, we came at the same time gasping and unable to speak.

Even though I was tired, sleep eluded me. The visions of what Janet and I might do the next day were vivid enough that I stayed awake, picturing the various alternatives in my mind and, like a child the night before Christmas, wishing the morrow were already here.

AMPUGOD
by Simon Shneider

An introduction to AmpuGod,...
How it all started...

AmpuGod created the amputation saw,
After seeing the amputation saw, he was proud on his
creation,
But he wanted to create more
The day after he realized, -that for doing amputations
He needed to have bodies
AmpuGod created Adam and Eve,
After seeing Adam and Eve, he was again proud on his
creations,
But AmpuGod wanted to create more
On the third day, AmpuGod wanted to create a stump.
He used his first creation with his second creation
So, AmpuGod created the amputation & the stump,
After seeing the stumps, again he was proud on his
creations,
But AmpuGod wanted to create more
On the fourth day, AmpuGod wanted to create metals and
rubbers,
After seeing the creations of rubbers and metals,
AmpuGod was again proud on his creations, but again
wanted to create more
AmpuGod needed to think.
He thought "Why did I created rubbers and metals?"
After a good night of sleeping and thinking, AmpuGod waked
up,
On that fifth day, AmpuGod brought the rubber and metals
together,
AmpuGod created wheelchairs, crutches and prosthetics,
from the metals and the rubber
AmpuGod was proud on his creations, but wanted to create
more.
On the sixth day, again after waking up, he created brains
and more people.
The brains he created were wannabe and devotee oriented,
The people he created received those new created brains.

AmpuGod was satisfied and exited.
On the seventh day, AmpuGod realized that his creations
were more then perfect.
He realized a new world, a world of Stumps and Happiness.
A world where everyone who he had created
wanted an amputation, or liked amputations.

So it came that AmpuGod started the world of perfect
happiness,
A world where less will be more,
A world where in Amputation and Stumps are the foundation
of unlimited Happiness.
A world where in Devotees and Amputees needed to live
with each other.

So Happy as his creations were, Also AmpuGod was
satisfied.
On day eight, AmpuGod created a new religion,
The AmpuGod religion,
A religion that would bring for thousands of years,
Amputees and devotees and wannabes closer to each other.
The religion of AmpuGod was created,
A religion were a stump is as an heart, as a breath,
Something you can't live without.
Again AmpuGod was happy with his creation,
But something was missing.
AmpuGod heard the people screaming.
Pain all over and around.

AmpuGod became sad, very sad.
He thought that his creation wasn't an happy creation.
After a good night sleeping,
AmpuGod realized that the pain wasn't from being an
amputee,
Now, on day nine,
That same day,
AmpuGod created Xylocaine /Lydocaine and injection
needles.
After his new creation, the people he had created before,

Started to use his new creation.
AmpuGod was more then satisfied, when he sew how the people
Used the new creation and became amputees without pain.
AmpuGod was so happy to see all those Satisfied Amputations.
Now, his new creation was 'whole'.
For thousands of years, people became amputees,
They married with devotees,
And wannabes became successful Amputees,
All in the Glory of AmpuGod.

The Glory of AmpuGod knows unlimited pure Stumped Satisfaction.
A satisfaction that not could be described to others,
To extenders

All Extenders that would show interest in AmpuGod or in his creations,
or in the world of Amputation & Stumps,
Would be welcomed with an amputation.
Having a Stump would be the only proof of appreciation & acceptation for AmpuGod.

But AmpuGod realized that his world could not be based on only wannabes.
On day ten, AmpuGod decided to create diseases.
He created bone cancer, birth defects, accidents and gangrene.
AmpuGod was again happy to see that those created diseases, helped his world.
The people he created, became now, much easier an amputee.

After this creation, AmpuGod sew that his whole creation was more then perfect,
So perfect that the most of his creations wanted to have more then one amputation.

Ten years later, AmpuGod observed his creation again,
He sew that the most people had became multiple
amputees.
He sew young girls with bone cancer, ready to have their
innocent leg being removed,
And seeing them so exited about this amputation that
needed to be done,
He sew that they were more then happy.
He sew boys in wheelchairs, without legs,
And seeing them so happy, because they could not walk,
AmpuGod was proud on his creations.

Because Amputation is our Destination,
We all believe in AmpuGod.

The secret sect of AmpuGod.

'But I really want my leg off', screamed Anny: 'Why don't you get it?'.

'You are so crazy as someone can be crazy!', was Paul's reaction.

Paul was the husband from Anny, and already years they lived an happy marriage.

An happy marriage ... till a few weeks ago.

Since that time Anny want her left leg amputated. High above the knee.

Nobody knows why she want that.

Paul called a few days to his doctor, but also he couldn't give any serious answer on the fact why really Anny want her leg off.

Anny is 22 years old and since a few months she works at the historic museum in her city.

Paul works at the local mail office. He is 25.

For sure Anny don't have any disease. The doctor investigated her completely.

No gangrene, no bone cancer,... just an healthy young woman.

'What is wrong with you?', screamed Paul, watching in her direction.

'I want my leg off, and if no one helps me, I will cut it of myself!', responded Anny.

Paul started to cry. He didn't know what to do, what to think.

'You don't need to cry', Anny said: 'I really need my left leg amputated, before the next full moon'.

'What next full moon?', Paul really didn't know about what she was talking.

'You don't get it, you don't understand anything', she said again: 'I will have my leg off for him!'.

The part –for him, Paul had heard: 'Who him?, what him?'.

'My master, you idiot', Anny responded: 'The Master of Amputation, my God'.

'Your God?, he wants you to be an amputee?', asked Paul then.

'Indeed, my master is the AmpuGod; The Creator of the Amputated Paradise, the master of a perfectly life with less limbs' were Anny's words.

'You are nuts', reacted Paul:' I gone call an ambulance and you go straight to the psychiatric hospital'.

On the moment that Paul had said those words, he disappeared on the place were he was standing. Gone, into nothing. Gone forever?.

'I will have my leg off', was the reaction on all this, coming out of the mouth from Anny. She didn't mind that Paul was gone, not knowing were he went to.

Was he dead, or were was he?. Maybe she knows where he was or what happened, but for sure she didn't mind.

Anny stand up, went to the kitchen and took a big butchers knife.

She brought it to the direction of her left leg.

On the moment she wanted to cut through her leg, above the knee; -She heard a voice saying: 'No!!!'.

Only she could hear the voice, it was a voice in her mind. A voice that could be heard only by the proud members of the sect of AmpuGod.

About AmpuGod and the fact that there were long time ago, -a few thousand years; people who believed in amputation for a better live, was an old book that she had found a few weeks before in the museum were she works.

During all the time Anny went to work, more and more she came in contact with the master of the old religion; The AmpuGod himself.

When someone started to believe in this old religion, or there was only −even a little bit interest in it, automatically AmpuGod came to that person.

On one of the late nights that Anny was working, she had used mumbling the word: 'interesting', while she was watching at some old graphics that were in the book she found. Designs of amputees, most of them with a kind of wooden prosthetic.

Hearing the word 'interesting', was for AmpuGod enough to get in contact with this soul on earth to find out how deep the interest of that person could be.

Through a kind of contact with Anny's soul, AmpuGod found out, that she was for sure prepared to have a leg removed, to become a member of the sect of him.

But in the book was also mentioned that the believers of AmpuGod needed to have their amputation done, before the next full moon.

If that would not happen, they would end up in a terrible unhappy live.

That the voice of AmpuGod had spoken through the soul of Anny, was for sure. At the moment in the kitchen, she realized that he had invited her to go to the museum.

'Midnight', Anny thought, and again realizing that this –around midnight invitation, only could came from the master himself, from AmpuGod.

When we take a deeper look into the religious book of the sect of AmpuGod, that Anny found, then we understand why her leg need to be removed.

The law of the AmpuGod bible says that four-limbed people are not allowed in his world of perfection. That for every amputation, there will follow great unlimited happiness. To join the religion of AmpuGod, woman always needed to start with a leg. What leg, -left or right, wasn't important. But for sure it needed to be above the knee, and very high.

Also the amputation needed to be done in front of AmpuGod. He needed to be able to see that his new believer was more then ready to enter his community.

'Midnight it will not be so far', was Anny thinking.

'My last two-legged steps will be on the way to the museum'.

Anny prepared herself to go to the museum. It wasn't that far from midnight.

She went first to the bathroom, washed her left leg, and shaved the hairs from it.

Also in the AmpuGod's bible was mentioned, that every new amputation could be only done, when the limb was completely clean and shaved.

With a marker, the person that became a member, needed to mark the line were the amputation needed to be done.

410

How higher the amputation level, how bigger the happiness and love from AmpuGod would return to the soul of the AmpuGod member.

After having this all done, Anny went to the museum. She had a key from a side door; went inside and went to the place were she found weeks ago, for the first time, the book about AmpuGod.

AmpuGod was already on the location, and so, also her husband Paul.

Paul was clearly hypnotized and had a big butchers knife in his left hand.

A big wooden, and old table in the middle, was the place where it all would happen. The place where Anny would offer her left leg for her master and God; The AmpuGod.

Anny didn't recognize her husband. −Or she recognized him, but understood that he was in the hands of AmpuGod.

The law for couples was more then clear. In the bible Anny read once that if one person with a partner become a member, automatically AmpuGod will reach the partner's soul, and will take him or her away, till the day that the believer becomes an amputee.

Not only Anny was there. In front was AmpuGod sitting on his thrown. The thrown was made from skin, coming from amputated limbs. Left and right from him were all different followers from his religion. Most of them were young people, on crutches, prosthetics, -even some of them in a kind of wheelchair.

'Come...', said AmpuGod, watching in the direction of Paul.

Paul walked slowly, but sure in the direction of his wife.

Anny laid down on the wooden table, and watched in the direction of her master, with the words: 'I believe in you my God, for you and your love, I offer my leg'.

While she watched in the direction of her master, Paul went on the backside of the table, so that AmpuGod could follow and see what he was doing.

That all was very important, because on the moment that the leg would separate from the body, that would be the moment that Anny became a proud and religious member of the holly believe in AmpuGod. It would be the moment that

411

she would receive unlimited happiness and love from AmpuGod.

The moment that Anny would become an amputee, was there.

High above his head out, -Paul hold the knife, that cut a fraction later, through her leg.

Her leg was no more part of her body. It was separated for good. The ultimate sign for the AmpuGod.

There was no blood, only a little bit pain, and a miracle seemed to happen. The wound closed immediately and became a stump.

A very short stump.

Now it was Paul's turn.

He needed to offer his right arm for the master.

Man who became a member of the AmpuGod his religious, needed to start with an arm.

All man needed to amputate their own limbs.

Also Paul received immediately afterwards his stump and unlimited happiness.

But for sure it wasn't anymore possible now to stay living there in the city they came from.

They both needed to follow AmpuGod in his footsteps.

Anny received a pair of wooden crutches. She was very happy with her new one-legged body.

This way, AmpuGod, followed by Anny and Paul, and all the other sect members disappeared. On the way to their unlimited happiness and love, that they received from AmpuGod; -on their way to the Stumped Paradise.

The book?. The book staid at the museum. Almost every historical museum worldwide have such a book. Only that a lot of people don't know that.

The book always staid on the place were the believer found it. —Ready and waiting on new believers and souls that will join AmpuGod and his fateful religion s

THE LEG THAT WANTED TO BE AMPUTATED
&
NO MORE LEGS, NO MORE BEER

By Simon Schneider

The leg that wanted to be Amputated

Long time ago, there was once a leg. An healthy leg.

The leg was a left leg, and had a name.

The leg's name was Krista; -This because it was a leg that belonged to a woman.

The leg had indeed the same name of the woman from who the leg was.

The leg was a left leg and wasn't very happy.

The leg had the age of 23. indeed, exactly the same age as from the woman, from who the leg was.

Since a very long time, Krista, -the leg, was in a huge depression.

The only thing the leg could think on, was a radical amputation.

The unhappy leg didn't felt herself comfortable with the body it was hanging on.

For those, and so many other reasons, the leg really wanted to be removed.

'But how to tell my owner, that I don't want to be with her anymore?', was the leg thinking: 'I need to find a way'.

A few months later, and after a long way of thinking,

The leg found a solution.

Inside the leg started to accept less blood from the owner.

'In this way, I will be disconnected soon', was the leg thinking.

Day after day, and night after night, the leg changed from color.

The leg became after a time, so black and started to smell.

Krista, the woman and owner from the leg, felt that there was something wrong.

When the pain started to get very bad, Krista decided to go to the doctor.

After a few and deeply investigations, doctor Shmertz; -That was his name,

-needed to inform Krista, that her leg needed to be amputated urgent.

'Finally!', was the leg thinking, while poor Krista, in this case the owner, -started to cry.

The morning after, at 6.43 AM, Doctor Shmertz removed the leg high above the knee.

After amputation, the both Krista's waked up,

slowly but sure, coming out of their narcotic situation.

The leg felt herself happy: 'Finally I am no longer together with that body'.

The other Krista needed to discover at the same time how her beautiful leg, that she loved so much, wasn't no longer there.

She started to cry. Again and Again.

But hours later, when doctor Shmertz removed the bandage slowly from the wound,

She discovered something totally different then she thought. She discovered a beautiful stump.

Very soon Krista, -the woman on one leg, became close friends with her cute little stump.

She even gave it a name. The name was Stumpy.

Stumpy was so short, so cute and also so soft.

Little as Stumpy was, she followed Krista everyday, hanging proud between two crutches.

Stumpy enjoyed the attention she got from so many people.

Almost on every walk, she observed how many people were staring at her.

Also Krista was so happy with the attention and respect she got from so many people.

She refused to wear a prosthetic.

Stumpy was very happy with that smart decision of her owner.

This because Stumpy didn't liked to be locked up.

Also, when Krista would use a prosthetic, then the people on the streets, during the many walks they both did together, could not see Stumpy.

When Krista touched her new friend Stumpy, then Stumpy became always more exited.

Krista and her Stump, lived for many happy years together,

So happy, that they never thought about separation.

No more legs, no more beer...

After years of sadness, Kelissia, a 24 years old female wannabe that wanted already for many years her amputations, became an amputee.

Kelissia lives in Shreveport, a city in the state of LA, USA. For years Kelissia wanted her legs off. Very high above the knee. Kelissia, was for years a substitute teacher. Many times she told to her students that she wanted to become a legless woman. During all the years of being a sad down-to-earth wannabe, Kelissia stepped in her brand new jeep and crossed over the highways of Louisiana, this in the direction of Texas, where her father was priest of the Evangelic church. Her father was very depressed and asked God many times for his help.

This because his daughter also informed her father about the deep amputation wishes Kelissia had already for years. Once she arrived in the church of her father, Kelissia asked again to her father to understand her dream.

But her father didn't wanted to listen. So depressed as she was, she droved back home. That day she started to drink. Back home, drinking a few beers and 20/20, what is a strong alcohol in the USA, she was sitting in front of the computer. ´What can I do´, was Kelissia thinking. How more drunk she went, how deeper she was thinking on meeting a real legless amputee. Kelissia thought: ´If I can't become an amputee, then I will find myself an amputee on the internet´. After a few more beers, Kelissia went on dating sites for Disabled people. After hours searching for a man with stumps, she met Ricardo.

Ricardo was a very intelligent man, without legs. He became an amputee by wish and was already for years stumped. ´I am so jealous on you´, was what Kelissia told to Ricardo. Ricardo was originally from Cuba, but lived already since 10 years in the USA.

Ricardo lived first in Florida, where he met Dr. Walter, a very famous wannabe surgeon who loved to remove healthy limbs.

That time Kelissia didn't know yet that there was such a wonderful dynamic wannabe surgeon.

After a lot of talking and more beers, Kelissia started to fall in deeply and real love. Ricardo invited her to his house in Colorado, where he lived at that time.

A few days later. Kelissia prepared the big travel to Colorado. Her dog Oreum, she left with her parents. Hours later and a flight later, she met Ricardo in his orange wheelchair on the airport.

´You are so beautiful´were Ricardo's first words: ´Probably the most beautiful woman from the whole USA´.

Kelissia was very happy with those words and thought how much more beautiful she would be if her legs would be totally gone.

´I want to be like you Ricardo´, she said and started to kiss Ricardo.

Ricardo's stumps were shaking, so happy he was. He never was kissed before by such a beautiful woman, such a perfection. Silently, that not everyone on the airport could ear it, Ricardo informed Kelissia that he would help her to become a real legless woman. After a few days of meeting and knowing each other, Ricardo discovered that Kelissia was a huge drunk. On one day she could drink about 80 cans of cheap beers.

´This is very sad´, was what Ricardo told to Kelissia. After more talking's, Ricardo decided to go with Kelissia to Florida, this to meet Dr. Walter.

Ricardo called Dr. Walter that night and informed him to prepare everything to do a very high double above the knee amputation.

Dr. Walter was very excited. His hobby was only amputation. For him it was pure satisfaction to see how easy it was to remove limbs, to separate them from bodies.

Ricardo told to Kelissia: ´If you become an amputee, you need to promise me, to never drink anymore´. That was for Kelissia no any problem.

The day after they went with an airplane to Florida, were Dr. Walter's ambulance was already waiting on the Miami airport.

Soon as Ricardo and Kelissia arrived in the healthy limb

removal hospital, she went to the surgery room where Dr. Walter was already waiting on her.

´Say farewell to your legs´, were the last words of Dr. Walter. After that, Kelissia felled in a deep amazing sleep.

Hours later she waked up.... Discovered that her legs were gone, forever.

´I am an amputee! My legs are gone!´, Kelissia screamed it out from totally happiness: ´I am never able to walk again!!!!´. Kelissia was so happy that she started to cry. She was thinking on her dog Oreum, and she wished that her dog could see the complete happiness Kelissia discovered.

Later that wonderful day, Ricardo and Dr. Walter came into the room of Kelissia.

But very long Dr. Walter could not stay, this because his cat Bellykitty was waiting on her boss at home.

But Ricardo stayed in the hospital with Kelissia. For hours they touched each other stumps and decided to get married. Kelissia agreed. A complete happy live, without drinking was what she really wanted.

The future changed their whole live. Kelissia decided to stop teaching. She hated students anyway. For sure 2 legged students. Ricardo, who had a Spanish radio station, for the Spanish speaking people in the USA and always had a brilliant mind, decided to start together with Kelissia their own Prosthetic and Wheelchair Historical museum. But for that, a lot of money was necessary. Ricardo sold his brand new radio transmitter and Kelissia pawned everything she had in the local pawn store. The people from the pawn store liked Kelissia very much. After that, they opened finally their own prosthetic and wheelchair museum.

Even Dr. Walter flied over from Sunny Florida to celebrate the opening. That night Dr. Walter started with a speech about wannabe happiness and the perfection happiness of stumped lives. He explained that he only corrected what God had did wrong. He removed what God offered to much.... limbs. It was a very happy end that day. Kelissia lived with Ricardo together for many happy legless years.

Happy

SEPARATION

Can be called

AMPUTATION

Or... some jokes around the subjects Amputees,
Amputation and Wheelchairs...

Left side amputation...
Did you hear about the man who had the whole left side of his body amputated????
Don't worry, he's ALL RIGHT now.

The penis amputation...
An American tourist goes on a trip to China. While in China, he is very sexually promiscuous and does not use a condom. A week after arriving back home in the States, he awakes one morning to find his penis covered with bright green and purple spots. Horrified, he immediately goes to see his doctor. The doctor, never having seen anything like this before, orders some tests and tells the man to return in two days for the results.
The man returns a couple of days later and the doctor says, "I've got bad news for you. You've contracted Mongolian VD. It's very rare and almost unheard of here. We know very little about it." The man looks a little perplexed and says, "Well, give me a shot or something and fix me up, doc." The doctor answers, "I'm sorry, there's no known cure. We're going to have to amputate your penis."
The man screams in horror, "Absolutely not! I want a second opinion!" The doctor replies, "Well it's your choice. Go ahead if you want, but surgery is your only choice." The next day, the man seeks out a Chinese doctor, figuring that he'll know more about the disease. The Chinese doctor examines his penis and proclaims, "Ah yes, Mongolian VD. Very rare disease." The guys says to the doctor, "Yeah, yeah, I already know that, but what can you do? My American doctor wants to operate and amputate my penis!" The Chinese doctor shakes his head and laughs, "Stupid American doctor! American doctor, always want to operate. Make more money, that way. No need to operate!" "Oh thank God!" the man replies. "Yes!" says the Chinese doctor, "You no worry! Wait two weeks. Dick fall off by itself!

The Leg Amputation...

A man recovering in hospital bed after a leg amputation due to a chronic illness.
Surgeon and house officers were doing their daily rounds in the ward. Surgeon walk up to his bed with his team read his notes and said,"Good morning Mr Jones".
"Morning doc" said the man,
"Well, I have good news and bad news for you Mr Jones, What do you like to hear first, good news or the bad news?"
Tell me the good news first, doc" said the man.
"well good news is your bad leg is getting better" said the doctor.
"So, what's the bad news doc?" asked the man.
"bad news is that we cut the wrong leg" said the surgeon.

Amputee Escaping...

During WWII a fighter pilot was shot down over Germany and he was captured by the Nazis. He was hurt pretty bad so he the German doctor amputated his arm. He had a request that they would drop his arm over his base in England. So the Germans did. Then next week they amputated his other arm and he asked for the same thing. So the Germans did. The next week they amputated his leg and he again asked for them to drop it over his base in England. The German doctor replied, "Nein, Ve do dis no more!" The pilot asked why not, and the German answered, "Ve tink you trying to escape!" Aviation
Revenge "Dying Husband: Kethrine, please marry Peter after my death.
Wife: Why?
Husband: Because i want to take revenge from him.

What's the definition of tight?
Throwing a bomb under someone's wheelchair and telling them to run for their lives.

One too many...

An Irishman has been drinking at a pub all night. The bartender finally says that the bar is closing. So the Irishman stands up to leave and falls flat on his face. He tries to stand one more time, same result. He figures he'll crawl outside and get some fresh air and maybe that will sober him up. Once outside he stands up and falls flat on his face. So he decides to crawl the four blocks to his home and when he arrives at the door he stands up and falls flat on his face. He crawls through the door into his bedroom. When he reaches his bed he tries one more time to stand up. This time he manages to pull himself upright but he quickly falls right into bed and is sound asleep as soon as his head hits the pillow. He awakens the next morning to his wife standing over him shouting at him. "So, you've been out drinking again!!" "What makes you say that?" he asks, as he puts on an innocent face. "The pub called, you left your wheelchair there again."

Is he drunk?

2 cops walk inside a bar to have a drink. The old guy next to them falls off his chair and gets back on. The bartender says, "He's been doing that for a half an hour! I think he's drunk." So the two cops bring him to their car and a wallet falls out of his pocket. The guys ID is in it and they found out where he lives. They bring him home, ring the doorbell and an elderly woman opens the door. The cops ask the woman, "Is this your husband?" and she replies, "Yes. But where's his wheelchair?"

*   *   *

Special thanks to:

DisabledPlanet.com (modelpicture cover Bruna)
And
DisabFriends.com
(a Social Network for people with a Disability)

www.ingramcontent.com/pod-product-compliance
Lightning Source LLC
Chambersburg PA
CBHW050739030726
47505CB00002B/330